Prize Stories
1989
THE O. HENRY AWARDS

Prize Stories 1989

THE

O. HENRY AWARDS

Edited and with
an Introduction by

William Abrahams

ANCHOR BOOKS
DOUBLEDAY
NEW YORK   LONDON   TORONTO   SYDNEY   AUCKLAND

AN ANCHOR BOOK
PUBLISHED BY DOUBLEDAY
a division of Bantam Doubleday Dell Publishing Group, Inc.
666 Fifth Avenue, New York, New York 10103

ANCHOR BOOKS, DOUBLEDAY, and the portrayal of an anchor
are trademarks of Doubleday, a division of Bantam Doubleday Dell
Publishing Group, Inc.

Library of Congress Cataloging-in-Publication Data
Prize stories. 1947–
    New York, etc. Doubleday.
    v. 22 cm.
Annual.
The O. Henry awards.
None published 1952–53.
Continues: O. Henry memorial award prize stories.
ISSN 0079-5453 = Prize stories
    1. Short stories, American—Collected works.
PZ1.011   813'.01'08—dc19   21-9372
                                        MARC-S
Library of Congress   [8804r83]rev4

ISBN 0-385-24634-X (pbk.)
Copyright © 1989 by Anchor Books, Doubleday, a division of
Bantam Doubleday Dell Publishing Group, Inc.
PRINTED IN THE UNITED STATES OF AMERICA
APRIL 1989
FIRST EDITION

BG

Contents

Publisher's Note

This volume is the sixty-ninth in the O. Henry Memorial Award series.

In 1918, the Society of Arts and Sciences met to vote upon a monument to the master of the short story, O. Henry. They decided that this memorial should be in the form of two prizes for the best short stories published by American authors in American magazines during the year 1919. From this beginning, the memorial developed into an annual anthology of outstanding short stories by American authors, published, with the exception of the years 1952 and 1953, by Doubleday & Company, Inc.

Blanche Colton Williams, one of the founders of the awards, was editor from 1919 to 1932; Harry Hansen from 1933 to 1940; Herschel Brickell from 1941 to 1951. The annual collection did not appear in 1952 and 1953, when the continuity of the series was interrupted by the death of Herschel Brickell. Paul Engle was editor from 1954 to 1959 with Hanson Martin co-editor in the years 1954 to 1960; Mary Stegner in 1960; Richard Poirier from 1961 to 1966, with assistance from and co-editorship with William Abrahams from 1964 to 1966. William Abrahams became editor of the series in 1967.

In 1970 Doubleday published under Mr. Abrahams' editorship *Fifty Years of the American Short Story,* and in 1981, *Prize Stories of the Seventies.* Both are collections of stories selected from this series.

The stories chosen for this volume were published in the pe-

riod from the summer of 1987 to the summer of 1988. A list of
the magazines consulted appears at the back of the book. The
choice of stories and the selection of prize winners are exclu-
sively the responsibility of the editor. Biographical material is
based on information provided by the contributors and obtained
from standard works of reference.

Introduction

We live in an age of insatiable publicity, when there is hardly an aspect of contemporary life, from politics to popcorn, that is safe from its voracious reach. It is not surprising, therefore, that even the writing of the short story, that private, personal, and idiosyncratic literary achievement, has become "a target of opportunity." The emphasis, predictably, is on the writers themselves—as people, so to speak—and only incidentally on what they actually have written. Indeed, it is startling to realize how little publicity attaches to the particular story itself, even when its author has become, temporarily, "a story," someone to be written about and photographed.

We have had alarming examples of the rite in operation: each season one or two young writers, fresh from university creative writing courses or from comparable strategic venues, are magically seized upon, taken up, thrust into the limelight, and then, having had their moment there, are let go, dropped, making way for the new discovery—and the talent that blazed up in those early stories seems to have burned out. That is sad enough in itself—surely so for the sacrificial victim—but what is even more deplorable is the notion that each season represents a fashion in stories—the year of the Minimum alternating with the year of the Maximum, as it were—and only *those* need to be written (or read) to be in vogue. Nothing could be farther from the truth.

Beyond fashion, the truth about the American short story in recent decades—and here, of course, I am generalizing from a wide-range perspective—is that it has been (and continues to be) accessible to many voices, expressive in many different modes, tones, themes, styles, structures, and concerns. Yet for all their individual differences, these stories do, whether consciously and deliberately or obliquely and with no such overt intention, reflect something of the time, our time, in which they are written and in which we live. That indeed is part of their fascination, for they present aspects of our time to us in ways that we may have only dimly perceived before. And at a great remove from the noisy misperceptions broadcast to us in official stereotypes, condescensions, platitudes, and slogans. A story, making no claims beyond itself, can illuminate experience, rarefied or commonplace, with the sort of truthfulness that doesn't figure in the calculations of communicators.

Certainly this is true of the twenty stories assembled in the present volume. The tradition of the O. Henry series, going back almost seventy years, dictates that three of the stories should be singled out as first, second, and third prizewinners, and that has been done. But I hasten to add that all twenty included here are O. Henry Award stories, and their placement is in no way meant to suggest an order of merit. The arrangement is simply aimed at showing to best advantage the variety in the contemporary American short story. Now and later they are here to be discovered, or as I would prefer to say, to be explored.

We are all, in the matter of short stories, explorers. For readers and writers, each in their own way, the story represents a kind of continuing exploration. One comes to it for its revelation of a truth of its own, however familiar the material out of which it is created may at first seem to be. In fact, if a story were no more than a mirror of ourselves, it would hardly survive a first reading. We would know it all already, and the individual secret would remain out of reach. Even the most dexterous manipulations of the mirror can't conceal stereotyped formulas—from which we may draw a reasonable conclusion: that a manufactured story can be programmed, but a created story, such as those here, cannot.

Reading these twenty stories, one recognizes the double nature of the exploration involved: the writer blazes the trail, the reader is persuaded to follow it. Does the writer, beginning the story, committing himself or herself to a first sentence—that significant blaze!—does the writer know where, ultimately, the trail will lead? Let us acknowledge an element of mystery here, a margin of meaning beyond what a writer may at first consciously have intended (or what a reader may have expected).

Consider, as a single classic example, the story "House Hunting" by Joyce Carol Oates. The title itself evokes a humdrum, or thrilling, or disturbing quasi-universal experience. And the elements of Ms. Oates's story are, on the face of it, quite simple: a young married couple who have recently lost their infant child; a decision in response to this tragedy to move across the country and resettle; the husband going on ahead as a kind of advance party to look for a house where they will resume the ordered pattern of their lives. Thus summed up, how ordinary and predictable the story might seem; yet how unpredictable and extraordinary it proves to be, and not simply because the author, as who does not already know, is so much the master of her art. Very subtly (and I do not propose to go into the details that are so essential a part of it) the hunt for a house moves beyond the boundaries of its announced subject. Yes, the hunt goes on, but something more is being sought. House hunting, we gradually apprehend, becomes a metaphor for life itself, and the house a habitation for the soul. The enigma of creativity accounts for much, and it seems plausible to say that Ms. Oates was exploring the story even as she was writing it.

I am certain, too, that something comparable might be discerned in each of these stories—but I do not mean to indulge in an editor's privilege to scrutinize what ought first to be enjoyed. There remains only to say of all twenty stories that they have been chosen not to illustrate a point or confirm a theme, but simply for their special, individual excellences. I leave to readers the pleasure of discovering those for themselves.

This year for the first time the biographies of the authors have been gathered together in a special section at the end of the book, along with comments by several of them about how the stories came to be written.

Invaluable assistance in preparing this volume has come from John M. Dean in California, and from Sally Arteseros and Teresa Scala in New York.

WILLIAM ABRAHAMS

Peacocks

•

ERNEST J. FINNEY

When he ran he kept his eyes closed as long as he could. The connection between himself and the dirt path that paralleled the orchard was what kept him from running into a tree. The loamy soil was just soft enough to carry his heelprint. Enough to keep the connection. On the other side of the path was the levee that kept the water in the slough away from the orchard. Whenever he felt himself veering up the bank, he forced himself to keep his eyes shut until he was sure he was back on the path by the plum trees his grandfather had planted. He knew them as well as anyone could. He'd been up in every single tree. He was well connected with the orchard and his grandfather.

It was easy keeping his eyes closed because he knew where he was going. He could run forever this way: his feet kept sending his imagination the right direction. But the pain was getting worse, his kidneys were burning red hot. It was hard to breathe, but he made himself keep going. He wanted to make it all the way back to the house for the first time. Grandpa would be sitting on the porch waiting, watching his pets. He tried to outrun it, went faster. He must be almost past the last section, Queen Rosas. When the bile started coming up he remembered what Jesse, his coach, said: it doesn't really hurt until after you stop, so keep going. Then he started vomiting and opened his eyes so he wouldn't get any on his shoes. He leaned forward, his

arms stiff against his knees, spitting, trying to get it all out.
Gasping, feeling his whole body hurt. When he could breathe, he
stood up and started for the house. He still had another half
hour left of his workout.

He could see the roof. The house was just right for the two of
them. All on one floor, so his grandfather didn't have to climb
steps, like in the main house. Each had his own door off his
bedroom into the bathroom. Plenty of privacy for his grandfather, who never came out into the kitchen in the long johns he
wore summer and winter. He dressed for his first cup of coffee.
The place was small enough to heat easily in the winter and cool
with one fan in the summer. He had set up his telescope on a
platform outside the attic window. And the porch was perfect
for his grandfather, two steps from the ground and his peafowl.

Grandpa was watching him come up. The peafowl were pecking and scratching in the flower bed. The cocks were too young
to have any of the big feathers. He got a kick out of how his
grandfather treated them. Named the three males after the
Three Stooges. The nine females had no names. Had trained
Moe to hop up on the porch rail and beg for the cracked corn he
kept in his shirt pocket.

He started out first. "Well, how's the stock, are they all fed
and watered? Getting ready to roost for the night?" He untied
the rope around his waist and started jumping, easy, just lifting
the toes of his shoes enough to let the rope pass under.

"Can't say," Grandpa answered. "They're so slow. If they
don't hurry up and grow some of those tail feathers I'm ready to
give up on them. I won't be responsible. They're just like chickens.

"Now that I'm semiretired and only a consultant in the plum
business, I thought I'd raise these birds. I'd seen them in the
catalogue for years, but never felt I was ready to buy." Elmo
kept jumping, the sound of his grandfather's voice caught up in
the rhythm that the rope and his feet were moving to. They both
knew they had heard this before. "I thought they were a sign of

prosperity: when a person raised something he wasn't planning on eating and selling, it gave you a certain distinction."

Elmo looked over at his grandfather. He'd changed again. Not just thinner than before, but he seemed like he was shrinking too. He was shorter than the six and a half feet he used to be. Elmo himself still had a foot to go to catch up, but there wasn't the difference there used to be.

When he heard the car, it was too close for him to get away. He kept jumping, faster now, trying not to watch her ease out of the car. Her stomach was so big she had the seat all the way back. She reached inside for the hot dish with a blue towel over the top. Grandpa had stood up, stiff-legged, and he went to meet her. "Well, Greta, you didn't have to go to any trouble, but we appreciate it, of course." She stopped nearly every day with something.

"It's no trouble," she said.

He turned the rope slower, not to miss anything.

Grandpa took the bowl. "I got the others washed up," he said. "I'll get them."

"That would be nice. I forget where they are. I keep looking for them."

"I got a little behind," he said, opening the screen door with his foot, carrying the bowl with both hands.

She turned awkwardly to watch Elmo jump. It looked like she was leaning back so far, to compensate for her stomach, that she would go over backwards. "How have you been, Elmo?" she asked.

"I'm fine."

"We don't see you much any more."

He jumped slow now, barely bringing the slack loop around. "I've been busy," he said. Then he heard the pickup. He didn't turn around, just kept jumping. James stopped right next to him, so he had to bring his arm in to miss tangling the rope on the truck mirror.

"Like old home week," James said. Grandpa came out the

screen door carrying a cardboard box rattling with Pyrex bowls and tin piepans. Elmo kept jumping.

"What I want to know is why don't you two come up and eat with us instead of making her bring the food down to you?"

The rope caught on Elmo's head and he let it hang on his shoulders, breathing hard. "We don't ask her to bring it," he said.

"Well, she can stop, then," James said.

"I don't mind," Greta said. "It's only a couple of miles."

"How did the pruning go?" Grandpa asked James, taking the box over to Greta's car.

"We're half done. Another three weeks, unless we can get the prima donna to help."

Elmo didn't answer; he wasn't going to fall into that trap again. "I do my share" sounded like an admission of guilt when he said it to James. And then James would snicker. The sound made him want to close his eyes.

James got out of the truck, hooked the heel of his boot on the bumper. He had a gut on him now. Almost as big as Greta's. His leather belt cut into the middle of it as if it were separating a couple of sausages. James looked bigger than any two heavyweights Elmo had ever seen. "What exactly have you been doing?" James asked. "Let's hear it; I'm interested."

Elmo saw the look on Grandpa's face, as if he was going to see something awful. Greta was holding her stomach from underneath with both hands. "Ever since we've come back from our honeymoon, you act like you're a guest here. When I can find you. You live down here—that's all right with me—but you're not doing your share. Those plum trees can't take care of themselves. Grandpa can't work any more. Greta can't either. That leaves you and me."

He didn't have to answer; he could just look at James. Infuriate him. His face would turn as red as the bulb on the porch thermometer. James was too easy. "I've been pretty busy," he said. "Going to school." Saying it out loud, he realized he'd been catching the school bus for eleven years now. It sounded like he needed more, so he added, "I was elected class president. I have to stay for council meetings. And I have sports."

James snickered. "What sports?" He'd been All League in his freshman year, playing football. All State in the shotput.

"I'm on the boxing team."

James laughed out loud. Elmo felt himself start to lose the connection he had with the ground.

"I had to sign a card," Grandpa said. "He's got a punching bag in the shed. I've got four clippings from the school paper too, if you want to see them."

"When are you going to fight next?" James asked.

There was no way out. "Next month at the Elks'."

"I've got to see that," James said, getting back in the truck. "Come on, let's go," he yelled over to Greta.

"That woman can cook," Grandpa said. He'd barely touched the Swiss steak Greta had brought over. Elmo was sopping up the last of the gravy with his fifth piece of bread. "Maybe we ought to go up there for dinner when she invites us. Say on a Sunday."

"You go ahead," Elmo said.

"He's your brother."

"Remember when we went up there?"

"It takes a lot of adjustment when you're first married," Grandpa said. "Two different people."

"Did you ever slap around our grandmother?" Elmo asked. He had to ask; it was worse not to. "I was just wondering," he added.

Grandpa took his time answering. "I was guilty of a lot of things, but not that."

They hadn't seen anything that time. Just heard the yelling, waiting for someone to open the door. Greta had been crying, face pink, eyes floating in tears. They sat down at the table and James started. "I never met anyone so stupid. I tell her to pick up my boots and get the case of shotgun shells I ordered. She forgets both of them. Drives all the way into town for a hot fudge sundae. Dumb."

"That's not necessary," Grandpa said.

"It is, believe me. She's stupid."

"If anyone is stupid it's you, James," Elmo said. "She graduated from high school; you didn't."

"Well, well," James said, smiling, "look who's speaking up."

"That's enough," Greta said.

"You're not big enough to take seriously," James said to Elmo.

No one said a word the rest of the dinner. He wouldn't go back. He didn't want to be connected with that business.

The next time, he came home from school and Greta was there, her lip cut, her eye swollen almost closed. Grandpa was putting hot cloths on the side of her face. "Do this for me, Elmo; I'm going to talk to James." He had no choice. He squeezed the cloth out, folded it into a rectangle, and put it over her eye. What was the connection between them? Earlier she had been like an older sister to him. No. That's what he made up for his grandfather, after she married James. But she should have married him—that's what he thought at the time. At fourteen. With seven years' difference between them. She should have waited for him. But now the connection between them was much less. He was almost a spectator. Someone who was watching a movie, then went home when it was over. "Oh, Elmo," she said, taking hold of his wrist. He didn't know what to do, how to act. He didn't understand this. How could anyone do something like that if he loved a person? Would he ever do that?

When Grandpa came home, she went back up to the house. "I told him," Grandpa said, "what kind of a man it took to hit a woman. I made him listen. Made it as plain as I could. I explained I wasn't going to have anyone on my place like that. It's not you boys' yet."

It stopped for a couple of months. Then Greta went to the

hospital with her nose broken. She said she fell. James took off, was in town drinking with his friends. Grandpa went after him. Elmo drove, parked in front of the Rio cocktail lounge, and followed him inside. James was sitting with Claude at the bar, swigging beer out of a green bottle. "I hope you're satisfied," Grandpa told him. "She went back to her folks."

"Good," James said. "I was getting tired of her anyway," and he laughed.

Grandpa backhanded him across the face hard. It was like hitting a tree. The place quieted down. "You sober up," Grandpa said. "I want to see you at six out in that orchard. Or don't you come back." Then he walked out. Elmo stood there for a minute, staring at his brother. He didn't want to leave him. Then his grandfather called out at the door, "Come on, Elmo."

He was doing his math at the kitchen table when the phone rang. "What's wrong with him? Elmo, is that you?"

"It's me, Joyce." He didn't want to hear what was coming from Greta's stepmother. It was amazing, all these connections. It reminded him of TinkerToys; you just kept adding more and more, going up and up. Was it natural—all these connections people had? Greta, his sister-in-law, her real mother dead, had her father Eddie, and of course Joyce, three stepsisters, and James her husband, and she was going to have a baby. They all meant something. Where he had his grandfather. And James. Sometimes. But more, say, than the photos of his mother, whom he couldn't remember; she'd left when he was little. Or his father, whom he could remember, that he'd found dead. His parents were like someone you didn't know that you read about in the newspaper. Interesting. But nothing to do with him.

"I'm not letting her come back there, Elmo. You can tell him that for me. Not when he mistreats her like this. And I can tell you, Eddie is upset; he's ready to come down there. Somebody better start talking some sense into that boy before it's too late."

He wrote down *James* on the paper. Grandpa's name. Then his own name. Grandpa was fifty years older than he was. James

was nine years. Was time important? He needed more information for an equation. For an answer. "Who was that?" Grandpa
asked, coming out of his bedroom. Elmo wasn't going to tell
him. He was having to go in to the doctor almost every week
now. He was skin and bones.

"It was Joyce."

Grandpa shook his head. "What can we do?" He kept a shining new thirty-gallon galvanized can in the entryway full of feed
for the peacocks. He lifted the lid and filled the pocket of his
wool shirt with cracked corn. Went out. Elmo could hear him
tilt his chair back and the sound of the first peacock hopping up
on the porch.

He watched from the kitchen window as another peacock
jumped up on the railing and displayed its train of feathers for
Grandpa. It was like having your own rainbow handy to look at.
They made him uneasy, those birds. The way they waited for
you to admire them. As if there were more to it than that. They
didn't belong here. They didn't have any connection to this
place. He couldn't imagine anything else that came close to a
peacock. He tried, too. Combining different kinds of ducks from
the marsh, a kingfisher and a red-winged blackbird, spring plum
blossoms with California poppies. It was no use. The harder he
tried, the less anything would come. He'd seen something almost
close enough once, but never got the chance to decide. It was a
painting by someone with a name he couldn't pronounce. Two
fat naked women in a field drying themselves after taking a swim
in a pond. It wasn't only the colors or the figures; it was the
feeling there was something else that was there that you couldn't
see. But someone had cut the picture out of the magazine before
he could bring it home from school to compare with the peafowl.
One time when his grandfather went to town he tried to catch
one. He was going to chase it down, get ahold of one, get a closer
look. But it took off, train of feathers and all. It was the first time
he'd seen one leave the ground. It flew better than a pheasant. It

was like seeing a hydrangea bush take off. He kept away from
them after that.

He wasn't nervous; it was just that he wasn't used to so many
people watching. The whole Elks' club was filled, must be a
thousand people. He had heard them from the storage room
where they were dressing. He'd stayed in there after the bouts
started, following the fights by the yelling, which was off and on
like someone was opening and shutting a door. Then he moved
over to the doorway.

He hadn't wanted Grandpa to come. But he'd insisted. James
had to stick his big nose in. "What's wrong—you don't want
him to see you get whipped?" It wasn't that; he was going to
win. But he'd never watched him fight before, and it was going
to make him feel exposed. Immodest. As if all the efforts they
made to be clothed, even when they got up in the middle of the
night to pee, were for nothing.

James brought him. They were sitting down in front, both of
them so big the people around them were already trying to shift
their folding chairs so they could see. Grandpa was still taller
than James. By getting fatter, James seemed shorter at the same
height. Elmo knew if he made six feet it would be a miracle.

After they awarded the trophies for the bouts before him and
the cheering died down, he came down the aisle. This was all
familiar. Jesse there with the stool. He didn't look at the other
fighter coming into the ring. He wouldn't do that until the bell.
There was no connection between them. He wasn't responsible.

They went out to the middle for instructions. The other
fighter tried to stare him down. He decided it would be better to
fight outside under the stars. The announcer gave their names
and the other fighter's tournament win in a trip to Chicago. Not
only wouldn't it be so smoky—there'd be the constellations he
knew. Jesse was taking his robe off his shoulders, wetting his
mouthpiece before putting it in.

He moved to the exact center, watching. The whole trick was

not to allow his eyes to go to any part of the other boxer but his nose. He imagined he was a flying railroad spike aimed at the middle of his opponent's head. There was the usual feeling out. It was going to depend on who was just a little quicker and who was in better shape for three two-minute rounds. That's what Jesse always told them.

Jab, he had the reach. His opponent's face began to get red; his eyes seemed to shift around, trying to get out of his head. "Stick 'im," Jesse kept yelling from the corner. It was almost too easy. The other fighter was getting concerned because he wasn't hitting anything. Getting wild.

He breathed easy, sitting on the stool after the first round. He'd heard James yelling "Killum, killum." Now he was yelling "Don't let up on him, don't lose him." There was a certain satisfaction in doing everything right, in order, exactly as he'd planned. He didn't understand why, but he always had the feeling he was the only one in the ring. That would be another good reason to fight outside.

He went out the second time, moving toward the center, knowing what was going to happen. His opponent came out fast, charged, swinging furiously. Then he threw his right hand, the leather connecting, making a satisfactory sound as it struck. His opponent sat on the canvas with a bewildered look on his face, his coach waving a towel, the referee yelling, the spectators in an uproar. He leaned against the ropes, not breathing hard yet, wondering if he should order two or three cheeseburgers after. He hadn't eaten any dinner.

The other fighter got up. He didn't want to look surprised, didn't register anything. He went back out. It was the only time in any of his nine fights that anyone had got up. But the kid's eyes were fixed now, and Elmo came in hitting him with both hands at will.

The referee stepped in and pulled Elmo away, his arms locked around Elmo's chest. The crowd went crazy; then there was a new burst of yelling as the referee put Elmo's arm up. This had been the main event. He got the winner's trophy, which was the same as the one they gave the loser. He always thought that was funny. Then the judges selected their fight as the best of the evening and they both got another trophy. More yelling. James and Grandpa were at the ring-side when he climbed down.

"You looked good," James yelled above the noise. "I never thought you had it in you." Grandpa patted his shoulder. Jesse came over. "He's a natural," he told them. "He's got fast hands and can hit with either one. You saw that. He's easy to coach, I'll tell you that. He can go all the way to the national finals if he wants." Elmo nodded, deciding he'd get all three cheeseburgers.

There was something pleasant about people coming up and congratulating him. People in town. Kids at school. Betty, a girl he'd ridden the school bus with, eight years to grammar school and two and a half so far to high school, came up blushing. "You pack a wallop, my father told me to tell you." He never knew what to say, except thank you. For her he said something different: "That's a kind thought."

Since Greta left, Grandpa had been cooking. Liver. Heart, braised. Spent all day scrubbing tripe on a washboard and soaking it in salted water for stew, red stew with potatoes and carrots. Brain fritters. Kidney pie. It was as if he was trying to find something Elmo wouldn't eat. "This is what I was raised on because it was cheap. Rich people threw this away with the guts," and he'd hold up a piece of liver with his fork. He didn't eat much, but he made Elmo eat. And James, when he stopped in at dinnertime. He'd stopped drinking and going to town after work. He'd been up to see Greta once. But she wouldn't come back.

A couple of weeks after his fight at the Elks' club they were sitting around the table after a dinner of brains and scrambled eggs. "That was tasty," Elmo told his grandfather.

"You're just trying to get on my good side so I'll make them again tomorrow." They both laughed. They were cracking English walnuts for dessert. Elmo put his halves on the oil-cloth near his grandfather's plate. They looked like dried flowers there. It was one thing he would eat. Lately when he told his stories he'd been going back, Elmo noticed, to his wife or his sister, never staying in the present very long if he could help it.

"I want you to consider quitting that boxing business," Grandpa said. Surprised, Elmo waited. Cracked another nut. "You took that other boy apart at the Elks' club. Just like you were pruning one of our plum trees." He pointed out the window toward the orchard. "It was too easy for you. You were like an executioner up there."

"I don't pick my opponents," Elmo answered.

"Some people shouldn't do things without knowing the same thing could happen to them. You're one of them. If it were James, I wouldn't waste my breath. He'd do the opposite. So would I, probably, for that matter. But I'm going to leave it up to you."

"I don't understand what you mean."

He lowered his voice, as if someone could overhear them. "You have to be careful, Elmo. What you do. You're my grandson. In the end it's going to be you that gets hurt."

Elmo slowly shook his head.

"You're too smart, Elmo," he said louder. "And now your hands are too smart." He got up. "I cooked this lovely dinner; you wash up," he said, going for the feed can.

He kept running, working out after school. It was habit, mostly, but he couldn't decide whether to quit or not. He kept going over what his grandfather had said. What difference did it make if hitting someone were easy or not? Betty offered to give him a ride home after a student-council meeting. She had the family Plymouth for the day. Her father had the dealership in town, but they lived on thirty acres of pears down the road from the plum orchard. They stopped at the A and W, and kids in other cars came over to say hello. They passed James on the way to town.

He honked when he saw Elmo. "Who's that?" Betty asked. "I don't recognize the pickup."

"Don't know," Elmo said.

Grandpa was sitting on the porch. His pet peacock Curly was on the rail, its plumage spread out. He got up out of his chair when Elmo introduced him, a few kernels of cracked corn dropping off his washed-out wool shirt. He took off his fedora to shake hands with Betty. "I know your father," he said. "You'll notice we have nothing but Dodge pickups."

"Best farm truck on the road," Betty said.

"She's slightly biased, Grandpa." Elmo went to get some cracked corn for her to feed to the peafowl. They ate right out of her hand from the first try.

"They must like you," Grandpa said. "They won't do that for everyone. Won't do that for Elmo."

"Because I run them off the porch with a broom. You don't hear them at four A.M. screeching."

After Betty had driven off, Grandpa said, "Nice girl."

"You're just saying that because your peacocks liked her," Elmo said.

"You don't see a flaming redhaired girl with two million freckles every day."

Teasing, Elmo asked, "You notice things like that still?"

"I'm not dead yet," Grandpa said, whacking Elmo on the shoulder with the fedora.

There was a boxing tournament in the city over the weekend. Elmo mentioned to Jesse that he wanted to move up a class to welterweight. "You're giving away your edge; they're bigger kids. They'll outweigh you." Elmo waited until he was through. Jesse was a gardener at the high school who had boxed in the navy. His team was the only one at school that was winning this year. Jesse almost strutted when he went into the teachers' lounge for coffee. "Don't worry, I know what I'm doing," Elmo said.

He won five matches and the division title. His picture was on local TV with Jesse, who was shorter than he, picking him up in a bear hug around the waist after the last fight. He was interviewed in the dressing room by a sports writer who covered high-school athletics for the city paper. When he got home, people he didn't know phoned to congratulate him. Grandpa didn't say anything, handed him the phone.

Betty phoned him. "I saw you on TV," she said.

"I guess I'm just a celebrity."

"My father said you could be in the Olympics."

"Me and Joe Palooka. I don't know if I want to go that far. It's kind of like astronomy. I used to think that people were almost like constellations. You can only know so much about them, as much as you can see, and then you have to rely on your imagination. I was wrong; because people are so much closer, it makes it harder to understand them."

"You're losing me, Elmo. But go on."

"I'm losing myself," he said. "Hitting someone in the ring is like making contact with a constellation. Draco, say. You get to know more. You see what I mean? There is a connection. But not as much as, say, between your sisters and you."

"Keep going."

"Maybe boxing is getting down to the essentials. Between yourself and who you think you are."

"I'm changing the subject," she said. "Did you get the assignment in math?"

He laughed. "You know better; I finished that on the bus."

"That was a silly question. A scholar like you. I have to go now. You phone me next. My mother thinks it's undignified."

"I promise," Elmo said.

Grandpa went into town for an appointment, and the doctor put him in the hospital. "They want to run a few tests," he told Elmo when he came into his room. "They must know I had some more money left." Elmo sat next to the bed to be able to hear him whisper: "Take care of my pets for me."

"I will, Grandpa."

"Don't be stingy with the feed."

"I won't." There was nothing to be worried about, Elmo kept telling himself.

The necessary three parking places were empty, and he maneuvered the truck just right, ten feet from his grandfather's window, then hurried inside. "I got a surprise for you," he said. His grandfather lay on his side, looking in the wrong direction. He started to turn toward him. Elmo knocked on the window with his knuckles for the bird. He had tethered the peacock up on top of the case he'd brought him in. He didn't think the stupid bird was going to cooperate. Just then he raised his train and the plumage spread out like a fan catching the summer light. The iridescent blues and greens moved like water.

"That's old Moe," Grandpa said, sitting up. He was looking better after this operation than he had after the first. He might be gaining weight. But he was still white as a sheet. He'd been in here the whole summer. The peacock collapsed its feathers. "Greta's just left; brought the baby in. He's going to be big like me and James," he said. "On the other hand, Greta's tall too, of course. Said she's pregnant again. That's rushing it, I'd say." Elmo stood still at the window, waiting for the peacock to answer his knocking again. "How's the picking going?"

"Right on time. We're in the California Blues."

"You'll be going back to school next week."

"If James gives me permission." Elmo laughed. "He's got Claude helping in the plums; he'll get by. Greta comes when she can."

"How are they getting along now? I didn't want to ask her."

"All right, I guess." He didn't want to tell him about the latest episode. How could they do that: call each other names, throw things, hit each other. Was he missing some connection between them?

"They wanted to name the baby after me," Grandpa said. "I said don't. Three Jameses are enough. Gary is a good name."

Elmo looked down at his grandfather. Listening to him, he could feel his eyes tear up, his eyelids blinking them away. He bent down and hugged him. When Elmo let go, he saw his grandfather was embarrassed.

Greta had left him a pan of meatloaf and potatoes. He sat at the kitchen table eating, not bothering to get a plate. Between going in to the hospital and working in the plums he hadn't been doing much else. He was so tired when he came in he sometimes fell asleep eating. He decided to phone Betty. He had meant to a dozen times. He hadn't seen her since school let out in June. He knew she'd got a job in town as a lifeguard at the pool.

She answered the phone on the first ring.

"May I speak to Betty Jean Briscoe, please?"

"This is she."

"This is Elmo Clark. Would you be interested in attending a movie classic, Creature of the Lost Lagoon, this next Friday evening?"

"Is this a date we're discussing here, Mr. Clark?" She started to giggle. He could hear her whisper to someone in the background "I have a date, I have a date."

"I think it would come under that category."

"Then I accept."

She could have said no. But then on the other hand he could be underestimating his own resources. He was looking at himself in the mirror over the sink. The pimples were gone except on his forehead, and his hair hid them. Five-o'clock shadow; he needed to shave once a week now. If he fought again he'd be a middleweight; he'd gained. But he was through with that. He looked closer, from a different angle, at his reflection. If he did look like his grandpa's sister Lorraine, she must have been a knockout.

Someone honked his horn out front. It could only be Mickey Conlin. He went out, the peacocks bobbing out of his way. "You want to go hunting tomorrow morning?" Mickey called out before he got near. Mickey was sitting in a new red sportscar

convertible Elmo didn't know the name of until he got close.
Mickey's father had leased the marsh from his grandfather for
his duck club five years ago. He brought clients over from the
city to shoot. Mickey was convinced he and Elmo were the
same. Because they were both sixteen. He had been in the auditorium when Elmo had boxed in the city. He had his younger
sister Virginia with him.

"Some of us have to work for a living," Elmo said, resting his
hands on the door. It was what his grandfather would have said.

"Come on, Elmo, the place is loaded with doves."

It gave him some pleasure to refuse—probably, he thought,
because Mickey wanted him to come so much. "Can't. If I don't
help James, my name's mud. You've got Virginia, she's lucky.
You going to hunt tomorrow?" he asked her. She didn't answer.
"You got your .410 with you?"

She finally nodded, then spoke. "Yes. I remember how you
showed me, Elmo. Keep the butt tight against the small of my
shoulder." At nine she was already a better shot than Mickey.

"Don't shoot in the trees where there's still plums."

"I won't," she said.

"Next time," he said, backing away from the car.

Elmo brought his grandfather home Friday morning. Helped
him out of the car. "I can walk," he said, holding onto Elmo's
shoulder. All the peafowl came across the yard in mincing steps,
the males expanding their feathers. "They're happy to see me,"
he said, hauling himself up the steps by the railing. He sat down
in his porch chair, and Elmo went back to the truck for his
things. The peafowl came up on the porch, wanting to be fed.
Elmo got the juice can of cracked corn and handed it to him.

"No matter what happens, I'm not going back to the hospital," he said as if he were ending a long conversation on the
subject. "I'm staying right here."

"The doctor says you're fine," Elmo said.

"That's right," Grandpa said. "He said that the last time too."

· · ·

It was almost time for him to leave to pick up Betty. "You're sure you don't want to go along?" he asked his grandfather. They both laughed.

"You don't need a chaperone, and that movie you told me about would keep me up nights."

"You're going to be all right?"

"If I'm lonely I'll phone Greta. If I get hungry I'll cook me up one of my peacock friends out there. Did I tell you I met someone in physical therapy that told me he actually had one of those critters for dinner? I was telling him about mine and he told me the story. I didn't tell you this yet?"

"No you didn't," Elmo said, not looking at the clock.

"Thought it would taste like pheasant. Cooked two. With orange slices, stuffed them with carrots and onions, like we do with ducks. Low heat. Basted them with their own drippings and white wine. Put it out on the table in front of his guests. Had his carving knife all ready, sharpened it with the steel." Grandpa made the motions of sharpening. "Tried to take a slice off. Wouldn't cut. Kept trying. Everybody waiting. Put it back on the cutting board and got a heavier knife; didn't do the trick. Tried a cleaver next, brought it down, never dented it. He had to take the guests out to a restaurant." The last time he told it, Elmo remembered, the peacock had been put on a chopping block and hit with an ax.

Mr. Briscoe opened the door, looked past him. "How many miles you got on that pickup?" he asked.

Elmo was ready; he remembered coming to birthday parties here: Mr. Briscoe had once wrapped up a colt for Betty in tissue paper and led it into the dining room. "One hundred and seventy-two thousand and six tenths of a mile, give or take a few feet."

"You Clarks, you're running it into the ground; I can't make any money off you. I can't even remember when I sold that truck." He sounded indignant. He led Elmo into the front room

and pointed to the couch for him to sit down. Elmo perched on
the edge. He never had a chance to be nervous; Betty came right
out and he stood back up. Being out in the sun must have made
her freckles multiply, he decided. There were at least a million
more, the color of red ants.

"Did he sell you a new pickup yet?" she asked him.

"Not yet." He wished he could seem as at ease as she was.

"How come I haven't seen your name in the paper lately?
Give up boxing?" Mr. Briscoe asked.

He was going to say, "No time. I've had to work." But for
some reason he heard himself going into a longer explanation. "I
liked it at first because a person has to concentrate so much,
with the conditioning and the training. The actual fighting was
secondary." Mr. Briscoe was looking puzzled. "Then I got so I
liked getting ready more than the actual boxing, so I've decided
not to do it any more. I just work out now."

Betty's mother came out of another room. She'd put on lipstick, he noticed. She had the same red hair and freckles as Betty
had. "How's your grandfather? I heard he was in the hospital."

"He's home now, feeling much better."

Betty took him by the arm and led him toward the front door
and opened it. "Say hello for me," Mrs. Briscoe said at the door.

Mr. Briscoe followed them down the walk. "Tell him I can get
him a good deal on this year's model."

"You promised," Betty said as she got into the pickup. Elmo
shut the door for her and went around.

"I know," Mr. Briscoe said, "but it's not every day I see you
hold your breath when I start to say something. I couldn't pass
it up." He started laughing, took his glasses off to wipe his eyes.

Elmo drove down their road wondering how long it took an
individual family like the Briscoes to develop the connections
with each other and how long with an outsider. Would an outsider not having the same past ever be connected well enough?
Greta wasn't a good example. Maybe the connection between a
person and object was more important. His grandfather's

peacocks. Or a person and what he thought. Just what he could think up inside his own head. The connection between himself and himself.

"What are you thinking?" Betty asked.

"Just when was the last time I changed the oil in this old wreck. What were you thinking?"

"If I hid my shampoo so my sister wouldn't use it."

They took back seats, right under the wall where the beam of light came out of the projectionist's booth. He must have sat next to her at least a hundred times on the school bus, in classes. But he felt uncomfortable, as if he had no control over his body. His stomach might gurgle, he might pass gas, drool, snort. He shifted himself again.

"You can hold my hand, Elmo," she said, "I'm done with the popcorn." He picked it up. It was warm, and he could feel the echo her pulse made from the flat of her thumb. After the cartoon was over and the movie started she whispered, "You can kiss me if you like, but only with a modicum of passion."

"Do you think I need all this direction?" he said. She closed her eyes, he noticed as he leaned toward her. He kissed her once and said, "You're going to have to wipe your mouth of the popcorn butter, Miss Briscoe, if I'm going to be able to gain purchase on your lips."

Walking back to the pickup, they passed the Rio. James must have seen them, because he and Claude came outside. James was yelling after them "Lookee here, what do I see?" and slurring his words. Elmo had to stop; there were people passing. James was so drunk his fly was half-open and he had to brace himself with one hand against the blue tiled front of the bar to stand. Claude, weaving slightly, stood alongside him. "Aren't you going to introduce me?" James asked.

He wasn't embarrassed, Elmo told himself. This was nothing. "This is my brother James," he told Betty, "and his friend Claude. Betty Briscoe." He had been holding her hand but now let it go.

"Pleased to make your acquaintance, Betty," James said. "Out on the town, huh. Why don't you come in and I'll buy you a drink." He tried to straighten up, and took a few steps toward them. Took Betty by the arm. "Come on, I know your old man." He tried to take a step backward and almost fell, pulling Betty with him.

"That's enough," Elmo said, getting between them and pushing James away.

"Who do you think you're pushing?" James said, and he tried to shove Elmo back, lost his balance, and fell over onto the sidewalk.

Claude punched Elmo from the side and knocked him down on all fours. "Son of a bitch," he said as he kicked Elmo in the stomach. Elmo noticed Betty had her hands over her face. He would have liked to reassure her. This was just funny. If he could get his breath to laugh, he would. There was no connection between her and what was happening. She shouldn't be bothered by this.

"Wait a minute," James was saying. "Just wait a minute." He got back up. "That's my little brother." Elmo got back up too, holding his stomach. His head was ringing like a bell, as if his tongue was the clapper. Claude had stepped back, both hands clenched and down low like an old-time boxer, ready for him. He wasn't as drunk as James. He blinked his eyes. Elmo aligned himself with the north star and moved in.

Claude swung too soon, and he stepped in and under, bringing his fist around. The skin over Claude's cheek bone split, and he felt his knuckle pop against the bone. Then, noting he was still aligned, he brought his right hand around. Claude crumpled like a piece of wastepaper.

James came toward him, weaving back and forth, his hands to his sides. Elmo hit him in the face. It was like hitting a sponge. "How do you like that?" Elmo told him, saying it every time he struck, until some customers came out from the bar and stopped it.

He remembered Betty then. She wasn't there. He walked as
fast as he could to where the truck was parked, but she wasn't
there either. He just started walking, not knowing where to look
next. He looked in the couple of stores still open as he passed,
going all the way back to the movie. He was worried now. She
couldn't walk home; it was too far.

He phoned her house. Her mother answered. "Mrs. Briscoe,
Betty and I seem to have got separated somehow."

"Her father went to pick her up. She phoned here. She was
upset."

"Thank you, Mrs. Briscoe," he said, not knowing what else to
say.

James's face looked like a plum that had been stepped on. He
wouldn't come into the house so Grandpa could see him. Talked
to Elmo from inside the cab of his pickup. "Whatever happened," James said, "it was probably my fault. I don't even
remember what I did," he said. Elmo didn't believe him. "You
don't know how bad I feel about this. I'm married and have a
kid and another one on the way. I have to decide what comes
first." Elmo was embarrassed. James was serious. "I was thinking this morning, what if I lost Greta. I'm going to straighten
up." He started the pickup. "Claude said you got lucky last
night. I told him we were lucky you didn't kill us both. If it
makes any difference, I'm sorry. I'm sorry about the girl. I remember that much. I'm sorry, Elmo."

He was going to phone Betty but he put it off. Decided to wait
until school started. They both had U.S. history first period. She
sat at the front. After class he caught up with her outside in the
hallway. He didn't know how to start out. He just walked along
beside her while she ignored him. She finally stopped and sat
down on a wooden bench. He sat beside her. "I don't know what
you want me to say," he started out.

"We don't act like that in my family," she said. "We don't go
in for excess. You were as much to blame as they were." She had

placed her books on her knees. This was not important, he decided, starting to enjoy the situation. There was no connection between them. "You Clarks are always doing something. You're famous in the county for it. When I was a little girl, I heard about you. I used to watch you on the bus and think I might catch you changing into something else."

She's being dramatic, he thought, and he started to laugh. She jumped up and walked away, surprising him. He yelled after her, "You have too many freckles anyway. I can't see you without trying to count them." She kept going, never turned around. "It's a nuisance," he called after her.

"I feel like I've been pregnant all my life," Greta said, sitting in the kitchen with Elmo. He didn't answer; he was thinking of Betty, whom he'd taken to the drive-in movie last night. Greta had to repeat herself. Elmo managed to nod and grin. They heard Grandpa's feet hit the linoleum floor. Elmo got up fast. "I'm getting the hell out of here," his grandfather said. "You and me are going to take off, Elmo. I'm not staying here any more." Elmo took him by the shoulders and eased him back in bed. "Are my clothes handy, Elmo?"

"They're handy, Grandpa," he said, putting the covers up around his grandfather's chin. "You rest some more; then we'll make some plans. These trips take some time." He went back out into the kitchen.

"His mind wanders," Greta said. "What did the doctor say yesterday?"

"He wants to put him in a rest home. Again. He thinks he's had another stroke. He'll come back, get better; he's not that way all the time, you know that."

"Do you want me to come tomorrow morning?"

"If you would. I got them to let me go just eight to twelve. You don't mind?"

"No, it's no trouble. Gary sleeps all morning. I'm too round to do much but sit." All the peafowl were waiting by the screen

door to see if anyone would feed them. The birds scattered as
they went out to the car.

When Elmo came back inside his grandfather was sitting up
again. There were veins that stayed out on his forehead now,
surrounded by brown spots the size of quarters. His eyes stared
out of his head, fixed at what he saw. He was looking around the
room, lost. "Where were you, Elmo? I was looking all over for
you."

"I was out shucking some early corn, for a surprise."

"Lorraine and I used to shuck corn. I was better than she was.
I did twenty bushels in one day. Don't deny your family, Elmo."

"I won't, Grandpa."

"She was a good sister to me. Couple of years ago I tried to
phone her, planning on making up."

"I didn't know that."

"She had no number." He lay back down and closed his eyes.
"I was too late."

James came in while he was boiling the water for the corn. It
was staying light longer now; it was almost 7:30. "How is he?"
James whispered. "Maybe we should take him into town, like
the doctor said."

"He wants to stay here. I can take care of him," Elmo said.

"Greta said you can't stay cooped up here all the time."

"I don't mind. She's going to come in the morning so I can go
back to school. They got after me."

"Claude's got the packing shed ready to go. I'm going to give
it a week before we start picking the Red Julys. I could come in
the afternoon until then."

"No, half a day of school is enough," Elmo said.

James got up. "Call us, Elmo; I can get here in a minute."

When the corn was done, he took a knife and cut the kernels
off a cob into a bowl and added butter and salt and pepper. He
sat by his grandfather's bed. "Open up, Grandpa, I've got some
corn for you. Open up." He put a few mashed kernels in between
his lips and saw them slide back out when he tried to swallow.

His grandfather began to ramble on with his eyes closed, how he'd caught three porcupines eating up his young trees. Put them in a gunnysack and hauled them out by boat to a small island. Couldn't knock them in the head, he said.

When he drifted off Elmo went back to the kitchen and ate an ear of corn. It was sweet. The peacocks were roosting; he heard them shifting their tail feathers. He ate the rest of the corn, then sopped up the butter with a piece of bread. "Elmo," his grandfather called out, "are you there?"

"I'm here, Grandpa. I'm here." He did his homework. Then he tried to remember the time difference between east and west. It would be eleven o'clock there. He picked up the phone anyway. He got the operator and told her what he was after. She said she'd phone back. He did the dishes, waiting.

The phone rang. "I found a Vivian, but no Lorraine."

"Would you try her?" He listened to the rings. They made him think he was going back into the past. Carrying all his grandpa's stories.

"Hello," someone said.

"Are you any relation to Lorraine Johnston?"

"May I ask who's inquiring?"

"My name is Elmo Clark. I live in California."

"My mother was named Lorraine. She died four years ago."

"Did she ever mention a brother? My grandfather's name is Jim Clark."

"I remember Uncle Jim. He came out here to see us. I'm her daughter. I must have been nine or ten when I saw him last."

"It's complicated," Elmo started out. "My grandpa is sick, and he's been mentioning your mother. His sister. I thought I might get them together, but I guess it's too late."

"I don't know what to tell you."

"There was a disagreement," Elmo went on, wanting to finish it. "Over a stickpin that belonged to your grandfather and was supposed to go to my grandfather."

"I don't remember anything like that."

"I'm sorry to bother you like this; it's just that he's sick. I wanted to see if I could tie up some loose ends, I guess."

"I've been to California. I have a niece in San Diego."

"Well, if you come out again, be sure and stop," Elmo said. "We'd be happy to see you."

Elmo was giving his grandfather a sponge bath the next morning, before Greta came. "I must be in sorry shape if I can't even wash my own neck," he said in his old voice, as if he hadn't had a stroke.

"You're just lazy," Elmo said. "You remember me shaving you last time?"

"You almost cut my nose off." He laughed. "You got coffee out there, or you going to keep it for yourself?"

"You finish and I'll get you a cup." He kept talking, wanting it to last. "Greta's coming over in a little while."

"What for? They having trouble?"

"No, no, she gets tired staying up there at the house by herself. She'll bring the baby and you can keep her company while I go straighten out that teacher on a few calculus problems."

"I like Greta," he said. Elmo came back with a cupful of hot coffee. He took a big gulp. "Now that's what I call coffee." He took a deep breath. "I never thought I'd get over your grandmother dying. We had been married less than fifteen years. But I had to, because of your father. When he killed himself, I had you and James to keep me getting up out of bed. You see what I'm getting at, Elmo."

"I see," Elmo said, "but you're not going anywhere."

He hadn't been in school in almost three weeks. But Betty took notes and got his assignments, then gave them to the bus driver, who put them in the Clark mailbox and picked up the homework. She sat next to him in math. "Truant," she said, when she walked into the classroom and saw him back. "I'm so far ahead of you now in the race for valedictorian you won't even be close enough to hear me give the speech."

"I'm the one that taught you how to invert in dividing fractions. In the fourth grade, remember that? How soon they forget their betters."

She reached across the aisle and gripped his wrist. "I missed you, Elmo." It surprised him for a minute; he didn't think she was going to let go. The teacher had come in and was writing on the chalkboard.

He wouldn't let himself think about her. He wasn't in control when he did. She wasn't in the fantasy that made him have to pull out his shirt in front to get up out of his seat, or jam both fists in his front pockets to hide the bulge. She made him forget things. Big things like why he had to go home after school. Or little things like how many trees did they have of Abundance. She made him forget. He didn't know if he had his eyes open or closed sometimes. If late at night, unable to sleep, he was seeing the peacocks in his grandpa's bedroom or if he was imagining it.

There was no math problem he couldn't find the answer for. He had to remember that. It was important. All he had to do was make himself think. Put his mind to work. Let his imagination pick up the answer and bring it back to him. He had even gone to church with the Briscoe family. When Betty had asked him, he'd said yes. He hadn't been in church since he was eight or nine—and then because one of the town churches sent a bus out for the kids. He waited every Sunday out by the mailbox because of the cookies. Each woman in church brought a different kind. There were peanut butter, date, oatmeal, brownies, lemon, raisin, and some with frosting and multicolored sprinkles. The bus had broken down after about a year and they never fixed it. He never went after that. He sat next to Betty, feeling her leg against his, the rest of the Briscoes lined up on either side. When they sang Betty held the book open and he could hear the sound of her voice next to his ear. He closed his eyes and imagined the springtime orchard, with him running. The singing was like what he saw then. The shape of the wind as it blew the spray of petals against him. The petals falling on his head and shoulders until he opened his eyes. His grandfather laughing at him when he came back to the house. "Your Easter hat," he said.

After class they walked together. "How's your grandfather?"

"He's getting better. I was talking to his niece last night in New Hampshire. I think we might go there for a visit. See that end of the family. As soon as he gets a little stronger."

"It's warmed up early this year. Time for our first swim." She waited; when he didn't comment, she went on. "I can hardly wait to dive off the barge. I could meet you up there today."

"I'll see," he said.

"I'm going to go anyway," she said.

When he got home everyone was asleep, Greta on the chair, the baby on the couch, and Grandpa in his bed. The oven was on and he could smell cake. She must have been baking all morning. He cut himself a slice of Greta's homemade bread, spread it with butter, then sprinkled a spoonful of sugar over the top. Went back out, taking big bites out of the bread. The peacocks all followed him, but he ignored them.

He started working on the twelve-foot wooden ladders for the coming season. The pickers busted hell out of them. He couldn't blame them, heavy as they were. He started replacing the broken steps. Taking his time. Examining each ladder, sorting out the ones that needed work.

James came by, stopped. "It's hot for May," he said. "It's going to hit eighty."

"They're all asleep," Elmo said.

"We're going to eat with you tonight, if that's all right. She's got enough grub cooked to feed a picking crew."

"I'll be back by then," Elmo said. "I'm going to take a ride soon as I finish these."

She was already there. He saw her father's car parked up on the levee. Then, coming down the bank, he saw her, already changed and sitting on the barge. He hurried. The wooden barge had drifted in here years before. It was tilted up so one edge was almost in the water. He'd been coming here since he was in the sixth grade; James had brought him. He would never have found it by himself. The tules closed in around it on three sides like tall grass. A raft of yellowed tules and driftwood that looked solid enough to walk on floated at the far end of the slough.

He could hear the lap of the water as he changed into his swimming suit in the cabin. He noticed her clothes halfway stuffed into a brown bag. Someone had put a quilt over the old mattress that had always been there. He folded his trousers on their crease and put his shirt over the back of one of the chairs. He made himself go back up the stairs and out into the sunshine.

He lowered himself next to her on the edge of the barge, put his feet in the water too. "It's too cold to go in," he said.

"You can't let your senses overcome your mind," she said back. He laughed; he had told her that once. "Have you ever seen a naked woman, Elmo?"

"Mamie Eisenhower," he said, and added when she started giggling, "in my religious dreams."

She started talking in an Okie drawl too. "Have you ever known a woman? In the biblical sense?" she asked.

"I think you're going beyond the bounds of good taste," he said, splashing her with his foot.

"Have you?" she asked in her normal voice.

"A gentleman never reveals a lady's name or past." He looked over and saw her face was flushed. She really wants to know, he thought. Not looking at her, he said, "Claude took me over to the city."

"How was it?"

He thought. "I don't know," he said. "On one level, interesting to do what I'd been hearing about since I was five and thinking about since I was eleven. On the other hand, I would say under those circumstances it was a little overrated, but I'm just starting out."

"What was her name?"

"I don't think she ever told me. But she was a Christian, which gave me some comfort—she was wearing a cross."

Embarrassed, Betty laughed. "I was wondering if we might try it one of these days," she said.

He could barely talk: the words wouldn't come out right. His mind felt like it was shutting down. "You sure you're ready for the big step into adulthood? This is the final pubic rite of passage." He didn't correct the word; he couldn't think of the right one.

She hadn't noticed. "I'm ready," she said. "Some days I feel like I'm ready to bust."

"Any particular day?" he asked. Neither was looking at the other.

"Maybe today," she said, getting up and walking back across the barge. He heard her go down the steps into the cabin. He sat there awhile before saying in a loud voice, "Well, I can't think of anything better to do on a sunny day like this."

"Where in the hell have you been?" James yelled, coming out of the house when Elmo drove up. "He's in there crying because he thinks you're not coming back." Elmo ran, scattering the peafowl. Greta was by the bed holding his hand, with the baby in her lap. Both the baby and his grandfather were sobbing as if their hearts would break. "I was out checking on the railroad fares," he said loud as he could, to be heard. "I think we can get tickets straight through, changing at Chicago. We can each take two suitcases," he said all in one breath.

His grandfather looked at him, stopped crying. James had taken the baby into the other room. "They still have sleepers?" he asked, his face all wet. Elmo nodded. "It's going to have to be the train," Grandpa said with a big sob; "you're not going to get me on an airplane."

He stayed home the next day, phoned Greta to say she didn't have to come. He did their wash in the old wringer washer. It was another warm day and he hung the clothes outside to dry. When the sun was directly overhead he brought out the rocker and set it on the porch. Then he picked his grandfather up,

wrapped him in two blankets, and took him outside. He didn't
seem to weigh anything.

"Well, sir, take a look at those peacocks of yours. They are
nearly the perfect pet; all they do is eat and sleep. They must
need all that rest and nourishment just to show off their feathers
once or twice a month." He looked over at his grandfather, who
was staring into space, eyes open, unblinking. The words made
no connection. He remembered them verbatim from when his
grandfather had spoken them.

He went in the house and changed the sheets on his grandfather's bed and then took him back inside. Tried to get him to eat
something. "All right for you, Grandpa, you're going to have to
eat twice as much for dinner." He went back in the kitchen with
the bowl.

Betty phoned at 3:30. After he said hello she said, "Well, I'm
glad you didn't die for love." He was able to laugh. "I've got
your assignments; do you want me to bring them out? I didn't
get to the bus on time."

"Put them on the bus tomorrow," he said. "I need a rest from
all that brain work."

"I'd like to see you," she said in a lower voice. "Just stop and
visit." He didn't answer. Nothing would come out. "How's your
grandfather?" she finally asked.

"He's fine. I took him out today and he had a good time,
sitting on the porch. I better get the wash in off the line," he said
before she could say anything else, and he hung up.

He had all the clothes in the basket when Greta drove in and
got out of her car carrying a Pyrex bowl and something wrapped
in a towel. "I made some carrot cake, Elmo," she called out.

"He's going to like that," he said, following her inside. She
put the things down and went into Grandpa's room. Elmo put
the basket of clothes down, opened the towel, then the wax paper. It had white frosting.

"Elmo," Greta said. He licked his fingers, went toward the
doorway.

"Grandpa," Greta said, leaning over him. She took a face mirror out of her purse and held it up to his nose.

"What are you doing, Greta?"

She felt around his wrist and put her ear to his chest, then shook him by the shoulders. The old head rolled. "Call the doctor, Elmo," she said. "Grandpa's dead."

"No, he isn't; he's fine, he's just asleep." Elmo went over and straightened the blankets. He could hear her call the doctor, then James. Elmo brought a kitchen chair in and sat beside the bed, holding Grandpa's hand. "You're not going to guess what we're going to have for dessert," he said. "Your favorite, carrot cake. She put white icing on, a thick layer. It's going to be so rich we're going to need a lot of hot coffee."

James came into the house, slamming the door shut. He was breathing hard and the sound filled the bedroom. He put his big fingers on Grandpa's neck. Left them a long time. "He's dead, Elmo."

He knew he was being calm and reasonable. "He's not dead, James. I'm talking to him."

"I know dead, Elmo. He's dead."

"He wouldn't leave me here, James, I know that. Not alone. He's not dead." James went out.

"I was thinking, Grandpa, about our trip out east. To the eastern seaboard, as you say. I think the fall is better. I'd like to see those leaves you're always talking about. We should go out there before it gets too cold. I don't want to run into any of those storms. I'm too partial to this California sunshine."

The doctor, who was also the county coroner, came in, felt around with his stethoscope, then carefully took the folded-down sheet as Elmo watched and put it up over his grandfather's head. "He's gone," he said, "he's gone."

Elmo took the sheet down. "He's all right," he said, laying his head on his grandfather's chest.

"Your grandfather had some arrangements with one of the

funeral homes in town. I'm going to send for them now, take him back with us."

"He's staying right here," Elmo shouted, sitting up. "He's going to get well. No one's going to take him anywhere." He jumped up, knocking over the chair, and put up his fists. The doctor backed out the door into the kitchen.

Greta tried to come in. "Elmo."

"No, Greta, he's staying right here."

He heard them talking and they all went out. He locked the front door and turned off the lights. "It's early," he said aloud, "but we both need our rest. We've got a big day ahead of us tomorrow." He sat down at the kitchen table to wait.

He'd been up and around when the knocking started. Had got the water just right and was shaving his grandfather. "Elmo, it's me, Joyce, I want to come in."

"Hold on," he called back. "I'm almost finished here." He wiped his grandpa's face off with a towel and went to the door.

Joyce stepped in as soon as he opened it, with James and Greta right behind her. Eddie and Claude stayed on the porch. The kitchen was crowded. James and Joyce went into his grandfather's bedroom. "I was getting him ready," Elmo said, following.

"I can give you a hand," Joyce said.

"He was awful shy," Elmo said.

"I know what you mean."

"Maybe you could brush his blue suit. It's hanging in his closet." Elmo went back and took the basin of shaving water and dumped it into the bathtub, washed out the pan, filled it with warm water.

When the suit was brushed he put it on his grandfather. Joyce knotted the tie and Elmo put it around his neck, buttoned the top button of his shirt. He couldn't think of anything else.

Eddie and Claude had gone back to the main house. James was sitting at the table with Greta. Joyce was folding the wash.

When no one was looking, Elmo slipped a piece of carrot cake wrapped in wax paper into his grandfather's pocket. Then he walked out and sat on the porch, his feet up on the rail, throwing single pieces of cracked corn to the peafowl.

When the sun was over the edge of the orchard, two men came in the hearse and wheeled a gurney into the house and then came back out. Elmo didn't look. Didn't move. Kept throwing feed, making the peafowl run for it.

"Let's go up to the house, Elmo," Joyce said. "We could all use some breakfast."

"I have a few things I have to do first," he said. "I'll be up later."

"You promise," Greta said, putting her hand on his shoulder.

"I promise," he said.

He sat there a long time. His head was emptied out. There was no connection between what he could see and what was going on inside. He closed his eyes for a minute. There was no relief there. When he opened them there was the same thing. The yard, the peacocks, the road and then the orchard. If only I could imagine the hardest math problem, he thought, and then come up with the right answer, I could do anything. But there was nothing but his grandfather in his head. Inside. Like the chick inside an egg when you hold it up to the light. That was never going to come out. There was no more room to imagine an answer. He threw the last of the feed, got up and went into the house.

He found his twelve-gauge in the pantry. He took his time, loaded, filled his jacket pockets full of shells. By the time he got back to the porch there were only five or six in sight. They must know, he thought, aiming. He got those and two more behind the house.

He dragged the dead ones, as he killed them, to a big pile of tree trimmings, higher than his head, that hadn't been burned yet. He swung them up by their legs to the top. The others couldn't get away; he took his time. Where could they go? What could they become? A tree?

When James came driving up in the pickup, he was surprised. Then he realized they must have heard the shots from the main house. One took off from behind the rhododendron bush, and he blasted it. Slowly James opened the truck door. "Just stay right there, James," he yelled. "I'm attending to my own business here." James sat still, his legs hanging out the open door, his elbow on the window frame, watching.

He nailed the last ones by the clothesline. They seemed like they were waiting for him there. He emptied the rest of the five gallons of diesel around the base of the pile and capped the can. He snapped the kitchen match alight with his thumbnail, then threw it in. There was a whoosh, and the still-green plum trimmings sizzled and foamed as heat from the flames climbed up the pile. He looked for the peacock feathers, but there wasn't any sign of them that he could see.

House Hunting

•

JOYCE CAROL OATES

How subtly the season of mourning shaded into a season of envy. To their knowledge they had never been envious people, but suddenly they caught themselves staring at families, young parents with their children, a mother holding her baby—strangers whose happiness grated with the irritation of steel wool against the skin. One Sunday in a city park Joel saw Kim staring at a couple with very young twin girls, her eyes narrowed and her pale lips drawn back from her teeth. He looked away as if he'd seen something forbidden.

It was a season too of opaque skies, wet air, slick dead leaves underfoot. Rain drumming against windows in the night, mists that rarely burned off before noon. They had lived in this beautiful city on the West Coast for nearly eight years, and this was the first winter they found nearly unbearable. And the routines of their lives, which had once seemed so exciting. And the routines of their friends' lives. And the handsome little Victorian house they'd bought at such a bargain on a street not then fashionable, and renovated, and decorated, and furnished—nearly unbearable. The period of their young adulthood was finished, and they decided to move back East.

. . .

It was not difficult for Joel to arrange to be transferred to the
Philadelphia branch of his company: he was a salesperson but a
salesperson of a very high order. The products he sold cost millions of dollars and were contracted for years in advance of
delivery. Kim was a commercial artist who could find work anywhere. Or maybe, since they had money, she might not work at
all . . . that period of her life too seemed to be winding down.
She was thirty-four years old. She looked, as she said, precisely
her age. She had intended to take only a month's maternity leave
from the small public relations firm with which she worked but,
as it turned out, she had been away twice that long, and at an
unscheduled time—the baby had been born six weeks premature. Now, as she said, she was permanently out of the rhythm
set by her coworkers and rivals. New seasons, and new promotion campaigns, and new strategies of selling. . . . She couldn't
keep up because she'd become repulsed by it, and she wondered
if she had been repulsed by it all along, without knowing.

"You hypnotize yourself into loving your life because it's what
you are doing and because it's life," she said. There was an edge
to her voice these days, a perpetual bemusement and irony, that
Joel had come to dislike. He particularly disliked, and feared,
pronouncements of this kind—flat, abstract, impersonal. They
allowed of no access, no quarrel.

But he said, "I love you."

He said, "We'll do whatever you want to do."

He was thirty-six years old. Young for his age. Athletic, aggres-
sive, affable. With sandy graying hair trimmed short, small
shrewd alert features, his skin rich, warm looking. He loved to
laugh and people loved to hear him laugh—his pleasure in happiness seemed so sincere. He had a quick temper which he kept
under control, in public; as a small child he'd been susceptible to
violent tantrums, short-lived but frightening. Even now, in his
maturity, he was susceptible to a flaring-up of what he thought

to be his "other" self, his childish despicable ignorant self, erupt-
ing, as it seemed, out of nowhere and leaving him exhausted and
guilty and ashamed afterward. Kim said, "I hate you in that
state. I'm terrified of you." She said, "You should see your face
when you're shouting—so *ugly.*" She told him she felt at such
times that she couldn't trust him, that she didn't even know him;
she wouldn't want such a man, so little in control of himself, to
be the father of any child of hers. And Joel was angered the
more but knew to keep it hidden, swallowed down hard. He
apologized; he was hurt, baffled, repentant, but resentful, accus-
tomed since childhood to being forgiven. Wasn't there a natural
rhythm, a ritual, of transgression and forgiveness? The loss of
control of one's self and the restoration of control?

She wasn't serious, Joel said. Speaking quietly, with what he
knew to be exquisite control.

She had better not say certain things, he said, it was impossible after all to unsay them.

"I say what I think," Kim told him.

She was by nature a quiet girl, very quiet, still and premedi-
tated, but at such times, her cheeks flushed as if they'd been
slapped and, her eyes bright, she seemed to take pleasure in
defying him, in prolonging their quarrel. If he began one of their
scenes, she must end it.

He embraced her, and she pushed him away. He embraced her
again, and she pushed him away. Then a third time, perhaps,
burying his face in her neck, murmuring "Sorry sorry sorry"
until he could feel her begin to relax, still tense and in defiance of
him but beginning to relax, and often he dared run his fingers up
and down her sides, tickling her, making her laugh, breathless
and flushed as she was. Once he made her laugh, he had her
won. They wrestled together like puppies: Kim would slap at
him, pummel him, he'd allow her to get the better of him, taking
pleasure in being slapped as he deserved, so long as the blows
were harmless, playful, affectionate. Sometimes, heated and

aroused, they felt a sort of anarchy between them, for what was there to prevent them from doing anything they wished? Anything they knew to do, to each other? If they made love at such a time, wordless, clutching, triumphant, it was as if they didn't know each other: they were strangers suddenly intimate, rather heartless. And what pleasure in being, for once, heartless—as if the body was after all the only way they could know each other.

After they lost the baby, Joel's temper tantrums stopped. Or were temporarily in abeyance. Weeks, months, nearly a year had gone by and he hadn't flared up in the old way, nor did they make love in the old way but were apt to lie together in each other's arms in a state of mutual exhaustion or melancholy or, oddly, contentment, a sense that they'd come to rest after grief, played it out, drained themselves of sorrow as they'd drained themselves of tears. Of course this wasn't really the case and they both knew it, but what pleasure in their lying together in each other's arms, adrift in separate dreams, on the very edge of sleep, or extinction.

One day in March they were packing to leave for a three-week visit in the East—to see relatives, to meet with Joel's new associates in Philadelphia, to begin house hunting—when Kim told Joel she wasn't going with him; she couldn't do it.

He was dazed, stunned, having thought in that brief instant that she meant that their marriage was over. That she wouldn't be coming East with him at all.

But she meant only that she wasn't coming now, for the three weeks. She wanted to stay by herself in the house; she wanted to be alone.

Joel smiled instinctively as he always smiled when he was thrown off balance. Several times he said, "I don't understand."

Kim said there was nothing to understand.

"But what's wrong?"

"Nothing is wrong. I want to be alone for a while."

"Why didn't you say something before now?"

"I didn't know before now."

"Before this *instant*—?"

"Don't talk to me in that tone of voice," she said, turning away.

Her copper-plated earrings, the size of silver dollars, swung and flashed against her cheeks. Her voice rose sharp and despairing.

She began to pace around their bedroom, not looking at him, resisting him. She lifted her heavy hair and beat at it from beneath with her fists as she sometimes did when she was anxious. She said she wanted him to go alone; she wanted to stay behind, alone; she was exhausted.

"Exhausted by what?" Joel said, dreading her answer.

"Just exhausted."

She shrank from him when he tried to touch her.

Still, his instinctive reaction was to smile. Like a skull's smile, Joel's wide staring grin.

She told him she needed space to breathe in. Always, they were alluding to the baby even when they spoke of other things. There was no escaping it—no escaping each other. She wanted to be alone for a while, for three weeks or maybe more, she was desperate to be alone and if he loved her he would respect her wishes.

When he tried to touch her she shrank from him. He felt her frantic heat, heard her quickened breath. He said, hurt, stung, angry, "You want a separation—you don't love *me*." She said, "I love you, but I don't know if I want to love you." "What does that mean?" "I'm exhausted." "What does *that* mean?" She backed away. She was still slapping at her hair, breathing hard. When her stony gaze moved onto him it seemed she looked at him without recognition; he was simply something standing in her line of vision.

"You know what I mean," Kim whispered.

. . .

They were to leave for Philadelphia at 7:30 the next morning, but he ran out of the house, stayed away until nearly 2:00 A.M. When he came back, mildly drunk, still angry, Kim was asleep in their bed, breathing now deeply and heavily. He envied her, resented her. He too was exhausted, after all.

In the bathroom he checked Kim's barbiturates but couldn't judge how many she had taken; or if she'd taken any.

He avoided looking too closely at his face in the mirror. When he drank too much his skin became mottled and flushed; the veins in his eyes pressed forward. He had been a beautiful child for what seemed a very long time and now, as an adult man, he worried he was still too attractive for other men to take seriously.

But he made them take him seriously: didn't he know how!

He went into the bedroom and woke Kim and she shrank from him, terrified, as if she'd forgotten their quarrel. As if she thought he might strike her. Her cringing, her high wild little screams, provoked him the more, but he knew enough not to lose control. He shouted at her but did not hit her—drew his hand back—stood frozen, transfixed. "All right, I'll go alone— I'll leave you alone if that's what you want," he said. "If that's what you want." Kim was too frightened to speak—she lay with one arm raised to shield herself from him. He felt immediately repentant; he felt like a damned fool.

He said, "If I don't have you I don't have anything. You know that." He spoke bitterly, calmly. It was not a statement of love nor even of reproach, but a mere statement of fact.

Their baby, whose name they never afterward uttered, weighed only three pounds eight ounces at birth and had not lived a week. Despite the ingenious medical strategies, the costly machinery, the suffering. For there was suffering: you could tell yourself that an infant so absurdly small, born with malformations of the heart, lungs, and kidneys, very likely brain damaged as well, did not possess the consciousness to register pain in the usual sense of the word. Without awareness of self, can there be awareness of suffering? And if the self *is* mere suffering . . . ? Joel was to wish he had not seen the tiny creature encased in its glass cage, since seeing it involved seeing also the strawlike translucent tubes hooking it up to life: tubes feeding both the body and the head. The infant was "premature" yet had the look of being prematurely aged, bearing the doom of the species.

Joel stared and stared, unable to break away. The creature was not so much his as it was himself.

He was in the East, he said, to see about buying property. In Bucks County, perhaps; or in a suburban village. He wasn't a wealthy man, but he had a fair amount of money to invest and would have considerably more when his house in San Francisco was sold. What he wanted was—well, it was difficult to say. Something unusual, unconventional. Not necessarily in perfect condition: he and his wife liked to remodel, decorate. He would know it, he said, when he saw it.

Ordinarily he and his wife would have been house hunting together, Joel added. But his wife wasn't well at the present time.

The real estate agent, a Mrs. Brody, was all business and quick empathy, exhaling smoke as she jotted down information on her clipboard. A woman of indeterminate age, in her late forties, perhaps, trim, attractive, stylishly dressed, with hair tinted the color of champagne, frosted nails, a husky throaty voice. She was sorry, she said, to hear that Joel's wife was unwell. Did they have any children? Plans for children? And could Joel be slightly more specific about the kind of house he wanted?

Joel said defensively, "As I told you—I'll know it when I see it."

Quickly Mrs. Brody said, "I understand." If she heard the emotion rising in her client's voice she gave no sign; she busied herself taking notes.

So began the brief intense period of Joel's house hunting.

For the next several days Mrs. Brody drove him about in her maroon Mercedes Benz to look at properties, as she called them, of particular interest, in the country northeast of Philadelphia and in one or another suburban village. Joel had sorted through what seemed to have been hundreds of listings; he'd selected a generous number, reluctant to discard any that seemed halfway promising. He was keenly excited yet also rather tense, edgy, acutely uncomfortable at first, sitting in the passenger's seat of Mrs. Brody's car, Mrs. Brody at the wheel. It seemed unnatural for him, particularly in his keyed-up state. If he and Kim were going somewhere, it was invariably Joel who drove.

And when Mrs. Brody brought him to the first house—red-brick, federal style, "restored" and rather shabbily grand—Joel felt an instant's panic at the prospect of going inside. Why was he here? What right had he to trespass? His heart was beating heavily and his face felt unnaturally warm. Mrs. Brody unlocked the door and turned to him with a smile. "This is a beautiful house," she said. "It's a shame your wife isn't with you, to see it."

There had been a derelict house in his grandparents' neighborhood, years ago: he'd passed by it a thousand times as a boy, weeds in the front yard, diseased trees, boarded-up windows and barricaded front door and that look of abandonment—patches of moss growing on the rotted shingles, tiny trees sprouting in the rain gutters. What was there about the house that so fascinated him as a child? He had sat on the curb staring. He prowled about. Threw stones that fell clattering down the steep slant of the roof. Once, ten years old, he'd dared poke about the rear of the house, stepping through mounds of broken rubble and glass, squatting to peer into a cellar window caked with grime—he'd frightened himself imagining a face staring up at him, waiting for him; he'd run away and never come back.

Even as he knew there was no one, nothing, there. For what

would it be?—all those years. No one, nothing. Eventually the old house was razed, the debris hauled away.

He telephoned Kim, he apologized for not having called sooner, he was excited, restless—couldn't sit still even with the phone in his hand—interrupting himself several times as he reported to her how his meetings with his associates-to-be had gone, how much they liked him, or seemed to; what sort of reputation he had. It was an excellent idea, their coming back East. This transfer was the wisest decision he'd made in years.

"Yes," Kim said in a neutral voice. "I think you're right."

"I *am* right," he said, "you'll see."

He waited for her to say something further—even to chide him for not having called until now. But she was silent.

He told her with suppressed excitement that he was house hunting. Again, she didn't respond. Then she said in a faint voice, "You are? Alone?" He said at once, "But I'm here alone." And again they fell silent. Joel stirred his drink with a forefinger: scotch on the rocks. He'd bought his own bottle that afternoon, ordered ice cubes from room service. Remembered too late, when the busboy delivered them, that ice cubes by way of hotel room service were enough for a dozen people.

He wanted to tell Kim about Mrs. Brody, joke a bit about the houses he'd seen that day, blurred now in his memory, each so promising at the outset and finally—in some cases, immediately—so disappointing, but she was vague and evasive, sleepy sounding. He wondered if she had taken a barbiturate; if in fact he had woken her from sleep. He said, "Are you all right?" and she said, "I'm fine," and he said, "I hope so," and she said, "Yes—I'm fine," and he said, "As long as you're all right," and she said, that slight ironic nettlesome edge to her voice, "I didn't say I was all right—I said I'm fine," and he laughed as if she had said something witty, which perhaps she had. "As long as you're fine, then," he said lamely, feeling clumsy and blunt as if tumescent (which he was not), "—with me gone." Kim made a sound that might have been assent, or protest, mild protest, mild and fleeting as a sigh. "—The house empty," he said. But this too was wrong, not what he meant to say. He corrected himself. "I mean—empty of me."

There was a pause. Kim said, "Who else would it be empty of?"

Joel said quickly, "Look—you *are* all right? Would you like me to come back home?"

"No," said Kim. "I'm fine. Didn't I tell you?"

After they hung up Joel sat on the edge of his bed and drank his drink. His thoughts followed one another slow and dense as clots in the blood but were not clear, could not have been translated into words. He felt both sick and elated. He tried to sift through a stack of property listings Mrs. Brody had left with him but he was too distracted, couldn't concentrate. He finished his drink and poured another and realized that he was waiting for the telephone to ring but why was he waiting for the telephone to ring?—he and Kim had just spoken. And there was no one else likely to call him, here.

Are you going to try again, he was asked. His parents asked him, and his older sister asked him, and even Kim's mother asked him, fearing, perhaps, to ask her daughter directly. The question was always tactfully raised; Joel grew to anticipate it. He told them frankly that he didn't know. He hoped so. But he didn't know. It was up to Kim after all, Kim was the one who had suffered most, or did he mean more—she'd suffered more than he had. (Obviously the baby had suffered most.) (But that was another story.) No, Joel said, speaking carefully so that he wouldn't be misunderstood,—no, he didn't know. He wouldn't know for a long, long time.

"Vacant houses are harder to sell than furnished houses," Mrs. Brody said, unlocking the door, leading him inside. "They look smaller, for some reason. Why, do you think? Why, if there's more space, do they look smaller?"

Joel said he didn't know. Maybe it was an optical illusion.

"It *is* an illusion of some kind," Mrs. Brody said. "I suppose it must be psychological."

He was shown vacant houses, and he was shown furnished houses. A Dutch colonial, and a brick Cape Cod, and an English Tudor, and another English Tudor, and a California style house built about an atrium, and a glass-and-redwood split-level, and a French Normandy, and a renovated stone farmhouse, and an aggressively modern house designed by a student of Frank Lloyd Wright. . . . Each was promising but none was, upon inspection, quite right.

"I hope I'm not exhausting you," Joel said gallantly. Though in fact it was he who felt the strain.

"Not at all," Mrs. Brody said, with a quick smile. "It's my job."

The woman was tireless, or seemed so. Brisk, pert, cheery, supremely in control. In her high-heeled shoes, handbag in the crook of her arm. She had the key to every lock: only let her fit it into the door; and the door opened, and she led her client inside: Joel, who was made to feel uncharacteristically passive, helpless. He didn't like the feeling. Then again, he did like it—there was something intimate and brazen, heady, as if with the air of the forbidden, about being led by a woman he didn't know into the houses of people he didn't know, escorted through rooms in which strangers lived their secret lives. The first several minutes were the most acute—he felt shy, absurdly ill at ease, excited. As if he were being brought to a test of some kind, a challenge or a riddle, and would not be equal to it.

Living rooms and dining rooms and kitchens (many gleaming with smart new tile floors, copper utensils that looked unused) and stairways and corridors and bedrooms and bathrooms and glassed-in porches and wood-panelled basements and laundry rooms (where the soiled clothing of strangers, in inglorious heaps, was frequently in view) and again living rooms, and dining rooms, and kitchens, and sometimes, in the older houses, butlers' pantries; and bedrooms, and bathrooms, and maids' rooms, and staircases, and two- and three- and even four-car garages. . . . Everything held promise but nothing pleased! Everything held promise but nothing pleased! He grew irritable, impatient, panicked that he wouldn't find what he knew was there, somewhere, waiting for him—if only he could find it. Several times he rejected houses with a flat, "No, sorry," not troubling to get out of Mrs. Brody's car. Then again, he asked to see one of the houses a second time even as—as he asked—he suddenly knew it wasn't the right house and he was wasting his and Mrs. Brody's time.

Though Mrs. Brody kept assuring him, "It's my job."

She assured him, "The customer knows what he wants and what he doesn't want."

She asked him to call her Charlotte. (" 'Charlotte Brody'—the name sounds like something out of a nineteenth-century novel, doesn't it?") He asked her to call him Joel, but didn't insist; she seemed more comfortable calling him Mr. Collier. Joel liked her, was inclined to trust her, yet, at the same time, had to remember that she was trying to sell him something—hoping to sell him property that would cost a half-million dollars and more—and what, he wondered, was the agent's commission on such a sale?

He tried to keep this fact in mind. It was a fact no salesperson would ever forget.

On the morning of the third day Charlotte Brody drove him twenty miles into the country to show him a house she thought he might like. And so it seemed as she parked her car and he stared—how his heart began to pound!—as much intrigued by the house's location as by the house itself. It was a modified Cape Cod, not, as Charlotte Brody warned, in the very best condition, but an excellent bargain, on the market for only twelve days and sure to be sold soon. Its location was the odd,

intriguing, charming thing: built on the downward slope of a
steep hill beneath a graveled road, overlooking a small lake, no
other houses visible in the area. To reach the house you had to
descend a considerable flight of steps. There were railings on
both sides painted a gay, brash green; the shutters were the same
color. As they approached the front door Joel's heartbeat accelerated—he could see right through the house, through a front
window to windows at the rear overlooking the lake! The air was
wintry, still, fresh, invigorating; the lake was glassy, dimpled
near shore with thin, discontinuous sheets of ice. Joel glanced
back, and up, at the stone steps. How vertical they were—how
steep. He saw Kim making her way down, cautious, gripping the
railing (which was not very steady), worried of losing her footing
—was she pregnant again? Charlotte Brody said, *"Isn't* it de-
lightful—a honeymoon cottage. And intelligently priced."

Joel followed Mrs. Brody inside in a haze of apprehension.
For some minutes he seemed scarcely to see what he was looking
at or to hear what he was being told. . . . Was this *the* house,
but oddly altered? The rooms cramped and rather shabby, the
ceiling too low, a smell of cooking in the air, dog hairs on all the
furniture? The kitchen fixtures antiquated? The colors all the
wrong colors—bold, primary, "arty," "modern"? Joel could
scarcely follow Mrs. Brody's animated talk of a mortgage available at 12 percent, boating privileges on the lake ("But no mo-
torboats allowed, I think that's wise"), the convenience of a
shopping center only five miles away. Off the main room was a
weatherized, but drafty, porch, and in a corner was an old spinet
piano, badly out of tune as you'd imagine—Joel struck several
notes. He had not played piano since going away to college. A
sensation of extreme weakness rose in him, as if he were about to
cry, or had in fact been crying.

The occupants of the house had tried to decorate it with a
certain flair: Turkish carpets, outsized pillows, walls crowded
with art. Joel had a vision of Kim rearranging the pillows, Kim
drawing the drapes back from the windows, Kim kneeling on the

hearth in front of the stone fireplace. . . . But was the woman Kim? Her husband entered the room as if at a gallop, tall, husky, big shouldered, sweater draped over his shoulders—no one Joel knew. He was faintly repulsed by them, disapproved of how they'd ruined this house of such promise, wanted only to be gone. To be led out.

Beneath the cooking odors, and the dog odors, there was an undercurrent of decay as well. Joel's sensitive nostrils picked it up. Was the lake polluted? Did it flood the house? He interrupted Charlotte Brody to say, "I assume it floods here sometimes, doesn't it? That isn't much of a retaining wall."

"I suppose—sometimes," she said. With a slight drop of her voice.

Later that day she asked whether Joel might want to call a temporary halt to house hunting?—it was such an intense, exhausting activity after all.

Joel said quickly and coolly, "Do you want to give me up? And if so, could you suggest another agent to take your place?"

Charlotte Brody was startled into silence, perhaps even stunned. For a moment she couldn't even reply. Then she said, in her level, throaty voice, "Certainly not. I was only thinking of you."

A split-level glass-brick-stone-stucco with cathedral ceiling, enormous fieldstone fireplace, 180° of plate glass overlooking a "sylvan woodland scene," "fully equipped wet bar" on the ground level, and Joel, suddenly impatient, and thirsty, suggested to Charlotte Brody that he make them a drink.

Naturally Mrs. Brody demurred—that sort of thing wasn't done. Joel said, "Oh, what's the difference?" He poked about behind the bar, whistling; ignored Mrs. Brody's protests. What difference could it possibly make? And who would know? The liquor cabinet was lavishly stocked; there was even a container

of fresh ice cubes in the freezer. "Scotch on the rocks, Charlotte," he said, "—who deserves it if we don't?"

She was staring, smiling, fiddling with the strap of her handbag. Uncertain of how to respond. Joel simply pushed the glass
in her hand. "I insist," he said.

She accepted it reluctantly. Joel clicked his glass against hers
and said, "Here's to—the future."

"Yes," Mrs. Brody said.

Joel took a large grateful swallow of his drink. "Assuming
there is one, of course."

Mrs. Brody sipped at her drink, or pretended to do so. With
an air of mild reproach she said, "There will be, Mr. Collier."

She was a handsome woman with a fair, just perceptibly faded
skin. Fastidiously made-up, the eyes especially—shrewd, intelligent, watchful. Her kidskin gloves were the color of vanilla, and
gave off that scent; her suit might have been by Chanel—a fine,
fine wool, rosy brown, expensive. Joel had been smelling her
subtly astringent perfume for days; he didn't know if he liked it,
or disliked it. If he liked her very much, or disliked her. She held
her glass high between them as if judging the innocence, or the
danger, of the moment. She was cordial, still—Charlotte Brody
couldn't be anything but cordial: the stamp of the professional—
but not altogether at ease in his presence. Preparing to sidestep
him should he—

As if, Joel thought, annoyed, he was that kind of—

He strolled whistling about the recreation room, drink in
hand. Asking Mrs. Brody a barrage of questions though it was
clear to him, and very likely to her, that he had no intention of
buying this house: it was not *the* house. Glass walls overlooking
a redwood deck overlooking an oddly shaped swimming pool,
now covered with a tarpaulin; in the near distance a dense stand
of pine. In one of the windows a woman's shadowy reflection
defined itself but he knew it could not be Kim's. It was no
woman he knew.

He, in this house, was no one he knew.

But he *did* feel good. The drink *did* hit the spot. In a few minutes he'd make himself another.

He said, abruptly, "I'm so lonely."

He said, "Oh God I'm so scared."

He was sitting, a leather chair with queer chrome-tubular legs, his knees weak and head spinning. Only one drink and his head spinning.

In weak moments the image of the glassed-in baby rose to consciousness, transparent tubes attached to its head because veins elsewhere were too tiny to endure the pressure of the IV fluids. Incubation but the incubation period was over, and this was the result. No one to blame. He was a reasonable man knowing this was so, but still. His wife had said quietly, "What have we brought into the world together except Death?" And he had had no reply.

He was leaning forward, his head on his crossed arms. Playing at being maudlin drunk, though certainly he wasn't drunk, not so quickly. He felt a woman's hand nearing the back of his neck. Her lacquered fingernails about to dig, lightly, into his flesh. Or would she lean over him, to kiss him, exposed, vulnerable, hopeful as he was. . . . But when he looked up Mrs. Brody was at the far side of the room, as if unaware of him, checking something on her clipboard. She wore half-moon reading glasses perched low on her nose; he couldn't quite see her expression. The room was very quiet. The windows were too high, too insistent. Dull wintry-white light, eye-aching, yet not illuminating, heavy with moisture. Joel wanted to shield his face.

It seemed to him that a good deal of time had passed, yet of course it was no more than two or three minutes.

His glass was empty, on the table before him. Mrs. Brody's glass, scarcely touched, was on the bar.

He heaved himself to his feet, sucking in his breath, in robust high spirits again. He would have walked out without thinking about the glasses, but of course Mrs. Brody remembered, washed them carefully at the sink, dried them, tidied things up.

That was the last-house-but-one. He'd forget it by the next morning.

The final house Mrs. Brody was to show him had been on the market, she said, for three years. And it was rather overpriced. She didn't think, in fact, that it was a property quite for him.

But Joel wanted to see it nonetheless. He was intrigued by the blurred photograph, the description of a "stately brick Georgian" with "historic" significance. "A Bucks County estate." Six bedrooms and a partially finished attic—"ideal for large family."

The drive took a half hour, beyond Jenkintown, beyond Abington, up north and east of Huntingdon Valley. Mrs. Brody was quiet as she drove, and Joel was quiet, drumming his fingers on his knees. He stared out the window and saw nothing. Traffic, roads, stubbled snowy fields, then again traffic, and hilly farmland, and a sky the color of tarnished silver. His nerves were taut and alert, his eyes burned, he felt himself on the brink of a revelation—though he had slept fitfully the night before, an alcoholic stupor for a few reliable hours, then broken-up patches of sleep until morning. At one point he woke dazed and groggy, not knowing where he was. He'd felt someone touch his shoulder as Kim sometimes did when he snored loudly. Or when, as she said, he seemed to stop breathing—she would be wakened by the absence of sound, the sudden quiet. A sharp clicking sound in his throat and he'd stop breathing, and after what seemed like a very long time he drew in a deep snorting breath as if he was desperate to suck up all the air in the room. . . . He had felt someone touch his shoulder, but of course there was no one there.

The evening before, Kim had told him on the telephone that she was going to spend some time with her married sister in Arizona; her sister was recuperating from some minor surgery and had invited her down, and Joel said that that sounded like an excellent idea—she always enjoyed visiting there, it seemed to do her good. He didn't ask immediately if she wanted him to join her in Arizona but talked for a while of other things, that day's house hunting for instance, keeping the talk general and vague and upbeat. Before they hung up he asked if she wanted him to fly to Tucson, instead of going directly back home, and Kim said, "I didn't think you could spare the time," and Joel said, "I suppose I can't."

Three acres of land, mainly woods, came with the house in Huntingdon Valley. As Mrs. Brody pulled into the circular driveway Joel stared and stared, unable to believe his good fortune. He thought, This is it.

Told himself extravagantly, Coming home!

"The architecture *is* distinctive, isn't it?" Charlotte Brody said, to break the silence. She couldn't determine if her client was deeply offended by the weatherworn look of the house, the crumbling foundation and sagging shutters, or whether, seeing past such contingencies to the solid structure beneath, he was deeply stirred. "Of course it needs work. . . ."

"Yes," Joel said quickly, as if to shut her up.

"In the hands of the right owners. . . ."

"Yes," Joel said. "I was thinking that too."

Inside, Joel was sharply disappointed that the house was very nearly vacant, and smelled of neglect. Only a few pieces of furniture in the downstairs rooms, draped in dusty sheets. No heat, of course—the air was damp and chill, colder, seemingly, than out-of-doors. A beautiful house, or it had been at one time, with large airy rooms, carved archways, hardwood floors. The ceilings were high, the floors bare: their footsteps sounded discomfortingly loud and their voices echoed, particularly Mrs. Brody's. The woman was talking nervously, incessantly, as if frightened of the silence. Joel wished violently he had come here alone.

He walked through the downstairs rooms, slowly, reverently, staring and blinking. Coming home! coming home! His vision misted over; he felt weak, shaky, yet altogether certain of what he must do. He would buy this house: make a bid. A shrewd but reasonable bid. Already he could imagine how the living room would look, the floors sanded and polished, the walls freshly papered, perhaps in William Morris wallpaper. Near-transparent curtains at all the windows to let the light in and the marble fireplace restored, if marble so discolored can be restored. They would buy new furniture in light neutral colors. . . .

He was intensely excited. He unbuttoned his coat, tugged at his collar. It seemed he could not look hard enough, yet he was having difficulty seeing clearly—his eyes had begun to water. And when Mrs. Brody fell silent he could hear something, or someone, in the background, singing? Children singing? Or was it a radio? Upstairs? In another wing of the house?

"What is that? Do you hear that?" Joel asked Mrs. Brody. She cocked her head, stood very still, heard nothing. The old house was silent. Outside, the sporadic cries of birds, crows—Joel had noticed a field of crows, close by—and in the distance, nearly inaudible, what sounded like the low dull roar of machinery. "It sounded like singing," Joel said. But now he heard nothing.

They walked on. Into the dining room: French windows facing a lawn that sloped to a border of juniper pine hundreds of yards away. Joel's vision misted over, he swallowed hard, seeing the lawn in summer, the grass freshly mowed, beds bright with flowers—

He heard the singing again. Faint and teasing. He interrupted Charlotte Brody's chatter to say, "There—there it is! You must hear it."

Charlotte Brody said cautiously, "Where is it coming from?"

"It sounds like children singing."

They listened. And now, to his annoyance, Joel couldn't—quite—hear it. "It might be coming from upstairs, or from the carriage house. Does someone live in the carriage house?"

"Not that I know of."

"A radio left on—"

"Yes. That might be it."

Joel was staring at a chandelier—brass and crystal, Irish made

—that hung down from the precise center of the dining room. It was layered in cobwebs and dust but still beautiful. How sad, though, that the dining room was vacant, the wallpapered walls discolored, the hardwood floor in such poor condition one might think it had been deliberately battered. Hammered at, chopped at, with mysterious instruments. . . .

Mrs. Brody led him through to the butler's pantry, and into the kitchen. Here, the sound was stronger: Joel decided it must be made by wires vibrating in the wind. A high maddening humming.

"Of course, the kitchen needs to be completely remodeled," Mrs. Brody said apologetically. "Modernized—Would your wife like a country kitchen?"

"What?"

"Country kitchen—"

Joel discussed kitchens with Charlotte Brody, hearing his voice level and clear and unhurried, his logic impeccable, even as he felt a tightening in his chest: a sickish apprehension. Each of these rooms was unknown to him yet—yet oddly familiar: he seemed to know what he would see, though, in fact, as he looked about, he saw nothing familiar; the house was totally foreign. He'd never felt so disoriented and yet—and yet!—so certain of himself. He was arguing with Kim, telling her they must make a bid on the house before someone else did; the house would be snatched away from them if they didn't hurry. A down payment of $200,000 could be easily arranged if their San Francisco house was sold quickly. . . .

They would have children to fill the empty rooms. Whose children, otherwise, would fill them?

They were climbing the uncarpeted stairs and Joel heard a faint scurrying overhead, and saw, or seemed to see, a shadowy figure in the hall above. Mrs. Brody noticed nothing, but then perhaps Mrs. Brody was not so alert as her client. She was telling him of the house's history: old misfortunes, and more recent ones; the difficulty the owner, an elderly widower who had disinherited his children, had given a number of local realtors over the years. He would not budge from his unreasonably high price and he would not, or could not, keep the house in a salable condition. . . . The shadow broke into shadows as Joel and Mrs. Brody approached, dispersed as if running for cover. Playful figures, very likely children; but of course nothing but light, refracted sunlight, a tricky play of light and shadow. The original house had been built in 1840, Mrs. Brody said, by one "Ichabod Dieter, Squire,"—he'd insisted upon calling himself "Squire"—and subsequently added to, remodeled, renovated over the decades. Its heyday, so to speak, was in the twenties, when the owners had plenty of money, owned five hundred acres of land, taxes were low, servants came cheap. She glanced sidelong at her frowning client. Could she sense the intensity of his interest? How improbably close she was to a sale? "Of course," she added, carefully, "a good deal of work needs to be done. In the hands of the right people—"

"Yes," Joel said. "You've already said that."

It should not have been surprising, yet it was, and keenly disappointing, that the upstairs—the "master bedroom" in particular—was in far worse condition than the downstairs. Bedrooms, bathrooms, a sewing room—the wallpaper was stained, the windowsills warped, the floors badly scratched. There were ghostly rectangles on the walls where mirrors and paintings had hung. Apart from fireplaces in several of the rooms, there were no unusual features on this floor; Joel looked in vain for something to admire. Of course, everything would have to be redone, in any case—new plastering, new wallpaper, new plumbing, new windows. The floors were so bad, they would have to be completely carpeted. And the light fixtures—

He was standing in the doorway of a large, high-ceilinged room speaking intensely with Mrs. Brody even as he stood in the intensive care ward for "premature" infants, "preemies" as they were called, being told something by a doctor which ran through

his head like a piece of short thread through a needle—try as he
could, he couldn't retain it. Too much! Too much to be borne!
He had understood that the floor beneath him could fall away at
any instant: that was what he had to concentrate on. Like this
floor, in Squire Dieter's house.

The physical body is the "floor." The head imagines itself
floating but is in fact merely balanced on its stalk. A desperate
device staring and blinking, taking in information, monitoring
the avalanche of information, that constitutes the "world."

Mrs. Brody's voice trailed off as she sensed her client's inat-
tention. She was opening a door that connected two rooms. "The
nursery, through here," she said, "I would guess."

Joel heard the high fine humming again, heard a teasing scuf-
fle down the corridor. He began to whistle. Went to stand at a
window, hands on his hips. I own this, he thought. The sky was
mottled, deep crevices of cloud, pockets of sunshine. O help me
God. God help me. It was another man's prayer—another man
who had stood here, at this window, long ago. In a house so
"historic," in these upstairs rooms in particular, a good deal of
living had transpired.

It was damply cold, their breaths steamed. Yet Joel was per-
spiring inside his clothes. Mrs. Brody had slipped on her tight
kidskin gloves that smelled of vanilla.

Mrs. Brody was about to suggest that they leave—Joel had
stood so long without speaking, rubbing his forehead with the
back of a hand—but he said, turning to her, "There's more to
the house, isn't there, than we've seen? A third floor?"

"A partially finished attic, yes," Mrs. Brody said. She hesitated. "Would you like to see it?"

"Of course," Joel said.

Was it *there* he'd meant to go all along . . . ?

Mrs. Brody led him along the hallway to a back stairway
where they climbed, wordless, up into the dark; the light switch
evidently didn't work. A powerful smell of mildew, mice, and
dirt assaulted their nostrils.

Mrs. Brody pushed a door open cautiously. She said, "I believe I saw this part of the house years ago, but I don't seem
to—" The room was flooded with light, which was a relief. They
stepped in. Joel blinked and stared, wiping his forehead with a
tissue. He was really quite agitated and no longer cared if Charlotte Brody noticed. She was speaking quickly, walking about in
her clattering high heels as if to distract them both. "—Excellent
for a study of sorts, a hideaway for the man of the house—Guest
room—Room for a teenager who values his or her—"

The room was large, but undefined. A mere rectangle. Dormer
windows on one side, a large circular window on the other.
Flooded with light. But mere space. Very dirty, cartons and mis-
matched furniture in one of the corners, dust balls, the dessi-
cated remains of insects. That strong, rank smell of mice and
age. Joel, breathless from the stairs, stood with his hands on his
hips. He'd climbed up so impatiently, with such dread and antic-
ipation, and—was this the room? *This?*—The last room in the
house? The place of revelation? Even the faint, teasing singing
had stopped. He heard only the crows somewhere close by.
Their raucous cries lifting and fading.

The circular window was unusually large, perhaps five feet
across, like a porthole, but with elaborate leaded spokes sug-
gesting a wheel or a stylized spider's web. The glass was layered
in grime, but sunshine streamed through nonetheless. Warm,
dazzling.

The floor was covered in worn linoleum tile in which there
were deep scratch marks, from a bed perhaps. Joel could see the
bed clearly—plain, merely functional, no headboard, exposed
metal rollers. A figure lying on it, too weak to move. Too weak
to turn his head.

Somewhere close by, improbably, an insect was buzzing. Joel
discovered a wasp on the windowsill of the circular windows—in
tiny convulsive death throes. He said, his voice lifting in faint
bemused wonder, "How can a wasp still be living at this time of

year?"—but Mrs. Brody was speaking of other things and did not hear.

Joel stood very still. There was nothing in this room but the space itself: mere space delimited by four walls.

But what otherwise might there have been? What had he hoped to see?

Sunlight spilling through the window, churning with dust as with maggots, atoms. Joel closed his eyes and felt the warmth on his eyelids. His heart was pounding very hard: he knew why he was here.

He stood swaying on the balls of his feet, sunshine beating on his face. Light, feathery, insubstantial as a breath, or a kiss. He knew: his life was pointless, yet he wanted to live. There was no purpose to it, yet he wanted to live. He was desperate, greedy, shameless—he wanted to live.

Mrs. Brody cleared her throat nervously. She asked him if he had any more questions about the house, and after a while he turned to her and said no. He'd seen as much as he needed to see.

She drove him back to his hotel and gave him her card, told him to telephone her at home, if necessary, if he wanted to see any further houses; or wanted to revisit any of those he'd looked at. He thanked her warmly. Shook her hand. Upstairs in his hotel room he ripped her card into several swift pieces and dropped them into the wastebasket.

He went to bed and slept for fifteen hours straight. Woke feeling wonderfully refreshed, suffused with a curious tender strength. Where was he? Why had he come here? What powers were given him? So close to extinction, to move an inch was to move a thousand miles.

Edie: A Life

•

HARRIET DOERR

In the middle of an April night in 1919, a plain woman named Edith Fisk, lifted from England to California on a tide of world peace, arrived at the Ransom house to raise five half-orphaned children.

A few hours later, at seven in the morning, this Edith, more widely called Edie, invited the three eldest to her room for tea. They were James, seven; Eliza, six; and Jenny, four. Being handed cups of tea, no matter how reduced by milk, made them believe that they had grown up overnight.

"Have some sugar," said Edie, and spooned it in. Moments later she said, "Have another cup." But her h's went unspoken and became the first of hundreds, then thousands, which would accumulate in the corners of the house and thicken in the air like sighs.

In an adjoining room the twins, entirely responsible for their mother's death, had finished their bottles and fallen back into guiltless sleep. At the far end of the house, the widower, Thomas Ransom, who had spent the night aching for his truant wife, lay across his bed, half awake, half asleep, and dreaming.

The three children sat in silence at Edie's table. She had grizzled hair pulled up in a knot, heavy brows, high cheeks, and two long hairs in her chin. She was bony and flat, and looked starched, like the apron she had tied around her. Her teeth were large and white and even, her eyes an uncompromising blue.

She talked to the children as if they were her age, forty-one. "My father was an ostler," she told them and they listened without comprehension. "My youngest brother died at Wipers," she said. "My nephew was gassed at Verdun."

These were places the children had never heard of. But all three of them, even Jenny, understood the word, die.

"Our mother died," said James.

Edie nodded.

"I was born, oldest of eight, in Atherleigh, a town in Devon. I've lived in five English counties," she told them, without saying what a county was. "And taken care of thirty children, a few of them best forgotten."

"Which ones?" said James.

But Edie only talked of her latest charges, the girls she had left to come to America.

"Lady Alice and Lady Anne," said Edie, and described two paragons of quietness and clean knees who lived in a castle in Kent.

Edie didn't say "castle," she said "big brick house." She didn't say "lake," she said "pond." But the children, dazzled by illustrations in Cinderella and King Arthur, assumed princesses. And after that, they assumed castle, tower, moat, lake, lily, swan.

Lady Alice was seven and Lady Anne was eight when last seen immaculately crayoning with their ankles crossed in their tower overlooking the lake.

Eliza touched Edie's arm. "What is gassed?" she said.

Edie explained.

Jenny lifted her spoon for attention. "I saw father cry," she said. "Twice."

"Oh, be quiet," said James.

With Edie, they could say anything.

.   .   .

After that morning, they would love tea forever, all their lives, in sitting rooms and restaurants, on terraces and balconies, at sidewalk cafes and whistle stops, even under awnings in the rain. They would drink it indiscriminately, careless of flavor, out of paper cups or Spode, with lemon, honey, milk, or cream, with spices or with rum.

Before Edie came to the Ransom house, signs of orphanhood were everywhere—in the twins' colic, in Eliza's aggravated impulse to pinch Jenny, in the state of James' sheets every morning. Their father, recognizing symptoms of grief, brought home wrapped packages in his overcoat pockets. He gave the children a Victrola and Harry Lauder records.

"Shall we read?" he would ask in the evening, and take Edward Lear from the shelf. "There was an Old Man with a beard," read Thomas Ransom, and he and his children listened solemnly to the unaccustomed voice speaking the familiar words.

While the twins baffled everyone by episodes of weight loss and angry tears, various efforts to please were directed toward the other three. The cook baked cakes and frosted their names into the icing. The sympathetic gardener packed them into his wheelbarrow and pushed them at high speeds down sloping paths. Two aunts, the dead mother's sisters, improvised weekly outings—to the ostrich farm, the alligator farm, the lion farm, to a picnic in the mountains, a shell hunt at the beach. These contrived entertainments failed. None substituted for what was needed: the reappearance at the piano or on the stairs of a young woman with freckles, green eyes, and a ribbon around her waist.

Edie came to rescue the Ransoms through the intervention of the aunts' English friend, Cissy. When hope for joy in any degree was almost lost, Cissy wrote and produced the remedy.

The aunts brought her letter to Thomas Ransom in his study

on a February afternoon. Outside the window a young sycamore, planted by his wife last year, cast its sparse shadow on a patch of grass.

Cissy wrote that all her friends lost sons and brothers in the war and she was happy she had none to offer up. Wherever one went in London wounded veterans, wearing their military medals, were performing for money. She saw a legless man in uniform playing an accordion outside Harrod's. Others, on Piccadilly, had harmonicas wired in front of their faces so they could play without hands. Blind men, dressed for parade, sang in the rain for theatre queues.

And the weather, wrote Cissy. Winter seemed to be a state of life and not a season. How lucky one was to be living, untouched by it all, in America, particularly California. Oh, to wake up to sunshine every morning, to spend one's days warm and dry.

Now she arrived at the point of her letter. Did anyone they knew want Edith Fisk, who had taken care of children for twenty-five years and was personally known to Cissy? Edie intended to live near a cousin in Texas. California might be just the place.

The reading of the letter ended.

"Who is Cissy?" said Thomas Ransom, unable to foresee that within a dozen years he would marry her.

James, who had been listening at the door, heard only the first part of the letter. Long before Cissy proposed Edie, he was upstairs in his room, trying to attach a harmonica to his mouth with kite string.

Edie was there within two months. The aunts and Thomas Ransom began to witness change.

Within weeks the teasing stopped. Within months the nighttime sheets stayed dry. The twins, male and identical, fattened and pulled toys apart. Edie bestowed on each of the five equal shares of attention and concern. She hung their drawings in her room, even the ones of moles in traps and inhabited houses burning to the ground. Samples of the twins' scribblings remained on permanent display. The children's pictures eventually occupied almost all one wall and surrounded a framed photograph of Lady Alice and Lady Anne, two small light-haired girls sitting straight-backed on dappled ponies.

"Can we have ponies?" Eliza and Jenny asked their father, but he had fallen in love with a woman named Trish and, distracted, brought home a cage of canaries instead.

Edie and the Ransom children suited each other. It seemed right to them all that she had come to braid hair, turn hems, push swings, take walks; to apply iodine to cuts and embrace the cry that followed, to pinch her fingers between the muddy rubber and the shoe. Edie stopped nightmares almost before they started. At a child's first gasp she would be in the doorway, uncombed and toothless, tying on her wrapper, a glass of water in her hand.

The older children repaid this bounty with torments of their own devising. They would rush at her in a trio, shout, "We've 'idden your 'at in the 'all," and run shrieking with laughter, out of her sight. They crept into her room at night, found the pink gums and big white teeth where they lay floating in a mug and, in a frenzy of bad manners, hid them in a hat box or behind the books.

Edie never reported these lapses of deportment to Thomas Ransom. Instead she would invoke the names and virtues of Lady Alice and Lady Anne.

"They didn't talk like roustabouts," said Edie. "They slept like angels through the night."

Between spring and fall the nonsense ceased. Edie grew into the Ransoms' lives and was accepted there, like air and water and the food they ate. From the start, the children saw her as a refuge. Flounder as they might in the choppy sea where orphans and half-orphans drown, they trusted her to save them.

Later on, when their father emerged from mourning, Edie was the mast they clung to in a squall of stepmothers.

. . .

Within a period of ten years Thomas Ransom, grasping at the
outer fringe of happiness, brought three wives in close succession
to the matrimonial bed he first shared with the children's now
sainted mother. He chose women he believed were like her, and
it was true that all three, Trish, Irene, and Cissy, were small-
boned and energetic. But they were brown-eyed and, on the
whole, not musical.

The first to come was Trish, nineteen years old and porcelain-
skinned. Before her arrival Thomas Ransom asked the children
not to come knocking at his bedroom door day and night, as
they had in the past. Once she was there, other things changed.
The children heard him humming at his desk in the study. They
noticed that he often left in mid-morning, instead of at eight, for
the office where he practiced law.

Eliza asked questions at early morning tea. "Why are they
always in their room, with the door locked?"

And Jenny said, "Yes. Even before dinner."

"Don't you know anything?" said James.

Edie poured more pale tea. "Hold your cups properly. Don't
spill," she told them, and the lost *h* floated into the steam rising
from the pot.

Trish, at nineteen, was neither mother nor sister to the children.
Given their priorities of blood and birth and previous residence,
they inevitably outdistanced her. They knew to the oldest
steamer trunk and the latest cookie the contents of the attic and
larder. They walked oblivious across rugs stained with their
spilled ink. The hall banister shone with the years of their sliding. Long ago they had enlisted the cook and the gardener as
allies. Three of them remembered their mother. The other two
thought they did.

Trish said good morning at noon and drove off with friends.
Later she paused to say goodnight in a rustle of taffeta on
Thomas Ransom's arm as they left for a dinner or a dance.

James made computations. "She's nine years older than I am," he said, "and eighteen years younger than father."

"He keeps staring at her," said Eliza.

"And kissing her hand," said Jenny.

Edie opened a door on a sliver of her past. "I knew a girl once with curly red hair like that, in Atherleigh."

"What was her name?" James asked, as if for solid evidence.

Edie bit off her darning thread. She looked backward with her inward eye. Finally she said, "Lily Stiles. The day I went into service in Dorset, Lily went to work at the Rose and Plough."

"The Rose and Plough," repeated Eliza. "What's that?"

"It's a pub," said Edie, and she explained what a public house was. Immediately this establishment, with its gleaming bar and its game of darts, was elevated in the children's minds to the mysterious realm of Lady Alice and Lady Anne and set in place a stone's throw from their castle.

At home, Trish's encounters with her husband's children were brief. In passing, she waved to them all and patted the twins on their dark heads. She saw more of the three eldest on those Saturday afternoons when she took them, along with Edie, to the movies.

Together they sat in the close, expectant dark of the Rivoli Theatre, watched the shimmering curtains part, shivered to the organist's opening chords and, at the appearance of an image on the screen, cast off their everyday lives to be periled, rescued, rejected, and adored. They sat spellbound through the film and when the words, The End, came on, rose depleted and blinking from their seats to face the hot sidewalk and full sun outside.

Trish selected the pictures and, though they occasionally included Fairbanks films and ones that starred the Gishes, these were not her favorites. She detested comedies. To avoid Harold Lloyd, they saw Rudolph Valentino in "The Sheik." Rather than endure Buster Keaton, they went to "Gypsy Blood," starring Alla Nazimova.

"I should speak to your father," Edie would say later on at home. But she never did. Instead, she only remarked at bedtime, "It's a nice change, going to the pictures."

Trish left at the end of two years, during which the children according to individual predispositions, grew taller and developed the hands and feet and faces they would always keep. They learned more about words and numbers, they began to like oysters, they swam the Australian crawl. They survived crises. These included scarlet fever, which the twins contracted and recovered from, and James' near electrocution as a result of his tinkering with wires and sockets.

Eliza and Jenny, exposed to chicken pox on the same day, ran simultaneous fevers and began to scratch. Edie brought ice and invented games. She cleared the table between their beds and knotted a handkerchief into arms and legs and a smooth, round head. She made it face each invalid and bow.

"This is how my sister Frahnces likes to dahnce the fahncy dahnces," Edie said, and the knotted handkerchief waltzed and two-stepped back and forth across the table.

Mesmerized by each other, the twins made few demands. A mechanical walking bear occupied them for weeks, a wind-up train for months. They shared a rocking horse and crashed slowly into one another on tricycles.

James, at eleven, sat in headphones by the hour in front of a crystal radio set. Sometimes he invited Edie to scratch a chip of rock with wire and hear a human voice advance and recede in the distance.

"Where's he talking from?" Edie would ask, and James said, "Oak Bluff. Ten miles away."

Together they marveled.

The two aunts, after one of their frequent visits, tried to squeeze the children into categories. James is the experimenter, they agreed. Jenny, the romantic. The twins, at five, too young to pigeon-hole. Eliza was the bookish one.

A single-minded child, she read while walking to school, in

the car on mountain curves, on the train in tunnels, on her back on the beach at noon, in theatres under dimming lights, between the sheets by flashlight. Eliza saw all the world through thick lenses adjusted for fine print. On Saturdays, she would often desert her invited friend and choose to read by herself instead.

At these times Edie would approach the bewildered visitor. Would she like to feed the canaries? Climb into the tree house?

"We'll make tiaras," she told one abandoned guest and, taking Jenny along, led the way to the orange grove.

"We're brides," announced Jenny a few minutes later, and she and Eliza's friend, balancing circles of flowers on their heads, stalked in a barefoot procession of two through the trees.

That afternoon, Jenny, as though she had never seen it before, inquired about Edie's ring. "Are you engaged?"

"I was once," said Edie, and went on to expose another slit of her past. "To Alfred Trotter."

"Was he killed at Wipers?"

Edie shook her head. "The war came later. He worked for his father at the Rose and Plough."

In a field beyond the grove, Jenny saw a plough, ploughing roses.

"Why didn't you get married?"

Edie looked at her watch and said it was five o'clock. She brushed off her skirt and got to her feet. "I wasn't the only girl in Atherleigh."

Jenny, peering into the past, caught a glimpse of Lily Stiles behind the bar at the Rose and Plough.

After Trish left, two more years went by before the children's father brought home his third wife. This was Irene, come to transplant herself in Ransom ground. Behind her she trailed a wake of friends, men with beards and women in batik scarves, who sat about the porch with big hats between them and the sun. In a circle of wicker chairs, they discussed Cubism, Freud,

Proust, and Schoenberg's twelve-tone row. They passed per-
fumed candies to the children.

Irene changed all the lampshades in the house from white
paper to red silk, threw a Persian prayer rug over the piano, and
gave the children incense sticks for Christmas. She recited poems translated from the Sanskrit and wore saris to the grocery
store. In spite of efforts on both sides, Irene remained an envoy
from a foreign land.

One autumn day, not long before the end of her tenure as
Thomas Ransom's wife, she took Edie and all five children to a
fortune teller at the county fair. A pale-eyed, wasted man sold
them tickets outside Madame Zelma's tent and pointed to the
curtained entrance. Crowding into the stale air of the interior,
they gradually made out the fortune teller's veiled head and
jewelled neck behind two lighted candelabra on a desk.

"Have a seat," said Madame.

All found places on a bench or hassocks, and rose, one by one,
to approach the palmist as she beckoned them to a chair facing
her.

Madame Zelma, starting with the eldest, pointed to Edie.

"I see children," said the fortune teller. She concentrated in
silence for a moment. "You will cross the ocean. I see a handsome man."

Alfred Trotter, thought Jenny. Us.

Madame Zelma, having wound Edie's life backward from
present to past, summoned Irene.

"I see a musical instrument," said Madame, as if she knew of
Irene's guitar and the chords in minor keys that were its reper-
tory. "Your flower is the poppy. Your fruit, the pear." The fortune teller leaned closer to Irene's hand. "Expect a change of
residence soon."

Edie and the children listened.

And so the fortunes went, the three eldest's full of prizes and
professions, talents and awards, happy marriages, big families,
silver mines and fame.

By the time Madame Zelma reached the twins, she had little left to predict. "Long lives," was all she told them. But what more could anyone divine from the trackless palms of seven-year olds?

By the time Cissy, the next wife, came, James' voice had changed and his sisters had bobbed their hair. The twins had joined in painting an oversized panorama titled, "After the Earthquake." Edie hung it on her wall.

Cissy, the children's last stepmother, traveled all the way from England, like Edie. Introduced by the aunts through a letter, Thomas Ransom met her in London, rode with her in Hyde Park, drove with her to Windsor for the day, then took her boating on the upper reaches of the Thames. They were married in a registry, she for the third, he for the fourth time, and spent their honeymoon on the Isle of Skye in a long, gray drizzle.

"I can hardly wait for California," said Cissy.

Once there, she lay about in the sun until she blistered. "Darling, bring my parasol, bring my gloves," she entreated whichever child was near.

"Are the hills always this brown?" she asked, splashing rose water on her throat. "Has that stream dried up for good?"

Cissy climbed mountain paths looking for wildflowers and came back with toyon and sage. Twice a week on her horse, Sweet William, she rode trails into the countryside, flushing up rattlesnakes instead of grouse.

On national holidays which celebrated American separation from Britain, Cissy felt in some way historically at fault. On the day before Thanksgiving, she strung cranberries silently at Edie's side. On the Fourth of July they sat together holding sparklers six thousand miles from the counties where their roots, still green, were sunk in English soil.

During the dry season of the year, from April to December, the children sometimes watched Cissy as she stood at a corner of the terrace, her head turning from east to west, her eyes searching the implacable blue sky. But for what? An English bird? The smell of fog?

By now the children were half grown or more, and old enough to recognize utter misery.

"Cissy didn't know what to expect," they told each other.

"She's homesick for the Sussex downs," said Edie, releasing the *h* into space.

"Are you homesick, too, for Atherleigh?" asked Eliza.

"I am not."

"You knew what to expect," said Jenny.

Edie said, "Almost."

The children discussed with her the final departure of each stepmother.

"Well, she's gone," said James, who was usually called to help carry out bags. "Maybe we'll have some peace."

After Cissy left, he made calculations. "Between the three of them, they had six husbands," he told the others.

"And father's had four wives," said one of the twins. "Six husbands and four wives make ten," said the other.

"Ten what?" said James.

"Poor souls," said Edie.

At last the children were as tall as they would ever be. The aunts could no longer say, "How are they ever to grow up?" For here they were, reasonably bright and reasonably healthy, survivors of a world war and a great depression, durable relics of their mother's premature and irreversible defection and their father's abrupt remarriages.

They had got through it all—the removal of tonsils, the straightening of teeth, the first night at camp, the first dance, the goodbyes waved from the rear platforms of trains that, like boats crossing the Styx, carried them away to college. This is not to say they were the same children they would have been if their mother had lived. They were not among the few who can suffer anything, loss or gain, without effect. But no one could point to a Ransom child's smile or frown or sleeping habits, and reasonably comment, "No mother."

Edie stayed in the Ransom house until the twins left for college. By now, Eliza and Jenny were married, James married, divorced, and remarried. Edie went to all the graduations and weddings.

On these occasions the children hurried across playing fields and lawns to reach and embrace her.

"Edie!" they said. "You came!" They introduced their fellow graduates and the persons they had married. "This is Edie. Edie, this is Bill, Terry, Peter, Joan," and were carried off in whirlwinds of friends.

As the Ransom house emptied of family, it began to expand. The bedrooms grew larger, the hall banister longer, the porch too wide for the wicker chairs. Edie took leave of the place for want of children in 1938. She was sixty years old.

She talked to Thomas Ransom in his study, where his first wife's portrait, painted in pastels, had been restored to its place on the wall facing his desk. Edie sat under the green-eyed young face, her unfaltering blue glance on her employer. Each tried to make the parting easy. It was clear, however, that they were dividing between them, top to bottom, a frail, towering structure of nineteen accumulated years, which was the time it had taken to turn five children with their interminable questions, unfounded terrors, and destructive impulses, into mature adults who could vote, follow maps, make omelets, and reach an accord of sorts with life and death.

Thinking back over the intervening years, Thomas Ransom remembered Edie's cousin in Texas and inquired, only to find that Texas had been a disappointment, as had America itself. The cousin had returned to England twelve years ago.

"Would you like that?" he asked Edie. "To go back to England?"

She had grown used to California, she said. She had no one in

Atherleigh. So, in the end, prompted by the look in his first wife's eyes, Thomas Ransom offered Edie a cottage and a pension to be hers for the rest of her life.

Edie's beach cottage was two blocks back from the sea and very small. On one wall she hung a few of the children's drawings, including the earthquake aftermath. Opposite them, by itself, she hung the framed photograph of Lady Alice and Lady Anne, fair and well-seated astride their ponies. Edie had become the repository of pets. The long-lived fish swam languidly in one corner of her sitting room, the last of the canaries moulted in another.

Each Ransom child came to her house once for tea, pulling in to the curb next to a mailbox marked Edith Fisk.

"Edie, you live so far away!"

On their first Christmas apart, the children sent five cards, the next year four, then two for several years, then one, or sometimes none.

During the first September of Edie's retirement, England declared war on Germany. She knitted socks for the British troops and, on one occasion four years after she left it, returned briefly to the Ransom house. This was when the twins were killed in Europe a month apart at the age of twenty-four, one in a fighter plane over the Baltic, the other in a bomber over the Rhine. Two months later Thomas Ransom asked Edie to dispose of their things and she came back for a week to her old, now anonymous, room.

She was unprepared for the mass of articles to be dealt with. The older children had cleared away childhood possessions at the time of their marriages. But here were all the books the twins had ever read, from Dr. Doolittle to Hemingway, and all their entertainments, from a ouija board to skis and swim fins. Years of their civilian trousers, coats, and shoes crowded the closets.

Edie first wrapped and packed the bulky objects, then folded into cartons the heaps of clothing, much of which she knew. A week was barely time enough to sort it all and reach decisions. Then, suddenly, as though it had been a matter of minutes, the boxes were packed and at the door. Edie marked each one with black crayon. Boys' Club, she printed, Children's Hospital, Red Cross, Veterans.

That afternoon, she stood for a moment with Thomas Ransom on the porch, the silent house behind them. The November air was cold and fresh, the sky cloudless.

"Lovely day," said Edie.

Thomas Ransom nodded, admiring the climate while his life thinned out.

If the three surviving children had written Edie during the years that followed, this is what she would have learned.

At thirty-five, James, instead of having become an electrical engineer or a master mechanic, was a junior partner in his father's law firm. Twice divorced and about to take a new wife, he had apparently learned nothing from Thomas Ransom, not even how to marry happily once. Each marriage had produced two children, four intended cures that failed. James' practice involved foreign corporations and he was often abroad. He moved from executive offices to board rooms and back, and made no attempt to diagnose his discontent. On vacations at home, he dismantled and reassembled heaters and fans, and wired every room of his house for sound.

Whenever he visited England, he tried, and failed, to find time to send Edie a card.

Eliza had been carried off from her research library by an archaeologist ten years older and three inches shorter than she. He took her first to Guatemala, then to Mexico, where they lived in a series of jungle huts in Chiapas and Yucatan. It was hard to find native help and the clothes Eliza washed often hung drying for days on the teeming underbrush. Her damp books, on

shelves and still in boxes, began to mildew. She cooked food
wrapped in leaves over a charcoal fire. On special days, like her
birthday and Christmas, Eliza would stand under the thatch of
her doorway and stare northwest through the rain and vegeta-
tion in the direction of the house where she was born and first
tasted tea.

Edie still lived in the house when Jenny, through a letter from
her last stepmother, Cissy, met the Englishman she would
marry. Thin as a pencil and pale as parchment, he had entered
the local university as an exchange fellow. Jenny was immediately moved to take care of him, sew on his missing buttons,
comb his sandy hair. His English speech enchanted her.

"Tell about boating at Henley," she urged him. "Tell about
climbing the Trossachs. Explain cricket." And while he described these things as fully as his inherent reserve would allow,
the inflections of another voice fell across his. Jenny heard
"fahncy dahnces." She heard "poor souls."

"Have you ever been to Atherleigh in Devon?" she asked him.

"That's Hatherleigh," he said.

If Jenny had written Edie, she would have said, "I love Massachusetts, I love my house, I can make scones, come and see
us."

On a spring afternoon in 1948, Thomas Ransom called his children together in the same study where the aunts had read Cissy's
letter of lament and recommendation. The tree his wife planted
thirty years ago towered in green leaf outside the window.

The children had gathered from the outposts of the world—
James from Paris, Eliza from the Mayan tropics, Jenny from
snowed-in Boston. When he summoned them, they had assumed
a crisis involving their father. Now they sat uneasily under the
portrait of their mother, a girl years younger than themselves.
Thomas Ransom offered them tea and sherry. He looked
through the window at the tree.

At last he presented his news. "Edie is dying," he said. "She is

in the hospital with cancer," as if cancer were a friend Edie had
always longed to share a room with.

They visited her on a shining April morning, much like the one
when they first met. With their first gray hairs and new lines at
their eyes, they waited a moment on the hospital steps.

James took charge. "We'll go in one by one," he said.

So, as if they had rehearsed together, each of them stood alone
outside the door that had a sign, No Visitors, stood there while
carts of half-eaten lunches or patients prepared for surgery were
wheeled past, stood and collected their childhood until a nurse
noticed and said, "Go in. She wants to see you." Then, one after
another, they pushed the door open, went to the high narrow
bed, and said, "Edie."

She may not have known they were there. She had started to
be a skeleton. Her skull was pulling her eyes in. Once they had
spoken her name, there was nothing more to say. Before leaving,
they touched the familiar, unrecognizable hand of shoe laces and
hair ribbons and knew it, for the first time, disengaged.

After their separate visits, they assembled again on the hospital steps. It was now they remembered Lady Alice and Lady
Anne.

"Where was that castle?" Eliza asked.

"In Kent," said Jenny.

All at one time, they imagined the girls in their tower after
tea. Below them, swans pulled lengthening reflections behind
them across the smooth surface of the lake. Lady Alice sat at her
rosewood desk, Lady Anne at hers. They were still seven and
eight years old. They wrote on thick paper with mother-of-pearl
pens dipped into ivory inkwells.

"Dear Edie," wrote Lady Alice.

"Dear Edie," wrote Lady Anne.

"I am sorry to hear you are ill," they both wrote.

Then, as if they were performing an exercise in penmanship,

they copied "I am sorry" over and over in flowing script until they reached the bottom of the page. When there was no more room, they signed one letter, Alice, and the other letter, Anne.

In the midst of all this, Edie died.

The Sky Fading Upward to Yellow: A Footnote to Literary History

•

You know what happens after someone like Worsham dies. In no time, hardly longer than it takes to say "important literary figure" or "publishing house," the wheels begin to turn. Maybe the first wife starts work on a memoir of the early years; the second or third wife gets busy preparing some letters or papers for publication. Eventually a letter soliciting information for a biography appears in *The New York Times Book Review* and *The New York Review of Books.* However it goes, the wives tend to get their due—their day in court; the wives and long-term alliances. Brenda was a short-term alliance, but she felt she deserved a page in Worsham's life story.

She thought about this a good deal. Whenever I was back in town on a visit, we talked about it. She was still there where we'd gone to graduate school, where we'd gone expecting, like so many others, to become writers, and where, one year, Robert Worsham was our teacher. It was customary there to bring big names out for a semester or a year, and he was a big name—in his fifties, but not long at the teaching business; at that point in his career he could pick and choose—a semester here, a summer

Copyright © 1987 by Jean Ross. First appeared in *Shenandoah.* Reprinted by permission.

conference there. He died three or four years later, suddenly, and before long a volume of his letters was in the works—"awfully soon," Brenda said decisively. She had a bunch of letters from him herself, but was not surprised that nobody asked about them. "Madeleine's in charge, and she may not know even now that I exist." (Madeleine was his wife.) But when Brenda learned that someone was at work on a biography, she began to expect a letter, a kind of summons. "I know he"—Rayner, the biographer—"has been in touch with people who knew about us." She was resigned, ready to be reasonable about it. "I could refuse to tell him anything, but sometimes if you don't cooperate, people will try to piece it together anyway and get it all wrong. *He* used to tell a story about that—"

"Anybody who's writing about him ought to be in touch with Bren," Jed, her friend, said. "She's the one who was closest to him that year—she knows things nobody else would know. What he was thinking about—his inner life." He looked at her fondly across our booth in Whaley's, a tavern that had once been the workshop hangout; Jed and I were on one side, Brenda on the other, her back against the wall, her legs out full-length on the seat. It was afternoon, but inside the light was dim; out on the bright street there was some spring street-work going on, with intermittent jackhammering, students jaywalking around the work, townspeople going up and down the sidewalk. Brenda often spoke in an almost affectedly soft voice, and she waited for a lull in the noise to murmur, "There was a week—when I was quite sure he was going to crack up. I was planning what to do, who to call—" She shook her head, shrugged, and reached for a cigarette, her hand trembling for an instant; I wondered precisely what old excitement, what regret for the past she was feeling.

Jed seemed so interested in the Brenda-Worsham connection that I wondered if knowing about it had helped attract him to her. I could imagine him writing a friend, "You'll like her—a remarkable woman, vital and gifted, once mistress of a famous novelist." He was a sculptor, a curly-haired, solidly-built man, not totally different from Worsham in appearance. He smiled at her encouragingly and said, "You have to put personal interests aside in a case like this. If he gets in touch, you'll have to level with him and show him the letters."

"Oh, you'll hear from him, surely," I said. I really thought she would.

But she didn't, and the subject came up again the next time I was through town. My folks were still living in Illinois then, and I got back to the Midwest at least a couple of times a year.

"He has to have been in touch with Andrea and Herb," she said. They were the ones from our bunch of Worsham students who had achieved some reputation; Andrea had published an interview with him, among other things. They knew about Brenda, for sure, but Andrea hadn't liked her much; anyway, she and the others might have considered it a breach of taste or judgment to bring up the Brenda connection now. (There was Mrs. W. off in the East.) Brenda seemed to be having the same thought. "I begged him, I implored him to tell Her—get the pain over now, it will be better for us all in the long run! I remember one night they talked on the phone half an hour, and when he came back into the room he said, 'How we batter and bruise each other with *words,*' and I really thought he might break down and cry. They'd had trouble before—they'd always had trouble. He said once, 'Madeleine talks as if my success is a species of morbid condition, brought on by a doting mother and a doubting father. She once said I must have been 'cruelly pro-grammed to strive for success.' '" Brenda pressed her lips to-gether, as if to keep from saying too much.

I'd just been reading the Worsham letters and hadn't found much in them about their troubles; but of course his wife had made the selection. "Too bad the timing wasn't better for you two," I said, "too bad you couldn't have found him sitting beside you in workshop, another student—"

She was taking some peanuts from a bowl on the table—we were once again in Whaley's—and she held them tight in her fist for a moment and looked at me suspiciously. "Oh, do you think I was drawn to his success? I can tell you, name and fame were not in it—I'd have seen him for what he was, anywhere. Reflected glory is *not* my thing."

"No, no, I didn't mean that," and I didn't—at least I don't think I did. "No, I just meant, what lousy luck, Brenda."

"B.—an aloof exhibitionist." That's what I wrote in my journal before I began to like her. (We were big on journals and descriptions then.) There was some truth in it: she wanted our attention, then seemed to throw it away. She was small, lithe, bright-eyed, with high-colored cheeks, as if she'd just scrubbed them almost too hard. She was from the East and had been to Europe, and had little anecdotes of Roman pensions and channel ferries; I remember hearing her say of someone, some obscure writer she'd met abroad, that he "spoke French in a soft, Belgian sort of way." I was a hearty small-town Midwesterner, sensitive about expressions with "corn" in them, such as "corn-fed," and hungry for a personal style; Brenda made me feel large and innocent, and I took her in carefully. After a while we hit it off together, and when the other woman in her apartment left town, she spoke of my moving in. Then she said the roommate might be back. That never happened, but other possibilities were developing.

One night late in the fall a bunch of us, six or seven, had dinner at her place; Worsham was the chief guest. Everybody brought something, and we ate off our laps and the coffee table, and took in what he had to say. He was a short, compact man, his head somehow especially compact-looking, as if it had a high specific gravity—solid as a rock; he had smoker's teeth and a slightly weathered face but looked remarkably young all the same. I thought it was exactly the way he ought to look, and when I saw, much later, a picture of him handsome in his twenties, I felt that the way we had known him was his true appearance.

We questioned him steadily: we wanted to know what to think about everything, especially all the other writers in the world. Who was Good?—who was worth our while? He didn't serve up the little insider's anecdotes we might have hoped to hear, though once in a while a question would make him laugh a short, sincere, cheerful laugh. "Him? Sure, he's good. It's too bad his life has turned progressively less interesting, since it's all he's got to write about." I remember he said something about reading a little Hemingway from time to time to "cleanse the palate. Like the sherbet between the courses. Not too much at a time, though." Someone asked about the novel he was working on, and he talked for a while about his grandfather, who figured in it. The grandfather had taken Robert Worsham and his brother with him on a trip to Canada when they were quite young, and the grandfather had taken sick; Robert had had to walk miles into the nearest town for help. It was early morning; he remembered the mist hanging over a stream, and the day beginning to warm up, and the feeling that he knew what it was like to be set free into adulthood, thrilling and frightening. He saw so much, he understood so much about himself and the rest of the world and described it so well that it made you long to see more—to go out and see and understand.

Some of the trivial talk that night has stayed in my mind, for some reason. It was a time of overalls and granny dresses, and Brenda had on a long flowered dress with a ruffle around the bottom, and brown lace-up boots that Worsham said looked like hightop shoes from the turn of the century. "When I see my daughter in overalls," he said, "I think of it as homage to the American farmer." Someone remarked that homage to the past was in style—those second-hand store dresses from the thirties and forties. And the Goodwill look—was that homage to the downtrodden? "What's Brenda's dress homage to?" someone said.

We waited for Worsham to answer; he was nice about paying attention to the silly things we said. "Oh—all the old-fashioned women, I suppose. A paradox in itself—" glancing at her quickly. A mysterious look passed between them; for a moment I was wild to know what it meant. Then he got up and opened another bottle of wine. He seemed to know where everything was in the kitchen without having to ask.

He was still there when the rest of us went home. His coat was on a chair by the door, but he seemed somehow settled in. It was late—we'd been waiting for him to leave—and it was cold, and LaDeane Hildebrand and I, who were going the same way, set off together, walking fast, moaning over the cold, our caps down over our ears, our scarves up over our chins. We trotted along rapidly not only from the cold, but because we were in a hurry to get far enough away to start talking. "Have they got something going, or are they just about to?" she puffed.

"God! He's only been here two months!" ("God" was something Brenda said a good deal.) "How do you suppose it happens! Wouldn't you like to know which one— But I thought he had a family back East. Well, some women are determined to find someone older, a married man—after all, *Father* was a married man—"

"Oh, come on, she just wanted to make him comfortable, give him a home away from home," LaDeane said, and we burst into wild laughter. "Of course this is only jealousy, you know that," meaning it couldn't be. Trotting on home, we shivered from excitement as much as from the cold; probably we both had trouble getting to sleep that night. But it was the only time I remember being catty about Brenda and Worsham. Later on our disapproval faded; soon our bunch of Worsham students felt too loyal to pass judgment. Maybe, in some odd way, this seemed to make him more one of us. It would be hard to say, considering their great discretion, how we knew what was going on, but then we were people who went in for observation; we could tell. If we didn't talk about it much, if we didn't know quite how to look at it, it wasn't for lack of thinking about it. I dreamed about Brenda's apartment; once, inside it in a dream, I told Worsham that Brenda had left town, like the roommate I'd been going to replace. He said it was all right.

Brenda and I went East together over spring break that year. Over vacations Worsham went back to New York, to domestic arrangements unknown to me and perhaps to Brenda as well. This time she was going East too. She'd bought an old car, a dull, lusterless brown, the color of dried mud, with an inefficient muffler that made it sound like a motorboat, Worsham said. ("We're coming in to the dock!" he cried once as we stopped in front of his place, when Brenda was giving him a ride home from Whaley's, where we usually gathered after class.) We drove East in the brown car, dropping Herb Soles in Athens, Ohio, then she proposed that we veer down into West Virginia to see a friend of hers. We didn't know much about driving in the mountains, and the last thirty or forty miles we had no brakes to speak of. The friend she was looking for wasn't around, but we got the brakes worked on, and while we waited we walked around town, then sat in a little cafe near the garage. I could see Brenda taking it all in. The beer salesman came, trundling his cases along; as he was leaving, the woman at the cash register, thirtyish and pretty, with a wretched permanent, gave him a hopeful smile and said, "Leaving us so soon?" and he thought for a moment and said, "Better come go with me." "Observe, Rachel, that's how it's done in the real world. You notice how much prettier she was when she was talking to him?" Brenda said. "A man and a maid, no music necessary," I said, an allusion to "Guy de Maupassant," an Isaac Babel story that I'd been reading in the car. And I thought that the man and woman back there had it easy, their thoughts and motives being so much simpler than Brenda's and Worsham's. About that I may have been wrong.

We went on to Nyack, where her mother lived; next morning, there was the Hudson down at the foot of the lawn, in the beautiful morning mist. Her mother looked at us dubiously, I thought, even after we got cleaned up—Brenda barefoot, wearing her faded Dostoyevsky tee shirt, me in my department store pants and pullover outfit, which I already knew wasn't quite right. Brenda took me into the city and showed me the sights very pleasantly, as if I were some visiting aunt.

I'd assumed that going East included seeing Worsham, and I'd half-expected to see him step out from some shadowy corner at the Cloisters, from the lunch line at a museum, or in the Japanese restaurant where we had dinner; perhaps I was even disappointed. Keyed up from being there and from trying to take it all in coolly, I said something gauche about wondering if he was in town. She smiled tolerantly.

"Have I heard from him? No, I have not. He's free and I'm free, we don't control each other. I told him I might be going home; I didn't give him the phone number because it would have been a direction. He can take extraordinary measures if he wishes to get in touch, but there's no obligation. We're free, both of us. No strings attached."

"That's wonderful," I said. "That's the way it ought to be. Free, absolutely free."

There were a couple of months left in the term when we got back. We had a great party near the end, afternoon to evening to morning, in the end tossing the glasses out into the yard, a ceremony the meaning of which I have forgotten, and I suppose all it meant to the neighbors was disorderly conduct. That afternoon we had sat around in the sun in somebody's backyard, Worsham sitting there smiling—a cheerful drinker, someone called him, and he said, "The Lord loveth a cheerful drinker." Once he nodded off for a few minutes. People were still asking him questions now and again: last chance for instructions before we parted company. I think we felt almost apprehensive about his going away and leaving us.

. . .

The biography of Worsham was a long time coming. After two or three years, portions of it appeared in a couple of quarterlies, and one of these covered the year he'd taught us. As I read it, I thought how fine that year had been, even more remarkable than we'd known at the time. It made me happy and sad at the same time.

Brenda was reading it too. She called me a few days later. "So much missing!" She meant herself and their relationship, and I had to agree that it was a noticeable omission.

"In the end I couldn't stand it," she said. "The night after I read it, I started writing what I know about that year, I really couldn't help it. I'm amazed at how much there is to say! But now I don't know whether to send it to Rayner or not. He's the logical person to have this, this and the letters I have—he's the official biographer, I suppose, so far, anyway. And the book hasn't been announced for next year so he probably hasn't finished it. Should I send it, do you think?"

"I don't know. I hadn't thought about it."

"I was keeping a journal at the time, and wrote down what we talked about, what was on his mind. It was seven months, more or less—one of the last good working years of his life, and he was finishing the last book and planning the one he didn't get to finish—I've got an amazingly complete record of that time, and it's a pretty important time."

Her tone was firm; I felt that she meant not only to set me straight, but now, years later, to set Worsham straight about a few things too. Oh, doesn't every woman, no matter how often she said they were free—doesn't she secretly, or perhaps unconsciously, expect the man freely to give up all the others for her?

I thought of them sitting side by side in a booth in Whaley's, smiling with a unanimity of gaze and an air of great happiness, as if they'd just had wonderful news that day. Wasn't it enough? It wasn't, thank God, my job to sort out what this meant in their lives over the long haul, but there it was, it had happened, with all its, I assume, joy of discovery. But she wanted more: a page in history; a paragraph; a footnote. She may even have felt it was a kind of belated gift that Worsham would have wanted her to have.

"Of course you know the whole story, Brenda—the untold story." I had expected this to sound funnier and less snide than it did, and I went on quickly, "Oh, I know there's a lot you can add. And that it's very interesting. But, you know, maybe you should let it sit for a while and see how it looks later." Maybe writing it all down would be good enough. "Of course, it's something you'll have to decide for yourself."

She'd expected me to say send it on, send it on, and she said stiffly, "It will certainly be my decision. I haven't finished it yet anyway."

My parents had moved from Illinois and I wasn't getting back to the Midwest much any more. Brenda and I had got into the habit of phoning maybe two or three times a year; these last few years the news had been that she and Jed had had a child, had separated briefly and then reconciled; that she was working part-time at the university press, had abandoned one novel and started another; that Jed's work could be seen now on a number of public lawns around the state. Sometimes it seemed a bit odd that she was still living in that town.

I was a little farther west, working on a wildlife-protection magazine; Tim and I had met and joined forces and built a house, doing some of the work ourselves; we'd moved into it, and were finishing things up. He's with a public interest research group—a do-er, rather different from most of my old graduate school friends. He's read a fantastic amount, and he says it's often a mistake to know the people who write the books—if the book's any good, what more do you need?

When I told him about the call from Brenda, he shrugged. "To blab or not to blab? Well, it was a lot like your everyday run-of-the-mill affair, wasn't it?—except that he was Somebody." He'd just come in from clearing the snow from the drive-way, and was in his sock feet, warming up at the stove. "To consummate the union with Success! There's something kind of primitive about it, don't you think? As if the magic will rub off on you."

"It didn't seem so run-of-the-mill at the time," I said. "It seemed terribly exciting and important! And he was really nice, a really nice person, beyond his books and all that—and she was drawn to the things in him that made him a success, not neces-sarily his *being* one." I heard myself sounding over-emphatic, a little too passionate about it all of a sudden. "Well—anyway, it's part of literary history now, like Sheilah Graham and Scott Fitz-gerald, or Hemingway and his inamoratas. Or maybe it's not like anybody else at all, but it's still interesting to a lot of people."

"That poor guy deserves to have his old flings cloaked in a decent obscurity as much as any suburbanite," Tim said. I couldn't tell whether he was serious or not; on certain subjects he likes to tease me.

It was three or four months before Brenda called again. "I've finished it," she said.

I thought she would ask me to read it, but instead she told it to me, reading from it here and there, sometimes a page or more. We were probably on the phone for an hour.

There were the things she thought might be useful to anyone writing about his work: a different ending he had considered for the book he was finishing; the plot of the one he'd started next, which was left unfinished, apparently a version of his parents' lives, beginning with his mother, before her marriage, in a sani-tarium at Lake Placid, where she had had some sort of romance. ("Like *The Magic Mountain,*" I murmured, and Brenda said, "Oh, not really.") Wouldn't all this be in his papers? But maybe not, or not all of it. She remembered—or her journal recorded—where they had been when he told her certain things: eating take-out food at her place; riding through the thawing countryside in the spring, after she got the car, which he called the Mud Hen.

"About us," she said. "I speak of the first time we had dinner together and went to my place afterwards and talked. And I say, 'We had dinner together again the next week. "It Happened One Night" was playing on the campus film series, and he said he wouldn't mind seeing it again; we had coffee afterwards. One night later that week there was a wonderful thick fog, and I called him and asked if he'd been outside, it was such a mysterious, magical night. He said he'd walk over to my place—it wasn't far—and we took a long walk together. We became lovers, and he often stayed over at my apartment.' Isn't that all right?"

"Oh, it's all right—"

But she was going on. She described an afternoon of sentiment, when he'd given her a ring. A ring from a machine, the kind you see beside the bubble gum machine up near the front of supermarkets or five-and-tens—you put in a nickel and get a little prize in a plastic bubble, one of four or five kinds. They got some of the wrong ones before they got a ring, and Worsham tried to give the excess to a child standing nearby, but the child moved away in alarm. They continued their walk, through downtown and across campus to the river; on the foot bridge they stopped, and he put the ring on her finger. It was December, and it was cold on the bridge, but a still, windless cold. They kissed and walked on, her hand in his pocket—she didn't want to put her glove back on over the ring. (I could picture it, a toy with adjustable prongs of the sort that break off if you adjust it too often, though that ensures that you'll toss it out before it turns green.) They went on to the art building, into the gallery; she remembered what he said about some of the pictures. When they went back over the bridge, it was toward twilight, the sky flushed orange along the horizon, fading upward to yellow, the river turning into a mirror, little greenish lights blossoming across the river.

The next year, after he was back East (reconciled with his wife?—Brenda didn't say; she dealt more in moments than continuity), she put the ring in an envelope and wrote on it the time and place and his name. Now she had written an account of the important moments.

The sky fading upward to yellow! And what he said about the pictures in the museum. I wasn't sorry to hear about those moments, I was glad to hear about them: in a way they were part of my past too, since I'd been there with them in that exciting year, and he was my teacher and she my friend. But how much did these things she was telling me matter?—maybe more than she thought, in one sense, and less in another; they mattered less if they mattered because of who he was. I thought, not then but later, of a line from that Auden poem about Yeats, changing it slightly: He was foolish like us.

And while she was talking I had pictured Worsham as he used to look walking along alone, maybe across the street from me, unaware of my notice. He had a tight, secretive walk, ambling along, hands in pockets; I imagined he was pondering lives known to him only, fictional people and events he was trying to understand and shape. That glimpse of him always gave me a moment of excitement and deep happiness. Now he was gone, the worlds in his head with him; soon the most casual readers would be poking into the recesses of his life, like sightseers with tickets going through an historic house. I thought of them with resentment: people who wouldn't have read much of him or appreciated fully what they read; people with a taste for gossip, ready to enjoy his weaknesses.

"Without this," Brenda said, "any account of that year is so incomplete that it's almost misleading."

"But there's always a lot missing—except maybe in Boswell. You know how those biographies are now, Brenda. Half the time it's just something to build a career on, no love lost on the subject—that's how it sounds, anyway. The facts without the essence. Without the understanding."

"How'll they get the essence if people won't tell them what happened? This man may not be Boswell, but what he's done so far is o.k."

"I guess he's all right. I couldn't tell what kind of job it would add up to in the end."

"He has good credentials, and access to the family's papers— why are you so negative about this? You don't want me to send this. Not even the letters? You feel it's all too private? But it's part of the past now, it's out of the realm of the private. Nor is what I'm doing unprecedented or at all unusual."

"Do what you like, Brenda, do whatever you want to. It doesn't matter that much! It's a trivial matter, it's not all this important to anyone else in the world but you." I meant this to give offense; I was fed up with her valuable recollections.

She let it pass. "It's what happened, it's true, it fills in the record—why should I play it coy? Oh, I could leave it to Jocelyn"—her daughter—"to read and dispose of years from now, but that would be ridiculous. I could toss it out; but I'm not going to. It's become history, and I wouldn't feel right destroying it."

"It belongs to the ages and all that?" For a moment the possibility of some long-term rupture hung there between us. "Well, you don't have to listen to me, do what you like. You're right, it's history. And it seems like a long time ago. What a good teacher he was!—he could see right to the heart of a problem. I remember he said once, 'This story's pretty good, Rachel, but it's too honest and straightforward. Keep us waiting, let it build. Don't spill the beans too soon.' Remember when your story about the house sitter was on the worksheet? That was a nice story. Brenda, have you ever thought about turning all this, about that year, into fiction?"

"Oh, I tried once, but I was still too close to it." She was still brisk, but I felt that she had liked the question.

"You might make something really good out of it. There's an authenticity about the *real* things, the way they really happen— the details." Oh, I hated myself as I said it; she might turn out some *roman à clef* of the sort people use to set life to rights. Still, it might keep her busy.

After we had hung up, I went on thinking about it. Maybe Rayner ought to have that memoir of hers. Let him have every last scrap of information there was, if he knew how to use it; if he would try to understand everything, or almost everything; if he could set forth the wonder and mystery of Worsham's life and gift. (Report him and his cause aright!) But I thought that if I had said that to Brenda, she might have replied that there was no knowing about that—that this was the way things worked, this was how it had to be.

It was more than six months before we talked again. Let the friendship lapse, I thought once or twice, in fits of irrational pique. At other times I had a bad conscience about what I had said to her. Would anyone else in the world see it that way? Maybe my notions came from some old buried envy, or a provincial mentality; maybe they were foolish and idiosyncratic notions of how the world ought to be. Toward Christmas I broke down and phoned her.

Everything was going along well, she said. They were leaving in a few days, going to New York to spend the holidays with her mother.

I'd promised myself not to ask if she'd sent her papers to the biographer, but of course I did anyway.

"Oh, not yet. I've been busy—working on a new novel, writing like mad." She laughed guiltily. "You might recognize a few of the people—not too quickly, I trust."

"That's wonderful. I hope it goes well," I said.

When the Worsham biography came out, it absorbed me for a week or two—reading it, then thinking about it.

Brenda called. "It's a pretty good job, you know," she said. I felt that she regretted not having sent him her papers, regretted that what we had just read wasn't what she would call the whole story.

"It's not a bad job at all," I said. "And yet it's not quite good enough, somehow, is it—not all that could be hoped for. Ideally."

"Will there ever be one good enough for you—for us?"

"Probably not. How's the novel coming?"

"I've put it aside for the moment. I got stuck—I needed to get away from it for a little while."

Something about the way she said it made me wonder if she wasn't really going to give up on it, and I thought that this might make her even sorrier that she hadn't got in touch with the biographer. It came to me that when the next Worsham biographer came along in a few years, she'd offer her papers. It wasn't in her to let them lie in a drawer somewhere and go to waste.

She would certainly have the good sense not to ask my advice next time; still, I might say go ahead, why not. Something about reading the biography—as workmanlike a job as it was, and as deeply engrossing at times—had made me feel the ultimate insignificance of the facts and recollections. What would a few additions or omissions matter, one way or the other? How hard it was to read the last few chapters and see the end coming! He's gone; the rest is trivial.

CV10

•

STARKEY FLYTHE, JR.

Walter could almost feel the rush of breath, hear the women roaring, mothers, girlfriends, sisters, sweeping up towards the flight deck, the warm fall day, San Francisco, 1945. A couple chasing a blue jump-suited baby girl just beginning to walk wobbled by him in exaggerated pursuit. He had been alone that day. Hadn't wanted to get off the ship or sleep anywhere but the chain-hung bunks inches above and inches below two other men whose smells and habits he knew better than his own.

He had been 17, 18 the next week. Lt. (jg) Stinson was dead. Three thousand men ("officers and men," they always said in casualty lists as if they died differently) yelled down at thirty thousand skirts, and nobody said anything to him. Buddies he'd held when they were bleeding, buddies who'd cried, told him heart secrets, secrets that still made his cheeks red, buddies had their sea-bags on their shoulders. They'd said good-bye the night before, at the party in the mess, and later in the hangar deck, the warm Pacific melting by, gold in the moonlight, peace, relief a kamikaze wasn't spiraling towards them overwhelming. There would be peace. Friends always. They would remember the dead. Morning, they'd forgotten all about it.

There had been a telegram for him in the USO clearing station from his uncle, aunt—they lived outside Indianapolis—his mother had died while he was at Marcus Bay and he hadn't known about it for three weeks. The telegram sounded like a message from the president. "Congratulations on a job well done. You are welcome to stop by here a day or so in the absence of other plans." He had wondered, never found out, whether his father was still alive. His father had left his mother when Walter was eleven. A sailor. That was why Walter had wanted to join. Quit high school. Find his father. Or, be like him.

Walter's legs trembled walking up the wood steps to the ship's entrance. He remembered the gangways. He'd paid $6.00 to get in, didn't want to ask if there was a discount for veterans who served on the ship. The woman ticket seller was in a glass box with a pass-through slot like a drive-in bank teller. "World's largest ship museum."

The hangar deck had been painted a sort of aqua. Walter felt he was in a place he'd lived in his whole life and never been. The first day at sea he'd had to go all the way forward with a stack of flight logs and he'd hugged the wall, he was so frightened by motion, huge engines being wheeled along to mechanics' stations, the men in forklifts avoiding collisions only by the roll of the ship as it steamed south, going nobody knew where. The ceiling had opened up then and a tennis court-size elevator descended, two F4U's, their wings folded like obedient insects, waiting to be worked on, huge in proximity though Walter had seen them tiny in the sky. This ship was the war. He might be killed. Wounded. That was worse, flyers said who'd already been in the Pacific theater and come back through Norfolk for rehab or mustering out if they'd been hurt bad—some said "good"— enough.

"Where the hell have you been?" the petty officer who took the logs from him said. "I called you down here forty-five minutes ago!"

Then he had got to know people. Men called out to him, "Ears!" Everybody had nicknames, Annapolis custom filtering down to enlisted men. He had mess mates, bunk mates, sick bay where he worked, a plane he was assigned to. When sorties were run, every man had a top-deck station except the engine room crew, and Walter had Stinson's. Walter had a job, a war to win, the scrambled-egg hats kept saying. Not a day had gone by, not one, not a single solitary day, that he hadn't said Stinson's name. "Hey, buddy," Stinson, officer, gentleman, pilot, had told him. "I'll stand up with you when we get back and you head down the aisle."

"Married?" Walter asked. "I might not . . ."

"Hoo! Everybody's going to. And I'll invite you to mine. I'm going to drink so much champagne my blood'll run clear. Hooo!"

Then Stinson, Lt. (jg) Wallace "Whippet" Stinson, had lifted off the flight deck on his first mission and the flight officer had worried the propellers wouldn't catch, the air was so humid: Stinson had come back seven pounds lighter. Not one man had been lost; they'd hit Marcus, hit the Japanese planes on the ground, the fueling depot, the port. And Stinson said he was so scared he was sitting in a pool of water in the cockpit and it wasn't sweat. Walter had pulled him out of the plane; Stinson turned his face aside so nobody could see his eyes. Only Walter had seen them: blank, dead.

The officers were snooty the first weeks out until proximity, dependence, fear closed the social-level gap. Stinson had been friendly. Walter remembered the eyes: warm, coffee-colored, not so dark they didn't catch the light when he smiled. He told Walter to call him "Whip." "They'll think you're saying Skip."

"Don't tell anybody!" Stinson had gripped Walter's arm so hard Walter thought the young lieutenant's hand—he would always be young in Walter's mind, though he'd been four years older than Walter—would draw blood. Stalking along the flight deck, parts of it covered with linoleum squares now and colored arrows so people wouldn't lose their way on the "museum" tour, Walter felt the wattle under his chin.

"Tell anybody what?" Walter had asked.

"That I'm afraid. That I'm scared. The sky's a poison lake.

Every tracer you see means three you don't. You won't even know when you won't even know." Walter had thought he was joking, this man, boy, now, who'd been to college, had a girl he was going to marry back home, a boy whose parents sent him money even over his navy officer's pay. "I mean it!" He said he was afraid as much of the other men on the ship as he was of the sky.

"So am I," Walter had whispered, but the hours of clamor, the turbines, anti-aircraft aak-aak, the earphones, the awful fear of not being able to pick out the sound that would kill you, deafened them. That was their friendship; they could not hear each other, but they talked to each other.

"God, Ears! I can't keep going up the rear end." That was his expression for night flights. "They want you to fly in formation. I'm supposed to be two inches off the wing—worse, *between*— the wing tips of two jerks who're myopic grain-alcohol drinkers. How do they get the stuff? You're not supposed to let it out of the dispensary."

"The head surgeon . . ."

Walter began to find his way, the ladders he'd gone up and down, a monkey, nearly three years, the passage to the lavatory where he'd sat, exposed to the rest of the crew; he saw a couple, their whole appearance a Hawaiian shirt, focusing on a Corsair set up for display, and just as Walter looked at them, simultaneously they touched their crotches, she to brush some ash from his cigarette—think of letting them smoke, here—and he for heaven only knew what reason—and Walter remembered the cook'd put something in the food to keep that part of the body out of the ship's mind.

"I don't want to get you in trouble," Walter had said. "You're not supposed to fraternize." The bronze plaques on the top deck, the "Hall of Fame," that only included officers and industrialists, war fat-cats, made Walter furious.

Nobody had ever liked Walter before. He had been the wrong size all the wrong years. Too small for B-team in 8th grade. Too big for Midgets in 7th. The difference between not being popular and not being liked hadn't occurred to him until he got on "The Fighting Lady"—the expressions they had! "So-and-so is still on patrol." "So-and-so made the supreme sacrifice."

Coming here—the South—was wrong, he thought, the first night. He had walked along the streets and walked, walked, been glad in a way his wife had died; she wouldn't have liked the idea of a pilgrimage to an aircraft carrier. She was younger, too young to remember the war, much else. Stinson hadn't been able to "stand up for him at his wedding." Walter remembered the day. Carlice, his wife, had had a bad complexion. She had cried and cried the day of the wedding because two big places had erupted on her cheek and chin. She had put some sort of cover makeup on the spots. It only accentuated them. He hadn't known how to say that night, as she lay crying beside him in the bed they would share thirty-five years, that it didn't matter. That the heart was somewhere underneath the skin. He had walked, thinking of that, of his daughter who tried to be dutiful though she was, he knew, slightly embarrassed by him. His ears? Job— learned in the navy—male nurse—the years before female tele- phone linemen, male stewardesses. He kept walking, as if he weren't getting anyplace and yet felt he could go on and on, passing little southern city-gardens. Stinson had had a farm. "Country place. When I fly over these tropical plants I wonder if they'd grow back in the States."

"You better keep your mind on your tail," Walter had told him. "You thinking about daffodils."

"Every gunner, every cook, every medic, clerk-typist is as- signed to a pilot and a plane. That's *your* baby! You'll serve that knight like the squires of old! He won't—can't—go into battle without you!" Walter could hear the deck officer lecturing them.

"Kids on the living room floor," Stinson had said, "running toy airplanes around on the rug. Varoom, varrooom!"

Walter would wind up the prop on the fighter, thinking any second he was going to get his skull sliced. He wouldn't be the first. Then he'd crouch by the side, or down in the gunneries while the navy-blue plane, wings unfolded, varoomed, varroomed, Whip standing on the brakes, the other planes beating behind him, Walter hoping the engine was warmed up enough though God knew in the heat, Alaska should've been ready. Then Walter would watch, his ears stinging, heart banging against his T-shirt, Stinson bump, bump, bump down the deck, over the great number CV10 painted near the end, and hobble off into the sky, the other planes screaming down the line seconds later.

The mission had not been a success: the Japanese knew where the fleet was by now; hiding behind atolls and steaming zig-zag all over the Coral Sea didn't work anymore. Kamikazes were bouncing off every carrier and cruiser. One—a near miss—had been fished out of the water on the starboard: the cockpit had been bolted down from the outside and the dead Japanese pilot's controls had been wired on. "Dumb sucker," Stinson said.

There was a big brouhaha over whether—he looked like a bee with his goggles, helmet, ear flaps tight around his chin—the Japanese should be given a Christian burial. "Oh, Jesus," Stinson said. "Shoot the works! Who knows who's next."

He was. Fewer fighters were getting back; those who made it had been through the wringer. The seaman artist who rated a cheer whenever he appeared topside with his rising sun template to paint zeroes and sunk ships on the quarterdeck vanished. The sick bay was packed. Walter knew the navy hymn by heart from funerals. "Remember the first syllable in that event," Stinson said. "Fun."

When Stinson hit the flight deck, it was moments after the Japanese had rained phosphorous over the ship. When you stepped on a piece of it, it burst into flame. Nobody could get to the planes to pull the pilots out of the way. The stop-straps were burned through. Walter was helping put a cast on a boy with a broken hip. They had him up on a winch. The cook was painting thick layers of plaster over the body. Walter would've laughed if he hadn't seen the boy's face. The smell of blood-soaked flight jackets cut off bodies mixed with sweat and nausea, the jerk and sway of the carrier as the skipper tried to out-maneuver the fire bombers. People were being sick and nobody had time to mop.

"No, Stinson ain't in yet," two medics said who'd brought another body—they thought it was alive—how could you fly in, make a perfect landing, and be dead? "And he probably won't be in. You hear the reports?" He got in. Seventy-eight wounds on his chest, back, legs. Flak. How could he talk? Walter wondered, much less upset than he thought he would be; working, patching up bodies made him think he could save anybody. The chief surgeon took a piece of metal half the size of a bicycle rim out of Whip's face.

"Don't worry," Walter said.

"We weren't the only ones," Stinson said, naked, his body like ocean with whitecaps, only red.

"The only ones?"

"Who were scared."

"Shut up a minute," the surgeon said, and took another metal rim out of his cheek.

"How do I look?" Whip asked.

"Leslie Howard." When Whip tried to smile, Walter saw half his teeth were gone. His face twisted the way a tree turned in strong wind.

He hung on. Walter wrote letters for him, read to him from Saroyan books. Running his hand over the names of the com- memorative tablets—Walter hadn't been able to find anything, his battle station, the places he thought he could never forget— he thought those had been the happiest days of his life. Some- body was dependent on him. Somebody spoke to him without saying a word. That sound—the noise between the noises—an- swered practically every question for him. The present. The war. Friendship. The rest of life. The name finally under his fingers, the block letters pressing into his knuckles more painful than any of the past. If the war had ended a different way, Stinson alive, Walter, they'd never have seen each other again. This way they would always be friends. Some men's lives never ended; they kept wandering around thinking something else was coming.

Walter knew it before Stinson. His color. The chief took in Stinson's appearance sideways. The ship news, a legal-size sheet whose inanity was undimmed by casualties, told of more, more victories. The Japanese were "broken" but didn't seem to know it.

The flag didn't go into the water. He knew sometimes parents didn't get the exact flag. Walter thought how hard getting food out to the carrier was, mail off, on, to keep ammunition, parts coming.

The hot wind that boiled the stomach mixed the words: Walter had never liked the chaplain though he'd dragged ten men out of a bulkhead fire, and never, Stinson said, "let you forget."

> . . . the Lord,
> who opened . . .
> a path through mighty waters,
> drew on chariot and horse to their destruction,
> a whole army, men of valour . . .

They always read that at the dumps. Walter's duties now included, if there was a moment in the bleeding, hauling out the prayer books. The white edges were dirty along the funeral service pages.

> they were crushed, snuffed out like a wick:
> . . .
> Here and now I will do a new thing:
> . . . Can you perceive it?

Walter stuck books—they were always flying off over the rail —in as many hands as could hold them. Four other packages. Whip would've said, "Odd man out." They began with him. Walter couldn't see the splash, to mark the spot in his mind.

The body there, a picture, stayed, a cage like the sunk ships

and plane-skeletons fish swam through. The boatswain's pipe—
Walter didn't know whether he was here or there, now, then—
keened. "Now hear this." They were showing a movie forward.

Walter went in, sat down. The dark slowly gave way around
him. He remembered going to a show with Whip—one of the
things officers, men could do together.

"Nothing makes you forget quicker than a flicker. Well, we
can't get a pint." Stinson's voice was right there, next to him. In
the images rolling, in competition with the waves, Stinson had
whispered, surprised, "Damn! I know I'm still on a ship."

Walter stared at the few tourists in the seats. Bored. Squirm-
ing. They had brought children. The film was a documentary—
had won an Academy Award. How phony the narrator's voice
sounded, false the sailors' smiles, passing down the mess line. He
recognized no one though the film was made when he was on the
ship. It went on. Walter felt proud, more like these people than
the boys who'd squeezed into the theater then, lined the walls,
hung from the girders, stuffed the aisles until the fire officer said
they had to clear out and a roar of protest sounded to panicky
sailors like the air-raid warning.

Slowly, Walter took in the steel beams, the X-girders, the
super structure of the flight deck above. He would wait till the
end of the movie though he might be the only one left in the
theater. He didn't feel as alone, as afraid as he had the day, those
years gone, when the carrier docked. He'd go back to the motel
—think of having someplace to go—and when the rates went
down he might phone his daughter, son-in-law. Or, watch television. Go for a walk, see whether he could make out the ship
from the other side of the bay.

After You've Gone

•

ALICE ADAMS

The truth is, for a while I managed very well indeed. I coped
with the house and its curious breakages, and with the bad
nights of remembering you only at your best, and the good days
suddenly jolted by your ghost. I dealt with the defection of certain old friends, and the crowding-around of a few would-be new
best friends. I did very well with all that, in the three months
since your departure for Oregon, very well indeed until I began
to get these letters from your new person (I reject 'lover' as too
explicit, and knowing you I am not at all sure that 'friend' would
be applicable). Anyway, Sally Ann.

(You do remember encouraging me to write to you, as somewhat precipitately you announced your departure—as though
extending me a kindness? It will make you feel better, you just
managed not to say. In any case, with my orderly lawyer's mind,
I am putting events or 'matters' as we say in order).

The house. I know that it was and is not yours, despite that
reckless moment at the Trident (too many margaritas, too palely
glimmering a view of our city, San Francisco) when I offered to
put it in both our names, as joint tenants, which I literally saw us
as, even though it was I who made payments. However, your
two-year occupancy and your incredibly skillful house-husband-
ing made it seem quite truly yours. (Is this question metaphysical, rather than legal? If the poet-husband of a house is not in

fact a husband, whose is the house?) But what I am getting at is this: how could you have arranged for everything to break the week you left? Even the Cuisinart; no one else ever even heard of a broken Cuisinart, ever. And the vacuum. And the electric blanket. The dishwasher and the Disposal. Not to mention my Datsun. "Old wiring, these older flats," the repair person diagnosed my household problems, adding, "But you've got a beautiful place here," and he gestured across the park—green, pyramidal Alta Plaza, where even now I can see you running, sunning, in your eccentric non-regular-runner outfit: yellow shorts, and that parrot-green sweatshirt from God knows where, both a little tight.

My Datsun turned out simply to need a tune-up, and since you don't drive I can hardly blame that on you. Still, the synchronicity, everything going at once, was hard not to consider.

Friends. Large parties, but not small dinners, my post-you invitations ran. Or, very small dinners—most welcome, from single women friends or gay men; unwelcome from wives-away husbands, or even from probably-perfectly nice single men. I am just not quite up to all that yet.

People whom I had suspected of inviting us because of your poet fame predictably dropped off.

Nights. In my dreams of course you still are here, or you are leaving and I know that you are, and there is nothing to do to stop you (you have already told me, so sadly, about Sally Ann, and the houseboat in Portland). Recently I have remembered that after my father died I had similar dreams: in those dreams he was dying, I knew, yet I could not keep him alive. But those father dreams have a guilty sound, I think, and I truly see no cause for guilt on my part toward you. I truly loved you, in my way, and I did what I could (I thought) to keep us happy, and I never, never thought we would last very long. Isn't two years a record of sorts for you, for maybe any non-marrying poet? Sometimes I thought it was simply San Francisco that held you here, your City Lights-Tosca circuit, where you sought out ghosts of Beats. Well, in my dreams you are out there still, or else you are here with me in our (my) bed, and we awaken slowly, sleepily to love.

Once, a month or so ago, I thought I saw you sitting far back in a courtroom; I saw those damn black Irish curls and slanted eyes, your big nose and arrogant chin, with that cleft. A bad shock, that; for days I wondered if it actually could have been you, your notion of a joke, or some sort of test.

In all fairness, though—and since I mention it I would like to ask you something: just why did my efforts at justice, even at seeing your side of arguments so enrage you? I can hear you shouting: Why do you have to be so goddam *fair,* what *is* this justice of yours?

But as I began to say, in all fairness I have to concede that I miss your cooking. On the nights that you cooked, that is. I really liked your tripe soup and your special fettucini with all those wild mushrooms. And the Sunday scrambled eggs that we never got to till early afternoon.

And you are a marvel at fixing things, even if they have a tendency not to stay fixed.

And, most importantly, a first-rate poet; Yale and now the Guggenheim people seem to think so, and surely as you hope the MacArthur group will come around. Having read so little poetry other than yours I am probably no judge; however, as I repeatedly told you, to me it was magic, pure word-alchemy.

I do miss it all, the house-fixing and cooking, the love and poetry. But I did very well without it all. Until recently.

The letters. The first note, on that awful forget-me-not paper, in that small, tight, rounded hand was a prim little apology: she felt badly about taking you away from me (a phrase from some junior high school, surely) but she also felt sure that I would 'understand,' since I am such a fair-minded person (I saw right off that you had described my habits of thought in some detail). I would see that she, a relatively innocent person, would have found your handsomeness-brilliance-sexiness quite irresistable (at that point I wondered if you could have written the letter yourself, which still seems a possibility). She added that naturally by now I would have found a replacement for you, the natural thing for a woman like me, in a city like San Francisco. That last implication, as to the loose lifestyles of both myself and of San Francisco would seem to excuse the two of you fleeing to the innocence of Portland, Oregon.

A couple of false assumptions lay therein, however. Actually, in point of fact, I personally might do better, man-wise, in Portland than down here. The men I most frequently meet are young lawyers, hard-core Yuppies, a group I find quite intolerable, totally unacceptable, along with the interchangeable young brokers—real estate dealers and just plain dealers. Well, no wonder that I too took up with a poet, an out-of-shape man with no CD's or portfolio but a trunk full of wonderful books. (I miss your books, having got through barely half of them. And did you really have to take the *Moby Dick* that I was in the middle of? Well, no matter; I went out to the Green Apple and stocked up, a huge carton of books, the day you left).

In any case, I felt that she, your young person, your Sally Ann, from too much evidence had arrived at false conclusions. In some ways we are more alike, she and I, than she sees. I too was a set-up, a perfect patsy for your charm, your 'difference.'

But why should she have been told so much about me at all? Surely you must have a few other topics; reading poems aloud as you used to do with me would have done her more good, or at least less harm, I believe. But as I pondered this question, I also remembered several of our own conversations, yours and mine, having to do with former lovers. It was talk that I quite deliberately cut short, for two clear reasons: one, I felt an odd embarrassment at my relative lack of what used to be called experience; and two, I did not want to hear about yours. You did keep on trying though; there was one particular woman in New York, a successful young editor (though on a rather junky magazine, as I remember), a woman you wanted me to hear all about, but I would not. "She has nothing to do with us," I told you (remember?). It now seems unfortunate that your new young woman, your Sally Ann, did not say the same about me.

Next came a letter which contained a seemingly innocent question: should Sally Ann go to law school, what did I think? On the surface this was a simple request for semi-expert advice; as she went on and on about it though, and on and on, I saw that she was really asking me how she could turn herself into me, which struck me as both sad and somewhat deranged: assuming that you have an ideal woman on whom Sally Ann could model herself, I am hardly that woman. You don't even much like 'lady lawyers,' as in some of your worst moments you used to phrase it.

Not having answered the first note at all (impossible, what could I have said) I responded to this one, because it seemed required, with a typed postcard of fairly trite advice: the hard work involved, the overcrowding of the field, the plethora of even token women.

And now she had taken to writing me almost every day; I mean it, at least every other day. Does she have no other friends? No relatives, even, or old school ties? If she does, in her present state of disturbance they have faded from her mind (poor, poor Sally Ann, all alone with you, in Portland, on a Willamette River houseboat), and only I remain, a purely accidental, non-presence in her life.

The rains have begun in Portland, and she understands that they will continue throughout the winter. She does not really like living on a houseboat, she finds it frightening; the boat rocks, and you have told her that all boats rock, there is nothing to be done. (You must be not exactly in top form either; I never heard you admit to an inability to remedy anything—even my Datsun; you said you could fix it and you did, temporarily).

You have found some old friends over at Reed College, she tells me; you hang out a lot over there, and you tell her that she would be very much happier with a job. Very likely she would, but you have taken her to an extremely high unemployment area.

She doesn't like your tripe soup (tripe is really yucky, says Sally Ann) any more than you seem to like her red peppers and goat cheese and cold pasta salads.

She doesn't understand your poetry at all, and doesn't know what to say when you read it to her. Well, this is certainly a problem that I too could have had, except that I dealt with it head on, as it were, simply and clearly saying that I didn't understand poetry, that I had not read much or ever studied it. But that to me your poems sounded marvelous—which they did; I really miss the sound of them, your words. But the point is, I was able to say what Sally Ann is not, although undoubtedly she feels very much the same.

You talk about me more and more, almost all the time, she tells me. Well, that is quite inexcusable, as I'm sure in your more rational moments you well know. What earthly point in telling Sally Ann how much weight I lost the first three months we lived together, or that my hair curls in the rain—or even my record at college, for heavens' sake?

You are at home less and less. And now Sally Ann confesses to me that she used to be a waitress at the Tosca; on some of the nights when I was at home, here in San Francisco (actually I used to be grateful for a little time to catch up on work), when I assumed you were just hanging out in North Beach you were actually courting Sally Ann, so to speak. Well, funnily enough, at this point I find this new information quite painless to absorb; it simply makes me miss you even less. But: Sally Ann wonders if I think you could possibly be seeing someone else now? She says that you've mentioned a French professor at Reed, a most talented woman, you've said. Do I think—?

Well, I most certainly do think; you seem to prefer women with very respectable professions, poor Sally Ann representing the single rule-proving exception, I suppose. Some sort of lapse in calculation on your part—or, quite likely Sally Ann had more to do with me than with herself, if you see what I mean, and I think you will. In any case, a fatal error all around.

Because it is clear to me that in an emotional sense you are battering this young woman. She is being abused, by you. I could prove it to a jury. And unlike me she is quite without defenses.

You must simply knock it off; you must cease and desist this abuse of Sally Ann. For one thing, it's beneath you, as you surely in your better, saner, kinder moments must clearly see (you're not all bad; even in my own worst moments I recall much good, much kindness, even). Why don't you just give her a ticket to somewhere, along with some gentle, ego-preserving words (heaven knows you're at your best with words) and let her go? Then you can move in your Reed College French professor and live happily there on your houseboat—almost forever, at least until the Portland rains let up and you feel like moving on.

As for myself, it seems only fair to tell you that I have indeed found a new friend, or rather, an old friend has reappeared in my life in another role. *(Fair.* As I write this I wonder if in some way, maybe, you were right all along to object to my notion of fairness? There was always a slightly hostile getting-even element in my justice? Well, I will at least admit that possibility). In any case, I am taking off on a small trip to Jackson, Wyoming day after tomorrow, with my old-new friend. About whom I can only at this moment say, So far so good, in fact very good indeed —although I have to admit that I am still a little wary, after you. However, at least for me he is a more known quality than you were (we were undergraduates together, in those distant romantic Berkeley days), and I very much doubt that you'll be getting any letter of complaint, regarding me. He already knows what he's getting, so to speak.

And so, please wish me well, as I do you (I'll keep my fingers crossed for the MacArthur thing).

And, I repeat, please lay off Sally Ann. Just let her go. All

three of us, you, me, and Sally Ann will be much better off—you
without her, and she without you. And me without the crazy
burden of these letters, which, if I were *really* fair, I would send
on to you.

History

•

FRANCES SHERWOOD

When I think of our brief marriage twenty-six years ago before
freedom rides and busing, it is like recalling pages out of a history book. In photographs Marcus, with his scalp-short hair, the
part properly shaved, his shoes shined to a mirrory sheen, looks
like a member of the Southern Christian Leadership Conference.
I, with my open white-girl smile, long bundle of blond hair and
dirty toes in California sandals, am a caricature hippie. But
those pictures come before sit-ins and flower children.

In 1960 all the newspapers in the nation's capital listed housing under White or Colored. Wherever I called, the landlords'
first question always was: White? Both, I'd answer. We are both.
Immediately on the other end, there would be a sudden intake of
breath as if I were a crank call or obscene or had let loose a big,
bad snake into the wire which was inching forward, making its
way up the wire to bite off an ear, pinch a nerve. They would let
down the phone that carefully.

"My husband is white," Mrs. Trakled had explained over the
phone, and she brought it up again when she was showing us the
upstairs apartment she had available. She and the Reverend
lived downstairs. It was an immaculate row house in a nice Negro neighborhood with clipped lawns, rose bushes, and green
and white striped awnings unfurled over freshly painted porches.

"The thing is," Mrs. Trakled said, "is that I am picky about my tenants." She looked at Marcus approvingly. "I understand you are studying to be a doctor at Howard University. My, my, a medical man." Marcus had worn a three-piece suit for our interview, carried an umbrella, and looked quite the Englishman —from the colonies. Mrs. Trakled was in purple. It was a plum dress for the Grand Tour with pleated handkerchiefs springing clusters of violets pinned to her shoulders. She looked like Mercury on errand, wings at ready-alert. "And you, my dear," she said, turning her motherly gaze on me, "working for the *Post?* I'm a professional woman, too."

Mrs. Trakled's sign hung in the front yard:

The Reverend Mrs. Trakled
Lessons in the Piano for Young Ladies

"Actually," she continued, "my husband is white-white. A man of the cloth."

I imagined ghost. Marcus gave me a look like Ku Klux Klan, but rabbit was more like it. The Reverend mysteriously materialized when we signed the lease across the grand piano. Albino, he was, and just about as old as Methuselah with blinking pink eyes and an embarrassed, bashful smile.

"The Reverend, once one of God's chosen orators, is now a man of few words," Mrs. Trakled explained. "We are from Mississippi, you see, and would you believe it, we couldn't get married down there, had to ride separate cars up to D.C., and here we are."

"It sounds like the Underground Railway," I said.

"What say?" The Reverend shuffled forth, leaned in towards me.

"They are newlyweds, Rev," Mrs. Trakled giggled.

"Underground Railway, really Joanna." We were packing like mad to make the move to the Trakled's. I could hardly wait.

"Can I help it that I was a history major?"

"Yes indeedy."

"Can you hug me, Marcus, in Virginia where you come from?"

"Are you crazy?"

I was. It came me leeway. Marcus, on the other hand, was Mr. Rational. In Control. It took me five minutes to stuff my meager belongings in my straw suitcase. We were staying at his ex-roommate's. Marcus folded all of his stuff neatly, arranging it in piles before putting it in his trunk. I noticed the letter from his mother. Back in Virginia, half a step out of Washington, she did not approve of me. Her letter had left enough space between the lines for me to evoke the whole scene, one Marcus had once described—the rickety front porch of the P.O. boasting a bevy of overalled, tobacco-chewing Guardians of Justice. On the side of her house hung an iron washtub and under the one tree in the yard was an old car seat, a spring sticking out like a corkscrew. Marcus said his mother made him wear a clothespin on his nose every Saturday and that he was scrubbed Saturday night hard enough to bleed (read bleach). Yet she didn't like me, I, who was in fact a natural.

My mother, at home in California amid her cats and dusty pottery, dashed off a quick note (more later) stating that she always knew I would marry somebody interesting. What she had in mind, I knew, was somebody larger than life—a Paul Robeson-John Henry type, a Byron or a Browning. Somebody dark and dangerous, and definitely très beau.

Marcus and I met at Howard University, E. Franklin Frazier's course, "Negro in the United States." It was a history course and I felt pretty historic myself, for I was the only white person in the class and from what I could see also on campus, save one exchange student from Oberlin who assiduously avoided me.

"How do you like Howard?" We were upstairs in the library, late spring, fans already set up on the long, lacquered tables.

Outside the opened windows, the air was still and dense even though it was eight o'clock at night.

"Fine," I answered, moving my hair out of my eyes, giving the man a good look. He wore wire-framed glasses. Nobody did then, and he had an old-fashioned, professorial look about him.

"Be honest." His wrists were thinner than mine and his fingers were long. You could play the harp in heaven, I thought.

"I'm always honest," I lied. Downstairs in the lobby there was a portrait of General Howard, blue eyes and sans left arm. The old Union general had gone from freeing slaves to killing Indians. The first students at Howard were not freed men, but Chinese. It was a place full of contradictions. Yet . . .

"It's like a white school," I said. Every afternoon light-skinned sorority girls linked arms and sang on the quad. It was like my college.

"So we're disappointed, are we?" He had a condescending, slightly humorous way of looking at me over the tops of his glasses. He made me feel amusing.

"Surprised," I said.

"We," and he gently put one of his long, brown fingers on my wrist as if feeling for the pulse, "are human just like everybody else. Not morally superior, particularly wise. Just people. Suffering is not a good teacher, all publicity to the contrary."

I should have listened to those words, for they would have provided a key to the language of our marriage. Instead, at that time, I didn't see how prim he was and only noted how different he was from my counterparts at the bookstore where I worked, those pale and pasty male versions of myself. Marcus was older, a hundred times more interesting, and of course, mysterious as Egypt. My heart did a fast flutter-butter, and I knew I was done for. Once before I had been in love, during college, and that had been pure disaster. He was Korean.

"I'm going to New York next week." Strains of the AKA song wafted up. A sister was passing by. The fans moved left and right on their stiff necks like sunflowers following the sun. I knew it was presumptuous to tell him I was going away, that is, as if he were interested, but I took the risk.

"I'll visit you," he said.

"If you say so."

"I mean it." And we exchanged names and addresses. His handwriting was small, elegant, a stylized code.

"Joanna Kandel," he read. "And where is this in New York?"

"The Village."

"Ah, of course."

"No really, it's just a cheap sublet, I can't let the opportunity . . ."

"Of course not."

"Are you laughing at me again?"

"Good gracious no." He raised his hands in surrender. "Why would I do that?"

The job I found in New York was worse than the one I left in Washington. Not at a bookstore, which is all a B.A. in history from the august Mills College netted me in Washington, but at a discount china store. I would say discounted discount china, and narrow as a ship's galley with place settings, each one an extraordinary bargain, rising to the ceiling like the Leaning Tower of Pisa. A stroll to the back of the store provided seasickness, too, and the bathroom was always at high tide.

"Qué pasa?" Some cute Puerto Rican guys worked as packers in the storeroom. I had to pass them all on the way to the bathroom.

"Degeneration of values in the western world, hombres," I'd answer, picking out a handy strip of Japanese newspaper from the packing crate. I read: "Likewise the eastern world. Nobody committing hari-kari anymore. What *is* this world coming to, yen for life reported on all fronts?"

They'd stare at my hairy legs and armpits as if they had never seen such before and give me the old thumbs-up. Yes, we understood each other. Ditto the other salesperson with whom I had a deep rapport. She was an Argentinean, refugee from the Peronistas, and had hopes of meeting a dentist in America, moving to Queens. I told her a little about Marcus. Not all, of course.

Friday nights and the city still baking a good 92, I would do the rounds of the air-conditioned bars, few and far between in 1960. I especially liked the ones with aquariums, green bubbling sea divers, startled sea horses. But no sooner would I get comfy on my stool than some lech would hunker up from the shadows, rest his chin on my shoulder. Oh yes, lust was the sawdust under our feet in those good old days. And I knew for sure somebody had to save me, for here I was in New York, New York, and I wasn't even having fun, couldn't even go for a decent drink. Sunday afternoons I spent in Washington Square Park watching city kids in scuba masks and flippers explore the briny depths of the three-foot fountain while I ate my Good Humor bar. Sometimes I went swimming at the Carmine Street swimming pool where all the sleek lovelies stretched out on the rough concrete like numbers on some celestial clock. That was the life.

One Friday night I was sitting on my chipped kitchen chair of my living-dining-kitchen wondering what to eat next when I heard a knock at my door. Only one person in the whole world knew where I lived.

That weekend we only went out for food and air. That was the time he told me about the P.O., Saturday baths, arrowheads and the statue of the Confederate colonel in the town square. I told him that as kids my sister and I jumped on our bed until it broke, and then we slept in a heap at a slant until one of my mother's boyfriends tied it up again with twine. That story did not seem to go over too well.

"Those chaotic days are over," he said. I wasn't sure what he meant, what new regime was in store for me, and I had never thought of my childhood as particularly chaotic, just fun. But I did think better of telling him the time my mother, my sister and

I drove through Mexico and the time we picked up a hitchhiker who dropped dead in the backseat of our car. When we drove back to the little seaside town near Ensenada where we had picked him up, nobody knew him, wanted to claim him, so we buried him ourselves on a promontory overlooking the beach. We made a cross since we figured everybody in Mexico was a Catholic and my sister said a few words just as she had when Stravinsky, our pet beagle, died.

Coming home from work on Monday after our weekend, knowing that Marcus was waiting for me in the apartment, and watching the other working people in the subway with their bags of groceries, tired feet, I felt that at long last I had joined the human race. I was going home too, had my own bag of groceries and a bouquet of daisies for Marcus, who after all was from the country. Climbing the stairs to the apartment, I expected the door to be open, but from down the hallway, I could see that not only was it closed, but that somebody had pasted something to the door. At a distance, it looked like the Declaration of Independence with lots of fancy signatures on it. Up close, I could see that it was a petition and eviction notice. All the mothers of the building, not the Ritz by any stretch of the imagination, alleged that I was a prostitute. Quietly, I unglued the document, stuffed it in my purse, and went inside. Marcus was packing, not because of the sign, which apparently he hadn't seen, but because he had to go back to Virginia, return to his job as a janitor.

At the train station, he said, "I've been accepted at Howard Medical School." People were looking at us standing together, and this was New York.

"I love you, Marcus." I thought I should set the record straight. It was true. I had all the symptoms. Dry throat, clammy hands, etcetera.

"Do you think we should get married," he said.

"I don't know." But I wasn't shocked at the idea. Love in my book did not necessarily mean marriage, but I was vaguely aware, even then, that Marcus's book was different. And I also knew, given the world, we had to be serious, all or nothing.

"I have GI benefits," he said. "Also I've saved. It's been proven that married men do better in medical school than single ones."

"I would work, too."

"Until I finish," he added.

Marriage *was* a thought. After a rather haphazard upbringing, I had gone to a girls' college where everybody on my floor was engaged by their senior year. Alumnae notes were full of tidbits about illustrious husbands and accomplished children, sometimes volunteer work. Yet, I could see that marriage with Marcus would not be tame and ordinary. It might very well be the grandest adventure of all. I could see myself plucking burning crosses from our front yard with my bare hands. Insults from ignoramuses would bounce off my strong chest. I would be a moral Paul Bunyan, showing them all, showing myself. It would certainly be better than living in New York, alone.

A Baptist preacher married us in Washington. Miscegenation was illegal in Virginia and we didn't have the money for California. Marcus's former roommate stood up for us, looking zonked out of his mind. I laughed through the ceremony, cosmic joy, I told Marcus, who was seriously miffed. I wore a paisley dress my mother had done up in a hurry, sent off. It was from an Indian bedspread, a pattern on the bottom of orange elephants trekking east. On my long yellow hair, I wore a wreath of laurels. Marcus was in his three-piecer, the one he wore for interviews and on Sundays for church.

On Sundays, I wore my bathrobe, was a slugabed, fixing Marcus's breakfast and then falling back in with the funnies and snacks, turning on the radio.

"Come stay with me and be my love," I would beg, fiddling with the little buttons on his vest. Sometimes I'd do a little jig on the bed, my mating dance I called it, which Marcus hated. He didn't want the Trakleds who slept right below us to think you-know-what.

Our bedroom overlooked a wonderful tree and towards November the yellow leaves plastered themselves to the window like large, yellow hands, fingers splayed. They made me think of children's drawings of fall you see in school windows, and yes, I wanted children, a whole slew of them. They would be beautiful, brown Gauguins and I would be the Pied Piper leading them along the beach. Not Virginia Beach, natch. But some beach, somewhere. Marcus wanted two children, a boy and a girl, after he had finished medical school, his internship and residency.

November and the afternoons turned very dark. I'd come home from my job at the *Post* to find a hallway of little girls waiting for their piano lessons in Mary Janes and braids so tight their eyes would slant up. On Saturdays when Marcus was studying in the library, I swept the leaves off the front porch, helped the Trakleds put on storm windows, learned how to make sweet potato pie and Mississippi mud cake. I took the Reverend's damp tobacco wads, lined up on the porch banister, inside. They looked like frozen bon-bons. When Marcus came home, he'd shower for hours it seemed, ate quickly, and then fell into bed, tucking up into a tight ball like the small armored bugs that curl closed at a touch. My new job in the library of a newspaper, called the morgue, where I clipped and filed newspaper stories all day, was more tedious than the china shop. At least there I had the Puerto Ricans, the homesick Argentinean. We were all disgruntled history majors, English majors dealing with yesterday's news, nothing deader, in the library. I began to hate the written word.

But around Christmas, Marcus and I were invited to a party. Finally I was going to meet his study group, talk to some real people. Picturing my mother's parties featuring wine, good talk, I dressed in comfortable slacks, a bulky sweater and my long scarf of many colors. I was prepared to spend the evening on the floor arguing about Marxism, folk music, Richard Nixon. Marcus wore his suit as always. Marcus was Marcus. Cuddling up to him on the streetcar going down Georgia Avenue, I thought of when we would be coming home that night. We'd be a little tipsy. It would be like New York again, that weekend, our courtship. But he inched over ever so slightly.

"Anymore and you'll be out the window," I said.

"Joanna."

"I know." He hated public displays of affection, considered them in bad taste. I moved back to my side. The trolley jiggled and jangled, careened around corners. (The tracks are all dug up now. And the trolleys are in museums.) I looked ahead. Washington at night was empty. You could not tell what part of the city was segregated, except in terms of buildings. There were good buildings and bad buildings, those with doormen, those without.

"I'm thinking of taking some courses again," I said. "At night when you're not home."

He didn't catch the hint.

"More history?"

"I won't make that mistake again. Maybe psychology." I knew what he thought of psychology. Not much.

He sniffed, said, "I'm going to have a lot of papers next semester."

"Meaning?"

"I was hoping you could help type them."

"Ah." But we had arrived. We got off the trolley, crossed the street, entered a dingy, unkept building, no doorman. I was not prepared.

When the apartment door was opened, I could see that I was way out of my depth. All the furniture was a creamy-white, soft and modern. Huge baskets of ferns hung from the ceiling. The lighting was subdued, the music jazz, cool, subtle jazz. The drinks were not jug wine, paper cups, that sort of thing, but a full bar, J.&B., a real bartender in uniform, obviously hired for the occasion. People were drinking martinis. The hors d'oeuvres, while not plentiful, were hot, complicated, and on silver trays. But the very worst part was that everybody except me was dressed to the teeth. I am talking about clothes with style and cut, the kind of thing you see in fashion magazines. I looked like an insult. Marcus should have warned me. I wished I could have just fainted right there on the spot so that I could be removed, on a stretcher, with a blanket thrown over my body. My only claim to class at the moment was my hair, which was the color of gold and lots of it, and Marcus, but when I turned, he was not there. He had vanished into the crowd. I could hardly blame him. Not at that moment.

"Scotch on the rocks," I requested of the bartender. I would have to be dead drunk to survive a minute.

"Hello there," a voice said behind me. I turned around.

"Hello." The woman was in a saronglike dress, pleating at the hips. The drape was perfect and the color was shades of green in crepe.

"My name is Casey," she said.

"Joanna." Her hair was in a Billie Holiday upsweep, but instead of a gardenia, she wore a spray of mistletoe over her ear.

"I'm Marcus's wife." She would know Marcus surely.

"I know." Her complexion and smile were reminiscent of Lena Horne. I couldn't believe this glamorous lady deemed me worthy of a conversation.

"What I've been wondering," and she arched her penciled eyebrows, "is don't they have men where you come from?"

I looked about in a panic. I looked for rescue, comfort, something, realized I was very much on my own.

"Excuse me, Casey." I was trying hard to hold the tears, keep some semblance of dignity. "I feel sick," I said.

"Then I ducked into the bathroom," I told Mrs. Trakled the next day over tea, candied violets. "I wanted to stay in there forever, incognito and incommunicado."

"Oh," Mrs. Trakled huffed. "Those high-brown Louisiana girls think they are something. Just jealous is all. Just jealous."

Mrs. Trakled's relatives looked down on us from their oval frames. They lined the dining room wall, daguerreotypes, in high-collared dresses, watch chains, struck poses. There was nothing of the Reverend, no trace to the past. Sometimes I thought of him spawned spontaneously in some backwoods swamps, a Mississippi grub, pale and translucent, turning in a single life from worm to man, cell to angel. Actually, Mrs. Trakled told me, he had been a preacher doing revivals when she met him, called in when the white pianist failed to appear.

"Do you think I should tell Marcus?" I hadn't. Not a word.

"Good heavens no. Don't tell him a thing. It would be a mistake."

That night the two of us were seated across from each other, a late dinner, eight o'clock. I had the oven on and open for added warmth. The wind was whistling outside and our bedroom windows were freezing up on the inside.

"Sometimes I wish I was in California, Marcus. Both of us."

"You act like it's my fault you're not."

"No I don't."

"Yes you do."

"Like hell I do." It slipped out.

"I hate vulgarity in a woman." I knew he did.

"I hate cruelty in a man," I replied.

"Oh, you people." He sighed, stood up.

"What people are you referring to, Marcus? California people? Other people? White people? For your information, I am *your* people."

"Joanna, what are you talking about?"

"Attitude. Yours."

"You are the one with an attitude."

"I am the one with a sense of family, the only one. Marcus, we are kin. You can't say, oh, you people to me. It makes you sound like that woman at the party."

"What woman?"

"The one who asked me if there weren't any men where I came from."

"Who said that?"

"Casey."

"Oh, she didn't mean anything."

"She meant plenty. Don't defend her. It was a mean thing to say."

"It didn't kill you, did it?"

"That's even meaner. Whose side are you on?"

He sat down, looked absolutely disgusted with me.

"I take you to a party," he said wearily. "I thought you would like it."

"I hated it."

"Great, that's just great."

I picked up his dish, took it to the sink.

"You know, Joanna, those are my friends, the people who help me, the people who would help you. If anything happened . . ."

"Marcus," I turned around from the sink. "Those people would not help me off the sidewalk if I was dying and you know it."

"So what about your friends. Tell me what they would do for me."

"My friends don't live in Washington," I said meekly.

"Where *do* they live, Joanna? Anywhere on earth?"

I couldn't tell him what people at work said when I showed them pictures of my husband. I hadn't even told him about my experiences in looking for an apartment. He didn't know what had happened to my world, that it was more than divided, that it had simply fallen away.

"I didn't see your mother sending us any wedding presents," he continued, "or your sister."

"My mother made my wedding dress."

"That Halloween costume?"

I had to sit down at that. "At least my mother congratulated me," I offered. "Congratulated us which is more, much more, than your mother did." But those words were weak. He was right about my sister, who had become in her maturity a big snob and rejected everything we had stood for growing up, however innocuous. We are the vanguard, my mother used to say, nosing our turquoise Pontiac down the coast highway. "Remember your mother's letter, Marcus? And I quote: Are you doing the right thing, Marcus? Unquote. She thought I was pregnant or something."

"You could have been. Easily."

"I'll let that go. The point is that you side with the woman at the party."

"There is a serious shortage of Negro men, so that when a white woman . . ."

"Has one of their own . . ."

"Do you know what people think of you, of me, Joanna?"

"Do *you* know? Anyway, I don't care what people think."

"I do."

"You care too much, that's your problem."

"We have to live in society."

"We are society, Marcus." I felt strong enough to get up again, start the dishes. Usually I let them soak, but Marcus recently had explained to me how unsanitary that was.

"The world out there, Marcus, is full of hypocrites and chicken-shits."

"It doesn't solve anything to say that."

"It puts it in perspective, though, Marcus, lets us know what is important, that we are more important." I looked over at him, remembering how I had felt that first time in New York when I opened my door to him. It was instant recognition, as if my door was really a mirror I was looking into. I had felt that close. Now, looking at Marcus, I felt a chill go through me, and it was like being confronted with a blank wall.

"When I become a doctor, Joanna . . ."

"The world will stop."

"You can make fun of it if you want. But do you know what one of my professors told me. He said that when he was doing his internship in a big city hospital, a northern city hospital, a woman came into the emergency room bleeding to death, but she would not let him stick a needle for a transfusion into her. She would rather bleed to death."

"Did she?"

"No, of course not. He got a nurse to do it."

I sat back down in the chair, put my head in my hands. I knew what was coming. "Tell me about Charles Drew, Marcus, isn't he the one, the one who discovered blood types and then bled to death on some southern road because the nearest hospital was white. Tell me all the stories, tell me all about it."

"You act like those things don't matter."

"I know they do, but that is not the difficulty we are having. I am not your enemy. And you can't play it both ways." The wind rattled the windows. "You seem to *be* like the woman at the party, like your mother, people who are outside, but want to be inside, yet hate the inside. It's . . ."

"And you, you are inside?"

"I am an outsider, too, can't you see that?"

"No."

"It's not just color, race." I felt outside of everything at that moment. But from my distance I could see that to Marcus I was an insider and that maybe it had been part of my attraction, and that I had taken him for an outsider, but that really in his heart he wasn't. "I'm on the fringe of things, Marcus, of all things, of your things, too. I need some company, can't you tell?"

The bare limbs of the tree were scratching against the window like skeleton hands trying to gain entrance. I looked down at Marcus's elegant hand, the one which would cut and snip, sew back up. Formaldehyde from the anatomy lab had pinched up the little pads at the end of the fingertips. His knuckles were wrinkled. With a surge of affection, I reached for the hand. But Marcus drew it back.

"For God's sake, Marcus, I don't want to cut it off."

Yet I felt like it suddenly. I could have. Instead, I ran into the bathroom and with two big swipes, using the scissors brought all the way from California, I cut off two feet of my hair which had taken me since junior high to grow. Then I marched back into the kitchen.

"See," I shouted, putting a fistful of hair before him. "A hair sandwich, how do you like them apples? See what you made me do? Happy now?"

"Joanna." He shook his head as if I was beyond all hope.

"I present you my hair." I tried to make it sound victorious, but my voice began to wobble and my whole body was shaking. Lying there on the table, my hair looked like some kind of prone animal, like a complete supplicant, a totally defeated, dead beast.

"You are so crazy, Joanna. You make everything so damned hard."

"You make it impossible. And you don't even care." I was feeling, also, light-headed as if like Samson, my strength resided in my hair. My neck felt cold, naked; my face was exposed. I was out there, stripped. Like a collaborator.

"You *don't* care," I wailed.

"Shh," he said, putting a finger to his lips, but not rising from his chair to hug and soothe me. "You'll wake the Trakleds."

I wailed all the louder. A line of roaches sneaked out from the crack by the side of the table, took note, waved their antennae. Marcus and I were the giants. This is what the children of gods do, fight, I wanted to tell them.

"Shut up, Joanna."

Then I really let loose, and in a few seconds there was a light tapping at the door.

"Joanna, honey, it is I, Althea, are you all right?"

I went to the door, opened it a little.

"Mrs. Trakled."

"Oh child, you've gone and cut your beautiful hair, your crowning glory."

"No, it's all right," I said sniffing. It was bad, but not that bad. "*Your* hair is short, Mrs. Trakled."

"That's different. I'm an old woman."

"No you're not." I noticed in my grief that her bathrobe, like all her clothes, was a variation on violet.

"Do you want to come down and watch wrestling on TV? Gorgeous George is on."

Gorgeous George was our mutual favorite. Nights when Marcus was not home and the Reverend retired early, Mrs. Trakled and I stayed up for wrestling and mint julips.

"Maybe some other time." I closed the door gently.

"Toodle-oo," she called, descending the stairs.

"Mrs. Trakled is my friend," I said, turning back to Marcus.

"You woke them up."

"They were up." I looked at the African violet on top of the fridge. It was a gift from Mrs. Trakled, part of her collection which she kept on a white tea cart. Music was her vocation, she explained to me, and horticulture her avocation.

"You've wakened them," Marcus persisted. "Two innocent people."

"They are not that innocent, Marcus." In fact, Mrs. Trakled told me that the Reverend liked to put a pillow under her hips, hike her up. And in fact, during the train trip north, he bribed the porter and he and Mrs. Trakled, then Miss Gibson, got together on one of the top bunks in the Pullman car. It was a metaphysical experience, I said to myself, their double-decker coupling, a preacher and his accompanist. Anyway.

"You know, Joanna, I sometimes wonder," Marcus said.

"Me too. I wonder too, Marcus. Tell me." He had never said it, not once, not on our wedding night, never. "Tell me, honestly, do you love me?"

There was a moment of silence, a long moment, too long. It wasn't real silence either. I could hear the tree scraping and a skittling along the baseboards. The roaches, lots of them, or mice. Another moment passed. I thought I could hear the plant on top of the fridge growing or at least straining towards us, its petals attuned to nuance, all hairs standing straight up. Then Marcus cleared his throat.

"Well?" I was waiting. This was it.

"I married you, didn't I?"

He looked up at me, for I was still standing, and I read such fear in his eyes that I wanted to comfort him, tell him it was all right. Because I knew then that there was no point, that it was all over.

Death of a Duke

•

BANNING K. LARY

The face was strange. The voice vaguely familiar.

"Hey Fox. Ol' Foxy, cum here."

I was heading into the gym to work off a little tension when I was distracted by a thin black dude in the lock-up section. The concrete slab serving as the gym's floor was split in two equal sections by a walkway lined with heavy gauge chain-link fence. One side teemed with convicts busy at basketball, handball and the weights. The other side was almost vacant. Only the gaunt stranger and another black were locked up in there. I started to pass.

"Fox. It's *me,* man!"

I felt it wise to check out anyone who was so insistent about attracting my attention, and I walked over. Two liquid brown eyes swam above baggy lower lids dressing an angular face. Sweat streamed from his steel-wool hair and ran down to collect in a pair of kerchiefs tied loosely about his throat. A red and a blue. This was significant because you couldn't buy them at the commissary and they were contraband on the unit. They would get you a case if the boss was feeling bitchy.

"It's Earl, man," he said. "From the Dexter Unit."

"Earl?" I still wasn't believing him. The Earl I remembered from Dexter was bigger, lots of flesh and fat and had a jolly face.

"I knew an Earl Peterson. 'Earl the Pearl' we called him. But we changed it to—"

"Duke of Earl," he cut me off. "After the song 'cause I was such a *bad* dude! I lived in H-2, twenty-one cell, bottom bunk. You were next door in twenty-two on top. Your cellie was Ebbie something. Big blond guy who worked in the laundry."

It was Earl all right. I began to piece it together—the voice, the face, the mannerisms—but the changes were numerous.

"You look different," I said. "Thinner, lean even. You've got some muscle tone. Before you were flabby. Used to walk with a cane."

"Yeah, well I been workin' out. See."

He flexed his muscles and made a face like a movie actor. I had to admit he had improved himself considerably. His biceps knotted up into high mounds, and lines of separation outlined his individual muscles in fine definition. I also noticed stretch marks left on him from the weight he had dropped.

"You lost some weight, Earl."

"Seventy pounds."

"That's pretty radical. But it's been a year."

"Yeah. Lot's of changes, m'man."

It was a cold crawling kind of smirk he flashed me then. Right at home on a face with hate-filled eyes. Something had changed deep inside him. He had been a jiver and a player, but he was able to enjoy himself too. All that was gone now. Replaced by a dark violence I could feel through the air.

"What are you doing over here in lock-up, Duke?" I asked.

"Had some trouble on the chain. Got into it with a dude goin' over to the hospital."

I remembered Earl liked to ride the hospital bus. He was a master hypochondriac and an expert at manipulating the doctor, who would send Earl on the day's ride to the hospital to be checked out by every specialist the state could provide.

"So what's the deal?"

Earl the Pearl displayed the basis for that nickname, facial muscles pulling his cheeks in tight over the bones. He was smiling, but his eyes were cold and mirthless.

"The other dude stayed at the hospital. Doctor's orders. Something about broken bones. I think he'll be there a while. Brought me back in shackles and stuck me in lock-up. Took away all my shit. Haven't even got a fan. The run is loaded with crazies who scream all night, throw food and piss, break out the windows and run around like psychos at shower time. Last night they tore up their fuckin' sheets and jammed up the shitters so the whole place got flooded. I wake up and step right into a puddle."

Earl was getting agitated. Foam was beginning to form at the corners of his mouth. His eyes were steady but wild. He stuck his fingers through the woven mesh and squeezed his knuckles white.

"You got to take it easy, Earl. Cool down. Already they've got you in lock-up. They can turn the screws to you, Earl."

"Let 'em start turnin' then, 'cause I had about all I can take. Time to fight back, I've been thinking. The Duke is takin' it no more. From anybody."

Talk like that always unnerves me, because I understand what can happen when a man reaches that point. The point where a man doesn't care any longer to exercise control and restraint over himself. The point where he feels he is backed into a corner and has nothing to lose. The point where a man starts to become dangerous—unpredictably, savagely dangerous. Earl was near to reaching that point if he hadn't already. I got the feeling an old homeboy like myself would not be immune from his fury should it break loose at any time soon. Suddenly I realized the sanity of the chain-link fence.

"I don't see it that way, Earl. This place to me is like quicksand, like one of those Chinese finger stretchers. The more you struggle, the deeper you go or the tighter it gets. But you can be cool and make your way through it and get out."

"Yeah, unless you're man enough to bust that finger stretcher right off. Tear it up. Rip it right off your fingers and your hands will be free."

"Only it's not straw in here, Earl. The chains in here are tempered steel. You're not Superman."

"Yeah? Who the fuck says I ain't?"

Earl had an answer for everything. I was beginning to see that my words were having no effect. His hatred was too deeply rooted and was growing like a cancer inside him. As if to bleed off some of the tension forming in the air around us, the silent mulatto inside the cage with Earl got up and started to work on the heavy bag with his fists. His blows thudded like quick snaps of thunder. Earl looked pleased he had support for his tirade. The one-man rebellion had been increased to two.

A job came open in the Major's office and I sent in the proper form for an interview. Ol' Jonesy had made his parole third time up after doing six flat on twenty. The Major called me down at six o'clock the next morning. I stood outside in the hallway for half an hour before I heard him boom "Come in" through the closed door. I entered quickly and stood in a respectful position before his desk. The Major was struggling to assemble some kind of printed report into a colored tagboard binder. Lieutenant Green, a younger white field boss, sat off to the side scraping mud from a boot into a trash can.

"What did you have on your mind there, Ol' Fox?" The Major questioned me condescendingly.

"Bookkeeper's job, sir. I am good with ledgers, numbers, strong in math, can type sixty words a minute, have a college degree, sir, used to run a construction company in the world."

The brief summary of what I thought would be my pertinent qualifications seemed to irritate him, and the stack of pages burst from his hands and spread out over the floor of the room.

"Damn!" The Major glared at me like it was my fault. I sensed my opportunity was at hand.

"Let me help you, sir," I said, bending down to gather the

sheets. I worked rapidly and in a moment had the offending
pages ordered and bound. I set it before him and employed my
best imitation of obsequiousness.

"There you are, sir. No problem."

Lieutenant Green looked up over his buck knife. I noticed his
big toe was poking through his sock on the foot where the
muddy boot was missing. He articulated his version of a command.

"That there's a stack of them books that needs puttin'
tagatha."

My cue.

"Yes, sir. Right away, sir." I sounded like a real Army man.

I sat down at the small table against the wall and began to
organize and collate silently. The two prison officers evaluated
my person verbally in their own brand of code.

"You know 'im?" the Major inquired of the Lieutenant.

"Naw. Seen 'im around."

Pause. Buck knife scraping mud. Desk chair rocking, squeak-
ing.

"Look like he's got some snap."

"Yup, maybe."

"Good with papers looks like."

"Yup."

"Be pretty hard to replace Ol' Jonesy."

"Jonesy was a good hand."

Pause. Buck knife folding. Foot squeezing into boot.

"Jonesy minded his own business. Never gave us any guff."

"Jonesy was awright."

"This one looks pretty good too."

"He might be able to cut it, Major."

"Why don't we give him a shot, Lieutenant?"

"O.K. by me."

The flow of words changed direction.

"Where you workin' now, Ol' Fox?"

"Garment Factory, Major," I said.

"What's a convict like you doing sewing overalls?"

"That's where they assigned me, Major."

"Makes a lot of sense. Don't it, Fox?"

I sensed a test of some kind in that question. It seemed designed to measure my true opinion of their system. A sincere, comprehensively evasive answer wrapped in respect was the ticket.

"Well, sir, they process a thousand or so men through Diagnostics every two weeks. There's a lot of factors involved and I'm sure it's hard to find the perfect slot for everybody. I think what they do is just try to get close and once you get to your unit you're supposed to use a little initiative and find the right spot for yourself. That's why I'm here this morning, Major. I'd like to work in a capacity that utilizes some of my skills and where also I can be of maximum service to the institution. That way we both benefit."

When I turned around and set the completed stack of bound reports on his desk, the Major's eyes were wide and his expression blank, like he was attempting to fathom some great mystery.

"There you are, sir," I said calmly, eagerly. "What's next?"

The Major glanced at the reports that had baffled him, then up at me. He seemed to be perceiving me in a new light.

"Get down to the laundry, Fox," he ordered, "and get some pressed clothes. If you're goin' to work in this office you can't look like you jus' fell off the turnip truck. What's your number?"

"H-17-223-83."

The Major made a move for the phone.

"Take off, Fox. Get the clothes and cum right back. Ol' Jonesy left things a mess and you look like the one to straighten them out. I'm callin' Garment right now and havin' you transferred."

"Yes, sir. Thank you, sir." A closing expression of anticipated gratitude. I skipped out through the heavy plate door and headed for the laundry. This was going to be easier than I had thought. He needed me.

Weeks rolled by and I adjusted to a somewhat civilized setting. The main difference was being away from the hatchetting machines and lint dust that in two minutes would settle a quarter-inch thick on a cup of coffee. The Major was right about things being a mess. Whether it had been Jonesy or someone else, it was hard to tell, but Jonesy took the blame. It's always that way when a guy goes home. He was always the dumbest clown to have hit the unit that decade.

It took a while to gain the Major's trust—and that at best was dependent upon his coarse vicissitudes of mood—but soon I was able to help effect certain changes. Little things, like moving one-legged men off top bunks, weren't too difficult to convince the Major about. Getting a guy with reoccurring hepatitis out of the food-preparation room was a little harder. But with back-up from medical records and case law indicating how the unit could get in trouble with the Federal examiners, the Major begrudgingly saw his way clear to make the change.

In prison the status quo is the rule except in emergencies. Only the emergencies receive any attention and hold hope of achieving results. To see the Major was hard, at best inconvenient. It was purposely made that way. If you were hurting bad enough you would stand on the wall for hours waiting, or come back four and five times to see him. Twelve years in the prison business had given the Major a certain wariness to bust just about any act of facade. Working as his bookkeeper, I was party to many of his interviews and eventually developed a special respect for his perceptiveness. But once in a while a convict was able to get over on him. The Duke of Earl was just such a convict.

I had not seen Earl since that day in the gym, but had been able to keep track of him through the move slips that crossed my desk. About three weeks after I became bookkeeper, Earl was moved from solitary over to D-Building, the skid-row block, home of the most violent and incorrigible prisoners. Our unit was classified medium-minimum security, and Earl would have been on a maximum unit like Dexter but for his medical problems. This was the infirmary unit, and when inmates like Earl had to be there they were sequestered in D-Building.

The problem was Johnny Boy. The pretty mulatto had been moved from solitary to A-Building and this interrupted what I found out was a rather heavy sexual thing between him and Earl.

Earl had held out for the first three or four years, thinking his appeal would come through, but when it got denied and caused him the heart-wrenching anxieties associated with the futile process of climbing the ladder to the Supreme Court, Earl needed sexual release, and needed it stronger than was his desire to wait for a woman. With a 75-year sentence, Earl would have to do at least twelve flat to come up for parole, but with his record, he could bet on several set-offs. That was fifteen years without sex, and Earl soon realized a pretty young boy was a hell of a lot better than his fading memories.

Johnny Boy had not been the first but was the current favorite of the Duke. Earl was in love and had eyes for no other. It wasn't my thing, I was getting out soon and could wait for a woman's touch, but I guess I could understand Earl's fascination with Johnny Boy. Slim but taut, *café au lait* coloring, dazzling green eyes and ripe full lips that frequently parted into a smile that must have said "I dare you" to Earl. But Johnny loved Earl too, and was down with twenty for murder. They were good together. I saw that the first day at the gym.

So, Earl came to see the Major about a move.

"What is it, Peterson?"

"I want to integrate, Major. Need your permission for the move."

Getting moved in with a friend was next to impossible, or the Major would have had them waiting a hundred deep. Integration was another story. It looked good when the races were mixing voluntarily. The Federal monitors ate it up. Made the prison's socialization process appear to be working.

I looked up from my ledgers when I heard Earl come on with this approach. It was a brilliant tactic.

"Who's the other inmate, Peterson?" the Major quizzed.

"John Randall. Sir. Lives in A4-21."

"Randall. Randall. Doesn't ring a bell. Pull his tag, Fox."

I went over to the master board that filled an entire wall and located Johnny Boy's bed tag in the slot under A4-21.

"Randall, John," the Major read. "Caucasian. Steward's Department. Where is this Randall, Peterson?"

"Sick call, Major. He's having medical trouble. That's why I want him in with me. He needs someone to look after him. He gets these fainting spells, Major. Is on special medicine."

The major seemed doubtful.

"Who's your cellie now, Peterson?"

"Don't have a cellie, sir. He went home yesterday."

Earl had all of his ducks in a row. He made things attractive to the institution and thus the Major himself. How he had gotten the race designation of Caucasian typed on Johnny Boy's bed tag was another trick. Later I found out that the night bookkeeper had been persuaded to change the word. Earl had gotten to him through his weakness for good weed.

"Make out a slip, Fox," the Major huffed.

I rolled it through the typewriter, imprinting both names, numbers and cell locations.

"O.K. Sign it, Peterson."

Earl made his obligatory mark.

"Have this John Randall come by and sign it and I'll authorize the move."

"But, Major," Earl said, "you're going on vacation tomorrow. If you would, sir, could you sign it while I'm here and I'll have John Randall come in as soon as he's feeling better. Lieutenant Green will be here."

The master stroke. The Major would never lay eyes on mulatto Johnny. The Major grabbed the paper and scrawled his unintelligible signature.

"O.K. Dismissed, Peterson. I got better things to do than spend another minute listenin' to your goat-smellin' ass."

"Thank you, Major," Earl fawned. But only I saw his sly smirk as he slid through the door . . . Duke of Earl.

Johnny went in the next day as planned and signed the move slip before the Lieutenant, consenting to the integration. Lieutenant Green was stumbling around trying to fill the Major's shoes and once he saw the Major's hand on the paper, passed it right through. I made up some new bed tags and went on about my business.

An hour later Earl and his mulatto were hot after it behind a bedsheet hung up over the bars. This was the beginning of the end for both of them, but you never would have known it then. They were just another happy couple.

Earl had been having his toenails cut out one at a time at a month's lay-in from work apiece, and Johnny Boy kept them supplied with goods from the Steward's Department and they set up shop. Earl gambled at dominoes in the day room while Johnny worked. In the afternoons after work, they'd go to the gym and pump iron hard for a couple hours, then shower and back to the cell for the evening's business. D1-25 was on the first floor all the way at the end of the run and was the perfect location to become headquarters for all kinds of illicit activities.

The Duke ruled over his enterprises fairly, but came down iron-handed on those who broke their word or crossed him. Everything depended upon his image and the Duke knew how to generate respect. He had given up on his appeal, and got set to do the long run and really had nothing to lose. If he had to do fifteen years flat, he was going to do it on his own terms. Earl was discreet in his dealings and the bossman left him alone. He was relatively new on the unit and hadn't caused any trouble since solitary. D-Block was rough anyway and the guards usually didn't like to come inside too far without official business. And then they never came alone.

Earl was a natural leader and organizer, and had boundless energy for carrying out his ventures and beating the Man. The Duke's reputation spread quickly, and he soon managed connections with about everybody who was anybody. He didn't deal with short-timers or fools, but every solid dude knew the Duke and treated him with respect. There weren't many who would back up their word with their life, but the Duke of Earl was concrete and attracted the players like flies. He got big, too big, real fast. And that was the problem.

Competition. Things had long been organized and were in operation long before Earl arrived, and the "powers that be" didn't take kindly to the rapid rise of the new kid in town. Steaks had always been available on D-Block for two decks, but Earl had them hot and seasoned. Marijuana joints were four decks of freeworld cigarettes but the Duke's brand would stone out three guys instead of one. Odds on football parlays paid five-to-one with the Duke but only four-to-one with Bumblebee. The Duke's punks were prettier.

Bumblebee. Six-foot-four, two-forty, could bench press 410 pounds and wore size thirteen triple-E brogans. Bumblebee had inherited D-Block from Wolfman four years back, when Wolf had finally discharged an 80-year sentence after serving twenty flat. Bumblebee—so called because of his similarity to a monstrous replica of that insect with his dark saucer-sized eyeglasses and teeth of pollen gold—lived at the roof of the world in D5-25, right above Earl five open tiers up. Bumblebee had been aware of the drain on his action from day one, but, to save face, voiced no worry to his runners or supplicants.

It wasn't until Magpie, Bumblebee's cellie and educated bookman, did some figuring and found that business was the lowest ever, that Bumblebee dispatched Highside, his A-number-one spy. A few days later Highside had found a workable crack in the Duke's organization.

Earl was at the hospital getting his sixth toenail removed when Highside sidled up to Johnny Boy as he was coming in from work.

"Johnny Boy, where's the Duke?"

"Hospital, Highside. What's up?"

"Somethin' special jus' cum in. Gotta find the Duke or he's gonna miss it."

"He won't be back 'til afta chow."

"That's too bad 'cause it's real pretty. Too bad you can't handle it."

That was the barb that got to Johnny Boy. He was tired of people thinking he was just the Duke's "gal" and nothing else.

"Sure, I can handle it. What's the deal?"

"Sinsimilla. Fresh and strong. Two ounces."

"You know the Duke always tests it first himself."

"I thought you said you could handle it."

"Who's got it?"

"Bumblebee."

"All right. Let's go take a look."

I know the dialogue is pretty accurate because a little bird told me. The little bird is an old man everyone calls Fossil who sweeps the runs and has powers of hearing like some illegal eavesdropping device the police might use. He is kind of a half snitch, half self-appointed peacemaker. Fossil's been known to give up a minor asshole from time to time so the big fish can continue to swim free and feed in the deep. He's been around since before half the guys in here were born and is considered a tradition, an exhibit like in a museum.

According to Fossil, Johnny Boy followed Highside up to D5-25 to see Bumblebee and to test the weed. Bumblebee came on real friendly and had a fat one already rolled and told Johnny Boy to smoke it and if he liked it he could make the deal in the Duke's place. Johnny Boy was playing the bigshot and smoked it deep and fast, saying he could take it no matter how strong it was. What Johnny Boy didn't know was that Bumblebee had laced the joint with a heavy hit of angel dust—a hit that would have knocked a donkey's dick in the dirt. It wasn't long before the pretty mulatto slid down glassy-eyed on Bumblebee's bunk, like his body was suddenly robbed of all its bones.

Bumblebee brutalized that poor boy that afternoon, asserting his territorial rights again and again for over two hours. Later the autopsy report would show that most of his inner organs had been ruptured. That was before Bumblebee stood outside his cell with Johnny Boy held high over his head and rattled the windows with his blood-curdling yell, continuing after the body had fallen and landed five stories below in front of D1-25.

Whether fate had its hand in play that day or not, Earl had been coming into the block at that moment, heard the yelling and saw the blur of falling tan flesh before the thud. The Duke threw his cane aside and started running, and when his eyes confirmed the broken body was Johnny Boy, his lover, the shrieking started and didn't stop until the Duke was dead.

A call came in from the building officer about then and I watched Lieutenant Green's face go white with fear.

"Seal off the block," he yelled into the phone. "I'm calling the riot squad."

The Lieutenant began dialing furiously, and in the confusion I slipped out the door and eased down to D-Block. The crash gates were locked tight when I got there and I joined the small crowd of inmates clustered outside the bars by the D-Block stairway. There was a noise but I couldn't recognize it, and then Earl ran by and I realized it was him screaming. It was an inhuman sound, a sound a hyena might make escaping into the night having torn its foot loose from the steel jaws of a heavy spring trap. The riot squad came up but not one of them was brave enough to go inside just then.

"Let's let 'em cool off a little first," I heard a helmeted corpsman say as he slapped the hardwood club into his other palm.

The Duke took the stairs three at a time, even though one foot was swathed in bandages. He carried a length of hollow pipe, flattened and sharpened like a spear, and a shorter shiv with a double-sided blade shiny at the edges. The Duke didn't see me. I don't think he saw anything but the rage that drove him. He had been expecting a showdown with Bumblebee, but not this way. The Duke had come to the end of himself, and all reason would have been useless.

Duke met Bumblebee halfway down 5 run and drove the spear through his mouth out the back of his head. Bumblebee had been weakened by the sex and exertions, but still managed to drive a shank under Earl's ribcage before the Duke toppled him over the railing. He landed about twenty feet away from us inside the bars, with a thud I could feel through my shoes.

A moment later Duke came down the stairs. His eyes were wide and he wore Bumblebee's shank rooted in a wet red stain on his left side. Bandage trailed out from his foot like an obscene tail, and no one could speak as he went to work with the short knife. The metal scraped concrete and the Duke stood up and started walking over to where we stood watching. He was dragging his left foot, and in his right hand he carried Bumblebee's head by the hair. He approached the bars and held up the head and pointed to it with the bloodied shiv.

"This guy has been fuckin' with me," the Duke said. Then he fell against the bars and slid to the floor.

Sinking House

•

T. CORAGHESSAN BOYLE

After Monty's last breath caught somewhere in the back of his throat, with a sound like the tired wheeze of an old screen door, the first thing she did was turn on the water. She leaned over him a minute to make sure, and then she wiped her hands on her dress and shuffled into the kitchen. Her fingers trembled as she jerked at the lever and felt the water surge against the porcelain. Steam rose in her face; a glitter of liquid leapt for the drain. Croak, that's what they called it. Now she knew why. She left the faucet running in the kitchen and crossed the living room, swung down the hallway to the guest bedroom, and turned on both taps in the bathroom there. Almost as an afterthought she decided to fill the tub, too.

For a long while she sat in the leather armchair in the living room. The sound of running water—pure, baptismal, as uncomplicated as the murmur of a brook in Vermont or a toilet at the Waldorf—soothed her. It trickled and trilled, burbling from either side of the house and driving down the terrible silence that crouched in the bedroom over the lifeless form of her husband.

The afternoon was gone and the sun was plunging into the canopy of the big eucalyptus behind the Finkelsteins' when she finally pushed herself up from the chair. Head down, arms moving stiffly at her sides, she scuffed out the back door, crossed the patio, and bent to turn on the sprinklers. They sputtered and

spat—not enough pressure, that much she understood—but finally came to life in half-hearted umbrellas of mist. She left the
hose trickling in the rose garden and went back into the house,
passed through the living room, the kitchen, the master bedroom
—not even a glance for Monty, no: she wouldn't look at him, not
yet—and on into the master bath. The taps were weak, produced
barely a trickle, but she left them on anyway, and then flushed
the toilet and pinned down the float with the brick Monty had
used as a doorstop. And then, finally, so weary she could barely
lift her arms, she leaned into the stall and flipped on the shower.

Two weeks after the ambulance came for the old man next door,
Meg Terwilliger was doing her stretching exercises on the prayer
rug in the sunroom, a menthol cigarette glowing in the ashtray
on the floor beside her, the new CD by Sandee and the Sharks
thumping out of the big speakers in the corners. Meg was
twenty-three, with the fine bones and haunted eyes of a poster
child. She wore her black hair cut close at the temples, long in
front, and she used a sheeny black eye shadow to bring out the
hunger in her eyes. In half an hour she'd have to pick up Tiffany
at nursery school; drop off the dog at the veterinarian's; take
Sonny's shirts to the cleaner's; buy cilantro, flour tortillas, and a
pound and a half of thresher shark at the market; and start the
burritos for supper. But for now she was stretching.

She took a deep drag on the cigarette, tugged at her right foot,
and brought it up snug against her buttocks. After a moment she
released it and drew back her left foot. One palm flat on the
floor, her head bobbing vaguely to the beat of the music, she did
half a dozen repetitions and then paused to relight her cigarette.
Not until she turned over to do her straight-leg lifts did she
notice the dampness in the rug.

Puzzled, she rose to her knees and reached behind her to rub
at the twin wet spots on the seat of her sweats. She lifted the
corner of the rug, suspecting the dog, but detected no odor of
urine. Looking closer, she saw that the concrete floor was a

shade darker beneath the rug, as if bleeding moisture, as it some-times did in winter. But this wasn't winter; this was high sum-mer in Los Angeles, and it hadn't rained for months. Cursing Sonny—he'd promised her ceramic tile, and though she'd run all over town to get the best price on a nice Italian floral pattern, he still hadn't found the time to go look at it—she shot back the sliding door and stepped into the yard to investigate.

Immediately she felt the Bermuda grass squelch beneath the soles of her aerobic shoes. Before she'd taken three strides—the sun in her face, Queenie yapping frantically from the fenced-in pool area—her feet were wet. Had Sonny left the hose running? Tiffany? She slogged across the lawn, the pastel Reeboks spat-tered with wet, and checked the hose. It was innocently coiled on its tender, the tap firmly shut. Queenie's yapping went up an octave. The heat—it must have been ninety-five, a hundred—made her feel faint. She gazed up into the cloudless sky and then bent to check each of the sprinklers in succession.

She was poking around in the welter of bushes along the fence, looking for an errant sprinkler, when she thought of the old lady next door—Muriel, wasn't that her name? What with her husband dying and all, maybe she'd left the hose running and had forgotten all about it. Meg rose on her tiptoes to peer over the redwood fence that separated her yard from the neigh-bors' and found herself looking into a glistening, sunstruck gar-den with banks of impatiens, bird-of-paradise, oleander, loquat, and roses in half a dozen shades. The sprinklers were on and the hose was running. For a long moment Meg stood there, mesmer-ized by the play of light through the drifting fans of water; she was wondering what it would be like to be old, thinking of how it would be if Sonny died and Tiffany were grown up and gone. She'd probably forget to turn off the sprinklers too.

The moment passed. The heat was deadening, the dog hysteri-cal. Meg knew she would have to do something about the sod-den yard and the wet floor in the sun-room, but she dreaded facing the old woman. What would she say—I'm sorry your husband died, but could you turn off the sprinklers? She was thinking maybe she'd phone—or wait till Sonny got home and let him handle it—when she stepped back from the fence and sank to her ankles in mud.

When the doorbell rang, Muriel was staring absently at the cover of an old *National Geographic* that lay beneath a patina of dust on the coffee table. The cover photo showed the beige and yellow sands of some distant desert, rippled to the horizon with corrugations that might have been waves on a barren sea. Monty was dead and buried. She wasn't eating much. Or sleeping much either. The sympathy cards sat unopened on the table in the kitchen, where the tap overflowed the sink and water plunged to the floor with a pertinacity that was like redemption. When it was quiet—in the early morning or late at night—she could distinguish the separate taps, each with its own voice and rhythm, as they dripped and trickled from the far corners of the house. In those suspended hours she could make out the comforting gurgle of the toilet in the guest room, the musical wash of the tub as it cascaded over the lip of its porcelain dam, the quickening rush of the stream in the hallway as it shot like a miniature Niagara down the chasm of the floor vent. She could hear the drip in the master bathroom, the distant hiss of a shower, and the sweet eternal sizzle of the sprinklers on the back lawn.

But now she heard the doorbell.

Wearily, gritting her teeth against the pain in her lower legs and the damp, lingering ache of her feet, she pushed herself up from the chair and sloshed her way to the door. The carpet was black with water, soaked through like a sponge—and in a tidy corner of her mind she regretted it—but most of the runoff was finding its way to the heating vents and the gaps in the corners where Monty had miscalculated the angle of the baseboard. She heard it dripping somewhere beneath the house and for a moment pictured the water lying dark and still in a shadowy lagoon that held a leaking ship poised on its trembling surface. The doorbell sounded again. "All right, all right," she muttered. "I'm coming."

A girl with dark circles around her eyes stood on the doorstep. She looked vaguely familiar, and for a moment Muriel thought she recognized her from a TV program about a streetwalker who rises up to kill her pimp and liberate all the other leather-clad, black-eyed streetwalkers of the neighborhood. But then the girl spoke and Muriel realized her mistake. "Hi," the girl said, and Muriel saw that her shoes were black with mud. "I'm your neighbor? Meg Terwilliger?" The girl looked down at her muddy shoes. "I, uh, just wanted to tell you that we're, uh—Sonny and I, I mean; he's my husband?—we're sorry about your trouble and all, but I wondered if you knew your sprinklers were on out back?"

Muriel attempted a smile—surely a smile was appropriate at this juncture—but managed only to lift her upper lip back from her teeth in a sort of wince or grimace.

The girl was noticing the rug now, and Muriel's sodden slippers. She looked baffled, perhaps even a little frightened. And young. So young. Muriel had had a young friend once, a girl from the community college who used to come to the house before Monty got sick. She had a tape recorder, and she would ask them questions about their childhood, about the days when the San Fernando Valley was dirt roads and orange groves. Oral history, she called it. "It's all right," Muriel said, trying to reassure her.

"I just—is it a plumbing problem?" the girl said, backing away from the door. "Sonny . . . ," she said, but didn't finish the thought. She ducked her head and retreated down the steps, but when she reached the walk, she wheeled around. "I mean you really ought to see about the sprinklers," she said. "The whole place is soaked, my sunroom and everything—"

"It's all right," Muriel repeated, and then the girl was gone and she shut the door.

. . .

"She's nuts, she is. Really. I mean she's out of her gourd." Meg was searing chunks of thresher shark in a pan with green chiles, sweet red pepper, onion, and cilantro. Sonny, who was twenty-eight and so intoxicated by real estate that he had to forgo the morning paper till he got home at night, was slumped in the breakfast nook with a vodka tonic and the sports pages. His white-blond hair was cut fashionably, in what might once have been called a flat-top, though it was thinning, and his open, appealing face, with its boyish look, had begun to show signs of wear, particularly around the eyes, where years of escrow had taken their toll. Tiffany was in her room, playing quietly with a pair of six-inch dolls that had cost sixty-five dollars each.

"Who?" Sonny murmured, tugging unconsciously at the gold chain he wore around his neck.

"Muriel. The old lady next door. Haven't you heard a thing I've been saying?" With an angry snap of her wrist, Meg cut the heat beneath the saucepan, and she clapped a lid over it. "The floor in the sun-room is flooded, for God's sake," she said, stalking across the kitchen in her bare feet till she stood poised over him. "The rug is ruined. Or almost is. And the yard—"

Sonny slapped the paper down on the table. "All right! Just let me relax a minute, will you?"

She put on her pleading look. It was a look compounded of pouty lips, tousled hair, and those inevitable eyes, and it always had its effect on him. "One minute," she murmured. "That's all it'll take. I just want you to see the back yard."

She took him by the hand and led him through the living room to the sun-room, where he stood a moment contemplating the damp spot on the concrete floor. She was surprised herself at how the spot had grown—it was three times what it had been that afternoon, and it seemed to have sprouted wings and legs like an enormous Rorschach blot. She pictured a butterfly. Or, no, a hovering crow or bat. She wondered what Muriel would have made of it.

Outside she let out a little yelp of disgust—all the earthworms in the yard had crawled up on the step to die. And the lawn wasn't merely spongy now, it was soaked through, puddled like a swamp. "Jesus Christ," Sonny muttered, sinking in his wing-tips. He cakewalked across the yard to where the fence had begun to sag, the post leaning drunkenly, the slats bowed. "Will you look at this?" he shouted over his shoulder. Squeamish about the worms, Meg stood at the door to the sun-room. "The Goddamn fence is falling down!"

He stood there a moment, water seeping into his shoes, a look of stupefaction on his face. Meg recognized the look. It stole over his features in moments of extremity, as when he tore open the phone bill to discover mysterious twenty-dollar calls to Billings, Montana, and Greenleaf, Mississippi, or when his buyer called on the day escrow was to close to tell him he'd assaulted the seller and wondered if Sonny had five hundred dollars for bail. These occasions always took him by surprise. He was shocked anew each time the crisply surveyed, neatly kept world he so cherished rose up to confront him with all its essential sloppiness, irrationality, and bad business sense. Meg watched the look of disbelief turn to one of injured rage. She followed him through the house, up the walk, and into Muriel's yard, where he stalked up to the front door and pounded like the Gestapo.

No one responded.

"Son of a bitch," he said, turning to glare over his shoulder at Meg as if it were her fault or something. From inside they could hear the drama of running water, a drip and gurgle, a sough and hiss. Sonny turned back to the door, hammering his fist against it till Meg was sure she could see the panels jump.

It frightened her, this sudden rage. Sure, they had a problem here, and she was glad he was taking care of it, but did he have to get violent, did he have to get crazy? "You don't have to beat her door down," she said, focusing on the swell of his shoulder and the hammer of his fist as it rose and fell in savage rhythm. "Sonny, come on. It's only water, for God's sake."

"Only?" he said, spinning round to face her. "You saw the fence—next thing you know the foundation'll shift on us. The whole damn house—" He never finished. The look on Meg's face told him that Muriel had opened the door.

Muriel was wearing the same faded blue housecoat she'd had on earlier, and the same wet slippers. Short, heavyset, so big in front she seemed about to topple over, she clung to the doorframe and peered up at Sonny out of a stony face. Sonny jerked round to confront her and then stopped cold when he got a look at the interior of the house. The plaster walls were stained now, drinking up the wet in long jagged fingers that clawed toward the ceiling, and a dribble of coffee-colored liquid began to seep across the doorstep and puddle at Sonny's feet. The sound of rushing water was unmistakable, even from where Meg was standing. "Yes?" Muriel said, the voice withered in her throat. "Can I help you?"

It took Sonny a minute—Meg could see it in his eyes: this was more than he could handle, willful destruction of a domicile, every tap in the place on full, the floors warped, plaster ruined—but then he recovered himself. "The water," he said. "You—our fence—I mean, you can't, you've got to stop this—"

The old woman drew herself up, clutching the belt of her dress till her knuckles bulged with the tension. She looked first at Meg, still planted in the corner of the yard, and then turned to Sonny. "Water?" she said. "What water?"

The young man at the door reminded her, in a way, of Monty. Something about the eyes or the set of the ears—or maybe the crisp, high cut of the sideburns . . . Of course, most young men reminded her of Monty. The Monty of fifty years ago, that is. The Monty who'd opened up the world to her over the shift lever of his Model A Ford, not the crabbed and abrasive old man who'd called her "bonehead" and "dildo" and cuffed her like a dog. Monty. When the stroke brought him down, she was almost glad. She saw him pinned beneath his tubes in the hospital and something stirred in her; she brought him home and changed his bedpan, peered into the vaults of his eyes, fed him Gerber's like the baby she'd never had, and she knew it was over. Fifty years. No more drunken rages, no more pans flung against the wall, never again his sour flesh pressed to hers. She was on top now.

The second young man—he was a Mexican, short, stocky, with a moustache so thin it could have been penciled on, and wicked little red-flecked eyes—also reminded her of Monty. Not so much in the way he looked as in the way he held himself, the way he swaggered and puffed out his chest. And the uniform, too, of course. Monty had worn a uniform during the war.

"Mrs. Burgess?" the Mexican asked.

Muriel stood at the open door. It was dusk, the heat cut as if there were a thermostat in the sky. She'd been sitting in the dark. The electricity had gone out on her—something to do with the water and the wires. She nodded her head in response to the policeman's question.

"We've had a complaint," he said.

Little piggy eyes. A complaint. *We've had a complaint.* He wasn't fooling her, not for a minute. She knew what they wanted, the police, the girl next door and the boy she was married to—they wanted to bring Monty back. Prop him up against the bed frame, stick his legs back under him, put the bellow back in his voice. Oh, no, they weren't fooling her.

She followed the policeman around the darkened house as he went from faucet to faucet, sink to tub to shower. He firmly twisted each of the taps closed and drained the basins, and then crossed the patio to kill the sprinklers and the hose, too. "Are you all right?" he kept asking. "Are you all right?"

She had to hold her chin in her palm to keep her lips from

trembling. "If you mean am I in possession of my faculties, yes, I am, thank you. I am all right."

They were back at the front door now. He leaned nonchalantly against the doorframe and dropped his voice to a confidential whisper. "So what's this with the water, then?"

She wouldn't answer him. She knew her rights. What business was it of his, or anybody's, what she did with her own taps and her own sprinklers? She could pay the water bill. Had paid it, in fact. Eleven hundred dollars' worth. She watched his eyes and shrugged.

"Next of kin?" he asked. "Daughter? Son? Anybody we can call?"

Now her lips held. She shook her head.

He gave it a moment and then let out a sigh. "Okay," he said, speaking slowly and with exaggerated emphasis, as if he were talking to a child. "I'm going now. You leave the water alone—wash your face, brush your teeth, do the dishes. But no more of this." He swaggered back from her, fingering his belt, his holster, the dead weight of his nightstick. "One more complaint and we'll have to take you into custody for your own good. You're endangering yourself and the neighbors, too. Understand?"

Smile, she told herself. Smile. "Oh, yes," she said softly. "Yes, I understand."

He held her eyes a moment, threatening her—just like Monty used to do, *just like Monty*—and then he was gone.

She stood there on the doorstep a long while, the night deepening around her. She listened to the cowbirds, the wild parakeets that nested in the Murtaughs' palm, the whoosh of traffic from the distant freeway. After a while she sat on the step. Behind her the house was silent: no faucet dripped, no sprinkler hissed, no toilet gurgled. It was horrible. Insupportable. In the pit of that dry silence she could hear him, Monty, treading the buckled floors, pouring himself another vodka, cursing her in a voice like sandpaper.

She couldn't go back in there. Not tonight. The place was

deadly, contaminated, sick as the grave—after all was said and done, it just wasn't clean enough. If the rest of it was a mystery—oral history, fifty years of Monty, the girl with the blackened eyes—that much she understood.

Meg was watering the cane plant in the living room when the police cruiser came for the old lady next door. The police had been there the night before, and Sonny had stood out front with his arms folded while the officer shut down Muriel's taps and sprinklers. "I guess that's that," he said, coming up the walk in the oversized Hawaiian shirt she'd given him for Father's Day. But in the morning the sprinklers were on again, and Sonny called the local substation three times before he left for work. She's crazy, he'd hollered into the phone, irresponsible, a threat to herself and the community. He had a four-year-old daughter to worry about, for Christ's sake. A dog. A wife. His fence was falling down. Did they have any idea what that amount of water was going to do to the substrata beneath the house?

Now the police were back. The patrol car stretched across the window and slid silently into the driveway next door. Meg set down the watering can. She was wearing her Fila sweats and a new pair of Nikes and her hair was tied back in a red scarf. She'd dropped Tiffany off at nursery school, but she had the watering and her stretching exercises to do and a pasta salad to make before she picked up Queenie at the vet's. Still, she went directly to the front door and then out onto the walk.

The police officers—she didn't realize for a minute that the shorter of the two was a woman—were on Muriel's front porch, looking stiff and uncertain in their razor-creased uniforms. The man knocked first—once, twice, three times. Nothing happened. Then the woman knocked. Still nothing. Meg folded her arms and waited. After a minute the man went around to the side gate and let himself into the yard. Meg heard the sprinklers die with a wheeze, and then the officer was back, his shoes heavy with mud.

Again he thumped at the door, much more violently now, and Meg thought of Sonny. "Open up," the woman called in a breathy contralto that she tried unsuccessfully to deepen. "Police."

Then Meg saw her, Muriel, at the bay window on the near side of the door. "Look!" she shouted before she knew what she was saying. "She's there, there in the window!"

The male officer—he had a moustache and pale, fine hair like Sonny's—leaned out over the railing and gestured impatiently at the figure behind the window. "Police," he said. "Open the door." Muriel never moved. "All right," he said, cursing under his breath, "all right," and he put his shoulder to the door. The frame splintered easily, water dribbled out, and both officers disappeared into the house.

Meg waited. She had things to do, yes, but she waited anyway, bending to pull the odd dandelion the gardener had missed, trying to look busy. The police were in there an awful long time—twenty minutes, half an hour—and then the woman appeared in the doorway with Muriel.

Muriel appeared heavier than ever, her face pouchy, arms swollen. She was wearing white sandals on her old splayed feet, a shapeless print dress, and a white straw hat that looked as if it had been dug out of a box in the attic. The woman had her by the arm; the man loomed behind her with a suitcase. Down the steps and up the walk, she never turned her head. But then, just as the policewoman was helping her into the back seat of the patrol car, Muriel swung round as if to take one last look at her house. But she wasn't looking at the house; she was looking at Meg.

The morning gave way to the heat of afternoon. Meg finished the watering, made the pasta salad—bow-tie twists, fresh salmon, black olives, and pine nuts—ran her errands, picked up Tiffany and put her down for a nap. Somehow, though, she just couldn't get Muriel out of her head. The old lady had stared at her for five seconds, maybe, and then the policewoman was coaxing her into the car. Meg had felt like sinking into the ground. But then she realized that Muriel's look wasn't vengeful at all—it was just sad. It was a look that said, This is what it comes to. Fifty years, and this is what it comes to.

The back yard was an inferno, the sun poised directly overhead. Queenie, cleansed of fleas, shampooed, and with her toenails clipped, was stretched out asleep in the shade beside the pool. It was quiet. Even the birds were still. Meg took off her Nikes and walked barefoot through the sopping grass to the fence, or what was left of it. The post had buckled overnight, canting the whole business into Muriel's yard. Meg never hesitated. She sprang up onto the plane of the slats and dropped to the grass on the other side.

Her feet sank in the mud, the earth like pudding, like chocolate pudding, and as she lifted her feet to move toward the house the tracks she left behind her slowly filled with water. The patio was an island. She crossed it, dodging potted plants and wicker furniture, and tried the back door. Finding it locked, she moved to the window, shaded her face with her hands, and peered in. The sight made her catch her breath. The plaster was crumbling, wallpaper peeling, the rug and floors ruined: she knew it was bad, but this was crazy, this was suicide.

Grief, that's what it was. Or was it? And then she was thinking of Sonny again—what if he were dead and she were old like Muriel? She wouldn't be so fat, of course, but maybe like one of those thin and elegant old ladies in Palm Springs, the ones who'd done their stretching all their lives. Or what if she wasn't an old lady at all—the thought swooped down on her like a bird out of the sky—what if Sonny was in a car wreck or something? It could happen.

She stood there gazing in on the mess through her own wavering reflection. One moment she saw the wreckage of the old lady's life, the next the fine mouth and expressive eyes everyone commented on. After a while she turned away from the window and looked out on the yard as Muriel must have seen it. She saw the roses, gorged with water and flowering madly, the impatiens, rigid as sticks, oleander drowning in their own yellowed leaves— and there, poking innocuously from the bushes at the far corner of the patio, was the steel wand that controlled the sprinklers. Handle, neck, prongs: it was just like theirs.

And then the idea came to her. She'd turn them on—the sprinklers—just for a minute, just to see what it felt like. She wouldn't leave them on long—the water could threaten the whole foundation of her house.

That much she understood.

The Hit

•

======   CATHERINE PETROSKI   ======

The long thin nose, the heavy brows, the shock of white frizzed hair standing on end like Beckett's—Yves Roland's is the kind of profile that is easy to caricature. It has been several times already, but then a filmmaker such as Yves Roland is a likely target. In the receiving line he turns a smile to the next well-wisher. His teeth are very small.

"No doubt about it—you're the hit of the festival, Monsieur Roland," the woman next in line says to him. Her *monsieur* is passable, the *r* actually quite good. "What a fabulous talk," she continues. "We're so lucky to have you here."

The woman saying all this to Roland appears to be somewhat fabulous herself: thin, very tall, and dark, in a black silk dress and an immense black straw hat. The kind of woman who looks as though one could never know everything about her. Hers is the only hat in the room, and Roland catches himself thinking what he would make of a detail like that on film. Along one side of the hat's crown lies a huge rose, pale pink, silk, that quivers as the woman speaks. Despite the woman's ease something in her eyes appears literally stunned. Was it Roland's talk? Had someone perhaps tricked her into the lecture hall and hit her with a small deadly mallet between the eyes?

The actual facts of tonight's lecture may have been something of an embarrassment to Festival administrators. More than the usual one or two odd ducks rose and left as Roland spoke. Had a crowd wandered into the auditorium by mistake, or on the wrong night? Or had it been Yves Roland's departure from the announced topic ("The Making of *Le Déluge"*), choosing instead to postulate the influence of the Occupation on French film-makers of the seventies and eighties. The woman in the rose hat moves to take her leave, to make way for the next to shake his hand, and Roland seizes her hand, shaking it again, finally rais-ing it to his lips. He is all charm. The woman is shaken. Shalimar fills the air thick and sweet, like too much blood.

Yves Roland turns then: full-face to the next person, another woman, totally different. Her face is flushed (or is it that false blush make-up?), her voice is expectant (or is it deliberately breathless?), and she tells him she has been waiting for this mo-ment for a long time. Ridiculous, he tells himself. He has seen this woman a hundred times. No, easily a thousand. Yet, not exactly. If he studies her, he will see how she is different.

Pictures in magazines didn't do him justice, nor did the TV. Everyone agreed to this. Always hidden minicams were catching Yves Roland fleeing, one hand up as if to shield himself from the blow he imagined coming. He would swear at cameramen in French. News editors seldom edited his profanities out. Roland was never sure whether they didn't know what he was saying, or did.

"Tell me what would bring you to a place like this?" the breathless woman asks him. He looks relieved that she is filling the silence. Maybe she doesn't like it here either.

"Money. Nothing more, nothing less."

"Oh, I can't believe that."

"It's true," he shrugs, smiles, turns his pants pockets inside out like Marcel Marceau. "See?" It is a practiced gesture, charming.

She laughs.

"And what brings you here?"

"My husband. Past tense. My ex-husband, now."

"Ah."

"And would anything keep you here, or make you come back?"

"A beautiful woman," he says. It is an answer that comes easily. Roland has always found that to be a superb answer, useful for a variety of questions. And her question was flirtatious enough. His face is perfectly still, except for the insides of his eyes.

"To each his own," she says. She laughs again, and he laughs.

"Let me get you some food, something to drink," he says.

"Oh, please, allow me." She does a Charlie Chaplin après-vous, and he does a Charlie Chaplin aprè-vous, and they trade several more until the whole room is looking. Then they laugh together, at the room, laughing at them.

"Tell me your name," he says to Clea.

". . . Monsieur Yves Roland." The Fête Cinematique greeted his introduction with the usual tumultuous applause. Another full house. The lighting tonight was too dramatic, but that too was the usual state. The details of Roland's days were, in a fashion, becoming frighteningly similar. Gone, it seemed, was the excitement of not knowing whether a film he wanted to do would be made, or whether the critics would like it, or if anyone would come to see it. After *Le Déluge,* Yves Roland could count on an audience no matter what he did, no matter what the critics said. Another blockbuster was another matter. But those aberrations depended on other things—timing, promotion—and not on the film.

Besides, of all that he had had his share, enough for two careers, and how much could one really enjoy? All that mattered now was work, which had become in recent years a serene and predictable mistress, like a lifetime mate. She could be depended on to lead him into those timeless chutes that took him out of real life into he knew not where. As long as those happened, he had no worry. So what if his young, passionate style had given way to something more considered. Continuity made up for the wild-eyed manner. There was no longer a question about being permitted to do what he wanted to do. He did it, and he was good at it.

Ah, *Le Déluge*, Roland's blessing and his curse. *Le Déluge* was ancient history. Yet always people asked the same questions, always about it. Had people stopped going to movies ten years ago? Refusing to answer, however, would be supremely ungracious. Perhaps the real price of success was always having to answer the same questions. Roland's answers were ready.

A: No, he did not anticipate doing a sequel to *Le Déluge*.

A: No, it was not true that he had found Monique Étoille in a Marseilles brothel, and no, he had not cast her as the lead in *IO*.

A: No, he had no immediate plans to become an American citizen.

A: No, Bergman and he were not bitter enemies. He hardly knew the man—did anyone?

A: Yes, he had children. Three. Nearly grown now. Nothing about them, please.

A: Yes, he had remarried. No, not at the moment.

A: No, he did not find it possible to work to one's fullest extent as an artist and be a marriage partner.

A: No, he was not antagonistic to gays.

A: No, he was not pro-gay. He believed that all people finally do what they must.

I am sorry, he would say then, I must catch a plane.

"And I came to the realization," she was saying, "that I was nothing better than a kept woman."

Roland gives Clea a professional scan. Blond and blue-eyed, all-American, the type always cast as the cheerleader, the girl next door, the eternal ingénue until she can no longer do close-ups even with the soft focus that everyone knows the reason for.

In real life this Clea's smile is fine. For the big screen, her teeth would have to be capped. Oh, the kept-woman thing again. "You were married how long?"

"Fourteen years. God, forever. He was a lawyer," she says. "Considering, he treated me very well in the divorce." She looks at him, Kansas and milkshakes and football Saturdays. He nods and notices Clea's stubby hands, nails bitten to the quick. "Not that I ever gave him reason to do otherwise. You know how lawyers are, though."

He knew. "But surely you are being too hard on yourself."

"Well, what else can you call it? He paid my bills, we went to bed. We stopped loving each other long before we stopped making love. Writing became my life." Clea's pink color intensified.

"Ah, you are a writer! I knew, I sensed that you were involved in something creative. So, what did your husband think of your writing?"

" 'That shit ruined our marriage'—that's what he said to me. Maybe it did."

"And what sort of writing do you do? Poetry? Stories?"

Clea's screenplay is about a man (a lawyer), well-regarded in his community, who is addicted to several controlled substances, which her treatment does not specify. Ritually, the man drives about in a fur-lined van in a drugged condition each night between the hours of 2 and 5 A.M. To what end is never exactly clear. Yves can't see an audience ever buying this, but he smiles and nods as Clea tells him. Maybe all will become obvious later. One learns to grant writers certain latitude in getting exposition out of the way. Matters of emphasis, theme, can be handled later with the special economy of film—a gesture, a series of images, nuances of expression, some central detail in the set. What else is a director for?

One night the addict backs out of his garage and accidentally runs over both his wife and her mother, who (innocent of any knowledge of the man's nocturnal habits) have spread their

Orvis sleeping bags on the warm concrete driveway in order to observe the Perseid. Despite his altered state, the lawyer realizes the gravity of his situation. He cannot deal with it. He rushes to his dealer, who perceives the man's desperation. The price of whatever it is skyrockets.

When Clea pauses, Roland asks her, "Have you ever tried coke?"

"No," she says. "I smoked some marijuana once years ago. Bill tried it too. Where would you get cocaine in a town like this? I wouldn't even know where to start."

Yves Roland knows it could be done, but sees that Clea thinks he wants her to get some for him. "You misunderstand me," he says, "but the point is, your play . . ."

"Oh, it's *just* a story," she says. Pairs of dimples.

He smiles.

Clea continues outlining the plot, but Roland doesn't listen. He doesn't want to know if her husband was right.

Around Yves Roland the words ebb and flow like a tide littered with so many broken shells and worn bits of old colored glass. It is part of the terra incognita he must face when he accepts these speaking engagements: the after-speech reception. Yves Roland thinks of how a wide-angle camera mounted on the ceiling would capture the advances and retreats of persons and groups. Water seeking higher ground. The crowd's eyes track him like those of lunatics enthralled by their moon, or like the faces of heliotropes following an afternoon sun. At the edge the woman in the rose-decked hat observes him, distanced and formal, like a tree-rose in a palace garden.

Then Roland knows: the rose hat is simply his first wife exactly, though if the two women were put side by side, nine people out of ten would not see the slightest resemblance. No, you have to have lived with a woman like that to know, a woman like Elli and like this woman in the rose hat. It is something Yves can't explain, and could never put on film. It is scent of pasture, like that of dairy cows, and their demeanor of passive resistance. The thought of Elli always makes Roland uncomfortable: Elli, who knew him too well, in ways he wasn't anymore. She refused to understand him, and he couldn't understand her. He needed his freedom. He was tired of her. Perhaps she was tired of him. There had been as many reasons to split as they had time to think up. Maybe, Roland thinks, everyone grows tired of his partner, only some conceal their boredom better than others. He yawns.

The festival chairman checks his watch. M. Roland's time's not up; another twenty-five minutes. And after all, his fee had in their eyes been a fortune.

Suddenly he wants the woman in the rose hat.

It is mad. The backs of his legs tell him to grab her, to tear her expensive dress, to carry her away he knew not where. He knows it is not the kind of thing she is used to. What has happened? It is altogether too absurd. The issue here is one of control and lack of control. Over self, over others, it doesn't matter. Roland wants to pull her hat from her head, wind his fingers in her hair, consume her, lose himself.

He yawns, stretches, faking boredom. Très fatigué, pardon, jet lag. He feels something at his elbow. It is Clea, a glass of wine, a cube of watermelon on a ruffled toothpick, and a second idea for a film. He takes the wine, sights her through the glass's rim.

"Where are your children?" he asks.

"Tim's with Bill. Missy's at camp." Clea lowers her eyes. Then she sees and looks up quickly. "Why?"

Oh, she knows. "Haven't you had enough of this party?" he asks. "Wouldn't you like to go somewhere quiet? Sri Lanka, the Hebrides, Bora Bora? You name it."

She laughs and then looks around. The crowd is staying. Many here know her, know her husband. She has stopped smiling.

Can he tell what she is thinking? Yves Roland, think of it.

Perhaps she recalls the revolutionary love scenes of his films, the arranged views of passion lighted artfully, draped with swaths of sheet, buttressed by mounds of pillows. Perfection. Shoulders, backs, legs, breasts, kisses, caresses, ecstasy, soft focus, low light. A dream come true.

"Well, O.K.," she says.

It will be a simple matter: these things are always simple matters. They won't go anywhere, really. Her house, his room. Yves reaches for Clea's hand, heading for the door.

Near the door the woman in the rose hat stands facing the other way, talking to the festival chairman, a bespectacled and intense young professor. As Roland passes her, he seems to trip, go off balance, but in fact he has calculated his misstep. He throws a block into the woman's elegant black silk back. She says "Oh!" and lurches forward, her hat jarred from its place and her wine spilling onto the chairman.

The chairman mutters through his teeth, "What a clumsy bastard." He is disgusted. Yves Roland isn't holding up his end of the deal.

Yves continues toward the door, reaching for Clea's hand, as though it is a magnet pulling him against his wishes.

"Mr. Roland," the chairman says, "it's early."

"I'm sorry, I never learn about red wine. Dreadful headache," he lies, stepping backward toward Clea. Yves is now in the hall. Clea is ahead of him, he is still reaching for her hand, practically running. It is as though they are in a silent high boxwood maze. Sound is irrelevant. All that matters is movement, action, and what lies directly ahead.

The chairman leans out the door. "Your envelope—" he says, waving as though he's flagging a train.

"You can mail me the check," Yves calls back to him. Whether they do or not makes no difference. It is, after all, only money.

American Express

•

JAMES SALTER

It's hard to think of all the places and nights, Nicola's like a railway car, deep and gleaming, the crowd at the Un Deux Trois, Billy's. Unknown brilliant faces jammed at the bar. The dark, dramatic eye that blazes for a moment and disappears.

In those days they were living in apartments with funny furniture and on Sundays sleeping until noon. They were in the last rank of the armies of law. Clever junior partners were above them, partners, associates, men in fine suits who had lunch at the Four Seasons. Frank's father went there three or four times a week, or else to the Century Club or the Union, where there were men even older than he. Half of the members can't urinate, he used to say, and the other half can't stop.

Alan on the other hand was from Cleveland, where his father was well known, if not detested. No defendant was too guilty, no case too clear-cut. Once in another part of the state he was defending a murderer, a black man. He knew what the jury was thinking, he knew what he looked like to them. He stood up slowly. It could be they had heard certain things, he began. They may have heard, for instance, that he was a big-time lawyer from the city. They may have heard that he wore $300 suits, that he drove a Cadillac and smoked expensive cigars. He was walking along as if looking for something on the floor. They may have heard that he was Jewish.

He stopped and looked up. Well, he was from the city, he said. He wore $300 suits, he drove a Cadillac, smoked big cigars, and he was Jewish. "Now that we have that settled, let's talk about this case."

Lawyers and sons of lawyers. Days of youth. In the morning in stale darkness the subways shrieked.

"Have you noticed the new girl at the reception desk?"

"What about her?" Frank asked.

They were surrounded by noise like the launch of a rocket. "She's hot," Alan confided.

"How do you know?"

"I know."

"What do you mean, you know?"

"Intuition."

"In*tui*tion?" Frank said.

"What's wrong?"

"That doesn't count."

Which was what made them inseparable, the hours of work, the lyric, the dreams. As it happened, they never knew the girl at the reception desk with her nearsightedness and wild, full hair. They knew various others, they knew Julie, they knew Catherine, they knew Ames. The best, for nearly two years, was Brenda, who had somehow managed to graduate from Marymount and had a walk-through apartment on West Fourth. In a smooth, thin silver frame was the photograph of her father with his two daughters at the Plaza, Brenda, thirteen, with an odd little smile.

"I wish I'd known you then," Frank told her.

Brenda said, "I bet you do."

It was her voice he liked, the city voice, scornful and warm. They were two of a kind, she liked to say, and in a way it was true. They drank in her favorite places, where the owner played the piano and everyone seemed to know her. Still, she counted on him. The city has its incomparable moments—rolling along the wall of the apartment, kissing, bumping like stones. Five in the afternoon, the vanishing light. "No," she was commanding. "No, no, no."

He was kissing her throat. "What are you going to do with that beautiful struma of yours?"

"You won't take me to dinner," she said.

"Sure I will."

"Beautiful what?"

She was like a huge dog, leaping from his arms.

"Come here," he coaxed.

She went into the bathroom and began combing her hair. "Which restaurant are we going to?" she called.

She would give herself, but it was mostly unpredictable. She would do anything her mother hadn't done and would live as her mother lived, in the same kind of apartment, in the same soft chairs. Christmas and the envelopes for the doormen, the snow sweeping past the awning, her children coming home from school. She adored her father. She went on a trip to Hawaii with him and sent back postcards, two or three scorching lines in a large, scrawled hand.

It was summer.

"Anybody here?" Frank called.

He rapped on the door, which was ajar. He was carrying his jacket, it was hot.

"All right," he said in a loud voice, "come out with your hands over your head. Alan, cover the back."

The party, it seemed, was over. He pushed the door open. There was one lamp on, the room was dark.

"Hey, Bren, are we too late?" he called. She appeared mysteriously in the doorway, bare-legged but in heels. "We'd have come earlier but we were working. We couldn't get out of the office. Where is everybody? Where's all the food? Hey, Alan, we're late. There's no food, nothing."

She was leaning against the doorway.

"We tried to get down here," Alan said. "We couldn't get a cab."

Frank had fallen onto the couch. "Bren, don't be mad," he said. "We were working, that's the truth. I should have called. Can you put some music on or something? Is there anything to drink?"

"There's about that much vodka," she finally said.

"Any ice?"

"About two cubes." She pushed off the wall without much enthusiasm. He watched her walk into the kitchen and heard the refrigerator door open.

"So, what do you think, Alan?" he said. "What are you going to do?"

"Me?"

"Where's Louise?" Frank called.

"Asleep," Brenda said.

"Did she really go home?"

"She goes to work in the morning."

"So does Alan."

Brenda came out of the kitchen with the drinks.

"I'm sorry we're late," he said. He was looking in the glass. "Was it a good party?" He stirred the contents with one finger. "This is the ice?"

"Jane Harrah got fired," Brenda said.

"That's too bad. Who is she?"

"She does big campaigns. Ross wants me to take her place."

"Great."

"I'm not sure if I want to," she said lazily.

"Why not?"

"She was sleeping with him."

"And she got fired?"

"Doesn't say much for him, does it?"

"It doesn't say much for her."

"That's just like a man. God."

"What does she look like? Does she look like Louise?"

The smile of the thirteen-year-old came across Brenda's face. "No one looks like Louise," she said. Her voice squeezed the name whose legs Alan dreamed of. "Jane has these thin lips."

"Is that all?"

"Thin-lipped women are always cold."

"Let me see yours," he said.

"Burn up."

"Yours aren't thin. Alan, these aren't thin, are they? Hey, Brenda, don't cover them up."

"Where were you? You weren't really working."

He'd pulled down her hand. "Come on, let them be natural," he said. "They're not thin, they're nice. I just never noticed them before." He leaned back. "Alan, how're you doing? You getting sleepy?"

"I was thinking. How much the city has changed," Alan said.

"In five years?"

"I've been here almost six years."

"Sure, it's changing. They're coming down, we're going up."

Alan was thinking of uncaring Louise, who had left him only a jolting ride home through the endless streets. "I know."

That year they sat in the steam room on limp towels, breathing the eucalyptus and talking about Hardmann Roe. They walked to the showers like champions. Their flesh still had firmness. Their haunches were solid and young.

Hardmann Roe was a small drug company in Connecticut that had strayed slightly out of its field and found itself suing a large manufacturer for infringement of an obscure patent. The case was highly technical with little chance of success. The opposing lawyers had thrown up a barricade of motions and delays and the case had made its way downward, to Frik and Frak, whose offices were near the copying machines, who had time for such things and who pondered it amid the hiss of steam. No one else wanted it and this also made it appealing.

So they worked. They were students again, sitting around in

polo shirts with their feet on the desk, throwing off hopeless ideas, crumpling wads of paper, staying late in the library and having the words blur in books.

They stayed on through vacations and weekends, sometimes sleeping in the office and making coffee long before anyone came to work. After a late dinner they were still talking about it, its complexities, where elements somehow fit in, the sequence of letters, articles in journals, meetings, the limits of meaning. Brenda met a handsome Dutchman who worked for a bank. Alan met Hopie. Still there was this infinite forest, the trunks and vines blocking out the light, the roots of distant things joined. With every month that passed they were deeper into it, less certain of where they had been or if it could end. They had become like the old partners whose existence had been slowly sealed off, fewer calls, fewer consultations, lives that had become lunch. It was known they were swallowed up by the case with knowledge of little else. The opposite was true—no one else understood its detail. Three years had passed. The length of time alone made it important. The reputation of the firm, at least in irony, was riding on them.

Two months before the case was to come to trial they quit Weyland, Braun. Frank sat down at the polished table for Sunday lunch. His father was one of the best men in the city. There is a kind of lawyer you trust and who becomes your friend. "What happened?" he wanted to know.

"We're starting our own firm," Frank said.

"What about the case you've been working on? You can't leave them with litigation you've spent years preparing."

"We're not. We're taking it with us," Frank said.

There was a moment of dreadful silence.

"Taking it with you? You can't. You went to one of the best schools, Frank. They'll sue you. You'll ruin yourself."

"We thought of that."

"Listen to me," his father said.

Everyone said that, his mother, his Uncle Cook, friends. It was worse than ruin, it was dishonor. His father said that.

Hardmann Roe never went to trial, as it turned out. Six weeks later there was a settlement. It was for $38 million, a third of it their fee.

His father had been wrong, which was something you could not hope for. They weren't sued either. That was settled, too. In place of ruin there were new offices overlooking Bryant Park, which from above seemed like a garden behind a dark château, young clients, opera tickets, dinners in apartments with divorced hostesses, surrendered apartments with books and big tiled kitchens.

The city was divided, as he had said, into those going up and those coming down, those in crowded restaurants and those on the street, those who waited and those who did not, those with three locks on the door and those rising in an elevator from a lobby with silver mirrors and walnut paneling.

And those like Mrs. Christie, who was in the intermediate state though looking assured. She wanted to renegotiate the settlement with her ex-husband. Frank had leafed through the papers. "What do you think?" she asked candidly.

"I think it would be easier for you to get married again."

She was in her fur coat, the dark lining displayed. She gave a little puff of disbelief. "It's not that easy," she said.

He didn't know what it was like, she told him. Not long ago she'd been introduced to someone by a couple she knew very well. "We'll go to dinner," they said, "you'll love him, you're perfect for him, he likes to talk about books."

They arrived at the apartment and the two women immediately went into the kitchen and began cooking. What did she think of him? She'd only had a glimpse, she said, but she liked him very much, his beautiful bald head, his dressing gown. She had begun to plan what she would do with the apartment, which had too much blue in it. The man—Warren was his name—was silent all evening. He'd lost his job, her friend explained in the kitchen. Money was no problem, but he was depressed. "He's had a shock," she said. "He likes you." And in fact he'd asked if he could see her again.

"Why don't you come for tea, tomorrow?" he said.

"I could do that," she said. "Of course. I'll be in the neighborhood," she added.

The next day she arrived at four with a bag filled with books, at least a hundred dollars worth, which she'd bought as a present. He was in pajamas. There was no tea. He hardly seemed to know who she was or why she was there. She said she remembered she had to meet someone and left the books. Going down in the elevator she felt suddenly sick to her stomach.

"Well," said Frank, "there might be a chance of getting the settlement overturned, Mrs. Christie, but it would mean a lot of expense."

"I see." Her voice was smaller. "Couldn't you do it as one of those things where you got a percentage?"

"Not on this kind of case," he said.

It was dusk. He offered her a drink. She worked her lips, in contemplation, one against the other. "Well, then, what can I do?"

Her life had been made up of disappointments, she told him, looking into her glass, most of them the result of foolishly falling in love. Going out with an older man just because he was wearing a white suit in Nashville, which was where she was from. Agreeing to marry George Christie while they were sailing off the coast of Maine. "I don't know where to get the money," she said, "or how."

She glanced up. She found him looking at her, without haste. The lights were coming on in buildings surrounding the park, in the streets, on homeward-bound cars. They talked as evening fell. They went out to dinner.

At Christmas that year Alan and his wife broke up. "You're kidding," Frank said. He'd moved into a new place with thick towels and fine carpets. In the foyer was a Biedermeier desk, black, tan, and gold. Across the street was a private school.

Alan was staring out the window, which was as cold as the side of a ship. "I don't know what to do," he said in despair. "I don't want to get divorced. I don't want to lose my daughter." Her name was Camille. She was two.

"I know how you feel," Frank said.

"If you had a kid, you'd know."

"Have you seen this?" Frank asked. He held up the alumni magazine. It was the fifteenth anniversary of their graduation. "Know any of these guys?"

Five members of the class had been cited for achievement. Alan recognized two or three of them. "Cummings," he said, "he was a zero—elected to Congress. Oh, God, I don't know what to do."

"Just don't let her take the apartment," Frank said.

Of course, it wasn't that easy. It was easy when it was someone else. Nan Christie had decided to get married. She brought it up one evening.

"I just don't think so," he finally said.

"You love me, don't you?"

"This isn't a good time to ask."

They lay silently. She was staring at something across the room. She was making him feel uncomfortable. "It wouldn't work. It's the attraction of opposites," he said.

"We're not opposites."

"I don't mean just you and me. Women fall in love when they get to know you. Men are just the opposite. When they finally know you they're ready to leave."

She got up without saying anything and began gathering her clothes. He watched her dress in silence. There was nothing interesting about it. The funny thing was that he had meant to go on with her.

"I'll get you a cab," he said.

"I used to think that you were intelligent," she said, half to herself. Exhausted, he was searching for a number. "I don't want a cab. I'm going to walk."

"Across the park?"

"Yes." She had an instant glimpse of herself in the next day's paper. She paused at the door for a moment. "Goodbye," she said coolly.

She wrote him a letter, which he read several times. *Of all the loves I have known, none has touched me so. Of all the men, no one has given me more.* He showed it to Alan, who did not comment.

"Let's go out and have a drink," Frank said toward the end of the day.

They walked up Lexington. Frank looked carefree, the scarf around his neck, the open topcoat, the thinning hair. "Well, you know . . ." he managed to say.

They went into a place called Jacks. Light was gleaming from the dark wood and the lines of glasses on narrow shelves. The young bartender stood with his hands on the edge of the bar. "How are you this evening?" he said with a smile. "Nice to see you again."

"Do you know me?" Frank asked.

"You look familiar," the bartender smiled.

"Do I? What's the name of this place, anyway? Remind me not to come in here again."

There were several other people at the bar. The nearest of them carefully looked away. After a while the manager came over. He had emerged from the brown-curtained back. "Anything wrong, sir?" he asked politely.

Frank looked at him. "No," he said, "everything's fine."

"We've had a big day," Alan explained. "We're just unwinding."

"We have a dining room upstairs," the manager said. Behind him was an iron staircase winding past framed drawings of dogs —borzois they looked like. "We serve from six to eleven every night."

"I bet you do," Frank said. "Look, your bartender doesn't know me."

"He made a mistake," the manager said.

"He doesn't know me and he never will."

"It's nothing, it's nothing," Alan said, waving his hands.

They sat at a table by the window. "I can't stand these out-of-work actors who think they're everybody's friend," Frank commented.

At dinner they talked about Nan Christie. Alan thought of her silk dresses, her devotion. The trouble, he said after a while, was that he never seemed to meet that kind of woman, the ones who sometimes walked by outside Jacks. The women he met were too human, he complained. Ever since his separation he'd been trying to find the right one.

"You shouldn't have any trouble," Frank said. "They're all looking for someone like you."

"They're looking for you."

"They think they are."

Frank paid the check without looking at it. "Once you've been married," Alan was explaining, "you want to be married again."

"I don't trust anyone enough to marry them," Frank said.

"What do you want then?"

"This is all right," Frank said.

Something was missing in him and women had always done anything to find out what it was. They always would. Perhaps it was simpler, Alan thought. Perhaps nothing was missing.

The car, which was a big Renault, a tourer, slowed down and pulled off the autostrada with Brenda asleep in back, her mouth a bit open and the daylight gleaming off her cheekbones. It was near Como, they had just crossed, the border police had glanced in at her.

"Come on, Bren, wake up," they said, "we're stopping for coffee."

She came back from the ladies' room with her hair combed

and fresh lipstick on. The boy in the white jacket behind the counter was rinsing spoons.

"Hey, Brenda, I forget. Is it *espresso* or *expresso?*" Frank asked her.

"Espresso," she said.

"How do you know?"

"I'm from New York," she said.

"That's right," he remembered. "The Italians don't have an *x,* do they?"

"They don't have a *j* either," Alan said.

"Why is that?"

"They're such careless people," Brenda said lazily. "They just lost them."

It was like old times. She was divorced from Doop or Boos or whoever. Her two little girls were with her mother. She had that quirky smile.

In Paris, Frank had taken them to the Crazy Horse. In blackness like velvet the music struck up and six girls in unison kicked their legs in the brilliant light. They wore high heels and a little strapping. The nudity that is immortal. He was leaning on one elbow in the darkness. He glanced at Brenda. "Still studying, eh?" she said. They were over for three weeks, Frank wasn't sure. Maybe they would stay longer, take a house in the South of France or something. Their clients would have to struggle along without them. There comes a time, he said, when you have to get away for a while.

They had breakfast together in hotels with the sound of workmen chipping at the stone of the fountain outside. They listened to the angry woman shouting in the kitchen, drove to little towns and drank every night. They had separate rooms, like staterooms, like passengers on a fading boat.

At noon, the light shifted along the curve of buildings and people were walking far off. A wave of pigeons rose before a trotting dog. The man at the table in front of them had a pair of binoculars and was looking here and there. Two Swedish girls strolled past.

"Now they're turning dark," the man said.

"What is?" said his wife.

"The pigeons."

"Alan," Frank confided.

"What?"

"The pigeons are turning dark."

"That's too bad."

There was silence for a moment.

"Why don't you just take a photograph?" the woman said.

"A photograph?"

"Of those women. You're looking at them so much."

He put down the binoculars.

"You know, the curve is so graceful," she said. "It's what makes this square so perfect."

"Isn't the weather glorious?" Frank said in the same tone of voice.

"And the pigeons," Alan said.

"The pigeons, too."

After a while the couple got up and left. The pigeons leaped up for a running child and hissed overhead. "I see you're still playing games," Brenda said. Frank smiled.

"We ought to get together in New York," she said that evening. They were waiting for Alan to come down. She reached across the table to pick up a magazine. "You've never met my kids, have you?" she said.

"No."

"They're terrific kids." She leafed through the pages, not paying attention to them. Her forearms were tanned. She was not wearing a wedding band. The first act was over or rather the first five minutes. Now came the plot. "Do you remember those nights at Goldie's?" she said.

"Things were different then, weren't they?"

"Not so different."

"What do you mean?"

She wiggled her bare third finger and glanced at him. Just then Alan appeared. He sat down and looked from one of them to the other. "What's wrong?" he asked. "Did I interrupt something?"

When the time came for her to leave she wanted them to drive to Rome. They could spend a couple of days and she would catch the plane. They weren't going that way, Frank said.

"It's only a three-hour drive."

"I know, but we're going the other way," he said.

"For God's sake. Why won't you drive me?"

"Let's do it," Alan said.

"Go ahead. I'll stay here."

"You should have gone into politics," Brenda said. "You have a real gift."

After she was gone the mood of things changed. They were by themselves. They drove through the sleepy country to the north. The green water slapped as darkness fell on Venice. The lights in some palazzos were on. On the curtained upper floors the legs of countesses uncoiled, slithering on the sheets like a serpent.

In Harry's, Frank held up a dense, icy glass and murmured his father's line, "Goodnight, nurse." He talked to some people at the next table, a German who was manager of a hotel in Düsseldorf and his girlfriend. She'd been looking at him. "Want a taste?" he asked her. It was his second. She drank looking directly at him. "Looks like you finished it," he said.

"Yes, I like to do that."

He smiled. When he was drinking he was strangely calm. In Lugano in the park that time a bird had sat on his shoe.

In the morning across the canal, wide as a river, the buildings of the Giudecca lay in their soft colors, a great sunken barge with roofs and the crowns of hidden trees. The first winds of autumn were blowing, ruffling the water.

Leaving Venice, Frank drove. He couldn't ride in a car unless he was driving. Alan sat back, looking out the window, sunlight falling on the hillsides of antiquity. European days, the silence, the needle floating at a hundred.

In Padua, Alan woke early. The stands were being set up in the market. It was before daylight and cool. A man was laying out boards on the pavement, eight of them like doors to set bags of grain on. He was wearing the jacket from a suit. Searching in the truck he found some small pieces of wood and used them to shim the boards, testing with his foot.

The sky became violet. Under the colonnade the butchers had hung out chickens and roosters, spurred legs bound together. Two men sat trimming artichokes. The blue car of the carabiniere lazed past. The bags of rice and dried beans were set out now, the tops folded back like cuffs. A girl in a tailored coat with a scarf around her head called, *"Signore,"* then arrogantly, *"dica!"*

He saw the world afresh, its pavements and architecture, the names that had lasted for a thousand years. It seemed that his life was being clarified, the sediment was drifting down. Across the street in a jeweler's shop a girl was laying out pieces in the window. She was wearing white gloves and arranging with great care. She glanced up as he stood watching. For a moment their eyes met, separated by the lighted glass. She was holding a lapis lazuli bracelet, the blue of the police car. Emboldened, he formed the silent words, *Quanto costa? Trecentosettantemila,* her lips said. It was eight in the morning when he got back to the hotel. A taxi pulled up and rattled the narrow street. A woman dressed for dinner got out and went inside.

The days passed. In Verona the points of steeples and then its domes rose from the mist. The white-coated waiters appeared from the kitchen. *Primi, secondi, dolce.* They stopped in Arezzo. Frank came back to the table. He had some postcards. Alan was trying to write to his daughter once a week. He never knew what to say: where they were and what they'd seen. Giotto—what would that mean to her?

They sat in the car. Frank was wearing a soft tweed jacket. It was like cashmere—he'd been shopping in Missoni and everywhere, Windbreakers, shoes. Schoolgirls in dark skirts were coming through an arch across the street. After a while one came through alone. She stood as if waiting for someone. Alan was studying the map. He felt the engine start. Very slowly they moved forward. The window glided down.

"Scusi, signorina," he heard Frank say.

She turned. She had pure features and her face was without expression, as if a bird had turned to look, a bird that might suddenly fly away.

Which way, Frank asked her, was the *centro,* the center of town? She looked one way and then the other. "There," she said.

"Are you sure?" he said. He turned his head unhurriedly to look more or less in the direction she was pointing.

"Si," she said.

They were going to Siena, Frank said. There was silence. Did she know which road went to Siena?

She pointed the other way.

"Alan, you want to give her a ride?" he asked.

"What are you talking about?"

Two men in white smocks like doctors were working on the wooden doors of the church. They were up on top of some scaffolding. Frank reached back and opened the rear door.

"Do you want to go for a ride?" he asked. He made a little circular motion with his finger.

They drove through the streets in silence. The radio was playing. Nothing was said. Frank glanced at her in the rearview mirror once or twice. It was at the time of a famous murder in Poland, the killing of a priest. Dusk was falling. The lights were coming on in shop windows and evening papers were in the kiosks. The body of the murdered man lay in a long coffin in the upper right corner of the *Corriere Della Sera.* It was in clean clothes like a worker after a terrible accident.

"Would you like an *aperitivo?"* Frank asked over his shoulder.

"No," she said.

They drove back to the church. He got out for a few minutes with her. His hair was very thin, Alan noticed. Strangely, it made him look younger. They stood talking, then she turned and walked down the street.

"What did you say to her?" Alan asked. He was nervous.

"I asked if she wanted a taxi."

"We're headed for trouble."

"There's not going to be any trouble," Frank said.

His room was on the corner. It was large, with a sitting area near the windows. On the wooden floor there were two worn oriental carpets. On a glass cabinet in the bathroom were his hairbrush, lotions, cologne. The towels were a pale green with the name of the hotel in white. She didn't look at any of that. He had given the *portiere* forty thousand lire. In Italy the laws were very strict. It was nearly the same hour of the afternoon. He kneeled to take off her shoes.

He had drawn the curtains, but light came in around them. At one point she seemed to tremble, her body shuddered. "Are you all right?" he said.

She had closed her eyes.

Later, standing, he saw himself in the mirror. He seemed to have thickened around the waist. He turned so that it was less noticeable. He got into bed again but was too hasty. *"Basta,"* she finally said.

They went down later and met Alan in a café. It was hard for him to look at them. He began to talk in a foolish way. What was she studying at school, he asked. For God's sake, Frank said. Well, what did her father do? She didn't understand.

"What work does he do?"

"Furniture," she said.

"He sells it?"

"Restauro."

"In our country, no *restauro,"* Alan explained. He made a gesture. "Throw it away."

"I've got to start running again," Frank decided.

The next day was Saturday. He had the *portiere* call her number and hand him the phone.

"Hello, Eda? It's Frank."

"I know."

"What are you doing?"

He didn't understand her reply.

"We're going to Florence. You want to come to Florence?" he said. There was a silence. "Why don't you come and spend a few days?"

"No," she said.

"Why not?"

In a quieter voice she said, "How do I explain?"

"You can think of something."

At a table across the room children were playing cards while three well-dressed women, their mothers, sat and talked. There were cries of excitement as the cards were thrown down.

"Eda?"

She was still there. *"Si,"* she said.

In the hills they were burning leaves. The smoke was invisible, but they could smell it as they passed through, like the smell from a restaurant or paper mill. It made Frank suddenly remember childhood and country houses, raking the lawn with his father long ago. The green signs began to say Firenze. It started to rain. The wipers swept silently across the glass. Everything was beautiful and dim.

They had dinner in a restaurant of plain rooms, whitewashed, like vaults in a cellar. She looked very young. She looked like a young dog, the white of her eyes was that pure. She said very little and played with a strip of pink paper that had come off the menu.

In the morning they walked aimlessly. The windows displayed things for women who were older, in their thirties at least, silk dresses, bracelets, scarves. In Fendi's was a beautiful coat, the price beneath in small metal numbers.

"Do you like it?" he asked. "Come on, I'll buy it for you."

He wanted to see the coat in the window, he told them inside.

"For the signorina?"

"Yes."

She seemed uncomprehending. Her face was lost in the fur. He touched her cheek through it.

"You know how much that is?" Alan said. "Four million five hundred thousand."

"Do you like it?" Frank asked her.

She wore it continually. She watched the football matches on television in it, her legs curled beneath her. The room was in disorder, they hadn't been out all day.

"What do you say to leaving here?" Alan asked unexpectedly. The announcers were shouting in Italian. "I thought I'd like to see Spoleto."

"Sure. Where is it?" Frank said. He had his hand on her knee and was rubbing it with the barest movement, as one might a dozing cat.

The countryside was flat and misty. They were leaving the past behind them, unwashed glasses, towels on the bathroom floor. There was a stain on his lapel, Frank noticed in the dining room. He tried to get it off as the headwaiter grated fresh parmesan over each plate. He dipped the corner of his napkin in water and rubbed the spot. The table was near the doorway, visible from the desk. Eda was fixing an earring.

"Cover it with your napkin," Alan told him.

"Here, get this off, will you?" he asked Eda.

She scratched at it quickly with her fingernail.

"What am I going to do without her?" Frank said.

"What do you mean, without her?"

"So this is Spoleto," he said. The spot was gone. "Let's have some more wine." He called the waiter. *"Senta.* Tell him," he said to Eda.

They laughed and talked about old times, the days when they

were getting $800 a week and working ten, twelve hours a day. They remembered Weyland and the veins in his nose. The word he always used was *vivid,* testimony a bit too vivid, far too vivid, a rather vivid decor.

They left talking loudly. Eda was close between them in her huge coat. *"Alla rovina,"* the clerk at the front desk muttered as they reached the street, *"alle macerie,"* he said, the girl at the switchboard looked over at him, *"alla polvere."* It was something about rubbish and dust.

The mornings grew cold. In the garden there were leaves piled against the table legs. Alan sat alone in the bar. A waitress, the one with the mole on her lip, came in and began to work the coffee machine. Frank came down. He had an overcoat across his shoulders. In his shirt without a tie he looked like a rich patient in some hospital. He looked like a man who owned a produce business and had been playing cards all night.

"So, what do you think?" Alan said.

Frank sat down. "Beautiful day," he commented. "Maybe we ought to go somewhere."

In the room, perhaps in the entire hotel, their voices were the only sound, irregular and low, like the soft strokes of someone sweeping. One muted sound, then another.

"Where's Eda?"

"She's taking a bath."

"I thought I'd say goodbye to her."

"Why? What's wrong?"

"I think I'm going home."

"What happened?" Frank said.

Alan could see himself in the mirror behind the bar, his sandy hair. He looked pale somehow, nonexistent. "Nothing happened," he said. She had come into the bar and was sitting at the other end of the room. He felt a tightness in his chest. "Europe depresses me."

Frank was looking at him. "Is it Eda?"

"No. I don't know." It seemed terribly quiet. Alan put his hands in his lap. They were trembling.

"Is that all it is? We can share her," Frank said.

"What do you mean?" He was too nervous to say it right. He stole a glance at Eda. She was looking at something outside in the garden.

"Eda," Frank called, "do you want something to drink? *Cosa vuoi?*" He made a motion of glass raised to the mouth. In college he had been a great favorite. Shuford had been shortened to Shuf and then Shoes. He had run in the Penn Relays. His mother could trace her family back for six generations.

"Orange juice," she said.

They sat there talking quietly. That was often the case, Eda had noticed. They talked about business or things in New York.

When they came back to the hotel that night, Frank explained it. She understood in an instant. No. She shook her head. Alan was sitting alone in the bar. He was drinking some kind of sweet liqueur. It wouldn't happen, he knew. It didn't matter anyway. Still, he felt shamed. The hotel above his head, its corridors and quiet rooms, what else were they for?

Frank and Eda came in. He managed to turn to them. She seemed impassive—he could not tell. What was this he was drinking, he finally asked? She didn't understand the question. He saw Frank nod once slightly, as if in agreement. They were like thieves.

In the morning the first light was blue on the window glass. There was the sound of rain. It was leaves blowing in the garden, shifting across the gravel. Alan slipped from the bed to fasten the loose shutter. Below, half-hidden in the hedges, a statue gleamed white. The few parked cars shone faintly. She was asleep, the soft, heavy pillow beneath her head. He was afraid to wake her. "Eda," he whispered, "Eda."

Her eyes opened a bit and closed. She was young and could stay asleep. He was afraid to touch her. She was unhappy, he knew, her bare neck, her hair, things he could not see. It would be a while before they were used to it. He didn't know what to do. Apart from that, it was perfect. It was the most natural thing in the world. He would buy her something himself, something beautiful.

In the bathroom he lingered at the window. He was thinking of the first day they had come to work at Weyland, Braun—he and Frank. They would become inseparable. Autumn in the gardens of the Veneto. It was barely dawn. He would always remember meeting Frank. He couldn't have done these things himself. A young man in a cap suddenly came out of a doorway below. He crossed the driveway and jumped onto a motorbike. The engine started, a faint blur. The headlight appeared and off he went, delivery basket in back. He was going to get the rolls for breakfast. His life was simple. The air was pure and cool. He was part of that great, unchanging order of those who live by wages, whose world is unlit and who do not realize what is above.

Here and There

•

DAVID FOSTER WALLACE

"Her photograph tastes bitter to me. A show of hands on the part of those who are willing to believe that I kiss her photo? She'd not believe it, or rather it would make her sad, or rather it would make her angry and she would say you never kissed me the way you kiss my chemically bitter senior photo, the reasons you kiss my photo all have to do with you, not me."

"He didn't really like to kiss me."

"On the back of the photo, beneath the remains of the reversible tape I had used to attach it carefully to the wall of my room at school, are written the words: 'Received 3 February 1983; treasured as of that date.'"

"He didn't like to kiss me. I could feel it."

"No contest to the charge that necking with an actual living girl is not my favorite boy-girl thing to do. It's not a squeamishness issue, has nothing to do with the fact, noted somewhere, that kissing someone is actually sucking on a long tube the other end of which is full of shit. For me it's rather a sort of silliness issue. I feel silly. The girl and I are so close, and the kiss contorts our mouths; noses get involved, bent: it's as if we're making faces at each other. At the time, with her, yes, I'd feel vaguely elsewhere, as a defense against myself. Admittedly this has to do with me, not her, but know that when I wasn't with her I dreamed of the time I could kiss her again. I thought about her constantly. She filled my thoughts."

"What about *my* thoughts."

"And then let's be equally candid about the utter lack of self-consciousness with which I'd kiss her elsewhere, slowly and in a way I'd found too soon she loved, and she'd admit she loved it, she does not lie, she'd admit to the pillow over her face to keep her quiet for the people in the other apartments. I knew her, I knew every curve, hollow, inlet and response of a body that was cool, hard, taut, waistless, vaguely masculine but still thoroughly exciting, quick to smile, quick to arch, quick to curl and cuddle and cling. I could unlock her like a differential, work her like an engine. Only when I was forced to be away at school did things mysteriously 'change.' "

"I felt like there was something missing."

"I kiss her bitter photo. It's cloudy from kisses. I know the outline of my mouth from her image. She continues to teach me without knowing it."

"My feelings changed. It took time, but I felt like there was something missing. He just works all the time on well-formed formulas and poems and their rules. They're the things that are important to him. He'd tell me he missed me and then stay away. I'm not angry, but I'm selfish, I need a lot of attention. All the time apart gave me a chance to do some thinking."

"All the time apart I thought of her constantly—But she says, 'My feelings have changed, what can I do, I can't with Bruce anymore.' As if her feelings controlled her rather than vice versa. As if her feelings were something outside her, not in her control, like a bus she has to wait for."

"I met someone I like to spend time with. Someone here at home, at school. I met him in Stats class. We got to be really good friends. It took time, but my feelings changed. Now I can't with Bruce anymore. It doesn't all have to do with him. It's me, too. Things change."

"The photo is a Sears Mini-portrait, too large for any wallet, so I've bought a special receptacle, a supporting framing folder of thick licorice cardboard. The receptacle is now wedged over the sun visor, along with a toll ticket, on the passenger side of my mother's car. I keep the windows rolled up to negate any possibility of the photo's blowing around, coming to harm. In June, in a car without air conditioning, I keep the windows rolled up for the sake of her photo. What more should anyone be required to say?"

'Bruce here I feel compelled to remind you that fiction therapy in order to be at all effective must locate itself and operate within a strenuously yes some might even say harshly limited defined structured space. It must be confronted as text which is to say fiction. Sense one's unease as you establish a line of distraction that now seems without either origin or end.'

"This kind of fiction doesn't interest me."

'Yes but remember we decided to construct an instance in which for once your interests are secondary to those of another.'

"So she's to be reader, as well as object?"

'See above for evidence that here she is so constructed as to be for once subject as well.'

"A relief of contrivance, then? The therapeutic lie is to pretend the real is the lie?"

'Affording you a specular latitude perspective disinterest the opportunity to be emotionally generous.'

"I think he should get to do whatever makes him feel better. I still care about him a lot. Just not in that way anymore."

"By late May 1983 her emotional bus has pulled out. I find in myself a need to get very far away. I am driving my mother's car on hot Interstate 95 in southern Maine, moving north toward Prosopopeia, the home of my mother's brother and his wife, almost at the Canadian border. Taking I-95 all the way from Worcester, Mass., let me curve comfortably around the west of Boston, far from Cambridge, which I don't wish to see again for a long time. I am Bruce, a hulking, pigeon-toed, blond, pale, red-lipped Midwestern boy, twenty-two, freshly graduated in electrical engineering from MIT, freshly patted on the head by assorted honors committees, freshly returned in putative triumph home with my family to Bloomington, Indiana, there to be kicked roundly in the emotional groin by a certain cool, taut, waistless, etc. Indiana University graduate student, the object of my theoretical passion, distant affection and near loyalty for three years, my prospective fiancée as of Thanksgiving last."

"All I said to him then was do you think we could do it. He had asked me if he could ask me someday."

"I was home again for Christmas: as of the evening of 12/27 we were drinking champagne, lying on her carpet, discussing potential names for potential children. She said for a girl she might like 'Kate.' "

"And then all of a sudden it's like he suddenly wasn't there."

"At this point she'd bring up how I seemed suddenly distant and cold. I would explain in response that I had gotten, suddenly, over champagne, an idea for a truly central piece on the application of state variable techniques to the analysis of small-signal linear control systems. A piece that could have formed the crux of my whole senior year's thesis, the project that had occupied and defined me for months."

"He went to his Dad's office at the University and I didn't see him for two days."

"She says that's when she began to feel differently about things. No doubt this new statistics person comforted her while I spent two sleepless, Coke-and-pizza-fueled days on a piece that ended up empty and unfeasible. I went to her for comfort and found her cool and hostile. Her eyes were dark and she was silent and trying with every fiber to look overtly unhappy."

"He only came to my apartment to sleep. He spent almost all Christmas break either working or sleeping, and he went back to Cambridge a week before he had to to work on his thesis. His honors thesis is an epic poem about variable systems of information- and energy-transfer."

"She regarded the things that were important to me as her enemy, not realizing that they were in fact the me she seemed so fiercely to covet."

"He wants to be the first really great poet of technology. He thinks art as literature will get progressively more mathematical and technological as time goes by. He says words as correlative signifiers are withering."

"Words as fulfillers of the function of signification in artistic communication will wither like the rules of form before them. Meaning will be clean. No, she says? Assuming she cares enough to try to understand? Then I say that art necessarily exists in a state of tension with its own standards. The clumsy and superfluous logos of the yesterday gives way to the crisp and proper and satisfactory of any age. Poetry, like everything organized and understood under the rubric of Life, is dynamic. The superfluous exists simply to have its ass kicked. The Norbert Wiener of today will be triumphant in the Darwinian arena of tomorrow."

"He said it was the most important thing in his life. What does that make me feel like?"

"It's here. It's now. The next beauties will and must be new. I invited her to see a crystalline renaissance; cool and chip-flat; fibers of delicate shine winking in aesthetic matrices under a spreading flourescent dawn. What touches, influences, and directs us is what applies. I sense the impending upheaval of a great cleaning, a coming tidiness foaming at every corner of meaning. I smell change and relief at cost like the musty promise of a summer rain. A new age and a new understanding of beauty as range, not locus. No more uni-object concepts, contemplations, warm clover breath, heaving bosoms, histories as symbol, colossi; no more man, fist to brow or palm to decollétage, understood in terms of any thumping, thudding, heated nature, itself conceived as colored, shaped, invested with odor, lending meaning in virtue of qualities. No more qualities. No more metaphors. Gödel numbers, context-free grammars, finite automata, correlation functions and spectra. Not sensuously here but causally, efficaciously here. Here in the most intimate way. Plasma electronics, large-scale systems, operational amplification. I admit to seeing myself as an aesthetician of the cold, the new, the right, the truly and spotlessly here. Various as Poisson, morphically dense: pieces whose form, dimension, character and implication can spread like sargasso from a single structured relation and a criterion of function. Odes to and of Green, Bessel, LeGendre, Eigen. Yes there were moments this past year when I almost had to shield my eyes as I looked in the mirror: I became in myself axiom, language and formation rule, and seemed to glow filament-white with a righteous fire."

"He said he'd be willing to take me with him to the top. And when I asked him what top that was he got mad."

"I was convinced I could sing like a wire at Kelvin, high and pale, burning cool as a hair on a lemony moon, mated to a lattice of pure meaning. Interferenceless transfer. But a small, quiet, polite, scented, neatly ordered system of new signals has somehow shot me in the head. With words and tears she has amputated something from me. I gave her the intimate importance of me and her bus pulled away, leaving something key of mine inside her like the weapon of a bee. All I want to do now is drive away to bleed."

'Which is neither here nor there.'

"No, the thing to see is that it's exquisitely *there*. That Maine is different, fundamentally other than both Boston and the Midwest. Unfamiliar sights are an unutterable balm. I see rocks veined with glassy color, immoderate blocks of granite whose cubed edges budge out from the scraggly surface of hills and slopes that lead out in gentle sines from the highway. The sky is a study in mint, soft and unassertive. Deer describe brown parabola by the sides of the forest stretches."

'I sense feeling being avoided not confronted, Bruce. Maybe here we might just admit together that if one uses a person as nothing more than a receptacle for one's organs, fluids, and emotions, if one never regards her as more than and independent from the feelings and qualities one is disposed to invest her with from a distance, it is foolish and wrong then to turn around and depend on her feelings for any significant part of one's own sense of well-being. Bruce why not just admit that what bothers you so much is that she has given irresistible notice that she has an emotional life with features that you knew nothing about, that she is just plain different from whatever you might decide to make her into for yourself. In short a person, Bruce.'

"Now a huge black bird curves through the corner of my sight and lets loose a strangely lovely berry rainbow of guano on the center of the windshield, near Smyrna, Maine, and under the arc of this spectrum from a remote height a unit of memories is laid out and systematized like colored print on the grey, chewed-looking two-lane road ahead of me. The trip I took with my family here to Prosopopeia, just two summers ago, and how she came along, how she and my sister discovered they could be such good friends, how she and I touched knees instead of holding hands on the airplane because my mother was seated next to her and she felt embarrassed. I remember with my gut the un-breachable promise of a whole new kind of distance implicit in the dizzying new height we all seemed to reach in the airplane on this very long flight, up to where the sky first turned cold and then darkened to cadet and we smelled space just above. How the shapes of a whole terrain of clouds, from inside the sky, took on the modal solidity of the real: shaggy buffalo heads; arched bridges of frozen cotton; the topology of states; political profiles; intricately etched turds. We flew away over the flat summer board games of Indiana and Ohio. Thunderstorms over Pennsylvania were great inverted anvils that narrowed darkly to rain far below our belly. I remember a jutting, carbuncular ruby ring on the finger of an Indian woman in the seat across the aisle, a stained dot on her forehead, and robes so full they seemed to foam. Her dark husband, in a business suit, with white eyes and white teeth and impossibly well-combed hair."

'And this top you would take the girl to? And why now that she is irrevocably absent does she become that top, the loss of which summons images of decapitation and harm?'

"I-95 proceeds north to Holton, Maine, then curves east into New Brunswick. I exit the highway at Holton, pay my toll, and, via a side street that leads between the Hagan Cabinet Company and the Atrium Supper Club, come out on County Route 1, again heading due north, through dense farmland, toward Mars Hill and then Prosopopeia. The sun sets gradually to my left over ranges of pale purple earth I learned two years ago are colored by the young potato plants. An irrigation generator howls and clanks by the road a few miles out of Mars Hill, and in this purple now an intricate circuit of tiny rivers runs red in the late light. Just further up 1 is a hand-lettered sign announcing hubcaps for sale, the improbable wares displayed in long rows, glinting dull pink on a fence and the sides of a barn, looking like the shields of an army of dwarves."

'The sun setting to the left, which is to say the West, meaning you remember the West, here, Bruce, meaning one becomes uncomfortable at this new silence from a subject in a West we have evidence you remember. One voice cannot shut off another, even in a structure of lies, if light is to be shed the way we profess to want.'

"Perhaps I should mention that at the toll booth for the Holton exit her photo's receptacle came free when I pulled down the visor to get the ticket, and curved over to me in the backwash of the air of the window I had to open, and got half-wedged between the brake and the floor. In reaching for it I dropped my money on the floor and somehow touched the accelerator with my foot. The car moved forward and nudged the miniature gate that lowers to stop a vehicle until state business has been satisfactorily transacted. The woman in the toll booth was out like a shot, a policeman in his cruiser by the road looked over and put down something he was eating. I had to scoop up my money and fork it over at the gate. The receptacle was bent and dusted with floor-dirt and cracker crumbs. The toll-taker was polite but firm. There was honking."

"The trip Bruce and his family invited me for to Maine year before last was the last time I think everything was totally good between us. On the trip out he pointed at things out of the airplane window and made his mom and me laugh. We kept our legs touching and he'd touch my hand too, very gently, so his mom wouldn't see him. At his aunt and uncle's house we went to a lake, and swam, and could of gone water skiing if we wanted. Sometimes we took long walks all day down back roads and got dusty and sometimes lost, but we always got back because Bruce could tell directions and times by the sun. We drank water with our hands out of little streams that were really cold. Once Bruce was picking us blueberries for lunch and got stung by a bee on the hand and I pulled the stinger out with my nails and put a berry on the place and he laughed and said he didn't care about anything. I had a wonderful time. It was really fun. It was when Bruce and I felt right. It felt right to be with him. It was maybe the last time it felt to me like there was both a real me and a real him when we were together. It was at his uncle's house, on some sweatshirts and clothes on the ground in some woods by a field, that I gave Bruce something I can't ever get back. I was glad I did it, but I think maybe that's when Bruce's feelings began to change. Maybe I'm wrong, but I think it kind of drove him away a little that I did it finally. That I finally really wanted to, and that he could see that I did. It's like he knew he really had me, and it made him go down inside himself even more, to have instead of just want. I think he really likes to want. I think maybe we were just meant to be friends the whole time. We knew each other ever since high school. We had driver's education together, and took our tests for our licenses in the same car, is how we really got to know each other. Except we didn't get really close until a long time after that, when we were both already in different colleges and only saw each other at vacations."

"I hit Prosopopeia just as the sun goes seriously down and all sorts of crepuscular Maine life begins rustling darkly in a spiny old section of forest I am happy to leave behind at the corporation limit. Before I head for my relatives' I stop at an IGA to buy some cold Michelob as a bit of a housewarming present. Michelob is a beer my uncle loves and does not really drink so much as inhale—it being at present practically the only thing he can inhale. He has emphysema now, quite bad, at fifty-five. Even the few steps from a chair to the kitchen door and a hearty handshake and the appropriation of one of my light bags is enough to make him have to begin his puffing exercise. He sits back down in his chair with my bag in his lap and begins to breathe, hard, rhythmically, between pursed lips, as my aunt hugs me and makes happy sounds punctuated by "Lord" and "Well" and "I" and then whisks all the bags away upstairs in one load. I keep my bent receptacle with me. My uncle goes for a wheezer of adrenaline spray on the kitchen table and resumes puffing as best he can, rather as though he were trying to blow out a flame, which is perhaps close to what it felt like for him. He has dropped more weight, especially in his legs, and his knees through his pants have a stick-like quality as he sits. Even thin and crinkled, though, he is still an eerie, breastless copy of my mother, with: grey-white hair, an oval high-cheekboned face, long, thin nose, perfectly straight lips, and blue eyes the shape of almonds. Like my mother's, these eyes can be light and beady as a bird's or sad and milky as a whale's; while my uncle puffs they are blank, loose, away. My aunt is an unreasonably pretty sixty, genuinely but not cloyingly nice, a lady against whom the only indictment might be hair dyed to a sort of sweet amber found nowhere in nature. She is back and asks me what I want to eat for supper. I say anything at all. A television is on, with no sound, by an ancient electric stove of chipped white enamel and a new brown dishwasher. My uncle says I look like I was the one carried the car out here rather than the other way around. I know I do not look good. I've driven straight for almost thirty hours, a trip punctuated only by the filling and emptying of various tanks. My shirt is crunchy with old sweat, I have a really persistent piece of darkened apple skin between my two front teeth, and something has happened to a blood vessel in one of my eyes from staring so long at roads—there is a small nova of red at the corner and a sandy pain when I blink. My hair needs a shampoo so badly it's almost yellow. I say I'm tired and sit down. My aunt gets bread from an actual breadbox and takes a dish of tuna salad out of the refrigerator and begins stirring it up with a wooden spoon. My uncle eyes the beer on the counter, two tall silver six-packs already spreading a bright puddle of condensation on the linoleum. He looks over at my aunt, who sighs to herself and gives a tiny nod. My uncle is instantly up and gets two beers loose and puts one in front of me and pops the other and drains probably half of it in one series of what I have to say are unattractive, foamy swallows. My aunt asks if I'd like one sandwich or two. My uncle says I'd better just eat up that tuna salad, that they've had it twice now and if it hangs around much longer they're going to have to name it. His eyes are back in him and he uses them to laugh, to tease, just like his sister. He looks at the photo receptacle by my place at the table and asks what I've got there. My aunt looks at him. I say memorabilia. He says it looks like it had a hard trip. The kitchen smells wonderful, of old wood and new bread and something warm and sweet, a faint tang of tuna. I can hear my mother's car ticking and cooling out in the driveway. My aunt puts two fat sandwiches down in front of me, pops my beer, gives me another little hug, with a joy she can't contain and I can't understand, given that I have just more or less *appeared* here, with no reason and little warning other than a late-night phone call two days ago and some sort of follow-up conversation with my parents after I'd hit the road. She says what a wonderful surprise having me come visit them and she hopes I'll stay just as long as I like and tell her what I like to eat so she can stock up and didn't I feel so good and *proud* graduating out of such a good school in such a hard subject that she could never in a dog's age understand. She sits down and we begin to talk about the family. The sandwiches are good, the beer slightly warm. My uncle eyes the six-packs on the counter again and goes into his shirt pocket for the snuff he dips ever since he had to stop smoking. There is cool, sweet, grassy air through the kitchen screens. I am too tired not to feel good."

"I felt so sorry when he said he was going to go out of town, maybe for the whole summer. But I got mad when he said now we were even, summer for summer. Because him leaving this summer is his choice, just like last summer was all his choices too. He stayed in Cambridge, Massachusetts, last summer, to work on starting his senior project, and he got a job in an engineering lab, and he didn't even ever really explain why he didn't want to come be in Bloomington for the summer, even though I'd just got my B.A. here. But he sent me a big bunch of roses and said for me to come live with him in Boston that summer, that he missed me so much, and I went through a lot of deciding, but I did, I used my graduation present money to fly to Boston and got a job as a hostess in Harvard Square at a German restaurant, the Wurst House, and we had an apartment in Cambridge with a fireplace that was really expensive. But then after some time passed Bruce acted like he really didn't want me to be there. If he'd said something that would be one thing, but he just started being really cold. He'd be gone all the time, and he never came in to eat when I was working, and when we were alone at home he didn't touch me for a week once, and he'd yell sometimes or just be cold. It was like he was repulsed by me after a while. I'd started taking birth control pills by then. Then in July he didn't come home or call for a day and a night, and when he did he got mad that I was mad that he didn't. He said why couldn't he at least have some vestige of his own life every once in a while. I said he could but it just didn't feel to me like he felt the same anymore. He said how dare you tell me what I feel. I flew back home a few days later. We decided that's what I better do, because if I stayed he'd feel like he had to be artificially nice all the time, and that wouldn't be any fun for either of us. We both cried a little bit at Logan airport when he took me on the bus. In Bloomington my family threw confetti on me when I got home, they were so glad to have me back, and I felt good to be home too. Then a day later Bruce sent roses and called and said he'd made a ghastly error, and he flew back home too and said he was very sorry that he had got obsessed with all sorts of outside things, and he tried to make me understand that he felt like he was standing on the cusp between two eras, and that however he'd acted I should regard as evidence of his own personal shortcomings, not as anything about his commitment to me. And maybe I guess I had so much invested in the relationship by then that I said OK that's OK, and he stayed in Bloomington over a week, and we did everything together, and at night he made me feel wonderful, it could really be wonderful being intimate with him, and he said he was making me feel wonderful because he wanted to, not because he thought he had to. Then he went back to Cambridge and said wait for me till Thanksgiving and I'll come back to you, so I did, I even turned down friendly lunch invitations and football tickets from guys in my classes. And then Thanksgiving and Christmas felt to me like the exact same thing as that bad part of the summer in Boston. My feelings just started to change. It wasn't all him. I just felt over a long time like there was something missing, and I'm selfish, I can only feel like I'm giving more than I'm getting for so long."

'Bruce, perhaps here is the opportunity to confront the issue of your having on four separate occasions late last fall slept with a Boston University sophomore from Great Neck, New York. Perhaps you might care to discuss a certain Halloween party?'

"Last summer was no fun, and when I'd tell him that at Christmas he'd get mad and tell me not to bring it up unless I was trying to really tell him something. I'd already started to be friends with the guy from Stats, but I wouldn't have even started hanging around with him if things had been good with Bruce and me."

"I sleep and eat and sit around a great deal, and the red in my eye slowly fades. I wash my mother's windshield. For a time I devote most of my energy to immersing myself in the lives and concerns of two adults for whom I have a real and growing affection. My uncle is an insurance adjustor, though he's due to retire early at the end of the summer because of the state of his wind: the family worries about the possibility of his car breaking down on one of the uncountable Aroostook County roads he crisscrosses every day, adjusting claims. The winters here are killers. I have the feeling that when my uncle retires he will do nothing but watch television and tease my aunt; from what I can gather these are already his two favorite hobbies. He talks to me over the few beers he's allowed every day. He tells me that he's always been a homebody and a family man, that he loved spending time with his family—the children now grown and gone—and that there have been plenty of fools in his firm who spent all their time on their careers and then what did they have, really? My aunt teaches third grade at the elementary school across town, and has the summer off, but she's taking two courses, a French and a Sociology, at the University of Maine's Prosopopeia branch downtown. For a few days after I'm rested I ride over with her to the little college and sit in the campus library while she's in class. The library is tiny, cute, like the children's section of a public facility, with carpet and furniture and walls colored in the muted earth-tones of autumn rot. There is hardly ever anyone in the library except for two very fat women who are doing the inventory on the books at the tops of their lungs. It is at once too quiet and too noisy to do any real work, and I have no ideas that do not seem to me shallow and unworkable. I really feel, sitting, trying to work on the ideas that have informed the last two years of my life, as though I'd been hit on the head with a mallet. I end up writing disordered pieces, or more often letters, that I know I will tear up. I soon stop going to the UMP library. Days go by, and my aunt and uncle are impeccably kind, but Maine becomes another here instead of a there."

'Explain.'

"Things become bad. I now have a haircut the shadow of which in certain light scares me. It occurs to me that neither my aunt nor my uncle has once asked what happened to the pretty little thing that came visiting with us last time, and I wonder what my mother has said to my aunt. I begin to be anxious about something I can neither locate nor define. I now begin having trouble sleeping; I wake up very early every morning and wait for the sun to rise behind the curtains of my room. When I do sleep I have troubling, repetitive dreams, dreams involving leopards, knees, some sort of formless protoplasm that jumps up and down in place, a bent old cafeteria fork with crazy tines. I have a slow dream in which she is bagging leaves in our front yard and I am pleading with her to be there for me again and she tells me to ask my mother and I go in the house and when I come out again with permission she is gone and the yard is knee-deep in leaves. In this dream I am afraid of the sky: she has pointed at it with her rake handle and it is full of clouds which, seen from here below, form themselves into variegated symbols of the calculus and begin to undergo manipulations I neither cause nor understand. In all my dreams the world is windy, disordered, grey."

'Now you stop kissing photos and writing letters and begin to intuit that things are, and have been, much more general and in certain respects sinister all along.'

"I begin to realize that she might never have existed. That I might feel the same way now for a different, or even no, reason. The loss of a specific reference for my feelings is wildly disorienting. Two and a half weeks have passed since I came here. The receptacle is lying on the bureau in my room, still bent from the toll incident. My affections have become a sort of faint crust on the photo, and I open the receptacle sometimes to see the silliness of what I've done since she did what she felt she had to. I now stay inside the house all day, avoid windows, and am not hungry. My testicles are drawn up constantly and begin to hurt. Whole periods of time now begin to feel to me like the intimate, agonizing interval between something's falling off and its hitting the ground. My aunt says I look pale. I put some cotton in my ear, tell her I have an earache, and spend a lot of time wrapped in a blanket, watching television with my uncle."

'Tell yourself what happens.'

"I begin to feel as though my thoughts and voice here are in some way the creative products of something outside me, not in my control, and yet that this shaping, determining influence outside me is still me. I feel a division which the outside voice posits as the labor-pains of a nascent emotional conscience. I am invested with an urge to 'write it all out,' to confront the past and present as a community of signs, but I lack the special sort of energy needed for this. For a few days I exercise instead, go for long, shambling runs in jeans and tennis shoes, move some heavy mechanical clutter out of my uncle's back yard. This makes me nervous and flushed and my aunt is happy; she says I look much better. I take the cotton out of my ear."

'All this time you're communicating with no one.'

"I let my aunt do most of the talking to my parents. I do, though, have one odd and unsatisfactory phone conversation with my oldest brother, who is an ophthalmologist in Baker's Beach, California. He smokes a pipe and is named Leonard. I like Leonard least of anyone in my family, and have no idea why I call him, collect, very late, and give him an involved and charitable edition of the whole story. We end up arguing: Leonard maintains that I am just like our mother and suffer from an unhappy and ultimately foolish desire to be perfect; I say that that has nothing to do with anything and that I fail to see what's so bad about wanting to be perfect anyway; Leonard says think how boring I would be if I were perfect; I defer to Leonard's extensive knowledge about being boring but point out that since being boring is an imperfection, it would by definition be impossible for a perfect person to be boring; Leonard says I've always liked playing games with words in order to escape the real meanings of things; I become almost hysterically excited and say that that's just the point and begin to spout run-on sentences about the impending death of lexical utterance; Leonard is unimpressed; things deteriorate; we wish each other well."

'Though of course your brother was only pointing out that perfection, when we get right down to the dark, cheese-binding heart of the matter, is impossible."

"There is no shortage of things that are perfect for the function that defines them. Peano's axioms. A Turing machine."

'Those aren't human beings.'

"No one has ever been able to convince me that that has anything to do with it."

'Could we possibly agree on whom you might ask now?'

"He said real literature won't be in words after a while. He said the icy beauty of the perfect signification of fabricated nonverbal symbols and their relation through agreed-on rules will come slowly to replace first the form and then the elements of poetry. He says words are dying and he can hear the rattle. I have all this in letters he sent me. He said poetic units that allude and evoke and summon and are variably limited by the particular experience and sensitivity of individual writers and readers will give way to symbols that both are and stand for what they're about, that both the limit and the infinity of what is real can be expressed best by axiom, sign, and function. I love Emily Dickinson and I said I didn't really understand but it seemed kind of cold to me, what he thought about poetry. I said a big part of the realness that poetry was about for me when I read it was feelings. I said I didn't know about him but I didn't think numbers and systems and variables could make people feel any way at all. Sometimes when I said that he acted like he was sorry for me and said I wasn't conceiving the project right, and he'd kiss me and play with my earlobes. But a couple times he'd had a lot of

beer and would get mad and say that I was just one of those
people that are afraid of everything new and think they're going
to be bad for people. He came so close to calling me stupid that I
almost got really mad. I'm not stupid. I graduated college in
three years. And I don't think all new things and things changing are bad for people."

'How could you think this was what the girl was afraid of?'

"Today, a little over three weeks here in Prosopopeia, I am sitting in my relatives' living room, with the cotton back in my ear,
watching the lunchtime news on a Canadian station. I think it's
nice outside. There is trouble in Quebec. I can hear my aunt
saying something from the kitchen. In a moment she comes in,
wiping her hands on a small towel, and says that the stove is
acting up. Apparently she can't get the top of the stove to heat,
that sometimes it acts up. She wants to heat up some chili for me
and for my uncle when he comes home for lunch. He'll be home
in the early afternoon. There's not much else for a good lunch in
the house, and she'd rather not go to the store because she has to
prepare for a quiz in class, and she can't get any burners to
work. She asks me if I could maybe have a look at the stove."

"I'm not afraid of new things. I'm just afraid of feeling alone
even when there's somebody else there. I'm afraid of feeling bad.
Maybe that's selfish, but it's the way I feel."

"The stove is indeed officially acting up. The burners do not
respond. My aunt says it's an electrical thingummy that comes
loose, that my uncle can usually get it working again but he
won't be home until she's already in class, and the chili won't be
able to simmer, reblend, get tasty. She says if it wouldn't hurt
my ear could I try to get the stove going? It's an electrical thingummy, after all. I say no problem. She goes for my uncle's tool-
box in the closet by the cellar door. I reach back and unplug this
huge, ugly old white stove and pull it out away from the wall
and the dishwasher. I get a Phillips out of my uncle's box and
remove the stove's back panel. This stove is so old I can't even

make out the manufacturer's name. It is possibly the crudest piece of equipment ever conceived. Its cord is insulated in some sort of ancient fabric wrap with tiny red barber-spirals on it. The cord simply conducts a normal 220 house AC into a five-way distributor circuit at the base of the stove's guts; a bundle of thick, wasteful wires in harness leads from each of the four top burner-controls and from the oven's temperature setting into outflow jacks on the circuit. The burner-controls determine temperature level at the selected point through straightforward contact and conduction of AC to the relevant burner's heating unit, each of which units is simply a crudely grounded high-resistance transformer circuit that conducts heat, again through simple contact, into the black iron spiral of its burner. There aren't even any reflecting pans under the burners. I tell my aunt that this is an old and poor and energy-inefficient stove. She says she knows and is sorry but that they've had it since before Kennedy and it's got sentimental value, and that this summer it had come down to either a new stove or a new dishwasher. She is sitting at the kitchen table, going over some French, apologizing about her stove. She says the chili needs to go on soon to simmer and reblend if it's going to go on at all, do I think I can fix the thingummy or should she run to the IGA for something cold?"

"I've only gotten one letter from him, all it says is how much he's taking care of a picture I gave him, and would I believe he kisses it? He didn't really like to kiss me. I could feel it."

"The harnessed bundles of insulated wires all seem well-connected to their burners' transformers, so I have to disconnect each bundle from its outflow jack on the distributor circuit and look at the circuit itself. The circuit is simply too old and pathetic and grimy and crude to be certain about, but its inputs and outputs seem free of impediment or obvious misconnection. My aunt is conjugating French ir-verbs in the imperfect. She has a soft voice, really quite lovely. She says: 'Je venais, tu venais, il venait, elle venait, nous venions, vous veniez, ils venaient, elles venaient.' I am deep in the bowels of the stove when she says my uncle once said it was just a matter of a screw to be tightened or something that had to be given a good knock. This is not especially helpful. I tighten the rusted screws on the case of the distributor circuit, reattach the main cord to the input jack, and am about to reattach the bundles of wire from the burners when I see that the harnesses, bundle casings, and the outflow jacks on the circuit are so old and worn and be-gooed that I can't possibly tell which bundle of wires corresponds to which outflow jack on the circuit. I am afraid of a fire hazard if the current is made to cross improperly in the circuit, and the odds are $1/2^{4}$ that anyone could guess the proper jack for each bundle correctly. 'Je tenais,' my aunt says to herself. 'Tu tenais, il tenait.' She asks me if everything is going all right. I tell her I've probably almost got it. She says that if it's something serious it would really be no trouble to wait until my uncle gets home, that he's a wonder with a tool and could have a look, and if neither he nor I could get the stove going we two could just go out and get a bite. I feel my haircut and tell her I've probably almost got it. I decide to strip some of the bundles of their old pink plastic casings for a few inches to see whether the wires themselves might be color-coded. I detach the bundles from their harnesses and strip down the first two, but all the wires seem to be the same dull, silver-fish-grey, and so old and frayed that they begin to unravel and stick out in different directions and become disordered, and now I couldn't get them back in the distributor circuit even if I could tell where they went, not to mention the increased hazard inherent in crossing current in bare wires. I begin to sweat. I notice that the stove's main cord's cloth insulation is itself badly worn and that one or two strands of copper 220-wire are protruding. The cord could have been the trouble all along. I realize that I should have tried to activate the oven unit first to see whether the power problem was even more fundamental than the burner bundles or the circuit. My aunt shifts in her chair. I begin to have trouble breathing. Frayed, stripped burner wires are spread out over the distributor like dirty grey hair. The wires will have

to be rebound into bundles in order to be reinserted and render
the burners even potentially workable, but my uncle has no tool
for binding, nor have I ever personally bound a system of wires.
The work that interests me is done with a pencil and a sheet of
paper, usually. Rarely even a calculator. At the level of today's
cutting-edge engineering theory almost everything can eventually be resolved by the manipulation of signs. I've never been
stumped on an exam. Ever. And I appear to have broken this
miserable piece of shit stove. I am unsure what to do. I could
attach the main oven's own conduction and temperature bundle
into a burner's outflow jack on the distributor circuit, but I have
no idea how hot that would make a burner. There is *no* way to
know without information on the resistance ratios in the metal
composition of the burners. The current used to heat a large
oven even to 'warm' could melt a burner down. I begin almost to
cry. My aunt is moving on to ir/iss verbs. 'Je partissais, tu partissais, il partissait, elle partissait.' "

'You're unable to fix an electric stove?'

"My aunt asks again if I'm sure it's no problem and I don't
answer because I'm afraid of how my voice will sound. I carefully disconnect the other end of each bundle from each burner's
transformer and loop all the wire very neatly and lay it at the
bottom of the stove. I tidy things up. Suddenly the inside of this
stove is the very last place on earth I want to be. I begin to be
frightened of the stove. Around its side I can see my aunt's feet
as she stands up. I hear the refrigerator door open. A dish is set
on the counter and something crinkly removed and through the
stove-slime I can smell a delicate waft of cold chili. I rattle a
screwdriver against the inside of the stove so my aunt thinks I'm
doing something. I get more and more frightened and irrational."

'Frightened of what?'

"I've broken their stove. I need a binding tool. But I've never
bound a wire."

'What does this have to do with anything?'

"It feels as though it has everything to do with it. I'm so scared behind this dirty old stove I can't breathe. I rattle tools."

'Is it that you love this pretty old woman and fear you've harmed a stove she's had since before Kennedy?'

"This is a crude piece of equipment."

'Whom else have you harmed?'

"My aunt comes back behind the stove and stands behind me and peers into the black hollow of the stove and says it looks like I've done quite a bit of work! I point at the filthy distributor circuit with my screwdriver and do not say anything. I prod it with the tool."

'What are you afraid of.'

"I don't think he needs to get hurt like this. No matter what."

"I think, behind the stove, with my aunt kneeling down to lay her hand on my shoulder, that I'm afraid of absolutely everything there is."

'Yes.'

Île Sèche

•

SUSAN MINOT

In the morning before sailing for Île Sèche, they went into town. The boathand dropped them off, then sped away to get ice.

The girl and the man strolled through the narrow streets, stepping aside to let the cars pass. Neither of them had been on St. Bart's before, but the man knew other islands and was pointing out charming aspects of the architecture. The man was tall, at least a foot taller than the girl, with grey hair and an eager pleasant expression, which suddenly vanished at the sound of a jackhammer down the road. The girl, following behind, looked the ingénue. She was an actress and that was her usual role. She was in the middle of asking a question when the man grabbed her out of the way of a car.

Meg flushed a little and walked on. How odd it was that they were here together. She did not know Charles Howe well, though she'd been hearing the name Charles Howe for years. It was not until her recent success off-Broadway that he'd swooped down on her from that lofty place where deals were made and plays produced. She was rather frightened, but, mostly, flattered. People warned her to watch out. Flashing a smile, Charles Howe said they were right. She laughed at his teasing. Almost a year ago, she'd been weeping in a bathtub, the only private place in the loft, because the fellow she was living with did not—not yet anyway—though he said he would, eventually—want to get married.

The man stopped at a motorbike shop. "Why don't you take one?" he said. "While I make my calls." Meg assumed the calls included the other girlfriend. A wind-surfing champion in California. Meg had not asked him about her.

A small traffic jam was forming. The jackhammer made a deafening noise. "So?" said the man. "Take a little spin?" He looked down at the girl.

She hesitated. They waited for someone to come over and help them.

"Do you or not?" he shouted above the noise. "Because if you don't . . ."

"Actually," she said and fingered the rubber grip of the handlebars.

"What?" he screamed.

She felt suddenly very far from everything. "I don't know," she said. "I don't think I trust myself on these."

"Well. Then. Then we shouldn't hang around. Better get a cup of coffee. Safer."

"They just make me nervous," she said, but that wasn't it. She'd ridden them before. It was something else.

He had already turned and was walking away. "Much safer. Yes, let's get a cup of coffee."

At the end of the street was a steep hill. "I think I'll keep going and walk up to the lighthouse," Meg said. They'd seen it from the boat, a white milk bottle with a red cap.

"Yes, you do that." He seemed relieved. He took her grocery bag, adding it to the one he carried. They set off apart.

Once away from him her step grew lighter and she practically ran up the hill. Up close the lighthouse was small. Down in the harbor she could see his boat, *Vapeur,* placid and certain, its bow pointing the same way as the other boats, but more lovely because it was his boat. At night his boat was like a cradle, the

clouds ghostlike through the oval windows. The wind flapped
the canvas.

That afternoon they anchored by the ribbed cliffs of Île Sèche.
The boathand brought them ashore in the dinghy, declining the
invitation to walk around the island with them. He wasn't one
for climbing in high places, he said with a bright expression, and
didn't like the look of those goats.

The beach where they landed was grey and white, the stones
fist-size, like paperweights. They tied on their sneakers. Meg saw
brain coral, with its maze pattern, and smooth rocks with
smooth holes bored partway through, and bits that looked like
petrified snowflakes. She reached for a goat bone that was like an
ivory shoehorn and *splat!* near her hand, a yellow foamy crap
from the sky landed on the smooth stones. A pelican, eerily close
to her, angled by on crippled wings. Then she saw the man was
heading up the hill.

It rose steeply. The dots they'd seen from afar became cactus
plants close up, swollen pincushions with tilted maroon chimneys and, in the dark red fur on top, one tiny shocking-pink
flower clashing with the red velvet. The man and the girl crossed
a wide bald place hammocked between two bluffs. The grass had
been bitten away. Startled goats flashed brown rears before gam-
boling off on thin legs. From the boat the bluffs had seemed
huge, a landscape in a Wyoming western. Up close they were
small enough to climb. It was the reverse of how perspective was
supposed to work, that things turned smaller when you drew
close to them. It had happened before with the lighthouse.

They climbed the steep bluff. The volcanic rock, melted thousands of years ago, was hardened into palm-size steps, soft and
sloping like melted wax. Charles Howe was behind her, a different climbing from the late nights in New York up deserted stairs.

They reached the tip in a thick wind. It was lovely to stand
there with the black rock dropping in folds beneath them. A
band of goats on the next peak eyed them.

On the man's large face was a rapturous expression. One hand was clamped on his sun hat. The girl was breathless.

"This is alright, isn't it?" he said.

"It's beautiful." She was smiling.

"Look." Charles Howe dismissed the horizon with his hand. "Nothing between us and England."

It was like no place the girl had seen, this primitive island with the pelicans angling by on their prehistoric wings. A blue haze hung at the horizon in a fine misty net. Meg had spent time on other islands, stepping off rocky beaches in Maine into the dark pines, discovering things in the dark shadows. Something as small as a mushroom, its hat ruffled at a dapper angle, could become the most remarkable thing, rare, something to examine.

The man stepped along the razorback. Meg noticed the shells cracked open by flying birds. To one side was a straight drop to the water pounding its head against the cliff.

"Wait," Meg said and was surprised at the weakness in her voice.

Charles Howe turned, frowning. "You alright?"

She nodded, stunned. There was nothing difficult about where they were walking, a sort of ledge. She'd walked narrow places hundreds of times, but the dark-shaded ocean was teeming straight down and his hardness threw her off. Her bearings suddenly went and her hand was suspended, toward him.

He grabbed her arm just as she tipped. He grabbed it hard and pulled her near and set her firmly again on her feet. Then he released her. She glanced desperately off. Neither spoke of it. It had hardly happened. Her heart was beating wildly.

The man set off, to be away from her. They went down the melted steps on the other side. The girl, feeling the bruise where he'd gripped her, felt light-headed and, catching her breath, calm. They stepped back on the ground, a crazed network of goat paths. She wanted to say something to him. "Look at the light," she said. The cactus plants were lit in fuzzy outlines, the tassel-ended grass flared in blond torches. Nothing moved.

"What?" said the man ahead of her. His voice was impatient again.

But she would not be scared. "Look," she repeated.

He turned around but did not look where she was pointing. He looked at her. His face was blank and inscrutable.

Still she refused to see it. She took in the sun. The air was fresh and balmy, and across the flat ocean stretched a bright carpet to the sun, which was lower now, and from this height made everything expansive and wide. She picked up a small stone and threw it near him, thinking it was what a playful, spirited girl would do. She was determined not to be defeated by him. And yet, something tightened in her chest.

They wandered apart, he drifting down, she staying higher along the ridge. There was no water on the island, only rain pooled in marshy valleys. No one could live on Île Sèche. It was barren and beautiful. The next bluff cast a dark blue shadow on the next hill. The goats hobbled over the volcanic rock, the cactus bristled. They too might skitter across the hillside, coming alive at night, growling in a low eerie way.

A white round thing bounced off some rocks and landed near the girl's feet. It was a sea shell. In the almond-shaped opening was a red claw folding up. As she watched, the claw pulled itself in slowly, its joints ancient, creaking, furtive. You don't notice me, it seemed to say, you aren't seeing me at all. Nearby, tucked beneath a ledge, was another shell, smaller, then another beside that, all of them hiding their blue-edged fingers like reclusive old women drawing knuckles under shawls, tightening around a precious brooch. Some shells were chalky-white with turret ends. Others were turban shells, swirled black and pearl, tipped like a meringue. The shells were everywhere, the plateau was covered with them.

She turned toward the bay where the boat was. She could make out the boathand's figure on the bow, slumped into a sailbag, reading or sleeping. Down in the anchorage the boat looked small. The little claws had climbed a long way.

Her heart choked at such a wonderful thing, she was bursting
with it. Again she found herself on a high place with water
below, something surging within her, and nearby, the man, ines-
capable. Where was he now? She looked around. There, she saw
the white sun hat at a distance down the slope. He was sitting on
a rock, facing the bay, watching his boat.

"You should see it up here," she called to him. "It's covered
with hermit crabs!" Her voice sailed through the quiet air, thin
and clear. He was not that far away, he could hear. There was
nothing between them, no trees, no wind, no bird sounds. The
rumble of the surf was somewhere, but far off, part of another
watery world, down by the cliffs, far away.

But the man was not a part of any world. He did not turn
around.

The girl had not believed before what his teasing voice had said.
Now she understood it in another way, with his back to her, his
white hat obtuse and silent. She could go ahead and exclaim
over the light, be a part of this open air, take in the sea, walk the
uneven surface of this hillside with its loose rocks and cactus
tubes and hermit crabs, but she should realize what part he was
playing in it—his own. He had brought her here, it was his boat,
they could puzzle out the constellations together, but that was
all. He was, said Charles Howe's back set to her, separate. He
would not be a part of her.

She walked, quickly.

Maybe, though, this was the better way to be. Certainly it had
not worked with the fellow before, melting into each other's
lives, then being miserable with the blurring. Something *should*
be different. There was something about this man, that when she
was in his arms they were always warm and long and she was
protected in them. It silenced her. He stroked her gently, his
profile staring off in the dark, and close to him, she could admire
his stubbornness, that he would not put up with ridiculous
things.

And there were many ridiculous things. She had become one of them.

She walked faster, stumbled, increased her pace.

They returned to the anchorage of Gustavia. The man had guests flying in the next day.

In the evening the man and the boathand went into town to buy supplies and the girl took a swim in the harbor. The sun, orange and low on the horizon, popped out of sight, turning the sky pink-violet. Clouds rose up, golden, fisted, dwarfing the islands. In the dim light the rocks guarding the harbor became flat and two-dimensional, the anchored boats dark silhouettes tied with bow lines. The girl swam around in the syrupy dimness for a long time.

"How was the water, lovely?" the boathand greeted her when she climbed up the ladder. He told her matter-of-factly the grocery store had been closed.

The man was bent over the ice chest. "Hash for supper tonight," he said with a stiff smile. "Who wants a delicious drink?"

After they ate, while the boathand was washing the dishes below, the man told the girl she shouldn't swim at dusk. "Imagine the explaining I'd have to do," he said, his dark eyes flat in the light of the oil lamp. "Responsible for the untimely death of a bright young actress. Your public would never forgive me."

The girl smiled back at him.

"But really," he said, fatherly, "you could have been run over. These outboards come speeding out of the harbor. They couldn't care less. It's the last thing in the world they're paying attention to."

She felt flattered. "I was staying close to the boats," she said, smiling. Was he scolding her?

He shook his head. "I know these guys. They're maniacs. They don't see you. They run you over. Their propeller chops you up."

"I realized it had gotten dark," she said. "I was being careful."

Charles Howe's face stiffened and his mouth twitched with an odd fury. "You can't be careful if it's someone else who's running you over," he said.

The girl turned to the oil lamp where the flame was stretching with the draught. She put up her palm by the glass opening. The flame bent from side to side, then grew upright and still. There was a clatter of pans down in the hatchway, but the man and the girl ignored it.

He spoke with a lighter more hollow tone. "I do have to bring you home in one piece." He was asking for her smile. She felt a foreboding but gave him the smile back, aware now that it was long out of her control. He stood up, satisfied, and went below to see what the boathand was up to. Whatever it was, Meg thought, the man would be disappointed.

The flame near her fluttered again, threatening to go out. Meg watched it and thought of the morning at the motorbike shop. How much she had resented him. She would not be coming home in one piece after all. She would be run over, chopped up by a propeller, an innocent swimmer in what she knew were dangerous waters. An ingénue.

Wrong Stories

•

MILLICENT DILLON

There was an incident; I have told it but I have not told it right.
The core of it is what eludes me in the telling, and yet the core of
it is what has stayed with me these ten years.

I was riding in the car with Freda and Martin up Central Park
West. They are my oldest and dearest friends. (What does that
have to do with this incident? I see I am embroidering already,
worried that I shall not present them in the light which will
make my feeling clear, or perhaps they will read this and misunderstand.)

I was riding in the car with Freda and Martin. Freda was driving. Yes, I am sure of that, she was driving. I was in the back
seat. Was she driving because it was night and she sees better
than he? Incidentally, she is a very good driver. I have to tell you
also—this I am sure is germane—that she is an extraordinarily
sympathetic human being. She devotes herself to others. Yet every now and then—it is mysterious—something sharp and unexpected will come out of her. I have known her for so long that I
take this sharp and unexpected as part of her. Once, or when I
was younger, I used to try to analyze it in terms of her past. I
have found that useless.

. . .

Let us say she was driving. I am not going to be held to this as if
I were on trial. No, surely not. If I fear trial, that is my own
problem. We had just left Columbus Circle and were going
north. (On trial. What would I be on trial for? But yet I am on
trial: to say as exactly and as clearly as possible what it was that
happened in that incident. If I do not—It will come back again,
in any case. I am not free not to give this account the most
absolute attention. Whether you will consider it and dismiss it,
or make the appraisal that I put the wrong weight upon things, I
do not know. I am obliged to tell this incident. I do not believe
that I believe that anyone is obliged to listen to it.)

We had been talking about safe streets. We came to a red light.
"That side of the street," Freda said, pointing to the West side,
"is safe, but this side, the park side, is not safe to walk on in the
evening. A young boy, a student (Did she say where he was
from? Holland? France? Europe, somewhere, yes, Europe, not
Asia), was walking along the street on that side when suddenly—" No, she did not say what happened. She skipped all
that. She shook her head. She simply said, "He was found the
next morning, paralyzed and blind. It was terrible." Then she
stopped. The light was changing. "He died the day after," she
said. "It was a relief to everyone when he died."

I had time to think, this is one of those unexpected things that
comes out of her that I do not understand. I had time to think
that as we had already begun to move—No, I remember now, I
was not in the back seat, I was in the front seat. It is a large car
with a large front seat. I was at the window. I am sure I was at
the window because of what follows. And Freda was beside me,
and it was Martin who was driving. Yes, of that I am sure now.

I turned my head and looked out the window. I know there
was no other body, either Martin's or Freda's, between me and
the window. Now I remember something else. We had been talking of something else before the safe streets. Or perhaps we

didn't talk of the safe streets and I only made that up so there would be a logical progression. I have a mania about logical progression, which makes it hard to be the way I am, to live the way I live, with these illogical presentiments and sentiments, these unexplainable obligations. We were talking about children. Yes, that is what it was. "And Laurie will be twenty-eight next month," Martin said. (Laurie is his child from his first marriage. They have never had any children together.) It was hard to believe. And I thought of how twenty-eight seemed so old to us when we—Freda and I—were girls together.

I looked out into the park, beyond the street trees, to the low stone wall and I remembered that when I was a girl, impoverished in an impoverished city, Freda, who came from a family which was better off financially, gave a birthday party for me in the park. The girls from school and she and I rode in a hansom cab. Ordinarily I did not come to this part of the park. My family lived farther north, on the east side of the park, on One Hundred and First Street, in a tenement. Next to it, facing Fifth Avenue, was an elegant building. Thomas Dewey lived there. I used to see him now and then walk out of the building, out from under the canopy, and across the street to the park. It was before he ran for president. It was before he was defeated—though for one brief instant, he thought he was president.

When Freda gave me that party, it was like joy in the morning to me. Let me say something about joy, what I think of it, and what I think of darkness. I believe there may not be that much difference. I have been accused of being one of those who likes to fall into darkness. I don't think this is quite true. Is it that darkness and light are not separated out for me? No, rather it is that at some crucial point, it is not whether it is joy or darkness that matters to me. Yes, yes, of course I know that, given the choice, I would rather sing, dance, be happy. But there is an edge at which joy and sorrow disappear, at which what is crucial in life annihilates these terms. I didn't mean to get into this. I was only trying to tell you what happened.

Joy in the park, joy in the morning, the air so sweet—it was May. I saw no cars, I heard no other song but the horse's hooves on the asphalt. Central Park became the world. The skyline of the city receded. It was a day given to me; the others had come to be with me to celebrate. And it mattered. Yes, it mattered.

But now the blackness, which I say and believe is inseparable from the light: I looked out into the park, onto the sidewalk, where the boy had been lying, blind, paralyzed. Something intervened. A second incident, a shadow incident, grew out of the first, superseded it. Though he had died on the sidewalk, he had suddenly been lifted—to Heaven? Hardly—but to above. This is very difficult for me to diagram spatially. The shift had to do with the word *relief,* as if at the moment that word was spoken, his dead body was levitated, and I with him, watching him, in some space in which my obligation was to continue to watch. I was levitated but I lived. I knew nothing about him. How could I draw my breath—in pain or out—to tell his story? Yet it was not his story, only the incident that I was obliged to tell. I am trying to be as clear as possible, knowing that the greater the clarity, the sharper the emptiness, and the more likely that you will shrink from me. (I am like one of those people—one sees them at a party—telling the same joke over and over. Or better, to be kinder, like the Ancient Mariner. Only my hands are not bony. They are short and stubby and there are age spots on them which I try now and then to erase with cream—but that is hopeless, hopeless.)

What I want to say to you is this: Ordinary experience is not ordinary. The unseen is not hidden.

Even as I say this, I don't like it any more than you do. I am a normal human being in that I like comfort and ease. I don't like to be cold or hungry or uncomfortable. I like to be warm, coddled, safe. For instance, sometimes I'd rather just turn on television and fall into those images that are not mine, so I don't have to think my thoughts, so I can get out of my obligation to tell what I must tell—over and over again the wrong story.

. . .

Coming back to the city, Ruth could no longer justify why she had run away from it. It still had its power over her, could even now turn her returning into another escape. After all these years in an ordinary house, on an ordinary street, in an ordinary town, she had not yet found safety in that place from this.

Through the bus window she caught the street sign, 68TH STREET, and then, before it, on the window pane, the reflection of the small gold buttons on her coat, shining in the late morning sun. Expecting October weather, she'd worn her wool coat, though it was very warm, just like summer. Perhaps because of the warmer weather everything seemed slower than she'd remembered it as being. When I was a girl here, she thought, how fast everything and everyone sped by. I was too slow, I couldn't sort out what mattered. But now I don't have to keep up, I don't have to wonder whom or what I will meet in the next minute, at the next stop, on the next corner. There was a relief in not having to be on watch every minute for what was to come and a satisfaction in that relief that she could not mistrust.

On the long seat behind the bus driver two black women were talking. One woman was very dark, her body heavy, almost massive, in a black coat. The other woman was lighter-skinned, slim, contained-looking. She wore a neat tan coat. Against some seasonal cold, Ruth thought, that we three share.

The heavy woman spoke to the slim woman of a boy who had died (was it her son?), of a daughter injured in a car crash, of a mother who had diabetes and was blind. The slim woman stood and pulled the cord to signal a stop. She held onto a pole, nodding, listening, not saying anything. "But the grandchildren, one has a good job teaching and the other is a secretary to the president of Sears and Roebuck. So it's all turned out all right," the heavy woman called out as the slim woman got off the bus.

"So it's all turned out all right" was a good omen, Ruth decided, to be stored up for the future, to counter any past.

At Fifty-seventh Street she got off and began to walk east, trying to keep pace with the others around her, avoiding matching her steps to theirs. Across the street she saw a building under construction, its front wall like a great tilted mirror. She stopped and stared at the reflections in the dark glass. Just like any tourist gawking at wonders, she told herself, as if I'd not lived here for so long. But then it wasn't "here" that I lived, she corrected herself. That was a different city.

She crossed Fifth and then Madison, moving more slowly now, or perhaps the others were speeding up. At Lexington she went north to Bloomingdale's. At the information booth she asked the way to "Men's Sweaters." She had seen one she liked advertised in the *Times* yesterday. Yuri's birthday was tomorrow and Alma had said he needed a sweater.

But when she got to the counter and saw the sweater, she didn't like the color or the texture. She looked through the other sweaters; she couldn't make up her mind which to get, if any. She wandered aimlessly through several departments. There's too much stuff here, she told herself, feeling at the same time, I don't belong here.

On the mezzanine all the telephone booths were occupied. One man had the door of his booth open. In a loud voice he was saying something about an estate that had to be settled. When the booth next to his became free, she went in and dialed Alma's number at work. The receptionist put her on hold and kept her there. She tried to call her back, to say, "I can't wait,"—though it wasn't exactly true, she didn't *have* to go anywhere—but if she clicked the receiver she might break the connection altogether.

"You got me at just the right time," Alma's voice came on the line. "I was about to go out and see a client. I wanted to tell you that you and Yuri and I have been invited to dinner by the Gellers. They're old friends of Yuri's and Max has the same birthday as Yuri. I'll be home early, around five-thirty and I'll see you then."

Alma's words snapped Ruth back into place. She felt as if

she'd been readmitted through Alma's connections to others, indeed as if she'd never been bypassed.

As she left the booth, she noticed that the man at the next phone was no longer there. On the yardage counter nearby a bolt of material of a subtle green color caught her attention. She reached out and touched it. It was soft, far more delicate than she had expected it to be and tears came to her eyes.

In the front seat of the car with Yuri and Alma, Ruth felt herself carried along in a comforting stillness. The window was open to the warm air and the last light of the sun, going down behind the Palisades, glowed in the smoky haze. She looked at the cars going past in the opposite lanes. "There's so much traffic," she said.

"On this highway, always. They're talking about redoing it. What a mess that will be." Yuri shook his head. "If you look down there, you can see the World Trade Building."

"Where?"

"You missed it." He turned off, down the ramp. "We'll get another look at it later."

"This used to be a safe street," he went on, as he looked for a parking place, "but not anymore. Max said that all the people on the block are getting together and paying five dollars a month for a guard to patrol from nine to twelve."

"Why not pay five dollars more and have it patrolled from nine to three?" Alma said. "It would be worth it."

Yuri shrugged. "It was never like this in the old days when I lived here."

"I never liked this neighborhood. It has no charm." Alma spoke with a definiteness and an asperity in her voice that Ruth did not remember. Perhaps they've had a disagreement, she thought.

"I liked it. There was a lot going on."

Yuri found a parking place in the next block in front of a warehouse. Ruth got out first and waited for them to get the

packages out of the back seat. Up ahead was a dead end. Though
it was not yet dark, the shadows there were very dense. Ruth
thought of what Yuri had said about it not being a safe street
anymore, but he and Alma seemed unconcerned, talking, taking
things out of the car. If they had had a disagreement, it was over
by now. Alma locked the car and they walked in the direction
away from the dead end. Ruth looked back once, as if to correct
herself, but there was nothing to be seen.

The Gellers lived in a brownstone with a steep staircase leading to the first floor. On the landing Yuri tried to open the outer
door, but it was locked. He knocked; there was no answer.
"What's the matter with Max? He knew we were coming." Yuri
leaned over the railing toward the front window and yelled,
"Hey, Max!" He yelled again and then whistled sharply.

Max opened the outer door. "It must have gotten locked by
mistake," he apologized. He was short and paunchy and almost
totally bald. Ruth had expected him to be bigger, she didn't
know why.

Alma embraced him. "Happy birthday, Max." When she introduced Ruth, he nodded and mumbled and then led them
down a long hallway. At the door to the kitchen Marie kissed
Yuri and Alma with great exclamations of joy. She was a heavy
woman who carried her weight easily. She turned to Ruth. "I'm
glad you were able to come. All of you, go in with Max. I'll be
with you, in a minute."

Alma and Yuri had told Ruth that Max was a collector, but
she was not prepared for the confusion of objects that she saw
when she entered the living room. The walls were covered with
paintings, some abstracts, some primitives, some vivid, some
somber, some nondescript—many of them were hanging crook-
edly. There were piles of books and papers around the walls. At
the center of the room a long beige couch faced two leather
chairs.

Alma gave Max two packages. He opened them and mumbled

something. Marie came in, bouncing with vitality, and gave one box to Max and one to Yuri.

"What's this?" Yuri asked.

"Isn't it your birthday tomorrow? Open it. You too, Max."

Max opened his and held up a tie with a large design in pink and orange. Yuri's present was also a tie, gray and black in a small diamond pattern.

"It's very nice," Yuri said.

"I like that one better than this one," Max said to Marie.

"I thought you'd like the brighter colors."

"It's too pink for me."

"We'll go to Saks' next week and you can exchange it and pick out what you want."

"I heard you were caught in a bank robbery," Yuri said to Marie.

"Yesterday, at the bank around the corner. I went in to cash a check and the next thing I knew, they said no one was allowed out of the bank. I kept telling them I had to be somewhere for an appointment, but they said no one was allowed out until they had further information. So I stayed there for a whole hour and a half. The ridiculous thing was that it had all happened before I got there. Somebody had crawled into the bank vault somehow. So why did they have to keep us?"

Enclosed with the others in the cluttered room, Ruth felt herself on an edge, part of what was going on, yet detached from it. Outside in the darkness someone was patrolling or would be soon. Yet even the question of safety, of these safe streets, was not her safety. It's not my life, she told herself—though it could have been.

"When do you start painting?" she heard Alma ask.

"Next week," Marie said.

"When you're ready to start moving the things from the walls, call me and I'll come down and help."

"Don't call me," Yuri said.

"We're finally going to redo this room," Marie said to Ruth.

"It used to have rough walls. But then we had them smoothed over and a silk paper put on. That was ten years ago. You can see how faded it is. Now we're going to take the paper off and have the walls made rough again. A little crazy but—" She laughed and opened her hands.

After dinner Alma and Ruth helped Marie with the dishes. Max came into the kitchen and moved some plates from one counter to another, then mumbled something. The doorbell rang and he went to answer it. There were sounds of "Happy Birthday," from the hall and a man and a woman waved to Marie from the doorway of the kitchen. "Go into the living room," Marie said. "We'll be right in. You go in too," she added to Ruth and Alma. "You've done enough. I'll be with you as soon as I get this coffee pot cleaned out from the last time I used it."

Burt and Hilda, a youthful looking couple with white hair and glowing pink skin, were sitting on the couch when Ruth and Alma entered. Burt had already taken off his jacket and was loosening his tie.

"If no one minds, I'll take off my shoes," Hilda said. No one minded. "Good, since I've already taken them off." She picked up a pillow, put it behind her and leaned back.

Burt began to talk about their summer place in New Hampshire. At intervals, he arched his back and lifted himself slightly off the couch. Then he'd settle back down again. Yet a few minutes later, as he was speaking, he lifted himself again. Suddenly he pointed to Yuri and Alma and Ruth. "Which of you three go together?"

"This week I am a lucky man with two such goodlooking women," Yuri said and everyone laughed.

"Max, do you remember, years ago, that woman—what was her name—she used to live on this street, she and three men?" Burt lifted himself and settled back again.

"Anna Belinsky," Yuri said. "I remember her."

"Did you live here too?" Burt asked.

"For almost ten years."

"But that didn't mean anything, that she was living with three men," said Max. "Milton wasn't potent and Herman—" He gestured with his hands to indicate that there was a question.

"But Raggio was potent," Burt said, lifting himself again.

"Yes, Raggio was potent."

"I haven't thought about that in a long time." Burt sounded as if he were out of breath. Maybe that's what the lifting is, Ruth thought, it has something to do with trying to get his breath.

"Do you remember Raggio was assassinated on Fifth Avenue? The papers said he was an anarchist and that Mussolini's men had been out to get him."

"That's what the papers said, but it wasn't so. It was some husband. We never knew, but we suspected—" Max's voice trailed off.

"Is this a new couch?" Hilda asked.

"Yes, it's new," Max said with sudden energy. "How do you like it?"

"It's very nice, but I keep sliding off it."

"That's because you've got the pillow behind you."

"It's worse if I take the pillow out. This isn't the couch you had here last time, is it?"

"The white one with the down pillows? That one we got at Bloomingdale's. When we got it home, it just wasn't comfortable. The pillows kept flattening out and the couch was getting filthy, even though they said it was Scotch-Guarded. I called Bloomingdale's and finally they sent a man out. He sat on it and said he couldn't see a thing wrong with it. So I got my lawyer to call their lawyer."

"Bloomingdale's' lawyer?"

Max nodded.

"Did it do any good?"

"They told me to cancel our outstanding bill—I think it was seventy dollars—and they said, 'Do us a favor, don't come back.'

This one I got at an auction. It's eight feet long and it was only three hundred dollars."

"What a good buy," everyone agreed.

Marie came in with the coffee on a tray. "What an idiot! Guess what I did. I went to the bakery and got a marvelous chocolate cake. I've been looking all over for the box with the cake in it. I just remembered, I left it on the counter. I can see it lying there."

"It doesn't matter."

"Really, we don't need it. We've just finished dinner."

"I feel like such a fool. But it was right after that business with the bank." Once again Marie told what had happened to her, repeating her words and gestures exactly.

"It sounds like that movie," Hilda said, *"Topkapi."*

"No, not *Topkapi, Rififi."*

"Yes, that was it, *Rififi.* That was a good movie."

"Do you know," Max said, "that in the last two weeks we've found three wallets thrown right under our steps? And the robberies weren't even here on this block. The wallets were just thrown here."

"How do you know the robberies weren't here?" Alma asked.

"The wallets had cards in them showing addresses in Great Neck."

"The people could have been visiting here."

"No I don't think so."

"What makes you think not?" Marie asked.

"I just don't think so."

"What's the difference?" said Yuri impatiently. "Great Neck wallets or not Great Neck wallets. Let's change the subject."

"Anyhow," Max mumbled, "we sent them back to the owners."

It was after eleven when Yuri and Alma signaled to Ruth that they were ready to go. Yuri said something to Alma and then she went over to speak to Max. "No, no," he said, "it's fine."

"What's the matter?" Marie asked.

"Yuri thought Max might want to exchange ties with him, since he likes the other one better."

"We'll go to Saks' next week and we can exchange it then."

Walking to the car with Yuri and Alma, Ruth felt as if she had left the semblance of safety behind. It was back there in the cluttered room, where the easy talk of exchanges of sofas and ties had taken place. I too made an exchange, the thought came to her, as she looked into the darkness of the dead end street. I turned one life in on another.

"While we're down here, I'll drive around so you can see some of the new buildings," said Yuri.

They went south, passing crowds of young people moving through the warm night. "There's the World Trade Building with all the lights."

They turned north on the Avenue of the Americas. "It's not much like the Sixth Avenue I knew," Alma said.

"Everything's changed."

Just ahead a sign was flashing, 75°.

"It's so warm for October."

They drove past Columbus Circle onto Central Park West. "Now it changes again," Yuri said.

"This side of the street," Alma said, pointing to the west, "is still one of the most elegant streets in the city. But that side, next to the park, is the most dangerous. Right here a young foreign student was walking alone late at night. He didn't know. When they found him in the morning, he was blind and completely paralyzed."

They stopped at the light and no one said anything. Then Alma spoke. "It was a relief to everyone when he died."

Why did she say that? Ruth wondered. It's not like her. She looked out the window onto the east side of the street, to the low stone wall at the edge of the park. A street light was shining into a dense group of trees. She thought of the young student lying there, not seeing, not able to move. He was alone and near death, separate and shut off, while here in the city everyone went about their lives as they always did, not knowing, relieved not to know.

The light changed and they started up again. Once more Ruth looked out onto the park, to the low stone wall. In four days she would go back . . . back. Back there seemed to have drifted into obscurity. Peering into the darkness of the trees, she thought she saw a gentle stirring in the leaves, like a breath, like the onset of a sigh.

. . .

Well, plainly, you can see it was wrong, all wrong. I didn't invent my details, I merely placed them. (Perhaps I am incapable of invention. Or is invention only another form of placing?) I had heard the two women talking on the bus, and I merely repeated what they said. I was wearing a red coat with gold buttons on that trip. Yes, I did go to Bloomingdale's. (How it drives me mad, all that stuff. Buy, buy, it says. Yet I have already done most of my buying. How can I throw out all that is old when it is not really worn? I take very good care of things. With me they endure long past their usefulness.)

Yes, there was a conversation at a dinner party about that couch from Bloomingdale's. Yes, a letter had come saying, "Do us a favor, don't come back." Yes, the wife did go to the bakery, yes, she did leave the cake there, yes, there was a robbery at the bank. And the man who made that curious gesture of lifting himself and putting himself back down again on that couch—he was there, and I kept wondering, Why is he doing that?

But the incident, you see how it goes wrong. It tries to become something else with that last line about the sigh at the end. That line popped into my head, close to something out of some jungle story of Conrad's, I can't remember which one. Perhaps I was thinking about the jungle when I thought of the park and that is why that line came to me and I borrowed it or stole it. (I think I might steal any word to make it mine, though never would I steal a thing.)

"What are you trying to prove?" a friend asked me, when he read my story. An incident, I wanted to say, but that did not seem a proper answer.

"The problem with this story is that Ruth has no background. Who is she? Where has she been? What has she done?"

Stubbornly I said—I too make unexpected statements—"I want it left that way."

"But what does the story mean if we don't know the world she comes out of?"

I couldn't answer. I only knew I needed her to be without a past. Almost always the characters in my stories spring fully grown without a history. Is it to prove that the past does not determine the present? But isn't it true that I don't have to tell you where I was born, who my parents were, what my father did? You know who I am just by listening to what I say. You know what I believe, how I am simultaneously pretentious and afflicted with an abysmal sense of my own inadequacies. You know who I am—by my words, by my rhythms, don't you?

Some years went by and I returned to New York again and again. I began to wonder if I shouldn't come back permanently to die here where I was born. But this year, from the moment of my arrival, everything seemed different.

I took a cab from Kennedy to Karl's apartment, which I was going to sit for two weeks. Karl is an old friend who was going to be away for a month. Another friend of his was staying there the first two weeks, and I was to stay the second. We were to take care of his bird.

Karl lives in Westbeth, the subsidized housing for artists at the corner of Bethune and West, next to the river. He has one of the penthouse apartments, one huge room, perhaps forty feet by twenty feet. One wall is lined with windows and before them, on a shelf that traverses the entire length, are large plants, some seven feet tall, thriving in the west light. The bird in its cage is in the corner. The south wall is lined with glassed-in bookshelves,

filled with sets of old books (Anatole France among them, I
remember). At the left end of this wall is a door that leads to the
roof, where Karl has built a wooden deck, surrounded by barrels
of flowering shrubs. From the edge of the roof, you look out onto
the lower skyline of Manhattan. At this height it seems very
beautiful and, indeed, serene. The river is narrow here—Jersey is
just across the way—but going south it widens and you can see
the shape of the Statue of Liberty quite clearly. Almost directly
south is the World Trade Building.

Robert, the young man who had been staying in the apartment, opened the door. He was strange looking, extraordinarily
thin, his eyes luminous in a face that seemed to have known
considerable suffering. (I found out later that he was a magician,
and had been training for some years to be a mentalist, an escape
artist, and a psychic.) Robert told me that Little Bird had just
been fed and was fine. He added that he had left a package that
someone was supposed to pick up and they would call in the
morning. He hoped I would enjoy my stay.

When he left, I noticed a shadow persisting in the room, a
darkness not quite physical. Puzzled, I went to sleep. In the
morning the darkness was still there. It had settled upon me
with a heaviness I could not shake off. Was it only the darkness
of the morning sky, threatening rain, and the oppressive humidity? I made a few telephone calls. I arranged to make arrangements, but that was as far as I could go. I read, I turned on the
radio and listened to a classical station. I made myself go out to
D'Agostino's to get some groceries.

Freda called and asked me to come uptown for dinner. Grate-
fully I accepted. The trip to Eighty-sixth Street on the bus took
an hour and a half. It was the day of that sudden terrible storm.
Everything crept in the downpour. I was wearing sandals. What
was the matter with me, what was I thinking, wearing sandals in
New York in October? My feet got wet and I felt as if I were
coming down with a cold. Martin lent me a pair of his socks. (I
lost one of them. I cannot believe I lost one sock.)

I returned that night to find the heaviness still there. In the morning I stayed in bed later than usual. I felt stupefied. Was I ill? I got up and looked out the window. The sky was clear, the sun was out. I opened the door to the roof and let the fresh air in. The phone rang. It was the woman who was to pick up the package. "I live in the building," she said. "I'll come right up."

"I'll bring it down," I told her. I have to go out anyhow, I better go out, I told myself.

I took the elevator down to the ninth floor and knocked on the door of 9W. The woman, Edith was her name, opened the door and invited me in when I gave her the package. She led me to a purple couch against the wall and she sat on a red chair against the window. The room had been divided into many spaces and levels. Beds, chairs, tables, pillows—so many pillows, purple and red—were scattered about.

Edith was in her mid-thirties, I guessed, a thin woman with long hair and a pursed mouth. As we talked, now and then, I looked behind her, out the window, which faced north, with a view of the river. I noticed a strangeness in the way she spoke. It was not exactly slurring, it was not exactly whining. It was as if complaint were being continuously edited out, as if a naturally high voice had been purposely tuned to a deeper, less revealing pitch. Her voice had the sound of other voices held back within it.

She talked about her apartment, how long she had been there, about the levels, built by her ex-husband, who had left her alone with three small children. I said I had seen a note on the bulletin board in the lobby about an emergency meeting to discuss a threat to the continuation of Westbeth. Yes, she said, the Reagan administration wanted to stop the subsidies. Everyone was very upset, they were forming a committee. Where would they go, where could they find a place to live in New York that they could afford? She spoke of the morale in the building. It had been bad these past few months. There had been three deaths at Westbeth recently. One, the mother of a friend of her daughter's, had committed suicide. The second, a woman in her fifties, had walked out in front of a truck and been killed instantly. The third was a young man who had thrown himself off the roof. He didn't even live in Westbeth, she said. He had just come there to throw himself off, so the police had informed them. She sighed and said, "It's easy to feel you're the only one who has troubles. But everyone—everyone has problems."

I did not go out, after all, but went back up to Karl's apartment. As I opened the door, I saw there was a bird flying around the room. In terror I thought, Little Bird has escaped, how will I ever catch him? He was beating against the window and flew across the room in a panic at my approach. I passed by the cage and saw that Little Bird was still there. He had never gotten out, it was a strange bird that had gotten in. I went to the door to the roof and opened it completely. Then I stepped back and waited. Finally, the bird found its way to the light and flew out.

Seeing Little Bird safe in his cage, I suddenly felt my own gloom lifting. Perhaps it was the realization or at least the suspicion that it was not *my* blackness that enshrouded me. It was something in the walls, something in the very building that I was picking up.

I went out and walked in the city. I found myself, finally, on One Hundred and First Street. The building where I had lived was no more. The apartment house on the corner of Fifth Avenue, the apartment house where Dewey had lived, was still there. When I was a child and passed that building I thought myself irrevocably shut out from it by its wealth, by my poverty. I could not put myself into that place in imagination. Often I could imagine myself in other places, but not there. It seems poverty can stop imagination in childhood. How curious. I can say this now because as I passed that building that day I was loosed from restraint. I could imagine what it was to live in that building, to be Dewey, to have gone to bed thinking you were president and to have awakened the next morning robbed of victory.

All that day my feelings went through a wild swing, from joy to darkness to joy. I know one is supposed to cultivate the middle course, but in fact it is these oppositions that come one upon the other, so quickly, like a vast and silent reversal, that intrigue me.

I returned to Westbeth. I had to wait a long time for an elevator. Two of them were out of order. Everyone seemed to be taking the wait goodnaturedly. Standing next to me was a woman holding her mail. I could see her name, *Sarah Baral,* on the envelope. "Oh," I said, "you are Sarah Baral. Karl told me to look you up while I was here."

"How did you know it was me?" she asked. I was about to say I read your name on your mail and then, squeamishly, I decided not to. We got into the elevator and when it came to her floor, she said, "Why don't you come in for a minute?" I followed her down the cavernous corridor. (All the corridors in Westbeth are cavernous. It was originally built to hold the telephone company, to store bank upon bank of wires.) She opened the door to her flat. It was small and it was dark. It had a number of windows, all on one side of the room, facing onto an enclosed courtyard. Because of the way the light entered, only from one direction, the room seemed to be no more than a corridor. In a moment I was living there, had lived there a life of one-sided light. I never lived here, I told myself—though I could have.

Sarah made a pot of tea. We sat at a small wooden table and she talked about her husband's work. He was a poet who died twenty years ago. She herself was a poet, recognized in some circles for her linguistic sensitivity. She supported herself and her poetry by working as a bookkeeper in a small firm. In her spare time she was writing a children's book on bald eagles. She wore her hair, just turning gray, in a braid around her head. She must once have been very beautiful. Her husband, Karl had told me, had been a fierce man, always arguing and haranguing others. She showed me his books. She seemed to treasure his work more than her own.

When I left her, I went up to Karl's floor. As I passed through the small vestibule between his apartment and the next—there are only two apartments on the top floor—I saw a huge painting leaning against the wall. The neighbor is an artist who paints blowups of movie stills. This was a blowup of a scene of a crowd of men on horseback, pioneers and soldiers and Indians. I recognized one of the soldiers as Preston Foster, an actor in the thirties. Behind him, a little to the right, was one face, only sketched in outline. It was not like the others, so real, so precise in duplication of the movie still. It was a face that was amorphous, uncertain—invented.

. . .

When Alma Efron returned to New York after so many years, there was a memory between her and the city. It rose like a mist, gainsaying what she was seeing, at this corner, at that crossing. It cropped up, a shadowy familiar, as she walked from Broadway to Sixth Avenue. It had no substance, yet it veiled other bodies. So just now she had bumped into a burly man with a red face. Excuse me, I'm sorry, she murmured. She wanted to say (not to the man, but to the memory) "Do you see what you're doing?" But how could memory see? She was its only eyes.

The sky darkened, exposing roughened surfaces, then grinding them to gray. The rain began to fall, slickening the grayness.

I'll take the bus, Alma thought. No, I'll take a cab. I should spend. What am I saving for? But a bus came along right then and she got on it and even found a seat. It pleased her, after all, to be in the company of others, one of many women wearing open-toed shoes, unprepared for the downpour.

Everyone was so well dressed, she noticed, looking about the bus. It never was that way when she was a child. Then so many (she too) wore discarded things. Even the city wore a discarded look. If I hadn't been a child at the time, would I have lamented for the city?

You can't lament for it now, she told herself.

It didn't need lamenting for, not with all those new buildings, slivers, solids, stone, slick and slicker in the rain, mirroring back this memory to her, this impediment.

She got off the bus right in front of a shoe store, Byron's. The shoes in the window were neither too cheap nor too expensive. They seemed just right for her.

The clerk, a ruddy middleaged man, greeted her with a hearty, "What can I do for you?" In the window she had seen a closed shoe, a shiny maroon pump. "Is that waterproof?" she asked, pointing it out to him.

"Sure is. It's called a rain shoe. New this season. What's your size? Let me see if I have it." He went over to a wall of boxes and came back with one box. "I don't have six and a half medium, I have seven. But they run small."

She put the shoes on and walked around on the carpet. "They seem just right. But they won't stretch, will they?"

"No, they won't stretch, they're nylon. Nylon doesn't stretch."

She walked back and forth on the carpet. "I'll take them. Can you send the ones I was wearing back home for me? I don't want to carry any more than I have to. My luggage is too heavy, as is."

When she gave him the address, he said, "From California, huh? Funny thing, just this morning a guy I know—hadn't seen him for twenty-five years—came in and said hello. He lives in Oakland. Is that far from you?"

"Not far."

"Twenty-five years and I recognized him right away, the minute he walked in."

"Hadn't he changed?"

"Grayer," he said and shrugged.

"You're going to like those," he remarked as she paid. "I can see you're the kind that cares about comfort and those are really comfortable. It's a good price too. Everything in the store is at a discount."

It was her cousin Rose who had told Alma about Libby's apartment, saying that Libby was going to be out of town for two weeks. "You'd be doing her a favor if you stay there. You can water the plants and feed the bird. It's a nice quiet little apartment."

It was little, it was quiet, it was not nice. So thought Alma, closing the door behind her. All three windows faced one way, onto an enclosed courtyard, its base level with the sills. Perhaps it was a trick of the waning light—the one-directional light—that made her feel that she was still outside, that in fact there was no inside here.

Briskly she took herself in hand. She pulled the shades, shutting out the courtyard and the wet blacktop and the windows opposite. She turned on the lights. She put her clothes in the closet (spaces within spaces—yes, that was a help). She went into the bathroom, looked in the mirror, combed her hair, curlier now with the humidity—but so gray, so gray—went out into the kitchen alcove, put water on to boil, touched the dirt around the roots of the plants (wet, still wet), and checked the bird. It fluttered at her approach, a tiny red and white and black thing.

She made herself a cup of tea and sat at the table with her shoes off. She turned on the radio, listened to the news, then turned it off. And there was the memory before her, insistently demanding attention.

As self-protection she reminded herself that this memory, to be exact, was not hers. It had not been evoked by her hearing, her smelling, her seeing, but had been allocated to her, secondhand. She and Arthur had been sitting on their patio with Rose and Harry (How many years ago had the two of them visited? Eight? Ten?). It was a wonderful early spring day. The wisteria was blooming on the overhang above with its lavender fall; in the distance the rolling hills were green and soft; here and there

a stand of trees was cradled. There was no haze at all. Everything was very clear, she remembered.

The conversation had turned to the snow Rose and Harry had
left behind them, and then somehow to the violence in the city.
Where they lived, on Eighty-sixth Street, was it dangerous? Arthur had asked. "You're careful, you look around," Harry had
said. "When I walk at night on the side streets after I park the
car, I have my keys in my hand like this." He closed his fist.

"I don't do that," Rose had said serenely. "I figure if something is going to happen, it will happen."

"But you're not foolish," Harry said with irritation.

"No, I'm not foolish, I don't go looking for trouble."

(All this while they soaked up the sun, the only sound a mock-
ingbird calling out, and in the distance a chain saw whirring.)

"The main cross streets are pretty safe," Harry went on.
"There are always a lot of people around until midnight at least.
But for the rest—you just have to know. On Central Park West,
for example, one side is dangerous even early in the evening, the
park side."

"There was a young boy, a foreign student, he didn't know
that," Rose said. "He was walking there at one or two in the
morning. They found him on the sidewalk, blind, totally paralyzed. It was terrible."

She was silent for a moment. "He died the next day." She
shook her head. "It was a relief to everyone when he died."

Sitting on the blue canvas chair in the bright sun, Alma had
seen the boy on the ground before her, blind, unable to move. In
an instant he would be dead, his death cause for relief. The
others had gone on to speak of everyday things but she had
remained behind. She must keep looking, must watch over him
as he lay there, at the edge of death.

Almost at once the image had retracted—she could not hold
to it—though the sense of obligation had remained. Now and
then at the most unexpected times the image would reappear.
She might be wiping off the counters in the kitchen or throwing

out the trash at night, and it would come to her as a vague and shadowy afterthought. But then when Arthur had left, it had returned in sharper outline, as if it were preparing to fill in the final detail. She had never thought of herself as a woman who was given to this kind of imagining and it frightened her. But then she had never thought of herself as a woman whose husband would leave her for a young girl either.

And now this memory that wasn't hers, that concerned death, was accruing life in the city, growing stronger, sharper, larger, as if it had finally found its rightful place. Now, now, it seemed to be saying, appropriating the world of real sight, real touch, real smell. She had the sense too that she was indulging it in its brashness, as if she were deriving satisfaction from the actions of an unruly child—she who had never had a child, who had never wanted one (though now he, Arthur, had a child).

"Yes, things are better, they're definitely better," said Harry.

The three of them, Rose, Harry, and Alma, were sitting at the table after dinner. Rose had cooked a wonderful meal, lamb and pilaf, a salad of watercress and mushrooms and red peppers, and chocolate cake, triple layered.

"All those cross streets that used to be so bad are being gentrified now," said Rose. "You can walk on them and not worry."

"Well, I'd still take precautions, I wouldn't do anything foolish," Harry said.

"You don't have to worry," said Rose firmly. Then she told Alma about the vegetable gardens on the next street. "They also have a farmer's market on Eighty-eighth every week."

"They're tearing down a lot of the old buildings all up and down Columbus and Amsterdam," Harry went on. "Some of them they're redoing. Did you see the one on the corner? You can imagine what the rents will be. Do you know what we pay here? Five hundred a month for a two-bedroom apartment in a safe building. If we moved out they could rent it for a thousand with no trouble. More."

It was raining again. They could hear the drops falling against the window and an even harsher sound, the rain drumming on the metal box of the air conditioner. "We should have that air conditioner taken out for the winter. That sound drives me crazy," Harry said.

"Why don't you stay here tonight?" Rose turned to Alma. "I can make up the bed in a minute."

"No, don't bother, I'll go back downtown, all my things are there. Besides, I've got my new rain shoes on so my feet won't get wet."

"I saw them, they're nice. But are you sure you don't want to stay? It doesn't bother you being alone in a strange apartment?"

"No."

"Even here in the apartment every time Harry goes away on business, it's hard for me. It's not that I'm afraid. I'm just used to having someone around. I don't like being alone."

"It's not all bad. It has its compensations," said Alma defensively.

"Oh, I'm sure. And besides, it is a nice little apartment."

When Alma got up to go, Harry said, "I'll walk you to the bus."

"No, no, it's still early."

"I have to go out anyhow, I forgot to get the paper."

He walked her to Columbus and she insisted that he leave her, why should he stand in the rain? The bus would be along any minute and there were other people waiting. After he had gone, she waited almost ten minutes, but the bus still hadn't come. Suddenly she crossed Columbus and walked east on Eighty-sixth street toward the park, turning once to see that Harry was not watching her, as if she were doing something surreptitious. I can get a cab on Central Park West, she told herself.

On Central Park West she turned south, keeping to the west side of the street. She thought about what Rose and Harry had said: that things were better, safer. She had been harboring this memory for so long, waiting to deliver it here where it belonged, only to find that the city refused it. She had been holding on not to what was essential, but to what was archaic.

Across the street she saw the low stone wall of the park in the misted light of the street lamps. The trees were black in the rain, shrouded. It came to her that she did not know the exact place where he had fallen, where he had lain until he was found. Was it Seventy-ninth, Seventy-eighth, Seventy-seventh? She felt a sense of panic, she had to know, yet how could she know? Her heart was sinking as if she were the one driving it down. She saw a cab at the next corner and, calling out, began to run. Her right shoe slipped off at the heel and she almost fell. When she righted herself, the cab had already sped away.

In Libby's apartment she turned on all the lights. She took off her shoes. Seven was the wrong size. She should never have let herself be persuaded. Nylon did stretch, no matter what he said.

She undressed, she went into the bathroom, she took a hot shower. She got into bed (the sofa became a bed) and tried to read. She looked up from the book. The memory was everywhere—on the table, in the chairs, on the ceiling, on the floor, in the walls.

She jumped out of bed and went to the window. She pulled the shade up so fast it snapped on its roller. Across the courtyard she saw lighted windows, their shades partially drawn. She made herself recall the floor to ceiling windows in her own house, looking out upon the patio and the overhang with the wisteria—so beautiful when it bloomed—and the hills in the distance. She said to herself, I left there last Monday, I am going back in a week, I have lived there how many years, a life of—No, she would not evaluate her life, what had been saved by marrying Arthur, what had been lost by leaving here.

She pulled the shade down, crept back to bed, and covered herself. The place, the place where it had happened, what was the exact place? The boy was walking late at night on the park side. Out of the business some men appeared. They demanded money. He resisted. They threatened him, they pushed him, they beat him, they used a knife. They took his money. (It had not occurred to her before that he had been robbed.) They left him to die.

She heard the little bird fluttering. She should put a cover over its cage. Birds needed to be covered at night. On a chair she saw a large piece of blue material. She threw the covers off and picked up the fabric. It was far heavier than she had expected, as if its threads were doubled or quadrupled in the weave. She draped it over the cage so the bird was completely hidden. She could still hear the bird fluttering.

When next she checked it, lifting the edge of the dense blue cover, the bird was quiet. It was in its little bamboo cup at the center of the cage, cradled.

.   .   .

In the act of writing the story, I thought, Now, this time, I have it right. But later, when I showed it to my friend, he said, "I still don't know enough about the woman. What's her name, Ruth?"

"No, it's Alma."

"Well, whatever her name is, I still don't know who she is. What is her life like? What's her husband like? It's too vague. It's more like a sketch for a story than a story."

Stubbornly I said, I did give her a life. She lives in California. She has a husband who has left her, who has married a younger woman. I gave the husband and the second wife a child. Maybe that was my error, I thought suddenly, to put in the child. It reduces the incident, makes the boy on the sidewalk only a substitute for the child she never had. Yes, the story was wrong, wrong again.

I was invited to visit a class in autobiographical writing for seniors by the mother of a friend of mine, Miriam Smith. You will find it interesting, she told me, to see how under the guidance of the teacher we are all writing about our lives. It's a wonderful release, I never thought I could do it.

The classroom was long and narrow, with windows on two adjacent sides. There were twenty women and two men in the room. Most of the women were in their seventies, I guessed, though a few were in their eighties. (On the face of one of the women the skin was tightly drawn about her mouth, wrinkling and pulling at the same time.)

I sat on the side of the table across from the long window and looked out upon a hillside surmounted by a group of white buildings of different heights. It was a bright Northern California day. The light was so sharp, the sky was a pure blue. You know how it is sometimes, you feel that if you keep looking into that blueness you will fall into it, but then it turns and lightens, expanding in brilliance until you almost can't see the blue at all.

On the faces of those about me were the marks of age in all its singleness and its uniformity. When one looks at the elderly at my age, one is almost in their body. It is as if they provide a place, just next door, being readied to be moved into. One holds it off, that moving, tries this or that as a delaying action, knowing full well there is no real holding off. I looked about me and smelled a strange smell in that room. It was half-medicinal, half-decay.

The teacher, Mrs. Houston, moved her lectern to the middle of the table, just opposite where I was sitting. Her back was to the long window. "Would it be helpful to those of you on that side of the table if I draw the curtains?" she asked. "Then there won't be so much glare when you look at me." Yes, they said, and the curtains were drawn. I could no longer see the white buildings or the hills or the sky, yet I too was grateful for the end of the glare.

Mrs. Houston began to call the roll. A woman in her late sixties or early seventies, she wore her hair in a short bob, straight and thick, pulled back to one side by a barrette. The students watched her and listened with close attention.

"The name of this course is 'Speak, Memory.' Those of you who have been here before know this but for the ones who are new I'll tell you that I stole the name from Nabokov's autobiography."

She asked if anyone had done any writing during the vacation. "No one? Well I guess I shouldn't expect you to, on vacation. I'll give you an exercise today so you can get those writing juices flowing again. This is what we're going to do. I want each one of you to pick an incident, any incident from your life. Then I want you to tell that incident in one sentence or two sentences at the most to the rest of the class."

"Out loud?" someone asked.

"Yes, out loud. Don't worry, it won't be hard. Then, after everybody had done that we are all going to start writing the incident—each one his or her own incident—expanding on what you told us. Okay? Think for just a moment and then we'll go around the room, one by one. Mary, why don't you start?"

"I'm not quite ready, I don't know—" Mary said nervously.

"Just go ahead, don't agonize, take the bull by the horns, you'll be surprised how easy it is once you get started."

"The day I saw my grandchild for the first time," Mary said quickly. "It was in the hospital, I was looking at him through the glass. I kept trying to see if he looked like my son or my daughter-in-law or like my husband or like nobody."

"Good, that's fine," Mrs. Houston smiled. "There you have your beginning. Dick, what about you?"

"The day—when I was about ten years old—" Dick drawled, "the day Albert Stanger and me blew up his Uncle Lester."

"You didn't really blow up his Uncle Lester."

"No, we didn't really blow him up. What we did is we got this flash powder and we set it up all along the path to his front door so when he walked out it was like a mine field around him."

"Did it go off?" someone asked.

"Sure it went off."

"But it didn't hurt him?"

"Nah, it didn't hurt him. We didn't want to hurt him. Uncle Lester was a nice guy."

"Well, that sounds as though it could be very exciting, Dick," said Mrs. Houston. "Martha?"

Martha leaned forward, blinking as if there were too much light, though the curtains had cut the glare. She began to say something but then she stopped. She put her hands up to her lips and sat in silence.

"Do you want me to come back to you, Martha?"

"No, I'm ready," she said, taking her hands away from her lips. A spasm passed over her face and she was silent again. Mrs. Houston said, "Why don't you—" but Martha interrupted her, the words coming headlong.

"One day I was in the garage. It was in the morning, about nine o'clock. I'd gone in there to put some clothes in my Goodwill bag. I had the garage door open and my back was to it. I didn't hear anyone come in, but then I felt someone grab me from the back. I never did see their faces. I kept turning my head, trying to see who they were. There were two of them. But I never did see. They started hitting me on the head for no reason. They just started hitting me. For no reason." She put her hands over her face and began to weep. The woman next to her put her arm around her shoulder and patted her, saying, "It's all right. It's all right."

Mrs. Houston said, "Are you sure you want to write about that, Martha? Maybe you shouldn't upset yourself."

"No," Martha said, drying her tears. "I do want to write about it. Maybe it will help me to write about it. Every time I go into the garage I still get nervous, though it's been a long time . . ."

Later I thought of the incidents that had been told: the painful ones and the funny ones, moving in their truth and in their brevity. They were what had happened to these men and women, out of their own lives, not out of another's. Listening, I

had believed them, had felt wonder with Mary, sly amusement
with Dick, pain with Martha. (Why did Mrs. Houston call them
by their first names? It made me feel uncomfortable, as if they
were being treated like children?)

But my own incident—that was not from my life but from
another's, that I was obliged to tell over and over again though
there was never enough detail or the right kind of detail to fill it
in, to flesh it out—Even as I told it I doubted myself in the
telling, knowing that it was the unseen I wanted to tell directly.
But it is not possible.

I should stop, give up, not try again.

Or is it possible that the others' incidents only seemed clearer?
If they had gone on to tell more detail, to turn incident into
story, would certainty have vanished? Once a sequence is set,
once a place is determined, once there is a beginning, once there
is an end, are all stories wrong?

That night I dreamed this dream:

I was taking care of Little Bird. It was cradled in its bamboo
cuplike basket. The door to its cage was open. I heard a disturbance behind me. I turned around to see what it was. There was
nothing there. When I turned back, I saw to my horror that
Little Bird had flown out of the cage. In anguish I ran after it. I
came to a meadow and there I saw Little Bird perched upon the
branch of a delicate bush. I went up to the bush. In silence I
pulled a branch toward me, not the one on which Little Bird
rested, but another one close to it. The branch with Little Bird
also moved toward me. Little Bird did not stir. I reached out for
it. I took it in my hand.

That sensation—it remained even after I awoke—of holding it
was one of the softest and sweetest I have ever known. I knew, in
the dream, that shortly it would choose to fly away, would in
time become a fierce creature in the wilds—an eagle? a lion?
(Species are not bound in dreams.) But I knew too that in its
fierceness it would never forget that it had once agreed to being
held.

Clandestine Acts

•

CHARLES SIMMONS

You couldn't get angry with Billy. You couldn't help liking him.
A lot had to do with his face. He was short, and slight without
being frail, and there was this completely fine and open face. He
had brown eyes and stiff brown hair; I could do a portrait from
memory, so vivid is my recollection of Billy's . . . virtuous
face. That's not the word. He had a face full of virtues.

King of Kings High School, where Billy and I and 400 other
boys were students, was Jesuit-taught. The time I'm thinking of
was just after we had gotten into World War II, when American
Catholicism—Irish-American Catholicism, that is—was at its
most rigid. The primary virtue for all of us was what we had
learned to call "purity"—freedom from sexual thought and
deed. Billy was very pure, and yet no one thought of him as a
prude. How was that possible with a bunch of adolescent boys?
Maybe he *was* prudish, but he didn't seem so, and I'm sure this
was due to his face. He was short, as I say, and he looked up at
us with a tentative eagerness. He wanted you to like him. He
wanted to be fun and have fun. All he asked was that you not
make it impossible. The easiest way to make it impossible, of
course, was with sexual innuendo or an outright dirty joke. That
was always a temptation. For instance, with two or three of us
looking on, you might say, "Knock, knock, Billy." Immediately
he would be suspicious. But you'd say, "Come on, Billy! Knock,

knock." "All right, who's there?" "Marmalade." "Marmalade who?" he'd say, ready now to be amused. "That's what Daddy wants to know!" His jaw would lock, he'd shake his head violently as if to get the impurity out, and rush off.

This was a kind of cruelty, I suppose, and yet we weren't cruel boys. To do such things to Billy was, I think, an expression of our mixed feelings about sex. We had all gone to Catholic grammar schools and been taught by nuns. We had been told from the first grade to emulate the saints—all of whom had been pure and some of whom had died for purity. Impurity not only put us in danger of eternal damnation, it offended Jesus, who loved us and had suffered on the Cross for us. Still, we were adolescent boys, constantly concerned with sex. We all felt—at least in my crowd —that great pleasure, and happiness too, awaited us in sex. As time went on and we went from 13 to 14 and 14 to 15, these mixed feelings were being resolved. Sex was going to be worth it at any price. The admonishments of our early years were receding and being replaced by imaginings and actual adventures, but the admonishments were still there, and our jokes on Billy were a way of playing out the uneasy change.

I said that you couldn't get angry with Billy. Billy himself never got angry. Nor would he badmouth anyone, not a student and particularly not a teacher. Everyone felt, for instance, that Mr. McMahon, the math teacher, was "a cube boob." Billy said he just had a speech defect. Father Leischner, the German teacher, was *"ein alter Scheisskopf."* "He's just old," Billy said, not knowing what the phrase meant, his modern language being French rather than German. Billy practiced the positive virtues too. King of Kings was a scholarship school; it was easy to get kicked out. Over the four years, a third of the boys were dropped on principle for being at the bottom of their classes. Billy helped anyone he could, staying after hours with a boy until the boy picked up or gave up. We tolerated Billy—we admired Billy— because he was good.

I don't know whether it was because there was little nudity at

King of Kings or because of Billy's physical modesty, but I found out about his deformity only by chance on a weekend I spent at his house. We were preparing for bed, and I walked into the bathroom not knowing he was there. He was drying himself after a bath. At first, I thought he was doing a kind of dance. He raised and lowered, raised and lowered the towel in front of him. Finally, he lowered it and kept it there. The bone in the middle of his chest stuck out. I later learned that this was a "chicken breast" and Billy was "chicken-breasted." He and I never spoke of it, and although it had been a shocking sight I don't think I thought of it until a year ago, when Billy died—and the picture of him standing there in the bathroom Saturday night, covering his bottom half, his more shameful half, with a towel and this ugly bone protruding from his chest, came back to me.

Billy, it turned out, played a decisive part in my life. One afternoon in the winter of our senior year, Donald Bosco, Frank McNutt, and I were hanging around late. None of us wanted to go home and prepare for the next day's history exam. At King of Kings, Latin, Greek, French or German, math, and English were the important subjects. The remaining two, history and religion, were minor subjects. Religion was not so much taught as discussed, and usually by an aging Jesuit. As for history, I think not enough of the young Jesuit scholastics, who made up most of the faculty, knew history well. Senior history was modern European, and what we were going to have to do that evening was run through the textbook and our notes. But we were weary from boning up for the major subjects, and I said that since it looked as if we were the only ones left in the school maybe we should slip into the headmaster's office and get a copy of the history exam. It would cut our work to half an hour and guarantee us a good mark as well—not that that was worth much, history being what it was.

The escapade was my idea. I was one of the school cut-ups, maybe *the* school cut-up. Was it high spirits only? I don't know that high spirits accounted for the chances I took.

Even as a freshman I'd played pranks. On Friday mornings
we were required to attend Mass and receive Communion. In
those days one had to fast before Communion, and the cafeteria
served breakfast after Mass. The cafeteria was in the basement;
upperclassmen tended to gather in one part, lowerclassmen in
the other. In both sections were four drinking fountains set in
long sink-like receptacles. At the turn of a knob, water rose
through a short cylinder from which protruded a half-inch of
solid, rounded metal. This kept the boys from covering the spout
with a finger and squirting water on one another. Every defense
provokes an offense, however, and one Friday morning after
breakfast I devised four small horseshoe-shaped plugs of folded
paper to fit around the metal protrusions and into the surrounding cylinders in the upperclassmen's fountains. After placing the
plugs, which allowed water to shoot forth through a small opening, two other freshmen and I stood back to watch. One after
another, nattily dressed upperclassmen came to the fountains to
drink and were drenched. After the shock and initial anger, the
victim joined the watchers and waited for new victims. The
game had gone on for five minutes or so when Father Flagello,
the prefect of discipline—a stocky, grouchy, middle-aged Jesuit
—approached to drink. It was a frighteningly heightened but
perfect conclusion to the joke. His brown face, gray hair, and
black cassock were soaked. He wiped himself, turned to the
smirking audience, saw there was nothing to do but leave, and
left.

Ten minutes later, as usual, the students assembled in the
school quadrangle. It was the one opportunity each week for the
headmaster, Father Dan, to discuss the common business of the
school. Father Dan had a square build and a florid Irish face; as
a layman he might have been a police captain. He had not gone
into the seminary from high school, as most Jesuits had; he had
attended college and then played semi-pro baseball for two years
before beginning his religious studies. His business that day was
the insult and injury to Father Flagello: ". . . and I promise

every man-boy of you that when the culprit is discovered he will be out on his ear. . . ."

I slipped from the quadrangle to an interior passage and hurried on to Father Dan's office. He soon arrived, sweaty from his harangue, and nodded at me. Although I was only a freshman, he knew me from having known my brother, who had gone to King of Kings some years before. "Father," I said, "I'm the boy you were talking about just now." It was pure confession.

He stared at me; I imagine he knew he was trapped. Finally he spoke: "I'll tell you this, boy. If someone else had gotten here first and told me who had done it, you would be out. *Out!*"

"Yes, sir."

He stood there silently for perhaps 30 seconds; he might have been thinking about what punishment less than expulsion was appropriate. If so, there was none. "All right," he said. "I'll tell Father Flagello. Go and apologize to him after classes!"

"Yes, sir," I said, and that was that. I never dealt with danger so well again. The sinner confesses; the priest absolves.

The visit to Father Flagello was not so elegant. After listening to my statement of contrition, he asked me if I was an only child.

"No, sir."

"But you are the oldest."

"No, sir."

"You have problems at home."

"No, sir."

"You had discipline trouble in grammar school."

"No, sir."

I think he was angrier at the denials than the soaking. So I went unpunished, and this was extraordinary: Boys were expelled from King of Kings for smoking in the bathroom or one day's truancy.

In the basement, Bosco, McNutt, and I were wrong in thinking that we were alone. Billy appeared as we were discussing my idea. We weren't surprised; he had probably been doing good deeds. Of course we invited him to join us, and of course he refused. We knew he would; we did it in the spirit of the dirty joke; to shock him.

After he left us, we went to the first floor. The headmaster's door was locked, as we had expected; the door to the supply room—which intruded into the headmaster's office—was unlocked, as we also had expected. The supply room was a makeshift space enclosed by shelved walls of bare pine, six-feet high. The winter light of late afternoon that came through the headmaster's windows and over the pine walls was just enough by which to see—we dared not light the bulb that hung from the ceiling. The shelves were neatly piled with yellow pads, envelopes, boxes of pencils, erasers, paper clips. I pushed them aside to make a ladder and climbed the shelves, leaving shoe prints on the bare pine, then dropped into Father Dan's office. There, on an oak table, were four groups of history exams, one for each class. The senior exam seemed the simplest, two essay questions on a single sheet, as opposed to short-answer questions for the others. I wish I could remember the two essay questions (I can tell you exactly, even now—45 years later—the lines from the "Iliad" I translated for the Greek exam). I took three copies, folded them in fourths, put them in my jacket pocket, and tried the headmaster's door. It opened from the inside. Waiting outside, in the hall, was Father Flagello. For a tough-looking man— I saw his face years later in Rome on an equestrian statue—he seemed frightened. Was a cornered student, like a rat, dangerous?

"What are you doing here?" he said.

Confession was not going to work on this bozo, nor would it have worked on Father Dan. This was big-time. I said nothing.

"Are you alone?"

I held out my hands palms-up and looked down at myself. I felt, for the moment, almost merry.

"Speak up! Speak up!"

Still I said nothing.

"Stand over there!" Like a cop, he indicated a spot away from the headmaster's open door. Keeping an eye on me, he shouted into the office, "Come out!" The supply-room door opened, and Bosco and McNutt came out. They might as well have had their hands up, for the look on their faces. If they had stayed put they might have gotten away, but being Catholic boys they had to obey, if not the rules, a command.

"Bosco, McNutt, and *you,*" he said, not choosing to pronounce my name, "go home! Stay home!"

No search, no interrogation. We said nothing to one another until we reached the bus stop, five blocks from the school. I forget what we finally did say. We exchanged telephone numbers. I offered them copies of the exam. Both declined, which gave me an ominous feeling of isolation.

I immediately told the whole story to my mother and my brother, who was home on Navy leave. My mother in turn told my father when he arrived.

This was a full-fledged family crisis. King of Kings was no ordinary school. It had been founded after World War I with a bequest from a wealthy Catholic woman. Year after year the brightest boys in the city's parochial schools competed for the 120 places in each new class. Rich and poor attended. There was no tuition, and the education was considered the best in any Catholic secondary school in the country. It was an honor for a Catholic family and a Catholic grammar school to place a boy at King of Kings. My brother, seven years older than I, had done very well there. All through grammar school it was impressed on me that I must go there too. I remember lying in bed after my nightly prayers, asking God whether I would get into King of Kings. I didn't seek a direct answer but would slyly inquire, say, what color sweater I would be wearing a few years hence. If it was maroon, the color of King of Kings, I would fall asleep content.

Am I misremembering? It seems to me that there was more wit and talent there than I have seen anywhere since. There was

Richie O'Connor, who could listen to a recording of an intricate piano piece once and reproduce it by ear. He had no interest in becoming a musician; he wanted to become a labor organizer and, I believe, did. There was Francis Duggan, who wrote, it seemed to me at the time, the most beautiful and sensuous poem I had ever read, about the sea meeting the shore. There was Tim Lyons, who played Portia, a male playing a woman playing a man, as in Shakespeare's time; there was a passage in which, on top of this three-layered portrayal, Portia imitates a woman, and Tim kept the genders distinct. I must mention Mr. Gramico, a layman and inspired Greek teacher, who was said never to have flunked anyone and to have had three nipples and 36 teeth.

During dinner the phone rang. We all knew it was the school. A young Jesuit scholastic, speaking to my father, said I should not come to school the next day or any day until we had further word from Father Dan.

After dinner my brother called Father Dan and made an appointment to see him the following afternoon. I think my brother went, rather than one or both of my parents, not only because he had been a success at King of Kings and had kept in touch with the school, but because he had a new Navy commission—one man in uniform dealing with another man in uniform. My brother did look splendid in his ensign's outfit.

The interview was not a success. Father Dan said that a considerable portion of the faculty had worked through the night composing and mimeographing four new history exams. They could not be sure that copies of all of them had not been distributed throughout the student body.

"How did they know I took any?" I said.

"They counted them," my brother said.

"Then they knew I only took the senior exam."

"You could have read the others. Anyway, you *did* take the senior exam."

"Whose side are you on?"

"What are they going to do?" my mother asked.

With some uncertainty my brother explained that Bosco and McNutt could be saved, "if you are willing to come forward and say that you asked the others for help."

"For help!"

"Because you needed the exam to pass."

"Needed the exam to pass! No one flunks history. History is a joke. And I never flunked anything in my life. What's going on? Where did this idea come from?"

"Father Dan talked with Bosco and McNutt. They're willing to corroborate if you're willing to come forward."

"Are you telling me I'm out no matter what?"

My brother nodded. "And the others can be saved."

During dinner my father had said nothing, I think because he was a Protestant. My mother was the Catholic, and everything about our schooling he left up to her. But now he said, "If they want the others, they keep him."

Before I went to bed he spoke to me alone and apologized for making my decision for me. He said that if I could save the others honestly and I wanted to, he would have no objections, but he didn't want me to lie. He also said he thought Father Dan's suggestion was "jesuitical."

In two days my parents received a letter from Father Dan formally expelling me. It was a stern letter, without expression of regret. I read it carefully, as you might read a letter announcing that you had won a contest. Twice it used the phrase "clandestine act." I didn't know what clandestine meant. Bad, I guessed, very bad, heinous. It wasn't until I came across it in a Wilkie Collins novel that I looked it up. I was amused that that fancy word means "secret" and derives from the queer little Latin adverb *clam.*

Bosco, McNutt, and I finished our senior year at different public schools. I was treated very well at mine. The assistant principal, an Irishman named O'Boyle, took an interest in me, assigned me to honors classes, and introduced me to the head of the dramatic society, who made me the villain in the spring play.

Half the teachers were women; my English teacher was young and pretty and that was a treat. But I had suffered the first irreparable loss of my life: I was no longer a "King of Kings boy."

I had planned to go to a Jesuit college, but what with one thing and another I chose a nonsectarian college, and it suited me fine. My mind filled up there. I worked with pleasure and sometimes exaltation.

My only connection with King of Kings after leaving was my brother, who has remained an active alumnus. He receives a yearly newsletter that reports on the doings of graduates. Billy became a Jesuit priest. After his ordination, he was sent to French Guiana to teach English at a French high school. After that, he was a retreat master in Albany and, before his death last year, a marriage counselor with a Catholic service group in the Boston area.

I learned about his death while visiting my brother in Delaware, to where he has retired. He told me that Billy, after leaving us in the basement that day, had gone to the priests' house across the street and alerted Father Flagello. Father Dan had made my brother promise not to tell me. "He was afraid you and the others would take it out on the boy."

"We wouldn't have done that."

"He couldn't be sure. Anyway, you can't now."

"What did he think about what Billy did?"

"He felt that some agency had directed him there."

"*Some agency!* You mean God?"

"I suppose so."

"So he approved of what Billy did."

"No, he thought Billy was hurt by it, was sacrificed to it, but had no choice."

"You realize that going to a non-Catholic college may have accounted for my leaving the Church? Did your 'agency' have that in mind!"

"We believe," my brother said, speaking for Catholics, "that

God works in mysterious ways. How do *you* feel about what he did?"

"Who, God?"

"No, for Christ's sake. Billy."

"I have no feeling at all," I said.

But later I understood that I felt admiration and pity.

Avid

•

JOHN CASEY

When Lucy Potter came back for the third time to her parents'
house on Pettaquamscutt Neck she spent hours in her old room,
at her old desk, staring across the mouth of the bay. Her hopeful
thought about herself was that she now saw more beauty in the
view than she'd seen before. Otherwise she felt terrible.

The young bank officer from her father's bank who'd helped
her out of her failed art gallery in Newport had said to her, "You
don't have to consider this a failure. Your business losses are
offset by capital gains on the property. It'll be a wash. You can
pick right up and try again."

She went home in May, back across the Newport Bridge over
the east passage, touched down on Conanicut Island, then up
again across the Jamestown Bridge over the west passage. South
along Scenic 1-A, then left onto the private way to Pettaquamscutt Neck. She unlocked the black chain that hung across the
way between the two stone pillars topped with anchors. Each
time she'd come home she'd had the key, each time she'd felt a
moment of bliss as she looked over the nine houses on the tilted
green field of the Neck, each house visible from this top point,
invisible from each other behind patches of blackberry, rasp-
berry, and beach roses and hedges of yew and arborvitae. She
could see the lip of the cliff, jumbled soft brown shale and hard
dark granite, the sparse grass crisped by salt spray. The top

railing of the stairway down to the boathouse was so smooth-worn and gray it was almost invisible. And then the wide mouth of Narragansett Bay opening to the sea, blue after blue after blue.

The Neck never changed faster than paint faded or hedges grew, but the sea was always changing. It changed so swiftly and easily it washed her sight: cloud shadows, cat's-paws, windward currents smoothing the water into slick silver-blue tracings, countercurrents setting it into contrary dark lines from time to time tipping into whitecaps. Each change swallowed by another. But always in the farthest blue she sensed her still present child-hood—not that it had been blissful but it seemed to contain the unbroken seed of her contentment.

The first time she'd come home to pull herself together she saw her mother first, who hugged her and said, "Your father will be so happy." The second time her father held both her hands and said, "Your mother's been waiting all morning." Each time they invited the Satterlees over for supper, and everyone was happy to see her and optimistic, as though her orderly arrival (that she'd locked the chain behind her, carried her bags out of the front hall up to her bedroom) was her promise to be good.

No one told her to be good. When she dropped out of college at nineteen and said she was leaving with Phil in his pickup truck to go live in Eureka, California, her father, after all the arguments, said, "If I was certain you were ruining your life, I'd try to stop you. But I have no such certainty." She'd left Phil after two years (a longer relationship than any other in their Eureka household of more or less four couples) but hadn't got home until almost a year later. It turned out her parents had been worried by phone calls from Phil asking where she was. Her father would say, "I'm quite sure she's all right, Phil," and Phil would say things like "I heard from a guy who came through here that she was at a really Fascist-type commune" or "I heard from a guy who came through here that she was at this place doing the macrobiotic diet and she looked really . . .

thin." Her father would say, "I'll tell her you called. The next time she calls we'll tell her you're worried."

It may have been the phone calls that tipped the balance against Phil. She was thinking of going back to him at least for a while, but her father's dry reporting of Phil's gooey drama made her wince. After she'd drifted around from Oregon to Mexico, she did go back to Eureka for a visit, was charmed by Phil again, spent the afternoon with him in a hammock on the upstairs back porch, overlooking the back yard of salvaged furniture overflowing from the household business. He said he loved her and wanted to marry her. She said no as patiently as she could. He said, "Give me another week, another day, with you." She said, "Here in the magic hammock?" They both laughed, and Phil said, "Yeah," in such a vulnerable and boyishly wicked way she couldn't tell him no.

That night she left for the East Coast with a man she met at a party downstairs. He mentioned he was driving to New York. She said, "Mind if I come? Let me get my backpack." It pleased her to be exact. Like getting her hair cut short—lifting strands of hair behind her ear on her middle finger, closing her first finger against it. Right there.

They drove non-stop to New York, one at the wheel, the other stretched out on the back seat. They drank coffee, sang, and gave each other neck rubs. The whole way she imagined the salt air, the color of the bay, the view from Pettaquamscutt Neck. She still had the key. She became single-minded. She would have stopped with this guy at a motel in Nebraska or Iowa, but east of the Mississippi she said no. He got too stoned to drive, and she took a double shift at the wheel. She was driving when they got to New York, so she went straight to Penn Station.

The rattle of her backpack frame woke him up. She said, "There's bound to be a train soon."

He worked his forehead for a few seconds. He said, "Maybe you'd like to spend a little time in New York."

She smiled and bent to kiss him. He knocked his cowboy hat askew getting his mouth to hers.

She was on her way. He said, "Hey . . ." and then laughed.

She slept on the train until New Haven; after that she was too excited by glimpses of salt water.

She took a taxi from Kingston to Pettaquamscutt Neck. There was her mother, then her father, and the Satterlees; her bed was made and turned down, a neat foresail of cotton sheet. She woke up at dawn and sat at her desk (this very desk) to watch the sun rise across the mouth of the bay behind Brenton Reef Light; the haze on the water was a bluish rose, the color of her lips when she looked in the mirror to see what her face showed for her three days of driving, for her three years away.

Some time had passed—she'd gone back to college, started painting, spent a summer at Skowhegan. Jack was after that.

The second time she came home to Pettaquamscutt Neck was when she was divorcing Jack. How could she have gone from easy Phil to hard Jack? That, too, was coast to coast non-stop. Her parents thought Jack was wonderful. They never said so; her mother had simply seemed to know all about him, though she never asked a direct question.

Lucy was twenty-five when she met Jack, twenty-seven when she finally married him. An ardent, dramatic courtship. One Saturday night after a date with her he sailed all the way across and down the bay from his house in Bristol—in a not very big boat—and arrived for Sunday breakfast. He must have left as soon as he got back to Bristol—an hour's drive up and around the bay—and then tacked down the bay the rest of the night in the light southwest wind.

Her mother, when Lucy asked her what she thought of Jack, had held back. Lucy said, "Well, you certainly seem to get along with him—better than—"

"Yes, but that's nothing against anyone else. It's just that Jack is a more familiar sort of fellow."

Lucy thought perhaps that was a perfectly acceptable part of her own pleasure.

Lucy asked Jack, "Weren't you sailing all night?"

"I loved it. Just coasted on down, singing all the way. You've heard of a serenade?" He sang, *"Dans mon coeur, la douleur* . . . Well, that was my *aubade,* the dawn song."

Jack's enthusiasm, his awkwardness, his corny affection ("If this is love, let's have some French") were all modified, even redeemed in Lucy's eyes, by his huge confidence ("Some people might worry about being corny. On me it looks good").

One thing Jack was was elaborate. The courtship was elaborate, the wedding plans were elaborate—Mr. Potter was taken aback by what Mrs. Potter got revved up to in her effort to match Jack's style. But Mr. Potter went along—it was the way they did things on Jack's side of the bay, after all. Mr. Potter and his best friend—Lucy's godfather, Russell Satterlee—got a lot of mileage out of being South County Yankee rustics marvelling at how grand things were over there. But they went along with everything Mrs. Potter and Mrs. Satterlee planned. Jack had enough courtship to spare to blow some their way.

Jack was a successful admiralty lawyer and he booked passage in the owner's quarters on a client's cargo ship to start off their honeymoon, which was two weeks in the Dominican Republic.

The third day out Jack told Lucy she was making the crew members uneasy by roaming around the ship in shorts and practicing her Spanish with them. She laughed. The next day she came back to their cabin after her stroll and found him in a black rage. At supper Lucy thought the captain, a perfectly nice man who had seemed pleased to have their company, was puzzled and embarrassed by Jack's tight silence.

When they went up to the quarterdeck they heard some of the crew singing along with the guitar. Jack said to the captain, "Are those men serenading my wife?"

The captain, in his soft Spanish voice, said, "Mr. Aldrich, let me assure you my men have the most perfect respect for Mrs. Aldrich."

Jack relaxed visibly.

Lucy thought this exchange so alien and antiquated as to be laughable, but she got mad when she and Jack got back to their cabin. Jack was calm. He said he'd be happy to tell her what he'd picked up over some years about Latino machismo that she just probably hadn't ever had a chance to encounter.

Lucy said, "I'm twenty-seven years old, for God's sake! I lived in a seaport in California for two years. I ran a business, I hitch-hiked all over, even in Mexico, which is certainly as Latino—"

"That was then," Jack said grimly.

She had seen at that moment that it would be easier to let him concoct his version of her—to let him think that she was an America previously inhabited only by natives who had dwindled without a trace, to let him think himself Manifest Destiny. He could celebrate the Fourth of July with oratory, patriotic marches, and a flag. She could get along without her own history, without a theory. If he wasn't upset, if he could shut the door on the outside world, Jack could become frantically adoring. She had no such intensities. She had none of Jack's outraged jealousy or his anguished longings.

He adored her elaborately. Once the sexual scene was set he was all for being teased, commanded, sent on detours—elaborate playful submission. Or it could be elaborate possession—he praised and kissed her fingers, her chin, her temple, behind her ear. "Avocado arm!" he said once, munching softly on her biceps. She asked him what he was talking about. She thought he meant green goose bumps. "No—the flesh!" he said, and pulled at the inside of the upper arm with his mouth. "The pale, creamy meat." And then sometimes a comic turn as he kissed her bare back. "Ach! Fiend! You've poisoned me! But before I die, revenge! And paradise!"

He could be ferocious, too, trembling and undone by desire.

Sometimes he seemed terrified, as though he were falling and only clinging to her body could save him.

She'd sometimes thought he was making it up. Her own feeling about desire had always been that it was a subtle undertow pulling her from her shore into someone else's current. She'd particularly liked the moments of being in up to her knees, feeling her sandy footing erode under her toes, around her heels.

But now, here at home on Pettaquamscutt Neck, she was in the midst of a craving she'd never felt before. Here where her hour of childhood had been grilled into the hot stone beach, the coarse grass and sand, the smooth gray planking of the boathouse deck and wharf. Where boredom and pleasure had alternated, not regularly as the tide, and not rationally (as her father and Mr. Satterlee seemed to think, in a design of effort and recompense)—perhaps not alternated; perhaps both had been touching her constantly and it was her skin that was inconstant. One minute she was sliding through the water, nosing her face mask up to the stone jetty, spying on eels, and the next, still holding her breath underwater, she was tired of being wet.

Then she would be sitting on the porch in her bathing suit still wet on her bottom, her shoulder and arm cooked dry in the short time it took to pick her way across the stones to the boathouse porch and up the wood stairs to the parched lawn. Picking up the arm of the record-player, her finger sticky with salt; it would take her two tries to get the needle in the groove for "I Want to Hold Your Hand." The air dry and hot around her wet hair in the gray and green shade of the porch. The crackling in the groove was delicious. Then she might be thrilled or bored by part or by all of the song. She might play it again, in any case.

So now she wondered how could she be having an affair here on the Neck? This current man was an intrusion. He'd rented a house—one or two of the nine houses were rented each summer, very carefully. Mr. Paxton—Rob—and Mrs. Paxton (the second Mrs. Paxton, with her own small child and adolescent stepchild) were from Philadelphia. He'd arrived in advance of his family and taken over one of the boathouses as a painting studio. White-haired and energetic, he'd pleased Mr. Satterlee with his early-morning rowing. Mr. Satterlee pointed out the dory to Lucy one pink early morning as it headed in across the glassy mouth of the bay. "I wouldn't lend my dory to just anybody," Mr. Satterlee said. "He handles her beautifully." They watched as Mr. Paxton swirled the dory around to a stop, shipped the oars, and clipped the painter to the ring in the middle of Mr. Satterlee's pulley system from the dock to a pile in deep water. Mr. Paxton launched himself into the water and disappeared from their view as he swam ashore under the cliff. He didn't come up the stairs.

Mr. Satterlee said, "We're so glad they rented to someone who's going to like it here"—meaning the renters were awfully lucky. But Mr. Paxton somehow had got across to the Satterlees and the Potters (the deans of the Neck) that Mr. Paxton would decide how lucky he was and that Pettaquamscutt Neck might just make it into his league of fjords and firths. That he'd managed to do this without antagonizing them all amazed Lucy.

He was in his early fifties, but restless and energetic in a way that at first reminded Lucy of her ex-husband—a Teddy Roosevelt of enthusiasms but with a stormy streak of ill-humor. Mr. Paxton turned out to be shrewder, more secretly appraising and aloofly amused.

Lucy met him when she was digging clams. He came out of the boathouse and down the strip of beach to the clam bed.

She kept on digging, rolling back the big barnacled rocks with her gloved hands and then driving her spade fork into the exposed mud with a jolt from her foot. She pried up a mound of mud and picked through it. A fat clam squirted as it pulled in its neck. She rinsed it off and put it in her bucket, its neck still shrivelling.

"Now, that is obscene," he said.

"Oh, that's not obscene," she said. "It's just scared."

He introduced himself and kept her company while she dug. He offered to turn over the rocks for her. She gave him her gloves. "Those barnacles will slice you, and you won't even feel it till tonight."

She threw away a clam whose two shells slid apart. It was all mud inside.

"How does that happen?" he said.

"A clam worm eats it. They crawl into the neck and eat their way all the way down to the body. When they're through eating they curl up inside for a little nap. You sometimes find them that way, but if you keep an eye open you'll see them digging through the sand."

After a while she found one for him. A good-sized one, six inches long and as thick as her little finger. It writhed as she held it just behind the head, the tail lashing and its bristles stroking as though it were trying to swim away. "Now look," she said. "This is obscene." She squeezed behind the head, and the thick front end of the worm peeled back. Its round mouth tube gaped. Then a pair of black hooked teeth—each the size and shape of a rose thorn—slid out and began scything across the dark pink hole.

She dropped it in the sandy mud and it burrowed in head first, gone in two seconds.

He laughed. "No wonder that poor little clam pulled his neck in."

"His?" Lucy said. "Clams are hermaphrodites. You shouldn't try to read too much into all this."

"You are the very model of a modern major-general," he said. "You're teeming with a lot of news. About all this dangerous life at the edge of the sea."

"Some of it is quite peaceful. Have you seen horseshoe crabs coupled?"

"No. What do they do?"

"They just lie there locked together. Right along the lee here." She pointed into the water. "Just rocking in these little waves."

"Do they enjoy it?"

She couldn't think of a clever answer. She looked down.

"Let me put it another way," he said. "Do they enjoy it?"

Her head came up as though he'd set the hook in her lip. She said, "Yes."

Lucy saw him again at the picnic the Potters gave to start the summer on the Neck. Beatrice Satterlee was talking into his chest; he was stuffing devilled eggs into his mouth and washing them down with beer. Lucy was passing a bucket to collect clamshells and dirty napkins. Rob Paxton turned his trunk and tilted his head back to watch Lucy approach.

"Lucy used to paint, too, didn't you, dear?" Beatrice Satterlee said. "Come here and talk to—"

"We've met," Rob Paxton said. "And I've seen you in your garden. These must be your raw peas we've been cracking our teeth on."

"Lucy would have us all on a regimen of health food," Beatrice said. "Whenever she spends a summer here—"

"You're here for the summer?" he said to Lucy.

"For a while."

"Do you have any good books? Or do you just dig? I didn't have room to bring books."

"You should ask Beatrice. She and Russell have the great library on the Neck. But I can't imagine what sort of books you're looking for."

She rather liked his measured rudeness. She'd been so blandly familial and quiet during May she was surprised to hear her own inflated voice on display.

The next day, when she was weeding her garden, she found a note taped to the empty packet of beet seeds marking the row: "Why don't you come down and cast a cold eye on the stuff I've been doing? RP"

She went to the boathouse that afternoon, but he wasn't there.

She went back to her room and wrote letters at her desk, looking up from time to time at the parade of boats sailing back

in from the sea. It was Sunday, the end of the first mild weekend
of the summer. She saw her parents' catboat. She saw her father
come about and stand to. Her ex-husband's Ensign came about
with a sudden flurry of luffing. She saw the people on both boats
wave and talk, then both boats fall off slowly, Jack's to put back
out into the west passage, her father's to starboard, circling
slowly in the lee of the promontory just south of the Neck.

Jack's boat was too far away for her to see who was with him.
Yet she was sure she'd heard the cracking of the sail, the sheet
running through the block just an instant before, still echoing in
the corners of her room.

Sailing bored her now. But the sound was soothing. And she
remembered the feeling of a following sea swelling up under the
stern, the hissing as the boat gathered speed sliding down the
front of the wave, the quivering of the tiller in her hand as the
boat half-surfed until the crest slipped by.

Perhaps the other person on Jack's boat was their old neighbor, Molly Enders. . . . Jack had once confessed to Lucy that
he'd kissed Molly Enders. Lucy hadn't cared enough by then to
be anything but irritated that he expected to gain something
from confessing, irritated that she herself was vaguely aroused
by the story. Jack always had a sneaker for Molly, as Lucy had
known better than Jack. Lucy had asked Molly to fill in for her
for Sunday tennis fairly often when Lucy had started spending
Sundays back on Pettaquamscutt Neck.

At first Jack was all heartiness. "Molly's pretty good—a really
game player."

Then baffled musing. "I wonder why Enders left her. And left
her with those two boys. What a tough situation!"

Lucy said, "She has a full-time nanny."

And the next Sunday Lucy had left again for the Neck.

"How was your game? Did you and Molly beat the
McEvoys?"

"They dropped out. I played singles with Molly."

Lucy found his tennis clothes dripping on the towel rack in the bathroom.

"Did you go swimming?"

Jack said from the bedroom, "What? Oh . . . No. I was sprinkling the court. Molly squeezed the hose—you know, the old trick. She let go and drenched me. So I sprayed her."

Lucy recoiled from having to suspect him. She saw for an instant the listlessness of her life.

"We were tussling for the hose. It was a silly reflex—kissing her. Silly schoolboy thing."

Lucy felt tired. Over the next months, whenever he tried to charm her or to interest her, she found it easy to let his efforts slide by.

Then he confessed to her that he had had an affair. She said, "With Molly Enders."

"No."

She didn't say anything for a while. In that short period of silence she saw that he was hurt, that he was baffled at how a bright, competent man like him could fail. She was amazed, too, that all his power was checked. She was the one who was feebler, more exhausted, but he was stalled, Lucy could feel it. He'd run aground on himself. She was light, bobbing loose.

There was a period when she felt bad that she didn't feel worse. The formula that came to her was "I hurt him, but I didn't wrong him."

He, of course, got to keep the house he loved. There were no children. She'd put that off. He was generous with a lump-sum settlement.

Her parents were sad. She reassured them that although it had not been possible to continue she had not suffered. Her father looked puzzled at that.

"Do you think I should have suffered more?" she said. "I was as stoical as you could want—"

"No, Lucy. No. I wasn't thinking that. I'm sure you know the difference between necessary suffering and useless suffering."

The day she got home she found her bed with the carved headboard made up and the covers turned down.

When she woke, the sun was up and, sitting against the headboard, she could see the mouth of the bay glittering. Beyond Beavertail to the southeast the sea and sky were both lighter and lighter bands of blue meeting in the pale haze of the horizon.

Now what she saw was as beautiful, only lit from the west— her father's sail, pale white in the shadow of the Neck, Jack's sail flat to the late sun as he left on a broad reach up the bay.

Why had she brought out the most miserable side of Jack? She was filled with anguish at the sight of him gliding away. She remembered that he was remarried. But he must think of her— why else did he go up the west passage under her window, when the east passage would take him home faster? She was filled with lost love for Jack, and at the same time for Phil. She'd left barbs in Phil, too, worse than just leaving him. He'd written her after she was married—a chatty note about the household in Eureka. He and his pals had made enough in their business to attempt a movie; they were on the verge of getting a matching grant if they could just get some of it developed. They'd all gone up to Northwest and filmed the Kwakiutl Indians salmon-fishing and dancing. They only needed a quick five hundred or a thousand.

Lucy had shown the letter to Jack, who'd already noticed the Eureka postmark.

"Send him the thousand. I'll write a check right now."

"What shall I say?"

"It doesn't matter. I think the check will speak for itself finally."

She'd mailed Jack's check.

She hadn't thought of how slowly but surely the check would work. She'd let herself bring out the worst in both Jack and Phil.

Phil's better side was free and blithe. Before she'd left for California with him, her father had taken him up to Providence to the Hope Club for lunch to discuss how she and Phil were going to provide for themselves. Her father was trying to put a regular and fair face on it all. She'd combed Phil's long hair and beard and found him a coat and tie in the attic. Phil had set off as if it were a great joke. Afterward, she picked him up. He grinned at her, but later in the day he asked her if it was right to clink glasses. "Your father held up his glass and said, 'I hope that things go well and that you both learn something,' and I stuck up my glass and clinked. Is that how you do it—you clink glasses?"

He wouldn't believe her when she said it didn't matter. Phil had always believed he was pulling her out of a life cluttered with forms; he said he despised them, but he'd always been a little uneasy that he might be indicted for an incorrectness before his natural charm and goodness got him off. She'd sent him Jack's check, which would fester in that uneasiness.

Poor Phil. Poor Jack. She'd caused them both so much trouble. It was odd: it didn't seem to matter if she was bad or good, she ended up causing pain.

She wondered what they'd seen in her. At this distance she saw what she'd seen in them: she could see herself getting into Phil's pickup or climbing onto Jack's boat and sailing happily away. She missed those beginnings terribly. Why did she always end up back here? Was she addicted to being a bright little girl, the sweetheart of Pettaquamscutt Neck? Or to being someone who waited for a suitor to break her chains?

As she wondered at that, and at the way she'd mangled Phil and Jack, she knew she was about to be bad in a way she hadn't been before, that might pay her back.

The next morning, she was up at dawn and down the cliff stairs to the dock. When Rob Paxton arrived, she got the extra pair of oars to the dory and climbed in. They didn't speak. She rowed hard—she could see his oar blades right behind hers, she could see the whirlpools his oars made swirling just behind hers in the still water. She could feel his breath on her back as they rowed

out, straight into the sun. After a while she faltered. Her back
was wet with sweat. He ran his knuckles up her spine against the
flow. He stuck one oar in the water and the dory wheeled
around. The sun was hot but still low enough to be in her eyes,
so that she couldn't see anything but glare in the sky and on the
water. Halfway back she stopped again. This time he held her
shoulder with one hard hand and put his mouth on the back of
her neck.

"What a salty little sprite."

That's it, she thought, the tone I expected—his voice dropping
down on her.

She rowed hard again, making the water pop and gurgle.

She was the one who tied the dory up to Russell Satterlee's
pulley system. She dove in and rolled onto her back. He looked
enormous as he dove in after her.

She swam to shore and picked her way out of the water and—
Rob always behind her—made a little helpless dash to the boathouse porch. She could be as amused as he was at the clichés of
seduction. She stood under the outside shower, pulled the top of
her bathing suit out to let the water wash down the front. He
stepped in beside her, singing "By the sea, by the sea, by the
beautiful sea."

They lay on the hot boards of the boathouse porch. When she
heard steps on the cliff stairs she went inside and peeped out the
window as Russell Satterlee went by to take the dory out for his
morning row. She heard Rob and Russell Satterlee speak. She
watched the dory head out—Russell stroking slowly, warming
up for his habitual hour. She didn't turn when the door opened,
she waited by the window looking out to sea, shifting her weight,
fingering the mullions with her unsteady fingers, confident that
Rob would descend on her, would kiss her with kisses that
would be ironic and corrosive.

She was right enough about that. But what happened next
surprised her. She'd been dutiful in her chores, she'd even helped
her father paint his catboat, she'd been so good and so still that

she'd become drowsy. She'd meant her trip to the boathouse that morning and her next visit by night to be no more than pinching herself awake. She'd done that now and then when she ran her little business in Newport—had little adventures that wouldn't do any harm. Gone for weekend cruises with a pleasant friend on a pleasant yawl or sloop. Air and salt water in their simple forms; suspended in them, sailing in neutral waters, she was simple, too, even mild and sweet.

She thought perhaps that was how it was meant to be—three days now and then, out to sea and back, no time to undo anyone.

Now this beefy, insidious man! From the upstairs-hall window she watched for the lights to go out in his rented house, the highest on the Neck. Then she went to her bedroom window on the bay side and waited to see if his shadowy bulk appeared at the head of the cliff stairs.

He'd left another note in the afternoon on the empty beet-seed packet: "Going down tonight to finish up another little painting. What will you make of it?"

She saw his dark sweater and white hair at the top of the cliff stairs. She tiptoed past her parents' bedroom. She hadn't made love with Phil the three days he'd stayed on the Neck before they left for California.

She wore her bathing suit and beach robe in case she ran into someone. She saw it all from the outside clearly and shrewdly— if someone came down the stairs she could slip out the door and be in the water before they came round the boathouse porch. Just a midnight dip in the bay. She looked down at her pale legs pushing between the skirt flaps of the robe, her bare feet finding their way over the grass, the stones, the stairs.

She had never used the cliff stairs for anything like this. Half-way down, she felt her notion of her childhood revolve. She thought how dully mistreated she'd been, how little fun she'd had, how alone she'd been with these rickety stairs, these wooden boats, all the tedious rules and basic principles of sea-manship and good character. She thought these thoughts know-

ing they were untrue but feeling that they had a power like truth
to scale the varnish from the wood, to rust the brightwork.

He was standing down by the water. She went into the boathouse and turned off his radio. She heard his slow steps on the
crumbled rock. She went over to the heap of sail bags in the
corner. Each one was marked with the name of its boat. Some
names were stitched in scarlet thread (her father's and Russell
Satterlee's), some stencilled neatly with waterproof ink, some
painted on with nail polish. There were more than a dozen bags
stuffed with jibs and mainsails, some Dacron, some canvas, and
the catboat's smooth-worn cotton. The canvas and cotton were
on top, soft and dry as toast from having been hosed off with
fresh water and hung in the sun that afternoon. Lucy spread her
beach robe across the sail bags. Rob turned the light out. Lucy
saw a red aftereffect of light over the sail bags. She wondered
why she'd never thought of this before, offering herself on the
edge of the sea, not chained to a rock (as in the picture of Andromeda in her parents' library) but face down on this jumble of
sail bags, clutching a whole bushel of sailcloth to her chest as
they sailed away, riding this dim white wave in the dark.

Afterward it occurred to her that, for all his heftiness, Rob
was the daintier and softer of the two of them; she was all sharp
energy, as avid and awkward as a man.

After Rob's family arrived everything was more difficult. He still
worked from early morning to noon. Then he'd bicycle the mile
or two to the Dunes Club beach to join his family. Sometimes in
the afternoons Lucy would see him playing father. She and Rob
didn't leave notes anymore. If she wished to meet him late at
night in the boathouse she would stick a pin in the beet-seed
packet. If he could come, he would put in another pin.

Lucy kept herself from looking for the second pin until she
went out just before supper to pick vegetables. If there were two
pins in the packet, she would stick them firmly back in the

wooden stake, her arm and fingers fierce with a feeling that was more like unleashing rage than anything else.

She once waited five days.

They had long conversations late at night. She found she could say anything. She liked telling him harsh things about herself, about her and Phil or Jack. She liked mocking life in Rhode Island: her father's careful habits, his good citizenship, the way he and Russell Satterlee were busy little bees on the board of the Perryville School, the S.P.C.A., and the Narrow River Preservation Society, the buzz that he and Russell Satterlee made applying "basic principles of seamanship" to the simplest little maneuver in their modest boats.

Rob reflected this harshness back at her, but subtly. He would draw her attention to her body in a cool, specific way. "You have your mother's eyes and nose. And general build. But your father shows up somehow . . . your way of speaking, I suppose. And this gesture—" He tucked his chin in and stroked his eyebrow with two fingers in a way she recognized. "Do you think they were ever as seething as you are under your Yankee front? Or are they all—I include the childless Satterlees, who also seem to consider you their bonny joy—quaint good citizens to the core?"

Lucy loved hearing him splinter the old folks, breaking their silly doting on her like kindling.

The one time Rob took her breath away with alarm was when he complimented her. "You know this is doing wonders for your looks. It's not that you're prettier but that there's an erotic lustre to your wiry tomboy looks." She felt dizzy that he could see a feeling of hers, and then describe it so handily, plucking it from her limbs now it was ripe.

It reminded her of the horrible feeling of strangeness she had when she was a little girl and she heard one of the grownups on the Neck say how pretty the view was. And another would agree, "Lovely, lovely," as though it were something there for a minute, passingly obvious, when for her it wasn't a view from the porch but a jumble of slow and fast, of incoherent particulars

as small as broken shells and first berries and the mottling of
scraped paint and, on the other hand, of forces so invisibly loom-
ing that their coherence was larger than any words she knew or
ever puzzled over—even those vague cardboard cartons of
phrases like "Your father's had a hard week," "It's been a good
summer," "next year."

Did these grownups not know? Or did they know so much?
("How wise we were to incorporate the Neck, Russell.")

And now, what was this man seeing? What did it mean, an
erotic lustre to her tomboy looks? Just another storage phrase
that packed up the grownup summer but not hers, not the incoherent particular (the stitching on the sail bags), not the sprawl-
ing blue distance that became invisible as it entered her. She
couldn't bear to hear his pat coherent noticing. Her excitement
at exciting him turned into a panic now. She'd never felt so
erotically charged, and yet at the same time blind to herself. He
mistook her silence. He said, "Another pleasure is your occasional misgiving. Your little disapprovals are truly wonderful."

She came back from that panic. But even when she was able to
express her ordinary alarm at how odd she thought this all was
she couldn't break the bantering tone of how she and Rob
talked. When she told him she'd never done anything like this
before, certainly not here on the Neck, that she thought perhaps
she should have just gone on being comfortably good, he said,
"Well, apparently being good isn't good enough for you." He lay
back and enjoyed his remark for some time.

Another several days passed. She finally stuck three pins in
the beet-seed packet. She was already in the boathouse when he
came down the stairs in the dark.

He told her he thought they'd better stop. She said, "O.K. But
what for?" She wasn't going to flinch.

He couldn't really say at first. He pursed his lips and grimaced
and started several sentences and then stopped. She asked him
several questions: "Are you afraid someone's found out?" No.
"Perhaps you're feeling guilty?" He laughed, but he began to

resist being questioned. After a silence he said, "There's a nastiness to it. It's bringing out something quite nasty in both of us. I
think your little sigh for your virtue the other day was just a
more genteel way of saying what I'm saying now. I think if
either of us could find more pleasure in being mean to the other
we'd do that instead. I feel a little tug in that direction—I think
you do, too. We could end up being a couple of nasty people
. . . and with a taste for it."

She was horrified. She wished to argue with him but knew
right away she didn't want to argue fairly; that is, to have to tell
the truth. She did wish to be mean to him . . . because she was
angry with him but also a tiny bit thrilled when he called her
nasty. She could imagine insulting him, being insulted in return
in a way that made her eyes narrow. She didn't like the idea at
all, and felt herself growing cold. She wished to have no more of
that idea.

She said, "Well, it's all very mysterious to me, but there's not
much point in talking on and on about it."

"You don't think I'm right?"

She said, "I really don't know enough about you to say."

Then she added, "I'm sorry, I simply don't understand how to
take what you say. But I think you're probably quite right that
we should leave it at that." She sounded as sternly and generously reasonable as her father.

It was midnight when she got back to her bedroom, but she
couldn't sleep. She was worried about everything again, but with
the additional anxiety that more and more small incidents were
going to occur to reveal to her more and more weaknesses and—
she adopted Rob's word, loosely—nastiness in herself. She used
to feel oppressed by her mistakes and bad luck, but she'd always
been hopeful that she was getting better or was due to arrive
soon in better circumstances. Now she feared what any small
incident might reveal to her.

How could that man have done this to her? That beefy piece
of vanity with soft hands, with that plummy voice.

How could he have been the one to call it off?

That was what made her revolted at herself—that he had re-coiled from her. She wasn't Andromeda chained to a rock, a gauze-wrapped innocence about to be attacked by a monster. In Rob's version *she* was the monster—an avid little clam worm about to gobble up his clammy substance.

She tried to dismiss his view. She couldn't. She still felt desire, fiercer than any she'd ever felt. It was crazy. She was crazy. But it was in her, a warm little worm of desire.

When she was younger, with Phil and Jack, she had wished to feel more. But now this unwanted granting of her wish! And even though Rob was a connoisseur of sharp pleasures, she frightened him.

She, too, was frightened, and angered. She walked around her room in a rage. She told herself that what she'd done with Rob was nothing. Nothing! It just seemed something because she'd done it here on Pettaquamscutt Neck. But it still writhed in her. She picked up a wooden coat hanger and hit her bare calf. The stinging made her eyes water, but it relieved her.

Each time she felt this little worm, she whacked her calf so hard it left a welt. Each time she felt a twist of shame at how avid she had become, she stung herself.

She looked at the marks on her calf. She remembered that her parents were giving a dinner party, to which she would be ex-pected to wear a dress. She looked through her closet for some-thing long enough to cover her calf. There—a floor-length skirt, a summer print with pale green and pink checks. This was ridic-ulous. What was she doing here? This was absurd. She was too tired to laugh. She dutifully went through her drawer of blouses until she found one to go with the skirt—a white blouse with a Peter Pan collar.

She felt hollow. She sat at the desk by the window and watched the eastern rim of the sky grow pale. She found this calming. She wasn't crazy. She'd just been through a lot. A friendly outsider would admire how much she'd been through, would say that it was perfectly natural to be momentarily upset. The *momentarily* was as soothing to her in her exhaustion as her pillow and turned-down sheets.

The next day she helped her mother prepare for the dinner—the second of her parents' two summer parties for the families on the Neck. Her parents invited half the Neck to the first, the other half to the second. The Satterlees did the same thing, but her parents and the Satterlees carefully rearranged who was in which half. Renters, popular novelties, were invited more than their fair share. Lucy thought that a friendly outsider wouldn't be able to notice the subtlety of these arrangements and rearrangements. All day long she kept considering what a friendly outsider would make of it all, would think of her life.

The Satterlees came fifteen minutes early, as was their habit when there was a party at the Potters'. Mrs. Satterlee slipped sideways through the gap in the yew hedge and progressed smoothly up the lawn, a tent of blue velvet with tiny feet. Mr. Satterlee walked beside her, putting an occasional hitch into his stride, even halting altogether and looking sagely out to sea in order to keep abeam of her.

Mrs. Satterlee immediately took Lucy aside, slipped her arm through hers and took her for a slow walk along the seaward edge of the lawn. Lucy shortened her stride, but she refused to bend over attentively. Beatrice Satterlee was only five-two, but she never looked up to talk to taller people. She stared straight ahead. She intimidated most of them into bending their heads down to hers.

Lucy was half listening to her when she was suddenly alerted by the phrase "You know how fond of you I am." The next thing Lucy heard was:

"I'm sure it's very romantic, my dear, to go slipping across the dewy lawn, but these things have a way of making themselves known, and I would not like your mother and father to have to consider a problem. I mean, it may or may not be a

problem for you—I'm sure it's possible to take it all quite
lightly, that's none of my business, of course . . . but it is not,
at least here on the Neck, *tout à fait comme il faut.*"

And, as if turning her craft smoothly into the swell of Lucy's
stunned, mute outrage, Mrs. Satterlee said, "You have always
been a great favorite of mine, and I wouldn't dream of speaking
this way to anyone I didn't care about deeply."

It wasn't because of Mrs. Satterlee's smooth change of course
that Lucy didn't get mad at her. Lucy felt a pang for Mrs.
Satterlee—how seriously she took herself, how seriously she regarded Pettaquamscutt Neck as a preserve of civilized comport-
ment. Lucy recognized reflections of her own feelings (the Neck
was one place she ought to be a good girl), and thought she was
no less foolish than Mrs. Satterlee.

Mrs. Satterlee, perhaps taking Lucy's silence for sullenness,
launched a third paragraph. "I think you share my feeling that I
am not just a nosy old neighbor." Mrs. Satterlee laughed lightly.
"I feel I can bring this subject up *en famille.*"

Lucy said, "If we keep talking about it much longer, you'll be
speaking entirely in French."

Mrs. Satterlee wasn't offended. "Well, it is a rather French
subject. You know I lived in France before the war. My father's
parish was the American community in Paris, and you can
imagine what that was like. He knew them all, you know. So I'm
not a puritan, my dear. I was exposed to all kinds of things; I
became *completely* broad-minded. *Tout comprendre, c'est tout
pardonner.* And I do understand, my dear. And I think you
understand me, too." She squeezed Lucy's arm. "Come along,
your mother will want us to mingle."

When they sat down to eat, Mrs. Satterlee was at the far end
of the table, next to Rob Paxton. Lucy could hear the duet of
their rich voices, each of them seeming to urge the other to
sforzandos of plumminess. It occurred to Lucy that in some
horrible way they resembled each other. Their subject, which

soon commanded the entire table, was the Narragansett Arts Festival scandal.

For years, the Arts Festival had been simply a chance for local weekend painters to set up booths and peddle their pictures to their neighbors. There were paintings of fishing boats at sea, beached dories, and quahog skiffs floating peacefully in foggy inlets. And of course there was driftwood sculpture. Then it had all become more serious—prize money and judges. This year, Rob Paxton had been prevailed upon to be a judge, and Mrs. Satterlee announced to the table how glad she was. But Mrs. Satterlee feared that last year's festival had been sabotaged by hippies. There had been booths selling chrome hookahs and a great many other . . . peculiar things. But worst of all had been last year's kite contest. The kites turned out to be extraordinarily beautiful, Mrs. Satterlee was the first to admit that. After all, she had volunteered to give out the prizes. Then the prize-winners had flown their kites. One of the kites represented with photo-realist detail a man in a derby hat and raincoat. When it went aloft the panels on which the raincoat was painted flapped open and revealed the man . . . revealing himself.

Mrs. Satterlee was now trying to enlist Rob Paxton in her efforts to make sure that that sort of thing would not happen again. He kept agreeing with her utterances, but somehow avoided actually being enlisted, even as he egged her on. He was amused.

Mrs. Satterlee said, "What I object to is not only that he was a sneak—I mean, we gave him the prize for one thing and he showed us quite another—but also that he meant to be cruel. And nasty. That is my point. He wasn't being jolly and bawdy in a good-natured way. I don't mind that he made a fool of me—" Rob arched one eyebrow. Lucy thought he must have practiced in front of a mirror. "I don't mind that so much as I mind the nastiness to the rest of the people in South County. He's a very clever fellow; he couldn't have not known the kind of people who come to the Arts Festival. Imagine the perfectly nice Irish and Italian mummies who brought their children to see art."

"I imagine that was part of his concept," Rob said. *"Épater le bourgeois."*

"There is a difference between astonishing the bourgeois and being deliberately disgusting." Rob lifted both eyebrows. "No, really, Mr. Paxton, this was . . . exaggerated. I'm afraid I can't make myself any clearer."

"And neither could he," Rob said, and grinned at the several people who laughed.

Mrs. Satterlee pursed her lips, silenced and cross. Lucy's father said, "I guess it could have been funny, but it just wasn't."

Mrs. Satterlee revived. She said, "This wasn't nudity at a play. It was just as much an act of exhibitionism as the criminal act itself, with the same deliberately inflicted nastiness. A complete exhibitionist, Mr. Paxton. An exhibitionist *de pie en cap."* Rob Paxton laughed. Mrs. Satterlee blushed and said, "It is the Old French word for *pied."* Rob Paxton chuckled on, and Lucy felt like belting him one. She thought Rob seriously nasty, but she had lost the right to indignation at his amusing himself at Mrs. Satterlee's expense.

Mr. Satterlee touched Lucy's elbow and cleared his throat. She turned toward him, thinking that he was making an effort to break up the general conversation.

"Ah," Russell Satterlee said, "I see we're having wine. Does that mean we're having chicken or fish for the next course?"

"Flounder," Lucy said.

Mr. Satterlee looked at the wine label more closely. "Did you deduce flounder from this wine?"

"I know we're having flounder because I bought it this afternoon."

"Ah. Not an expert witness but a yet more convincing witness —a witness to a key fact."

Lucy had always loved Russell Satterlee but found it excruciating to talk to him for long. He seemed to think he could hold the floor so long as he was praising his listener, no matter for how trivial a virtue or accomplishment. He also knew an enormous amount about sailboats, and he loved them so much he couldn't understand that anyone would want to avoid the smallest piece of nautical information, which seemed to Mr. Satterlee to emanate not from him but from some font of knowledge that he and his listener should enjoy together without the conversational elapsed time being charged to his account.

Russell Satterlee said, "The way you cleared up that question reminds me of a Swedish sailor I once met. Dick Jennings and I were out on his boat once . . . Do you know Dick Jennings? Wonderful fellow, and an awfully good sailor. Dick and I were out on his ketch . . ." Russell described the rigging, which was intricate, the weather, which was stormy, and several feats of Dick Jennings' seamanship, which were extraordinary. They ended up in a harbor of refuge at Block Island.

Lucy said, "Is Jennings the Swedish sailor?"

"No, no. I'm coming to him." Russell maneuvered the ketch to a mooring alongside a schooner, whose even more intricate rigging he also described.

Lucy thought she might faint with boredom. She tried to control her breathing. She didn't understand how she could be simultaneously bored and panic-stricken.

Russell said that Dick Jennings knew the owner.

Lucy said, "The Swedish sailor?"

Russell shook his head while continuing to describe the dinghy in which Dick Jennings and he rowed over to the schooner.

Russell said, "We went below, and there indeed was the owner, eating supper with two of the hired crew." Russell took some time out to deliver an essay on the salutary blend of hierarchy and democracy on a small sailing vessel. "We sat down, all at the same table, and the owner introduced us. The Swedish sailor nodded but did not interrupt his consumption of peas, which, in spite of the fact that we were rolling a bit, he was eating with his knife."

Lucy was glad to hear they'd reached the Swedish sailor, but her heart sank when Russell had Dick Jennings tell a story about how the Newport-to-Halifax race was won by a fancy bit of jib-handling near the finish. Dick Jennings told his story in as much detail as even Russell found complete.

Lucy tried to hear what Rob Paxton was saying to Mrs. Satterlee, but Russell's voice engulfed her as solidly as the sound of surf.

Russell said, "When Dick Jennings finished his story of the race, the Swedish sailor interrupted his consumption of peas with his knife only long enough to say, 'Mr. Yennings, dot's wrong.' Now, I hope I've made it clear from my description of him that Dick Jennings was not the sort of man who was in the habit of being told to his face that he was just plain wrong. But Dick was a guest on board and understood that although the Swedish sailor was hired crew and was eating peas with his knife, the Swede was on board his own ship. So Dick, without taking offense, very calmly and politely told the story again. . . ."

Lucy grew alert with fear. And indeed, as calmly and politely as Dick Jennings, Russell was telling the story all over again. Lucy felt scorched with boredom. She felt like a crumpled paper tossed into the fire, landing a bit to one side, curling and turning brown but taking forever to burst into flame.

Russell said, "Now, when Dick finished his account, really a very plausible and instructive account of seamanship in general and jib-handling in particular, the Swede looked up from his peas and said once again, 'Mr. Yennings, dot's wrong.' Well, I can tell you, I braced myself. Dick Jennings slowly turned toward the Swede and said, 'You know, I'm quite interested in what you have to say. Now, I heard this story from the skipper of the boat in question, and I'm known among my friends as having a pretty fair memory, and even as knowing a thing or two about boats. So I would be grateful, young man, if you'd tell me why it is that you seem to think I am, as you put it, wrong.' I can tell you, Lucy, my blood was ice water. But the Swede looked Dick right in the eye and said, 'De skipper he vas in de stern of de boat. I vas de yib man and I vas right up front. So, Mr. Yennings, I vas right dere.' " Russell laughed and faced Lucy. Lucy felt in a trance. She thought she might really have been hypnotized. Russell laughed a little more, and Lucy heard herself laugh. Russell grabbed her hand. "You have such a pretty laugh, Lucy." His hand was wide, callous, and hard as a board. "I've been meaning to talk to you seriously. I know you've had a rotten time, my dear, a very hard time." He listed her misfortunes to her, starting with her having been misled by that West Coast hippie, her unhappy marriage to that ill-tempered young admiralty lawyer, who'd disappointed them all so badly, and at last her valiant business effort.

She at first concentrated on his old dry, warm hand, but along the way she found what he was saying to her so blindly loyal that she was moved.

"It's much harder being a young woman these days than when I was young. Obviously I can't testify from direct experience, but I have observed this. And I'm considered a pretty fair judge of character, so when I say you are a remarkably fine young woman you can fairly well rely on its being so."

He released her hand. She wanted to hold his again. She was dizzy with a panic that his hand seemed to dispel.

He said, "Are you having a good summer? I can tell you it's a great pleasure looking out and seeing you digging away in your garden. You look as though you're back on an even keel."

She said, "I'm all right. Aside from thinking I'm going to go crazy, I'm just fine."

He seemed less surprised than she was at this statement. He said, "Let me tell you something about feeling crazy, Lucy. You aren't crazy just because you feel crazy. You're only crazy if you do something crazy."

That made her laugh. He said, "Now, wait—that's not as foolish as it sounds." She wasn't laughing because he'd said something foolish. What made her laugh was the preposterousness of his knowing her, of his loving her. (She'd heard Mrs. Satterlee say, "Oh, Russell adores Lucy! He'd put his hand in fire for her.")

Of course he knew her—not her heading West in Phil's pickup, not her in Jack's house and garden, not her in and out of business in Newport, but her as the bright girl in the dark house. It was preposterous, as preposterous as his knowing the sea, as his loving the sea—this lanky, watery-eyed old man with dry broad hands as hard and worn as oar handles, his head full of names of sails and admirable boats owned by admirable businessmen. But it was wonderful that he tried, that he ever clambered on board a sailboat and sailed away from land, that he thought of ways to praise her, that he took her hand or patted her knee.

Yankee bankers and lawyers, descended from Yankee traders and privateers, owning these dark houses on Pettaquamscutt Neck, knew her and loved her, told her to pay her debts and told her she was sane—forgave her and adored her.

But even as she felt this brimming high tide of dutiful affection, she felt it begin to run out fast the other way.

They were preposterous!

She could already see the barnacles on the rocks, then the sagging eelgrass flattening on the intertidal mud, the oozing debris of the high tide of her love of them and her self-loathing.

All that drained out of the bay. They didn't know her, and they didn't know what was really going on. When her father had told her before he took Phil to the Hope Club, "If I was certain you were ruining your life, I'd try to stop you. But I have no such certainty," she'd thought how amazing it was that he could see so far, encompass so much. But he hadn't seen anything at all! He was just feebly and blindly hoping. She'd thought he had a kingly conscience whose gentle reproofs and balanced love would reach her anywhere. So she never developed a conscience of her own. That was their fault, that she had no conscience.

Now she wanted a conscience, not in order to blame herself but in order to forgive herself. As they forgave themselves.

But now the tide rushed back in over the oozing flats she'd just uncovered.

She'd felt a sense of shame each time she'd failed, but her shame had brought her back to this snug little Neck. Here she was reproved and comforted. Sanded down, patched up and refitted. And then she could set out again. Her fault was she didn't really leave. She hadn't been completely present, either, in California or even just across the bay in Bristol.

Poor Phil, who thought she'd run away with him.

Poor Jack, who thought she'd married him.

What a fraud she'd been. She'd never left.

As she began to drown in this flood, she wished it out again. It wasn't her fault! If only she'd known these men were not her conscience, how much less a fraud she might have been, and how much more whole. She wouldn't have had to find her tiny little moments of happiness in grit and dust and ashes. Tiny little humbling chores to make her a good girl. What frauds these men were! Their modest disclaimers invited her to think they knew more—oh, worlds more!—than they said. Their calm pipe-sucking poses were tintypes of authority. They varnished themselves with plainness so they did not appear to think themselves great; they sat so assured of their common sense and plain virtue that they could allow turbulence to dance around them. In the face of a rant against them they could sigh. In the face of brutal, shrill disagreement they spoke softly. It was in this sneaky fog of modesty and this haze of careful tedium that they maintained themselves. They said,

Get a grip on yourself, now.

Steady as she goes.

Well, let's just hear what he has to say for himself, and then we'll see.

If we all just sit tight . . .

But they were as crazy as she was. Their "basic principles," their laws, rules, and regulations were crazy. They were obsessions, crazy incantations to make their inertia feel like the seat of the elect.

What was so wrong with her life, anyway? How dare they sit back and cluck over her! And then turn down her sheets when she came home.

She came to with the little breeze that blew in through three inches of open window, that fluttered the white curtains and bent the candle flames in their clear glass chimneys. The horrible accelerated rushing in and out, her outgoing accusatory fury and her incoming self-loathing dwindled, the turbulent chop of contradicting herself grew still. In this first calm instant she saw Russell's hand now again lying on hers on the white tablecloth between his dessert fork and her spoon. She thought, I can't feel it. I am losing my senses.

She moved her hand and felt his. She thought, It's just that his hand bored mine. His hand put mine to sleep. My hand is normal.

It was bright and calm again.

She and her mother would clear the table.

Her mother and father and the Satterlees had been lucky to love themselves, that was all. They'd been lucky to be so fond of themselves and the lives they'd fitted into. Soon they'd be shrinking as fast as the Neck. Faster. Her father and mother and godfather and godmother were useless to her now. She'd get as much use out of them as out of that creep Rob Paxton. She'd get as much use out of her wooden clothes hanger as out of her turned-down sheets.

Russell was now telling his Hurricane-of-'38 story, and Beatrice was punctuating it.

Lucy thought she should leave for college, or run off with her boyfriend, or get married, or start her own business, and it was a real surprise to her when she remembered she'd done all those things.

But she'd done them all before she really and truly left Petta-quamscutt Neck, before she'd realized she could leave.

She wished she could give up trying to decide whether she was bad and crazy or whether they were. That wasn't the question. . . . There wasn't any question that was the question, there wasn't any wish that was the wish that would make her more than she was, there wasn't any fairy godmother or prince or magic fish to change her. She felt herself alone inside her skin.

Russell absent-mindedly drew his pipe from his side pocket, and his rolled tobacco pouch with the Hope Club insignia on it from his inside breast pocket. He filled his pipe. His broad fingers pinched a match out from a waterproof cylinder with a tiny compass embedded in its screw top. He was always ready for heavy weather. Beatrice caught his eye with one sideways flick of her own, and he put the match away without lighting it. He kept his pipe in his mouth, rattling the stem in his teeth a little, like a patient old horse passing time with its bit. He would get a chance to light it when the men retired to the chart room. He would point with the stem to various places on chart 1210 (Block Island to Martha's Vineyard) in its mahogany frame on the wall, and he would puff away describing happy moments at sea to Rob Paxton.

Lucy decided to let him be. And to let Beatrice be when she took out her needlepoint in the living room with the women. Her parents and the Satterlees were shrinking no matter what, sweet shrinking old men and women who'd been lucky to have such a good opinion of themselves. Let them cling to their little cliff top, their dwindling cells still able to catch the light that broke across the bay.

Lucy got up and began to clear the table. How strange she felt, how strange it was to know this place after all—to know the raised patterns of the plate rims she felt with each thumb, to know just how hard to push her hip against the swinging kitchen door to make it stay open. She knew each voice and its place in the web of agreement. How strange that she'd thought she had to struggle to escape it—to close her eyes and bolt away, to behave badly or to go crazy. All she had to do was brush by it, coming or going. She didn't even have to say a word. Whatever grace or power she needed didn't depend on their letting her go or taking her back.

She drifted back into the dining room and picked up two more plates, her thumbs reading the rims again. Her father and Russell Satterlee had led the men to the chart room.

It came to her that all this would be hers one day. Of course she'd known that all along, but she'd never contemplated the sensation. How horrible of her to imagine . . . She amended dutifully: all this would be hers, diminished without them. But that was not what she felt. First she felt the comedy of herself as châtelaine, as a member of the corporation, knowing basic principles. And she felt a pivot on which weight balanced to weightlessness: all this would be hers, she was not theirs.

Mrs. Satterlee and her mother took the women to the living room. Lucy took cups and saucers from the shelf and forgave her father and mother for letting her think that because they loved her she was in their power. She felt the patterns on the cups and saucers under her fingertips. She felt a tenderness for her illusions. She could slip them off and leave them intact, as intact and fragile as china, as intact and fragile as the rest of her parents' lives, as Pettaquamscutt Neck beside the enormous sea.

To Be

•

— BARBARA GRIZZUTI HARRISON —

"Life is terrible," Joel said. This sentence gave him evident pleasure. "No, it is not," Laura said. He is indecent, she thought. "It
is full of joy and delight and our troubles are of our own making," she said. She did not entirely believe this, how could one.
But it vexed her to see Joel sitting in his sunny kitchen, rolling
his own cigarettes—he could well afford to buy cigarettes—dis-
coursing with relish on the terribleness of life, his own life in
smooth working order. He sits at a round oak table and sleeps in
a brass double bed, how can he say life is terrible, Laura
thought; he would probably declare against happiness in the
Pantheon. Laura had been wont, in times past, to judge people
by their response to the Pantheon, which she had experienced as
a place of perfect happiness and safety, as proof in fact that the
world was good. She would like to have skated on a sheet of thin
ice over the marble floor of the Pantheon while clouds drifted
over the round aperture above. Joel said her aesthetic apprecia-
tion—that is what he called it—was a matter of upper-class social conditioning; he put it to her that the Pantheon reminded
her of the dome of a Wall Street bank. "Why don't you read the
Autobiography of Benvenuto Cellini?" Laura now said, giggling
—a Wall Street bank!—"it will inspire you with joy." She had
herself just reread the *Autobiography of Benvenuto Cellini,* and it
had inspired her with joy. Miriam, Joel's wife, who was chop-

ping scallions at the marble counter, looked at Laura with pity.
The line between pity and condescension is a fine one, Laura
thought; and, the last thing Miriam and Joel wish to have
brought to their attention is that happiness is generally available,
she thought. They pitied Laura because, in their company, she
professed to believe in the availability of happiness, a profession
of faith which did not jibe with their own peculiar ideology.
Laura herself was unhappy.

"What?" she said.

Joel was talking, as Laura contemplated her unhappiness,
about some recent manifestation of Class Oppression and—this
was a new one—Tribality. Laura declined to talk about Tribality, whatever that was. "The world does not consist of conspiracies," she said, hoping to fend off the inevitable discussion of
who was in league with whom to destroy the Third World, of
which Miriam and Joel—for reasons that Laura had heard many
times but refused to make an effort of the imagination to com-
prehend—considered themselves satellites. Miriam and Joel
sighed in unison. "The world does not consist of people conspir-
ing," Laura said. Actually Laura was not quite sure she wished
to fend off a discussion of conspiracies, as, while she herself
made no great claim to sanity, she liked, from time to time, to
receive proof that Joel and Miriam were crackers. At least, she
thought, I am not smug.

"They're all the same people," Miriam said.

"*Who* are all the same people?" Laura said. "Is Benvenuto
Cellini in on the conspiracy?" she said.

Miriam and Joel exchanged glances. Miriam was scraping ginger with which to season a sirloin steak.

"For example," Joel said, "could you argue that the old lady
downstairs visits her troubles upon herself?" This rendered
Laura mute. The old lady downstairs was about to be evicted,
her children having abandoned her, which event Joel laboriously
traced to the far-reaching tendrils and the cunning contrivances
of the multinational corporations and in particular to southern

bankers. "I hate Freud and Marx with an equal passion," Laura said. "Perhaps we could give the old lady downstairs a share of the sirloin, it might considerably lighten her oppression."

"The Israeli Mafia is in league with the Soviets," Joel said, "and the role of the multinationals is clear when you consider. . . ."

"Why don't we invite the old lady up for dinner?" Laura said.

"The steak is ready," Miriam said, setting three places.

"What you lack," Joel said, "is a world view." That is true, Laura thought; and this plunged her into depression.

Laura had had a falling-out with Joel months before. He had tried to establish himself as her mentor at the community college where he held, tenuously, a post in the sociology department, and where Laura taught Freshman Italian. In addition to lacking a world view, Laura lacked a mentor (she was also, at this time in her life, short on friends); and for a while she amused herself, while trying simultaneously to take their preposterous views seriously, by listening to Joel and Miriam carry on about the impossibility of achieving happiness in a class-ridden society. Then one day she had said, "You are truly preposterous, you have no idea how real people live in the real world, the real world is not made up of oppressed and oppressors, it is made up of people—more or less happy, good or bad depending on their degree of ignorance—of whom I am one, and why I listen to you at all I can't imagine."

"You have been conditioned," Joel said.

". . . yes, at the beauty parlor," Laura said, after which they had not spoken.

This evening she had met Joel at the butcher's, and he'd invited her to dinner, and, her unhappiness having taken the form of lethargy, she had consented to go with him. This obliged her to walk up six flights of stairs to Joel and Miriam's shabby-by-intent apartment; and this predisposed her to anger, inasmuch as Joel and Miriam could well have afforded to buy the building in

which they lived, all this laboring up stairs being an affectation
in aid of exactly what Laura could not be expected to understand.

"Living in Italy disqualified you for understanding real life,"
Joel said.

Laura had lived in Rome, quite happily, for ten years, until
she had been robbed and raped in Trastevere. There she had
lived in a six-flight walk-up—and what cruel steps they were—
but the reward for her exertions had been a view of St. Peter's
and a terrace on which jasmine and oleander grew. "Rome, however," she said, "*is* the real world, why is any one place any less
real than any other place?"

"I thought you liked bean sprouts," Miriam said. "Have some
more."

"He pays lip service to social justice but he supports Opus
Dei," Joel said, "he" being the Pope.

In Rome Laura had seriously considered the demands of the
Catholic Church and had judged them outrageous. Were I a
Catholic, she thought now, I should have to love Joel and Mir-
iam, an impossibility. Then she thought of these words of Blake:
"To love thine enemies is to betray thy friends/That is surely not
what Christ intends." She saw the point. Seeing the point ruled
out having a world view—at least one that emanated from
Rome; and, having spoken the truth when she said she hated
Marx and Freud with an equal passion, where exactly did that
leave her?

"Have some more steak," Miriam said; "the dog doesn't like
ginger."

Laura went home to find her daughter reading Edith Wharton.
"How's Edith Wharton?" Laura said. Laura's daughter looked
up from her book and crossed her eyes. "When you were fifteen
months old," Laura said, "you spoke English and Italian. How
is it that now you hardly utter either, can you tell me that?"

Laura's daughter vouchsafed no reply. Perhaps she's forming a World View, Laura thought; God help me.

At two in the morning Laura decided to write down randomly ten things she loved:

Baroque churches—Gesú, St. Augustino, St. Ignazio. She counted this as one love.

Granite de café.

Penne all'arrabbiata.

Caravaggio.

Frank Sinatra.

"I Know Where I'm Going," a movie *circa* 1945 in which Wendy Hiller and Roger Livesey live Happily Ever After, she a fiercely independent, prickly, bank clerk's daughter who aspires to wealth, he a tender, impoverished Scottish laird blessed with exquisite manners and dedicated to the concept of *noblesse oblige.* ("A wartime propaganda film that conveys subtle messages about Class," Joel had said when she taped this movie on his VCR; "a way to lull the British working-class into believing the war would unite all classes." "I don't receive subtle messages," Laura had said; "subtle messages are lost on me. They loved each other and that's good enough for me.")

The New York skyline.

Her daughter's flesh.

Her father, dead.

Jasmine, white.

The Piazza in Piscinula. She thought of the three masked men who had robbed and raped her in an alley in Trastevere, crossed off Piazza in Piscinula, then, after some consideration, reinstated it.

Her list had come to eleven. She crossed off *penne all'arrabbiata.* Then she added:

Bittersweet chocolate and the Pantheon.

She looked at her list. It did not in her opinion add up to anything approaching a world view. Laura reckoned it might be therapeutic if she now made a list of ten important questions, important to her: Can stupidity ever be harmless? Is sensation more important than intellect? Is the one contingent upon the other? Her heart was not in it. Bored by the puerility of what she had caused to be on paper, she went to her daughter's room. The child was still reading Edith Wharton. "How would you like to go back to Rome?" Laura said. Laura's daughter dropped her book and ostentatiously feigned sleep.

The next night Laura received a call from a friend of Joel and Miriam's, a man called Steve whom she intensely disliked in spite of the fact that he'd been hospitalized for schizophrenia, which fact, Laura thought, ought to have triggered her compassion but did not. Can one be latently compassionate, she wondered, as Steve babbled on. In Italy there was a law that declared there were no insane people, as a result of which schizophrenics and other crazy people freely roamed the streets, a contributing factor to her returning home to New York, where also crazies roamed the streets. Steve wanted her to join a protest march, something to do with a blind man with a German Shepherd who was being evicted from his apartment. "I can't make it that night," Laura said, "sorry."

"I haven't told you what night," Steve said; "it's day."

"I can't stand crowds," Laura said.

"There probably won't be more than four or five of us," Steve said.

"In which case it will do no good," Laura said; "look, I'm very sorry, I'm busy marking papers." This was a lie.

Laura called Pan Am and TWA to find out what the airfare was to Rome. She made six separate calls to six separate agents, booked six tickets, two in first-class, two in business-class, and two in economy-class (which she refused to call *coach*).

At school the next day she avoided Joel; this was made easy for her, as Joel seemed bent upon avoiding her. In her afternoon class she conjugated the verb *essere:* To Be. *I want to be in bed with Joel.* This thought darted through her mind. It surprised but did not alarm her. She scrutinized it with interest. Laura had not been to bed with anyone since the night of the three masked men—two years. Joel, to whom in the early days of their friendship she had related the events of that night, explained it as a function of Class Oppression. Laura, he said, was merely a symbol to these men of all that had made their lives mean, and their violence had had little to do with her—*"per se."* A function of my walking down a dark alley, a function of my being in the wrong place at the wrong time, she thought. She had not felt like a symbol at the time. But she had permitted herself to draw some comfort from Joel's words; they gentled her into believing that neither had she, Laura, been chosen, nor (by her congenital wooly-mindedness which sometimes gathered itself into an orb —this is how she imaged it—of flaming concentration, but which had not done so on the night of the attack) had she, Laura, chosen her rape or her rapists. Laura thought of her mind as a series of twisting dark alleys in which were contained memory and desire and which sometimes led to a round place of blazing light. She often saw herself walking through her own mind; but she could never anticipate the coming of the light. What an idiot, she thought. Then she examined the sentence she had spoken silently, and thought: Who is the idiot in that sentence, Joel? or me?

Laura invited Joel and Miriam to dinner, the origins of this impulse being obscure to her. It seemed in some way connected with her daughter, Laura did not know how—Oh if life consisted only of conjugating verbs. Joel and Miriam would expect Italian food, Laura was an excellent cook. She decided to cook Indian food, curry being a mystery to her; she wanted to see Joel eating with his fingers, for reasons she thought might become clear to her sooner or later.

The curry, of repellent texture, color, and odor, dribbled on Joel's beard. He pronounced it too mild, which was the least of its problems. Laura watched in fascination as the yellow-gray stuff mingled with the black-gray of his beard. Miriam ate fastidiously insofar as that was possible. Laura's daughter ate with *Portrait of a Lady* propped up against her water glass. Joel began, as he helped himself to more of the mess, to expound upon the reasons for hunger in the Third World, a turn of events Laura had anticipated and in equal measure dreaded and hoped for, as she knew it would provoke her to wrath, an emotion she had, since the night of the ginger-steak, wished very much to experience in Joel's presence.

"I'm going back to Rome," Laura said, aborting the conversation about hunger, which had not succeeded in making her sufficiently angry.

"What do you think about that?" Miriam asked Laura's daughter.

"Ask her what she *feels,* thinking is not instructive in this regard," Laura said.

Laura's daughter turned the page of her book with her left hand.

Joel proceeded to talk about the origins of tribality on the subcontinent.

"I don't suppose anyone cares to take me seriously," Laura said. "I'm going back to Rome. A fact. A real fact. Hello? Anybody there?"

"How do you feel about Henry James?" Miriam asked Laura's daughter.

"Oh my God," Laura said. "Ask her to conjugate *to be* and *to feel* in Italian," she said. "Do you know there is no exact equivalent for the English *to feel* in Italian? I find that more interesting than Pakistan and Lord Mountbatten, to tell the truth."

Steve called while Joel and Miriam were helping themselves to thirds. "I'm afraid you have the wrong number," Laura said, disguising her voice with facility.

Laura's daughter said, in her clear, high voice, "My mother lies."

"That is true," Laura said. "I see you've found your voice, however."

"*Sono, sei, è, siamo siete, sono, sarò, ero, eri, era, eravamo, eravate, erano,*" Laura's daughter said.

Laura was suddenly immensely happy, and immediately began to question from which direction her happiness had come.

"What is the difference between happiness and joy?" she asked.

"It comes and it goes," Laura's daughter said.

"Which does?"

Laura's daughter crossed her eyes.

Laura asked Miriam to name ten things she loved—"or eleven." Miriam gave this request such earnest and prolonged attention, never once looking at Joel, that Laura was moved to silent mirth; her happiness expanded, as a result of which she pinched her daughter's thigh. Miriam was still pondering when Joel said, "Laura, may I see you alone? About that business at school."

Laura was on the point of asking, *What business?* but did not, and allowed herself to be led into the living room. There Joel kissed her, a very wet and very garlicky kiss which Laura entertained but did not return.

"Don't go," Joel said.

"We can't stay here forever, there's salad and dessert," Laura said.

"Don't go to Rome," Joel said.

"*Forse ché si, forse ché no,*" Laura said. "Wipe that goo off your beard."

In the kitchen Laura's daughter was singing. She was singing *Giovanitsa,* the Fascist youth anthem. Miriam, who did not know it was the Fascist youth anthem, was smiling benignly upon her.

"Dear me, where did you learn that?" Laura said.

"Grandpa," the child answered.

"Naughty of him," Laura said.

"Why was it naughty?" asked Miriam, handling the word naughty as if it were itself suspect; it was not in her vocabulary.

"I prefer my mother's lies," Laura's daughter said. Laura correctly interpreted this sentence to mean that her daughter did not like Joel and Miriam.

"What I want to know," Laura said, addressing her daughter, "is, do you have a world view?" Laura's daughter crossed her eyes. Joel dipped his napkin in his glass and applied it to his beard. Miriam asked for a finger bowl.

"*Finger*bowl!" Laura's daughter said. She tugged at Laura's hair, letting her hand rest for a moment on the back of Laura's neck.

Laura's feelings went on a collision course. Her feelings were: pity for Joel and Miriam, a pained love for her daughter's flesh, and—oh let it not be fleeting, she prayed—a clear and unmistakable roundness of joy.

The Watch

•

=============== **RICK BASS** ===============

When Hollingsworth's father, Buzbee, was seventy-seven years old, he was worth a thousand dollars, that summer and fall. His name was up in all the restaurants and convenience stores, all along the interstate, and the indistinctions on the dark photocopies taped to doors and walls made him look distinguished, like someone else. The Xerox sheets didn't even say *Reward, Lost,* or *Missing.* They just got right to the point: *Mr. Buzbee, $1,000.*

The country Buzbee had disappeared in was piney woods, in the center of the state, away from the towns, the Mississippi—away from everything. There were swamps and ridges, and it was the hottest part of the state, and hardly anyone lived there. If they did, it was on those ridges, not down in the bottoms, and there were sometimes fields that had been cleared by hand, though the soil was poor and red, and could really grow nothing but tall lime-colored grass that bent in the wind like waves in a storm, and was good for horses, and nothing else—no crops, no cattle, nothing worth a damn—and Hollingsworth did not doubt that Buzbee, who had just recently taken to pissing in his pants, was alive, perhaps even just lying down in the deep grass somewhere out there, to be spiteful, like a dog.

Hollingsworth knew the reward he was offering wasn't much.

He had a lot more money than that, but he read the papers and he knew that people in Jackson, the big town seventy miles north, offered that much every week, when their dogs ran off, or their cats went away somewhere to have kittens. Hollingsworth had offered only $1,000 for his father because $900 or some lesser figure would have seemed cheap—and some greater number would have made people think he was sad and missed the old man. It really cracked Hollingsworth up, reading about those lawyers in Jackson who would offer $1,000 for their tramp cats. He wondered how they came upon those figures—if they knew what a thing was really worth when they liked it.

It was lonely without Buzbee—it was bad, it was much too quiet, especially in the evenings—and it was the first time in his life that Hollingsworth had ever heard such a silence. Sometimes cyclists would ride past his dried-out barn and country store, and one of them would sometimes stop for a Coke, sweaty, breathing hard, and he was more like some sort of draft animal than a person, so intent was he upon his speed, and he never had time to chat with Hollingsworth, to spin tales. He said his name was Jesse; he would say hello, gulp his Coke, and then this Jesse would be off, hurrying to catch the others, who had not stopped.

Hollingsworth tried to guess the names of the other cyclists. He felt he had a secret over them: giving them names they didn't know they had. He felt as if he owned them: as if he had them on some invisible string and could pull them back in just by muttering their names. He called all the others by French names—François, Pierre, Jacques—as they all rode French bicycles with an unpronounceable name—and he thought they were pansies, delicate, for having been given such soft and fluttering names—but he liked Jesse, and even more, he liked Jesse's bike, which was a black Schwinn, a heavy old bike that Hollingsworth saw made Jesse struggle hard to stay up with the Frenchmen.

Hollingsworth watched them ride, like a pack of animals, up and down the weedy, abandoned roads in the heat, disappearing into the shimmer that came up out of the road and the fields: the cyclists disappeared into the mirages, tracking a straight line, and then, later in the day—sitting on his porch, waiting—Hollingsworth would see them again when they came riding back out of the mirages.

The very first time that Jesse had peeled off from the rest of the pack and stopped by Hollingsworth's ratty-ass grocery for a Coke—the sound the old bottle made, sliding down the chute, Hollingsworth still had the old formula Cokes, as no one—no one—ever came to his old leaning barn of a store, set back on the hill off the deserted road—that first time, Hollingsworth was so excited at having a visitor that he couldn't speak: he just kept swallowing, filling his stomach fuller and fuller with air—and the sound the Coke bottle made, sliding down, made Hollingsworth feel as if he had been struck in the head with it, as if he had been waiting at the bottom of the chute. No one had been out to his place since his father ran away: just the sheriff, once.

The road past Hollingsworth's store was the road of a ghost town. There had once been a good community, a big one—back at the turn of the century—down in the bottom, below his store —across the road, across the wide fields—rich growing grasses there, from the river's flooding—the Bayou Pierre, which emptied into the Mississippi, and down in the tall hardwoods, with trees so thick that three men, holding arms, could not circle them, there had been a colony, a fair-sized town actually, that shipped cotton down the bayou in the fall, when the waters started to rise again.

The town had been called Hollingsworth.

But in 1903 the last survivors had died of yellow fever, as had happened in almost every other town in the state—strangely enough, those lying closest to swamps and bayous, where yellow fever had always been a problem, were the last towns to go under, the most resistant—and then in the years that followed, the new towns that re-established themselves in the state did not choose to locate near Hollingsworth again. Buzbee's father had been one of the few who left before the town died, though he had

contracted it, the yellow fever, and both Buzbee's parents died
shortly after Buzbee was born.

Malaria came again in the 1930s, and got Buzbee's wife—
Hollingsworth's mother—when Hollingsworth was born, but
Buzbee and his new son stayed, dug in and refused to leave the
store. When Hollingsworth was fifteen, they both caught it
again, but fought it down, together, as it was the kind that attacked only every other day—a different strain than before—and
their days of fever alternated, so that they were able to take care
of each other: cleaning up the spitting and the vomiting of black
blood; covering each other with blankets when the chills started,
and building fires in the fireplace, even in summer. And they
tried all the roots in the area, all the plants, and somehow—for
they did not keep track of what they ate, they only sampled
everything, anything that grew—pine boughs, cattails, wild carrots—they escaped being buried. Cemeteries were scattered
throughout the woods and fields; nearly every place that was
high and windy had one.

So the fact that no one ever came to their store, that there
never had been any business, was nothing for Buzbee and Hollingsworth; everything would always be a secondary calamity,
after the two years of yellow fever, and burying everyone, everything. Waking up in the night, with a mosquito biting them, and
wondering if it had the fever. There were cans of milk on the
shelves in their store that were forty years old; bags of potato
chips that were twenty years old, because neither of them liked
potato chips.

Hollingsworth would sit on his heels on the steps and tremble
whenever Jesse and the others rode past, and on the times when
Jesse turned in and came up to the store, so great was Hollingsworth's hurry to light his cigarette and then talk, slowly, the
way it was supposed to be done in the country, the way he had
seen it in his imagination, when he thought about how he would
like his life to really be—that he spilled two cigarettes, and had

barely gotten the third lit and drawn one puff when Jesse finished his Coke and then stood back up, and put the wet empty
bottle back in the wire rack, waved, and rode off, the great backs
of his calves and hamstrings working up and down in swallowing shapes, like things trapped in a sack, like ominous things,
too. So Hollingsworth had to wait again for Jesse to come back,
and by the next time, he had decided for certain that Buzbee was
just being spiteful.

Before Buzbee had run away, sometimes Hollingsworth and
Buzbee had cooked their dinners in the evenings, and other
times they had driven into a town and ordered something, and
looked around at people, and talked to the waitresses—but now,
in the evenings, Hollingsworth stayed around, so as not to miss
Jesse should he come by, and he ate briefly, sparingly, from his
stocks on the shelves: dusty cans of Vienna sausage; sardines,
and rock crackers. Warm beer, brands that had gone out of business a decade earlier, two decades. Holding out against time was
difficult, but was also nothing after holding out against death. In
cheating death, Hollingsworth and Buzbee had continued to
live, had survived, but also, curiously, they had lost an edge of
some sort: nothing would ever be quite as intense, nothing would
ever really matter, after the biggest struggle.

The old cans of food didn't have any taste, but Hollingsworth
didn't mind. He didn't see that it mattered much. Jesse said the
other bikers wouldn't stop because they thought the Cokes were
bad for them: cut their wind, slowed them down.

Hollingsworth had to fight down the feelings of wildness
sometimes, now that his father was gone. Hollingsworth had
never married, never had a friend other than his father. He had
everything brought to him by the grocery truck, on the rarest of
orders, and by the mail. He subscribed to *The Wall Street Journal.* It was eight days late by the time he received it—but he read
it—and before Buzbee had run away they used to tell each other
stories. They would start at sundown and talk until ten o'clock:

Buzbee relating the ancient things, and Hollingsworth telling about everything that was in the paper. Buzbee's stories were always better. They were things that had happened two, three miles away.

As heirs to the town, Hollingsworth and Buzbee had once owned, back in the thirties, over two thousand acres of land—cypress and water oak, down in the swamp, and great thick bull pines, on the ridges—but they'd sold almost all of it to the timber companies—a forty- or eighty-acre tract every few years—and now they had almost no land left, just the shack in which they lived.

But they had bushels and bushels of money, kept in peach bushel baskets in their closet, stacked high. They didn't miss the land they had sold, but wished they had more, so that the pulp-wood cutters would return: they had enjoyed the sound of the chain saws.

Back when they'd been selling their land, and having it cut, they would sit on their porch in the evenings and listen to it, the far-off cutting, as if it were music: picturing the great trees, falling; and feeling satisfied, somehow, each time they heard one hit.

The first thing Jesse did in the mornings when he woke up was to check the sky, and then, stepping out onto the back porch, naked, the wind. If there wasn't any, he would be relaxed and happy with his life. If it was windy—even the faintest stir against his shaved ankles, up and over his round legs—he would scowl, a grimace of concentration, and go in and fix his coffee. There couldn't be any letting up on windy days, and if there was a breeze in the morning, it would build to true and hard wind for sure by afternoon: the heat of the fields rising, cooling, falling back down: blocks of air as slippery as his biking suit, sliding all up and down the roads, twisting through trees, looking for places to blow, paths of least resistance.

. . .

There was so much Hollingsworth wanted to tell someone! Jesse,
or even François, Jacques, Pierre! Buzbee was gone! He and Buzbee had told each other all the old stories, again and again.
There wasn't anything new, not really, not of worth, and hadn't
been for a long time. Hollingsworth had even had to resort to
fabricating things, pretending he was reading them in the paper,
to match Buzbee during the last few years of storytelling. And
now, alone, his imagination was turning in on itself, and growing, like the most uncontrollable kind of cancer, with nowhere to
go, and in the evenings he went out on the porch and looked
across the empty highway, into the waving fields in the ebbing
winds, and beyond, down to the blue line of trees along the
bayou, where he knew Buzbee was hiding out, and Hollingsworth would ring the dinner bell, loudly and clearly, with a grim
anger, and he would hope, scanning the fields, that Buzbee
would stand up and wave, and come back in.

Jesse came by for another Coke in the second week of July.
There was such heat. Hollingsworth had called in to Crystal
Springs and had the asphalt truck come out and grade and level
his gravel, pour hot slick new tar down over it, and smooth it
out: it cooled, slowly, and was beautiful, almost iridescent, like a
blacksnake in the bright green grass: it glowed its way across the
yard as if it were made of glass, a path straight to the store,
coming in off the road. It beckoned.

"So you got a new driveway," Jesse said, looking down at his
feet.

The bottle was already in his hand; he was already taking the
first sip.

Nothing lasted; nothing!

Hollingsworth clawed at his chest, his shirt pocket, for cigarettes. He pulled them out and got one and lit it, and then sat
down and said, slowly, "Yes." He looked out at the fields and
couldn't remember a single damn story.

He groped, and faltered.

"You may have noticed there's a sudden abundance of old coins, especially quarters, say, 1964, 1965, the ones that have still got some silver in them," Hollingsworth said casually, but it wasn't the story in his heart.

"This is nice," Jesse said. "This is like what I race on sometimes." The little tar strip leading in to the Coke machine and Hollingsworth's porch was as black as a snake that had just freshly shed its skin, and was as smooth and new. Hollingsworth had been sweeping it twice a day, to keep twigs off it, and waiting.

It was soft and comfortable to stand on; Jesse was testing it with his foot—pressing down on it, pleasurably, admiring the surface and firmness, yet also the give of it.

"The Russians hoarded them, is my theory, got millions of them from our mints in the sixties, during the cold war," Hollingsworth said quickly. Jesse was halfway through with his Coke. This wasn't the way it was with Buzbee at all. "They've since subjected them to radiation—planted them amongst our populace."

Jesse's calves looked like whales going away; his legs, like things from another world. They were grotesque when they moved and pumped.

"I saw a man who looked like you," Jesse told Hollingsworth in August.

Jesse's legs and deep chest were taking on a hardness and slickness that hadn't been there before. He was drinking only half his Coke, and then slowly pouring the rest of it on the ground, while Hollingsworth watched, crestfallen: the visit already over, cut in half by dieting, and the mania for speed and distance.

"Except he was real old," Jesse said. "I think he was the man they're looking for." Jesse didn't know Hollingsworth's first or last name; he had never stopped to consider it.

Hollingsworth couldn't speak. The Coke had made a puddle
and was fizzing, popping quietly in the dry grass. The sun was
big and orange across the fields, going down behind the blue
trees. It was beginning to cool. Doves were flying past, far over
their heads, fat from the fields and late-summer grain. Hollingsworth wondered what Buzbee was eating, where he was living,
why he had run away.

"He was fixing to cross the road," said Jesse.

He was standing up: balancing carefully, in the little cleat
shoes that would skid out from underneath him from time to
time when he tried to walk in them. He didn't use a stopwatch
the way other cyclists did, but he knew he was getting faster,
because just recently he had gotten the quiet, almost silent sensation—just a soft hushing—of falling, the one that athletes, and
sometimes other people, get when they push deeper and deeper
into their sport, until—like pushing through one final restraining
layer of tissue, the last and thinnest, easiest one—they are falling, slowly, and there is nothing left in their life to stop them, no
work is necessary, things are just happening, and they suddenly
have all the time in the world to perfect their sport, because
that's all there is, one day, finally.

"I tried to lay the bike down and get off and chase him," Jesse
said. "But my legs cramped up."

He put the Coke bottle in the rack.

The sun was in Hollingsworth's eyes: it was as if he was being
struck blind. He could smell only Jesse's heavy body odor, and
could feel only the heat still radiating from his legs, like thick
andirons taken from a fire: legs like a horse's, standing there,
with veins wrapping them, spidery, beneath the thin browned
skin.

"He was wearing dirty old overalls and no shirt," said Jesse.
"And listen to this. He had a live carp tucked under one arm,
and it didn't have a tail left on it. I had the thought that he had
been eating on that fish's tail, chewing on it."

Jesse was giving a speech. Hollingsworth felt himself twisting down and inside with pleasure, like he was swooning. Jesse kept talking, nailing home the facts.

"He turned and ran like a deer, back down through the field, down toward the creek, and into those trees, still holding on to the fish." Jesse turned and pointed. "I was thinking that if we could catch him on your tractor, run him down and lasso him, I'd split the reward money with you." Jesse looked down at his legs: the round swell of them so ballooned and great that they hid completely his view of the tiny shoes below him. "I could never catch him by myself, on foot, I don't think," he said, almost apologetically. "For an old fucker, he's fast. There's no telling what he thinks he's running from."

"Hogson, the farmer over on Green Gable Road, has got himself some hounds," Hollingsworth heard himself saying, in a whisper. "He bought them from the penitentiary, when they turned mean, for five hundred dollars. They can track anything. They'll run the old man to Florida if they catch his scent; they won't ever let up."

Hollingsworth was remembering the hounds: black and tan, the colors of late frozen night, and cold honey in the sun, in the morning, and he was picturing the dogs moving through the forest, with Jesse and himself behind them: camping out! The dogs straining on their heavy leashes! Buzbee, slightly ahead of them, on the run, leaping logs, crashing the undergrowth, splashing through the bends and loops in the bayou: savage swamp birds, rafts of them, darkening the air as they rose in their fright, leaping up in entire rookeries . . . cries in the forest, it would be like the jungle . . . It might take days! Stories around the campfire! He would tear off a greasy leg of chicken, from the grill, reach across to hand it to Jesse, and tell him about anything, everything.

"We should try the tractor first," Jesse said, thinking ahead. It was hard to think about a thing other than bicycling, and he was frowning and felt awkward, exposed, and, also, trapped: cut off from the escape route. "But if he gets down into the woods, we'll probably have to use the dogs."

Hollingsworth was rolling up his pants leg, cigarette still in hand, to show Jesse the scar from the hunting accident when he was twelve: his father had said he thought he was a deer, and had shot him. Buzbee had been twenty-six.

"I'm like you," Hollingsworth said faithfully. "I can't run worth a damn, either." But Jesse had already mounted his bike: he was moving away, down the thin black strip, like a pilot taking a plane down a runway, to lift off, or like a fish running to sea; he entered the dead highway, which had patches of weeds growing up even in its center, and he stood up in the clips and accelerated away, down through the trees, with the wind at his back, going home.

He was gone almost immediately.

Hollingsworth's store had turned dark; the sun was behind the trees. He did not want to go back inside. He sat down on the porch and watched the empty road. His mother had died giving birth to him. She, like his father, had been fourteen. He and his father had always been more like brothers to each other than anything else. Hollingsworth could remember playing a game with his father, perhaps when he was seven or eight, and his father then would have been twenty-one or so—Jesse's age, roughly—and his father would run out into the field and hide, on their old homestead—racing down the hill, arms windmilling, and disappearing suddenly, diving down into the tall grass, while Hollingsworth—Quirter, Quirt—tried to find him. They played that game again and again, more than any other game in the world, and at all times of the year, not just in the summer.

Buzbee had a favorite tree, and he sat up in the low branch of it often and looked back in the direction from which he had come. He saw the bikers every day. There weren't ever cars on the road. The cyclists sometimes picnicked at a little roadside table

off of it, oranges and bottles of warm water and candy bars by
the dozens—he had snuck out there in the evenings, before, right
at dusk, and sorted through their garbage, nibbled some of the
orange peelings—and he was nervous, in his tree, whenever they
stopped for any reason.

Buzbee had not in the least considered going back to his mad-
dened son. He shifted on the branch and watched the cyclists eat
their oranges. His back was slick with sweat, and he was rank,
like the worst of animals. He and all the women bathed in the
evenings in the bayou, in the shallows, rolling around in the
mud. The women wouldn't go out any deeper. Snakes swam in
evil S-shapes, back and forth, as if patrolling. He was starting to
learn the women well, and many of them were like his son in
every regard, in that they always wanted to talk, it seemed—this
compulsion to communicate, as if it could be used to keep something else away, something big and threatening. He thought
about what the cold weather would be like, November and beyond, himself trapped, as it were, in the abandoned palmetto
shack, with all of them around the fireplace, talking, for four
months.

He slid down from the tree and started out into the field,
toward the cyclists—the women watched him go—and in the
heat, in the long walk across the field, he became dizzy, started
to fall several times, and for the briefest fragments of time he
kept forgetting where he was, imagined that one of the cyclists
was his son, that he was coming back in from the game that they
used to play, and he stopped, knelt down in the grass and pretended to hide. Eventually, though, the cyclists finished eating,
got up and rode away, down the road again. Buzbee watched
them go, then stood up and turned and raced back down into the
woods, to the women. He had become very frightened, for no
reason, out in the field like that.

Buzbee had found the old settlement after wandering around in
the woods for a week. There were carp in the bayou, and gar,

and catfish, and he wrestled the large ones out of the shallow oxbows that had been cut off from the rest of the water. He caught alligators, too, the small ones.

He kept a small fire going, continuously, to keep the mosquitoes away, and as he caught more and more of the big fish, he hung them from the branches in his clearing, looped vine through their huge jaws and hung them like villains, all around in his small clearing, like the most ancient of burial grounds: all these vertical fish, out of the water, mouths gaping in silent death, as if preparing to ascend: they were all pointing up.

The new pleasure of being alone sometimes stirred Buzbee so that he ran from errand to errand, as if on a shopping spree or a game show: he was getting ready for this new life, and with fall and winter coming on, he felt young.

After a couple of weeks, he had followed the bayou upstream, toward town, backtracking the water's sluggishness; sleeping under the large logs that had fallen across it like netting, and he swatted at the mosquitoes that swarmed him whenever he stopped moving, in the evenings, and he had kept going, even at night. The moon came down through the bare limbs of the swamp-rotted ghost trees, skeleton-white, disease-killed, but as he got higher above the swamp and closer to the town, near daylight, the water moved faster, had some circulation, was still alive, and the mosquitoes were not a threat.

He lay under a boxcar on the railroad tracks and looked across the road at the tired women going in and out of the washateria: moving so slowly, as if old. They were in their twenties, their thirties, their forties: they carried their baskets of wet clothes in front of them with a bumping, side-to-side motion, as if they were going to quit living on the very next step; their forearms sweated, glistened, and the sandals on their wide feet made flopping sounds, and he wanted to tell them about his settlement. He wanted five or six, ten or twenty of them. He wanted them walking around barefooted on the dark earth beneath his trees, beneath his hanging catfish and alligators, by the water, in the swamp.

He stole four chickens and a rooster that night, hooded their eyes, and put them in a burlap sack, put three eggs in each of his shirt pockets, too, after sucking ten of them dry, greedily, gulping, in the almost wet brilliance of the moon, behind a chicken farm back west of town, along the bayou—and then he continued on down its banks, the burlap sack thrown over his back, the chickens and rooster warm against his damp body, and calm, waiting.

He stopped when he came out of the green and thick woods, over a little ridge, and looked down into the country where the bayous slowed to heavy swamp and where the white and dead trees were and the bad mosquitoes lived—and he sat down and leaned his old back against a tree, and watched the moon and its blue light shining on the swamp, with his chickens. He waited until the sun came up and it got hot, and the mosquitoes had gone away, before starting down toward the last part of his journey, back to his camp.

The rest of the day he gathered seeds and grain from the little raised hummocks and grassy spots in the woods, openings in the forest, to use for feed for the chickens, which moved in small crooked shapes of white, like little ghosts in the woods, all through his camp, but they did not leave it. The rooster flew up into a low tree and stared wildly, golden-eyed, down into the bayou. For weeks Buzbee had been hunting the quinine bushes said to have been planted there during the big epidemic, and on that day he found them, because the chickens went straight to them and began pecking at them as Buzbee had never seen chickens peck: they flew up into the leaves, smothered their bodies against the bushes as if mating with them, so wild were they to get to the berries.

Buzbee's father had planted the bushes, had received the seeds from South America, on a freighter that he met in New Orleans the third year of the epidemic, and he had returned with them to the settlement, that third year, when everyone went down finally.

The plants had not done well; they kept rotting, and never, in Buzbee's father's time, bore fruit or made berries. Buzbee had listened to his father tell the story about how they rotted—but also how, briefly, they had lived, even flourished, for a week or two, and how the settlement had celebrated and danced, and cooked alligators and cattle, and prayed: and everyone in the settlement had planted quinine seeds, all over the woods, for miles, in every conceivable location . . . and Buzbee knew immediately, when the chickens began to cluck and feed, that it was the quinine berries, which they knew instinctively they must eat, and he went and gathered all the berries, and finally, he knew, he was safe.

The smoke from his fire, down in the low bottom, had spread through the swamp, and from above would have looked as if that portion of the bayou, going into the tangled dead trees, had simply disappeared: a large spill of white, a fuzzy, milky spot—and then, on the other side of the spill, coming out again, bayou once more.

Buzbee was relieved to have the berries, and he let the fire go down: he let it die. He sat against his favorite tree by the water and watched for small alligators. When he saw one, he would leap into the water, splash and swim across to meet it, and wrestle it out of the shallows and into the mud, where he would kill it savagely.

But the days were long, and he did not see that many alligators, and many of the ones he did see were a little too large, sometimes far too large. Still, he had almost enough for winter, as it stood: those hanging from the trees, along with the gaping catfish, spun slowly in the breeze of fall coming, and if he waited and watched, eventually he would see one. He sat against the tree and watched, and ate berries, chewed them slowly, pleasuring in their sour taste.

He imagined that they soured his blood: that they made him

taste bad to the mosquitoes, and kept them away. Though he
noticed they were still biting him, more even, now that the
smoke was gone. But he got used to it.

A chicken had disappeared, probably to a snake, but also possibly to anything, anything.

The berries would keep him safe.

He watched the water. Sometimes there would be the tiniest
string of bubbles rising, from where an alligator was stirring in
the mud below.

Two of the women from the laundry came out of the woods,
tentatively, having left their homes, following the bayou, to see if
it was true: what they had heard. It was dusk, and their clothes
were torn and their faces wild. Buzbee looked up and could see
the fear, and he wanted to comfort them. He did not ask what
had happened at their homes, what fear could make the woods
and the bayou journey seem less frightening. They stayed back
in the trees, frozen, and would not come with him, even when he
took each by the hand, until he saw what it was that was horrify-
ing them: the grinning reptiles, the dried fish, spinning from the
trees—and he explained to them that he had put them there to
smoke, for food, for the winter.

"They smell good," said the shorter one, heavier than her
friend, her skin a deep black, like some poisonous berry. Her
face was shiny.

Her friend slapped at a mosquito.

"Here," said Buzbee, handing them some berries. "Eat these."

But they made faces and spat them out when they tasted the
bitterness.

Buzbee frowned. "You'll get sick if you don't eat them," he
said. "You won't make it otherwise."

They walked past him, over to the alligators, and reached out
to the horned, hard skin, and touched them fearfully, ready to
run, making sure the alligators were unable to leave the trees
and were truly harmless.

. . .

"Don't you ever, you know, get lonely for girls?" Hollingsworth asked, like a child. It was only four days later: but Jesse was back for another half-Coke. The other bikers had ridden past almost an hour earlier: a fast rip-rip-rip, and then, much later, Jesse had come up the hill, pedaling hard, but moving slower.

He was trying, but he couldn't stay up with them. He had thrown his bike down angrily, and glowered at Hollingsworth, when he stalked up to the Coke machine, scowled at him as if it was Hollingsworth's fault.

"I got a whore," Jesse said, looking behind him and out across the road. The pasture was green and wet, and fog, like mist, hung over it, steaming from a rain earlier in the day. Jesse was lying; he didn't have anyone, hadn't had anyone in over a year—everybody knew he was slow in his group, and they shunned him for that—and Jesse felt as if he was getting farther and farther away from ever wanting anyone, or anything. He felt like everything was a blur: such was the speed at which he imagined he was trying to travel. Beyond the fog in the pasture were the trees, clear and dark and washed from the rain, and smelling good, even at this distance. Hollingsworth wished he had a whore. He wondered if Jesse would let him use his. He wondered if maybe she would be available if Jesse was to get fast and go off to the Olympics, or something.

"What does she cost?" Hollingsworth asked timidly.

Jesse looked at him in disgust. "I didn't mean it *that* way," he said. He looked tired, as if he was holding back, just a few seconds, from having to go back out on the road. Hollingsworth leaned closer, eagerly, sensing weakness, tasting hesitation. His senses were sharp, from deprivation: he could tell, even before Jesse could, that Jesse was feeling thick, laggard, dulled. He knew Jesse was going to quit. He knew it the way a farmer might see that rain was coming.

"I mean," sighed Jesse, "that I got an old lady. A woman friend. A girl."

"What's her name?" Hollingsworth said quickly. He would make Jesse so tired that he would never ride again. They would sit around on the porch and talk forever, all of the days.

"Jemima."

Hollingsworth wanted her, just for her name.

"That's nice," he said, in a smaller voice.

It seemed to Hollingsworth that Jesse was getting his energy back. But he had felt the tiredness, and maybe, Hollingsworth hoped, it would come back.

"I found out the old man is your father," said Jesse. He was looking out at the road. He still wasn't making any move toward it. Hollingsworth realized, as if he had been tricked, that perhaps Jesse was just waiting for the roads to dry up a little, to finish steaming.

"Yes," said Hollingsworth, "he has run away."

They looked at the fields together.

"He is not right," Hollingsworth said.

"The black women in town, the ones that do everyone's wash at the laundromat, say he is living down in the old yellow-fever community," Jesse said. "They say he means to stay, and that some of them have thought about going down there with him: the ones with bad husbands and too much work. He's been sneaking around the laundry late in the evenings, and promising them he'll cook for them, if any of them want to move down there with him. He says there aren't any snakes. They're scared the fever will come back, but he promises there aren't any snakes, that he killed them all, and a lot of them are considering it." Jesse related all this in a monotone, still watching the road, as if waiting for energy. The sun was burning the steam off. Hollingsworth felt damp, weak, unsteady, as if his mind was sweating with condensation from the knowledge, the way glasses suddenly fog up when you are walking into a humid setting.

"Sounds like he's getting lonely," Jesse said.

The steam was almost gone.

"He'll freeze this winter," Hollingsworth said, hopefully.

Jesse shook his head. "Sounds like he's got a plan. I suspect he'll have those women cutting firewood for him; fanning him with leaves; fishing, running traps, bearing children. Washing clothes."

"We'll catch him," Hollingsworth said, making a fist and smacking it in his palm. "And anyway, those women won't go down into those woods. They're dark, and the yellow fever's still down there: I'll go into town, and tell them it is. I'll tell them Buzbee's spitting up black blood and shivering, and is crazy. Those women won't go down into those woods."

Jesse shook his head. He put the bottle into the rack. The road was dry; it looked clean, scrubbed, by the quick thunderstorm. "A lot of those women have got bruises on their arms, their faces, have got teeth missing, and their lives are too hard and without hope," Jesse said slowly, as if just for the first time seeing it. "Myself, I think they'll go down there in great numbers. I don't think yellow fever means anything compared to what they have, or will have." He turned to Hollingsworth and slipped a leg over his bike, got on, put his feet in the clips, steadied himself against the porch railing. "I bet by June next year you're going to have about twenty half brothers and half sisters."

When Jesse rode off, thickly, as if the simple heat of the air were a thing holding him back, there was no question, Hollingsworth realized, Jesse was exhausted, and fall was coming. Jesse was getting tired. He, Hollingsworth, and Buzbee, and the colored women at the washhouse, and other people would get tired, too. The temperatures would be getting cooler, milder, in a month or so, and the bikers would be riding harder than ever. There would be the smoke from fires, hunters down on the river, and at night the stars would be brighter, and people's sleep would be heavier, and deeper. Hollingsworth wondered just how fast those bikers wanted to go. Surely, he thought, they were already going fast enough. He didn't understand them. Surely, he thought, they didn't know what they were doing.

The speeds that the end of June and the beginning of July brought, Jesse had never felt before, and he didn't trust them to last, didn't know if they could: and he tried to stay with the other riders, but didn't know if there was anything he could do to make the little speed he had last, in the curves, and that feeling, pounding up the hills; his heart working thick and smooth, like the wildest, easiest, most volatile thing ever invented. He tried to stay with them.

Hollingsworth, the old faggot, was running out into the road some days, trying to flag him down, for some piece of bullshit, but there wasn't time, and he rode past, not even looking at him, only staring straight ahead.

The doves started to fly. The year was moving along. A newspaper reporter wandered down, to do a short piece on the still-missing Buzbee. It was rumored he was living in an abandoned, rotting shack, deep into the darkest, lowest heart of the swamp. It was said that he had started taking old colored women, maids and such, women from the laundromat, away from town; that they were going back down into the woods with him and living there, and that he had them in a corral, like a herd of wild horses. The reporter's story slipped further from the truth. It was all very mysterious, all rumor, and the reward was increased to $1,200 by Hollingsworth, as the days grew shorter after the solstice, and lonelier.

Jesse stopped racing. He just didn't go out one day; and when the Frenchmen came by for him, he pretended not to be in.

He slept late and began to eat vast quantities of oatmeal. Sometimes, around noon, he would stop eating and get on his bike and ride slowly up the road to Hollingsworth's—sometimes the other bikers would pass him, moving as ever at great speed, all of them, and they would jeer at him, shout yah-yah, and then they were quickly gone; and he willed them to wreck, shut his eyes and tried to make it happen—picturing the whole pack of them getting tangled up, falling over one another, the way they tended to do, riding so close together—and the pain of those wrecks, the long slide, the drag and skid of flesh on gravel.

The next week he allowed himself a whole Coca-Cola, with Hollingsworth, on the steps of the store's porch. The old man swooned, and had to steady himself against the railing when he saw it was his true love. It was a dry summer. They talked more about Buzbee.

"He's probably averse to being captured," Hollingsworth said. "He probably won't go easy."

Jesse looked at his shoes, watched them, as if thinking about where they were made.

"If you were to help me catch him, I would give you my half of it," Hollingsworth said generously. Jesse watched his shoes.

Hollingsworth got up and went in the store quickly, and came back out with a hank of calf-roping lariat, heavy, gold as a fable, and corded.

"I been practicing," he said. There was a sawhorse standing across the drive, up on two legs, like a man, with a hat on it, and a coat, and Hollingsworth said nothing else, but twirled the lariat over his head and then flung it at the sawhorse, a mean heavy whistle over their heads, and the loop settled over the sawhorse, and Hollingsworth stepped back quickly and tugged, cinched the loop shut. The sawhorse fell over, and Hollingsworth began dragging it across the gravel, reeling it in as fast as he could.

"I could lasso you off that road, if I wanted," Hollingsworth said.

Jesse thought about how the money would be nice. He thought about how it was in a wreck, too, when he wasn't able to get his feet free of the clips and had to stay with the bike, and roll over with it, still wrapped up in it. It was just the way his sport was.

"I've got to be going," he told Hollingsworth. When he stood up, though, he had been still too long, and his blood stayed down in his legs, and he saw spots and almost fell.

"Easy now, hoss," Hollingsworth cautioned; watching him eagerly, eyes narrowed, hoping for an accident and no more riding.

The moonlight that came in through Hollingsworth's window, onto his bed, all night—it was silver. It made things look different: ghostly. He slept on his back: looking up at the ceiling until he fell asleep. He listened to crickets, to hoot owls, and to the silence, too.

We'll get him, he thought. We'll find his ass. But he couldn't sleep, and the sound of his heart, the movement of his blood pulsing, was the roar of an ocean, and it wasn't right. His father did not belong down in those woods. No one did. There was nothing down there that Hollingsworth could see but reptiles, and danger.

The moon was so bright that it washed out all stars. Hollingsworth listened to the old house. There was a blister on the inside of his finger from practicing with the lariat, and he fingered it and looked at the ceiling.

Jesse went back, again and again. He drank the Coke slowly. He wasn't sweating.

"Let's go hunt that old dog," Hollingsworth said—it was the first thing he said, after Jesse had gotten his bottle out of the machine and opened it—and like a molester, a crooner, Hollingsworth seemed to be drifting toward Jesse without moving his feet: just leaning forward, swaying closer and closer, as if moving in to smell blossoms. His eyes were a believer's blue, and for a moment, still thinking about how slowly he had ridden over and the Coke's coldness and wetness, Jesse had no idea what he was talking about and felt dizzy. He looked into Hollingsworth's eyes, such a pale wash of light, such a pale blue that he knew the eyes had never seen anything factual, nothing of substance—and he laughed, thinking of Hollingsworth trying to catch Buzbee, or anything, on his own. The idea of Hollingsworth being able to do anything other than just take what was thrown at him was ridiculous. He thought of Hollingsworth on a bike, pedaling, and laughed again.

"We can split the reward money," Hollingsworth said again. He was grinning, smiling wildly, trying as hard as he could to show all his teeth and yet keep them close together, uppers and lowers touching. He breathed through the cracks in them in a low, pulsing whistle: in and out. He had never in his life drunk anything but water, and his teeth were startlingly white; they were just whittled down, was all, and puny, from aging and time. He closed his eyes, squeezed them shut slowly, as if trying to remember something simple, like speech, or balance, or even breathing. He was like a turtle sunning on a log.

Jesse couldn't believe he was speaking.

"Give me all of it," he heard himself say.

"All of it," Hollingsworth agreed, his eyes still shut, and then he opened them and handed the money to Jesse slowly, ceremoniously, like a child paying for something at a store counter, for the first time.

Jesse unlaced his shoes, and folded the bills in half and slid them down into the soles, putting bills in both shoes. He unlaced the drawstring to his pants and slid some down into the black dampness of his racing silks: down in the crotch, and padding the buttocks, and in front, high on the flatness of his abdomen, like a girdle, directly below the cinching lace of the drawstring, which he then tied again, tighter than it had been before.

Then he got on the bike and rode home, slowly, not racing anymore, not at all; through the late-day heat that had built up, but with fall in the air, the leaves on the trees hanging differently. There was some stillness everywhere. He rode on.

When he got home he carried the bike inside, as was his custom, and then undressed, peeling his suit off, with the damp bills fluttering slowly to the old rug, like petals and blossoms from a dying flower, unfolding when they landed, and it surprised him

at first to see them falling away from him like that, all around
him, for he had forgotten that they were down there as he rode.

Buzbee was like a field general. The women were tasting freedom, and seemed to be like circus strongmen, muscled with
great strength suddenly, from not being told what to do, from
not being beaten or yelled at. They laughed and talked, and were
kind to Buzbee. He sat up in the tree, in his old khaki pants, and
watched, and whenever it looked like his feeble son and the ex-
biker might be coming, he leaped down from the tree, and like
monkeys they scattered into the woods: back to another, deeper,
temporary camp they had built.

They splashed across the river like wild things, but they were
laughing, there was no fear, not like there would have been in
animals.

They knew they could get away. They knew that as long as
they ran fast, they would make it.

Buzbee grinned too, panting, his eyes bright, and he watched
the women's breasts float and bounce, riding high as they
charged across; ankle-deep, knee-deep, waist-deep; hurrying to
get away from his mad, lonely son: running fast and shrieking,
because they were all afraid of the alligators.

Buzbee had a knife in one hand and a sharpened stick in the
other, and he almost wished there would be an attack, so that he
could be a hero.

The second camp was about two miles down into the swamp.
No one had ever been that far into it, not ever. The mosquitoes
were worse, too. There wasn't any dry land, not even a patch:
but they sat on the branches, and dangled their feet, and waited.
Sometimes they saw black bears splashing after fish, and turtles.
There were more snakes, too, deeper back, but the women were
still bruised, and some of them fingered their scars as they
watched the snakes, and no one went back.

They made up songs, with which they pretended to make the
snakes go away.

It wasn't too bad.

They sat through the night listening to the cries of birds, and when the woods began to grow light again, so faintly at first that they doubted it was happening, they would ease down into the water and start back toward their dry camp.

Hollingsworth would be gone, chased away by the mosquitoes, by the emptiness, and they would feel righteous, as if they'd won something: a victory.

None of them had a watch. They never knew what time it was, what day even.

"Gone," said Hollingsworth.

He was out of breath, out of shape. His shoelaces were untied, and there were burrs in his socks. The camp was empty. Just chickens. And the godawful reptiles, twisting from the trees.

"Shit almighty," said Jesse. His legs were cramping, and he was bent over, massaging them: he wasn't used to walking.

Hollingsworth poked around in the little grass-and-wood shacks. He was quivering, and kept saying, alternately, "Gone" and "Damn."

Jesse had to sit down, so bad was the pain in his legs. He put his feet together like a bear in the zoo and held them there, and rocked, trying to stretch them back out. He was frightened of the alligators, and he felt helpless, in his cramps, knowing that Buzbee could come up from behind with a club and rap him on the head, like one of the chickens, and that he, Jesse, wouldn't even be able to get up to stop him, or run.

Buzbee was in control.

"Shit. Damn. Gone," said Hollingsworth. He was running a hand through his thinning hair. He kicked a few halfhearted times at the shacks, but they were kicks of sorrow, not rage yet, and did no damage.

"We could eat the chickens," Jesse suggested, from his sitting position. "We could cook them on his fire and leave the bones all over camp." Jesse still had his appetite from his riding days, and was getting fat fast. He was eating all the time since he had stopped riding.

Hollingsworth turned to him, slightly insulted. "They belong to my father," he said.

Jesse continued to rock, but thought: My God, what a madman.

He rubbed his legs and rocked. The pain was getting worse.

There was a breeze stirring. They could hear the leather and rope creaking, as some of the smaller alligators moved. There was a big alligator hanging from a beech tree, about ten feet off the ground, and as they watched it, the leather cord snapped, from the friction, and the dead weight of the alligator crashed to the ground.

"The mosquitoes are getting bad," said Jesse, rising: hobbled, bent over. "We'd better be going."

But Hollingsworth was already scrambling up through the brush, up toward the brightness of sky above the field. He could see the sky, the space, through the trees, and knew the field was out there. He was frantic to get out of the woods; there was a burning in his chest, in his throat, and he couldn't breathe.

Jesse helped him across the field and got him home; he offered to ride into Crystal Springs, thirty miles, and make a call for an ambulance, but Hollingsworth waved him away.

"Just stay with me a little while," he said. "I'll be okay."

But the thought was terrifying to Jesse—of being in the same room with Hollingsworth, contained, and listening to him talk, forever, all day and through the night, doubtless.

"I have to go," he said, and hurried out the door.

He got on his bike and started slowly for home. His knees were bumping against his belly, such was the quickness of his becoming fat, but the relief of being away from Hollingsworth was so great that he didn't mind.

Part of him wanted to be as he had been, briefly: iron, and fast, racing with the fastest people in the world, it seemed—he couldn't remember anything about them, only the blaze and rip of their speed, the *whish-whish* cutting sound they made, as a pack, tucking and sailing down around corners—but also, he was so tired of that, and it felt good to be away from it, for just a little while.

He could always go back.

His legs were still strong. He could start again any time. The sport of it, the road, would have him back. The other bikers would have him back, they would be happy to see him.

He thought all these things as he trundled fatly up the minor hills, the gradual rises: coasting, relievedly, on the down sides.

Shortly before he got to the gravel turnoff, the little tree-lined road that led to his house, the other bikers passed him, coming from out of the west, and they screamed and howled at him, passing, and jabbed their thumbs down at him, as if they were trying to unplug a drain or poke a hole in something; they shrieked, and then they were gone, so quickly.

He did not stop blushing for the rest of the day. He wanted to hide somewhere, he was so ashamed of what he had lost, but there was nowhere to hide, for in a way it was still in him: the memory of it.

He dreamed of going down into the woods, of joining Buzbee and starting over, wrestling alligators; but he only dreamed it— and in the morning, when he woke up, he was still heavy and slow, grounded.

He went into the kitchen, and looked in the refrigerator, and began taking things out. Maybe, he thought, Hollingsworth would up the reward money.

Buzbee enjoyed cooking for the women. It was going to be an early fall, and dry; they got to where they hardly noticed the mosquitoes that were always whining around them—a tiny buzzing—and they had stopped wearing clothes long ago. Buzbee pulled down hickory branches and climbed up in trees, often —and he sat hunkered above the women, looking down, just watching them move around in their lives, naked and happy, talking; more had come down the bayou since the first two, and they were shoring up the old shelter; pulling up palmetto plants from the hummocks and dragging logs across the clearing, fixing the largest of the abandoned cabins into a place that was livable, for all of them.

He liked the way they began to look at him, on about the tenth day of their being there, and he did not feel seventy-seven. He slid down out of the tree, walked across the clearing toward the largest woman, the one he had had his eye on, and took her hand, hugged her, felt her broad fat back, the backs of her legs, which were sweaty, and then her behind, while she giggled.

All that week, as the weather changed, they came drifting in, women from town, sometimes carrying lawn chairs, always wild-eyed and tentative when they saw the alligators and catfish, the people moving around naked in camp, brown as the earth itself—but then they would recognize someone, and would move out into the clearing with wonder, and a disbelief at having escaped. A breeze might be stirring, and dry colored hardwood leaves, ash and hickory, and oak and beech, orange and gold, would tumble down into the clearing, spill around their ankles, and the leaves made empty scraping sounds when the women walked through them, shuffling, looking up at the spinning fish.

At night they would sit around the fire and eat the dripping juiciness of the alligators, roasted: fat, from the tails, sweet, glistening on their hands, their faces; running down to their elbows. They smeared it on their backs, their breasts, to keep the mosquitoes away. Nights smelled of wood smoke. They could see the stars above their trees, above the shadows of their catches.

The women had all screamed and run into the woods, in different directions, the first time Buzbee leaped into the water after an alligator; but now they all gathered close and applauded and chanted an alligator-catching song they had made up that had few vowels, whenever he wrestled them. But that first time they thought he had lost his mind: he had rolled around and around in the thick gray-white slick mud, down by the bank, jabbing the young alligator with his pocketknife again and again, perforating it and muttering savage dog noises, until they could no longer tell which was which, except for the jets of blood that spurted out of the alligator's fat belly—but after he had killed the reptile, and rinsed off in the shallows, and come back across the oxbow, wading in knee-deep water, carrying it in his arms, a four-footer, his largest ever, he was smiling, gap-toothed, having lost two in the fight, but he was also erect, proud, and ready for love. It was the first time they had seen that.

The one he had hugged went into the hut after him.

The other women walked around the alligator carefully, and poked sticks at it, but also glanced toward the hut and listened, for the brief and final end of the small thrashings, the little pleasure, that was going on inside, the confirmation, and presently it came: Buzbee's goatish bleats, and the girl's, too, which made them look at one another with surprise, wonder, interest, and speculation.

"It's those berries he's eatin'," said one, whose name was Onessimius. Oney.

"They tastes bad," said Tasha.

"They makes your pee turn black," said Oney.

They looked at her with caution.

Jesse didn't have the money for a car, or even for an old tractor.

He bought a used lawn-mower engine instead, for fifteen dollars. He found some old plywood in a dry abandoned barn. He scrounged some wheels, and stole a fan belt from a car rotting in a field, with bright wildflowers growing out from under the hood and mice in the back seat. He made a go-cart, and put a long plastic antenna with an orange flag, a banner, on the back of it that reached high into the sky, so that any motorists coming would see it.

But there was never any traffic. He sputtered and coughed up the hills, going one, two miles an hour: then coasting down, a

slight breeze in his face. He didn't wear his biking helmet, and
the breeze felt good.

It took him an hour to get to Hollingsworth's sometimes; he
carried a sack lunch with him, apples and potato chips, and ate,
happily, as he drove.

He started out going over to Hollingsworth's in the mid-
morning, and always trying to come back in the early afternoon,
so that the bikers would not see him: but it got more and more to
where he didn't care, and finally, he just came and went as he
pleased, waving happily when he saw them; but they never
waved back. Sometimes the one who had replaced him, the trail-
ing one, would spit water from his thermos bottle onto the top of
Jesse's head as he rushed past; but they were gone quickly, almost as fast as they had appeared, and soon he was no longer
thinking about them. They were gone.

Cottonwoods. Rabbits. Fields. It was still summer, it seemed
it would always be summer; the smell of hay was good, and dry.
All summer, they cut hay in the fields around him.

He was a slow movement of color going up the hills, with
everything else in his world motionless; down in the fields, black
Angus grazed, and cattle egrets stood behind them and on their
backs. Crows sat in the dead limbs of trees, back in the woods,
watching him, watching the cows, waiting for fall.

He would reach Hollingsworth's, and the old man would be
waiting, like a child: wanting his father back. It was a ritual.
Hollingsworth would wave, tiredly: hiding in his heart the delight at seeing another person.

Jesse would wave back as he drove up into the gravel drive.
He would grunt and pull himself up out of the little go-cart, and
go over to the Coke machine.

The long slide of the bottle down the chute; the rattle, and
clunk.

They'd sit on the porch, and Hollingsworth would begin to
talk.

"I saw one of those explode in a man's hand," he said, pointing to the bottle Jesse was drinking. "Shot a sliver of glass as long as a knife up into his forearm, all the way. He didn't feel a thing: he just looked at it, and then walked around, pointing to it, showing everybody . . ."

Hollingsworth remembered everything that had ever happened to him. He told Jesse everything.

Jesse would stir after the second or third story. He couldn't figure it out; he couldn't stand to be too close to Hollingsworth, to listen to him for more than twenty or thirty minutes—he hated it after that point—but always, he went back; every day.

It was as if he got full, almost to the point of vomiting; but then he got hungry again.

He sat on the porch and drank Cokes, and ate cans and cans of whatever Hollingsworth had on the shelf: yams, mushrooms, pickles, deviled ham—and he knew, as if it were an equation on a blackboard, that his life had gone to hell—he could see it in the size of his belly resting between his soft legs—but he didn't know what to do.

There was a thing that was not in him anymore, and he did not know where to go to find it.

Oney was twenty-two, and had had a bad husband. She still had the stitches in her forehead: he had thrown a chair at her, because she had called him a lard-ass, which he was. The stitches in the center of her head looked like a third eyebrow, with the eye missing, and she hadn't heard about the old days of yellow fever and what it could do to one person, or everyone.

That night, even though she slept in Buzbee's arms, she began to shiver wildly, though the night was still and warm. And then two days later, again, she shivered and shook all night, and then two days later, a third time: it was coming every forty-eight hours, which was how it had done when Buzbee and his father had had it.

Onessimius had been pale to begin with, and was turning, as if with the leaves, yellow, right in front of them: a little brighter yellow each day. All of the women began to eat the berries, slowly at first, and then wolfishly, watching Oney as they ate them.

They had built a little palmetto coop for their remaining chickens, which were laying regularly, and they turned them out, three small white magicians moving through the woods in search of bugs, seeds, and berries, and the chickens split up and wandered in different directions, and Buzbee and all the women split up, too, and followed them single file, at a distance, waiting for the chickens to find more berries, but somehow two of the chickens got away from them, escaped, and when they came back to camp, with the one remaining white chicken, a large corn snake was in the rooster's cage and was swallowing him, with only his thrashing feet visible: the snake's mouth stretched hideously wide, eyes wide and unblinking, mouth stretched into a laugh, as if he was enjoying the meal. Buzbee killed the snake, but the rooster died shortly after being pulled back out.

Oney screamed and cried, and shook until she was spitting up more black blood, when they told her they were going to take her back into town, and she took Buzbee's pocketknife and pointed it between her breasts and swore she would kill herself if they tried to make her go back to Luscious—because he would kill her for having left, and in a way worse than spitting up black blood and even parts of her stomach—and so they let her stay, but worried, and fed her their dwindling berry supply, and watched the stars, the sunset, and hoped for a hard and cold winter and an early freeze, but the days stayed warm, though the leaves were changing on schedule, and always, they looked for berries, and began experimenting, too, with the things Buzbee and his father had tried so many years ago: cedar berries, mushrooms, hickory nuts, acorns. They smeared grease from the fish and alligators over every inch of their bodies, and kept a fire going again, at all times. But none of the women would go back to town. And none of them other than Oney had started spitting up blood or shivering yet. Ozzie, Buzbee's first woman, had missed her time.

And Buzbee sat up in the trees and looked down on them often, and stopped eating his berries, unbeknownst to them, so that there would be more. The alligators hung from the trees like dead insurgents, traitors to a way of life. They weren't seeing any more in the bayou, and he wasn't catching nearly as many fish. The fall was coming, and winter beyond that. The animals knew it first. Nothing could prevent its coming, or even slow its approach: nothing they could do would matter. Buzbee felt fairly certain that he had caught enough alligators.

Hollingsworth and Jesse made another approach a week later. Hollingsworth had the lariat, and was wearing cowboy boots and a hat. Jesse was licking a Fudgicle.

Buzbee, in his tree, spotted them and jumped down.

The women grumbled, but they dropped what they were doing and fled, went deeper, to safety.

"Shit," said Hollingsworth when they got to the camp. "He saw us coming again."

"He runs away," said Jesse, nodding. They could see the muddy slide marks where Buzbee and the women had scrambled out on the other side. The dark wall of trees, a wall.

"I've got an idea," said Hollingsworth.

They knew where Buzbee and the women were getting their firewood: there was a tremendous logjam, with driftwood stacked all along the banks, not far from the camp.

Hollingsworth and Jesse went and got shovels, as well as old mattresses from the dump, and came back and dug pits: huge, deep holes, big enough to bury cars, big enough to hold a school bus.

"I saw it on a Tarzan show," said Hollingsworth. His heart was burning; both of the men were dripping with sweat. It was the softest, richest dirt in the world, good and loose and black and easy to move, but they were out of shape and it took them all day. They sang as they dug, to keep Buzbee and the women at bay, hemmed in, back in the trees.

Buzbee and the women sat up on their branches, swatting at mosquitoes, and listened, and wondered what was going on.

"Row, row, row your boat!" Jesse shouted as he dug, his big belly wet, like a melon. Mopping his brow; his face streaked, with dirt and mud. He remembered the story about the pioneers who went crazy alone, and dug their own graves: standing at the edge, then, and doing it.

"Oh, say—can—you—see," Hollingsworth brayed, "by the dawn's—earl—lee—light?"

Back in the trees, the women looked at Buzbee for an explanation. They knew it was his son.

"He was born too early," he said weakly. "He has never been right."

"He misses you," said Oney. "That boy wants you to come home."

Buzbee scowled and looked down at his toes, hunkered on the branch, and held on fiercely, as if the tree had started to sway.

"That boy don't know *what* he wants," he said.

When Hollingsworth and Jesse had finished the pits, they spread long branches over them, then scattered leaves and twigs over the branches and left.

"We'll catch the whole tribe of them," Hollingsworth cackled.

Jesse nodded. He was faint, and didn't know if he could make it all the way back out or not. He wondered vaguely what Buzbee and the women would be having for supper.

The mosquitoes were vicious; the sun was going down. Owls were beginning to call.

"Come on," said Hollingsworth. "We've got to get out of here."

Jesse wanted to stay. But he felt Hollingsworth pull on his arm; he let himself be led away.

Back in the woods, up in the tree, Oney began to shiver, and closed her eyes, lost consciousness, and fell. Buzbee leaped down and gathered her up, held her tightly, and tried to warm her with his body.

"They gone," said a woman named Vesuvius. The singing had gone away when it got dark, as had the ominous sound of digging.

There was no moon, and it was hard, even though they were familiar with it, to find their way back to camp.

They built fires around Oney, and two days later she was better.

But they knew it would come again.

"Look at what that fool boy of yours has done," Tasha said the next day. She had gone to get more wood. A deer had fallen into one of the pits and was leaping about, uninjured, trying to get free.

Buzbee said his favorite curse word, a new one that Oney had told him, "Fuckarama," and they tried to rope the deer, but it was too wild: it would not let them get near.

"We could stone it," Tasha said, but not with much certainty; and they all knew they could not harm the deer, trapped as it was, so helpless.

They felt badly about it, and sat and tried to think of ways to get it out of the pit, but without shovels they were stumped.

They saw Oney's husband one horrible evening, moving through the woods, perilously close to their camp, moving through the gray trees at dusk, stalking their woods with a shotgun, as if squirrel-hunting.

They hid in their huts and watched, hoping he would not look down the hill and see their camp, not see the alligators hanging.

"Come on, baby," said Tasha, "find that pit." He was moving in that direction.

They watched, petrified. Oney was whimpering. His dark, slow shape moved cautiously about, but the light was going fast: that darkness of purple, all light being drawn away. He faded; he disappeared; it was dark. Then, into the night, they heard a yell, and a blast, and then the quietest silence they had ever known.

And then, later: owls calling, in the night.

It was a simple matter burying him in the morning. They hadn't thought of letting the deer out that way; they had not thought of filling it in and making it not be there anymore.

"You will get better," they told Oney. She believed them. On the days in which she did not have the fever, she believed them. There was still, though, the memory of it.

It was escapable. Some people lived through it and survived. It didn't get everyone. They didn't all just lie down and die, those who got it.

She loved old Buzbee, on her good days. She laughed, and slept with him, rolled with him, and put into the back of her mind what had happened before, and what would be happening again.

Her teeth, when she was laughing, pressing against him, clutching him, shutting her eyes. She would fight to keep it in the back of her mind, and to keep it behind her.

Jesse rode out to Hollingsworth's in the go-cart. He took a back road, a different route. The air was cooler, it seemed that summer could be ending, after all, and he felt like just getting out and seeing the country again. It was a road he had always liked to ride on, with or without the pack, back when he had been racing, and he had forgotten how fresh it had been, how it had tasted, just to look at it. He drove through a tunnel of trees; a pasture, on the other side of the trees, a stretch of pastel green, a smear of green, with charcoal cattle standing in it, and white egrets at their sides, pressed an image into the sides of his slow-moving vision. It was almost cold down in the creek bottom, going through the shade, so slowly.

He smiled and gave a small whoop, and waved a fist in the air.

The light on the other side of the trees, coming down onto the field, was the color of gold smoke.

He had a sack of groceries with him, behind the engine, and he reached back and got a sandwich and a canned drink. The go-cart rumbled along, carrying him; threatening to stop on the hill, but struggling on.

They went to check the traps, the pits, flushing Buzbee's troops back into the swamp, as ever.

"I'd hoped we could have caught them all," said Hollings-worth. His eyes were pale, mad, and he wanted to dig more holes.

"Look," he said. "They buried my mattress." He bent down on the fresh mound and began digging at it with his hands; but he gave up shortly, and looked around blankly, as if forgetting why he had been digging in the first place.

Buzbee and the women were getting angry at being chased so often, so regularly. They sat in the trees and waited. Some of the women said nothing, but hoped, to themselves, that Hollings-worth and Jesse would forget where some of the pits lay, and would stumble in.

Jesse and Hollingsworth sat on Hollingsworth's porch.

"You don't talk much," Hollingsworth said, as if noticing for the first time.

Jesse said nothing. It was getting near the twenty-minute mark. He had had two Cokes and a package of Twinkies. He was thinking about how it had been, when he had been in shape, and riding with the others, the pack: how his old iron bike had been a traitor some days, and his legs had laid down and died, and he had run out of wind—but how he had kept going, any-way, and how eventually—though only for a little while—it had gotten better.

The bikers rode past. They were moving so fast. Hills were nothing to them. They had light bikes, expensive ones, and the climbs were only excuses to use the great strength of their legs. The wind in their faces, and pressing back against their chests, was but a reason and a direction, for a feeling: it was something to rail against, and defeat, or be defeated by—but it was tangible. Compared to some things, the wind was actually tangible.

They shouted encouragement to one another as they jockeyed back and forth, sharing turns, breaking the wind for each other.

"I'm ready," Hollingsworth told Jesse on his next visit, a few days later.

He was jumping up and down like a child.

"I'm ready, I'm ready," Hollingsworth sang. "Ready for anything."

He had a new plan. All he had been doing was thinking: trying to figure out a way to get something back.

Jesse rode his bike to town, to get the supplies they would need: an extra lariat, and rope for trussing him up with; they figured he would be senile, and wild. Muzzles for the dogs. Jesse rode hard, for a fat man.

The wind was coming up. It was the first week in September. The hay was baled, stood in tall rolls, and the fields looked tame, civilized, smoothed: flattened.

They muzzled the dogs and put heavy leashes on their collars, and started out across the field. Owls were beginning to call again, it was the falling of dusk, and Jesse and Hollingsworth carried with them a kerosene lantern and some food and water.

When they had crossed the field—half running, half being dragged, by the big dogs' eagerness—and came to the edge of the woods, and started down into them, toward the swamp, they were halted by the mosquitoes, which rose up in a noisy dark cloud and fell upon them like soft fingers. The dogs turned back, whining in their muzzles, yelping, instinct warning them of the danger of these particular mosquitoes, and they kept backing away, back into the field, and would not go down into the swamp.

So Hollingsworth and Jesse camped back in the wind of the pasture, in the cool grass, and waited for daylight.

They could smell the smoke from Buzbee's camp, but could see nothing, the woods were so dark. There was a quarter-moon, and it came up so close to them, over the trees, that they could see the craters. Hollingsworth talked.

He talked about the space program. He asked Jesse if this wasn't better than riding his old bike. They shared a can of Vienna sausage. Hollingsworth talked all night. Chuck-will's-widows called, and bullbats thumped around in the grass, not far from their small fire: flinging themselves into the grass and flopping around as if mourning; rising again, flying past, and then twisting and slamming hard and awkwardly down, without a cry, as if pulled there by a sudden force, hidden: as if their time was up; all around them, the bullbats flew like this, twisting and then diving into the ground, until it seemed to Jesse that without a doubt they were trying to send a message: Go back, go back.

And he imagined, as he tried not to listen to Hollingsworth's babblings, that the bikers he had ridden with, the Frenchmen, were asleep, or making love to soft women, or eating ice-cream cones.

A light drizzle woke Hollingsworth and Jesse and the dogs in the morning, and they stood up and stretched, and then moved on the camp. Crickets were chirping quietly in the soft rain, and the field was steaming. There wasn't any more smoke from the fire. The dogs had been smelling Buzbee and his camp all night, and were nearly crazed: their chests swelled and strained like barrels of apples, like hearts of anger, and they jumped and twisted and tugged against their leashes, pulling Hollingsworth and Jesse behind them in a stumbling run through the wet grasses.

Froth came from their muzzles, their rubbery lips. Their eyes were wild. They were too hard to hold. They pulled free of their leashes, and raced, silently, like the fastest thing in the world, accelerating across the field and into the woods, straight for the camp, the straightest thing that ever was.

Jesse bought a bike with the reward money: a French bicycle, a racer, with tires that were thinner than a person's finger held sideways: it could fly. It was light blue, like an old man's eyes.

Hollingsworth had chained Buzbee to the porch: had padlocked the clasp around his ankle, with thirty feet of chain. It disgusted Jesse, but even more disgusted was he by his own part in the capture, and by the size of his stomach, his loss of muscularity.

He began to ride again: not with the pack, but by himself.

He got fast again, as he had thought he could. He got faster than he had been before, faster than he had ever imagined, and bought a stopwatch and raced against himself, timing himself, riding up and down the same roads over and over again.

Sometimes, riding, he would look up and see Buzbee out on the porch, standing, with Hollingsworth sitting behind him, talking. Hollingsworth would wave, wildly.

One night, when Jesse got in from his ride, the wind had shifted out of the warm west and was from the north, and serious, and in it, after Jesse had bathed and gotten in bed, was the thing, not for the first time, but the most insistent that year, that made Jesse get back out of bed, where he was reading, and go outside and sit on the steps beneath his porch light. He tried to read.

Moths fell down off the porch light's bulb, brushed his shoulders, landed on the pages of his book, spun, and flew off, leaving traces of magic. And the wind began to stir harder. Stars were all above him, and they glittered and flashed in the wind. They seemed to be challenging him: daring him to see what was true.

Two miles away, up on the hill, back in the trees, the A.M.E. church was singing. He couldn't see their lights, but for the first time that year he could hear them singing, the way he could in the winter, when there were no leaves on the trees and when the air was colder, more brittle, and sounds carried. He could never hear the words, just the sad moaning that sometimes, finally, fell away into pleasure.

He stood up on the porch and walked out into the yard, the cool grass, and tried some sit-ups. When he was through, he lay back, sweating slightly, breathing harder, and he watched the stars, but they weren't as bright, it seemed, and he felt as if he had somehow failed them, had not done the thing expected or, rather, the thing demanded.

When he woke up in the morning, turned on his side in the yard, sleeping, lying out in the grass like an animal, the breeze was still blowing and the light of the day was gold, coming out of the pines on the east edge of his field.

He sat up, stiffly, and for a moment forgot who he was, what he did, where he was—it was the breeze moving across him, so much cooler suddenly—and then he remembered, it was so simple, that he was supposed to ride.

It was early November. There was a heaviness to all movements, to all sights. It was impossible to look at the sky, at the trees, at the cattle in the fields even, and not know that it was November. The clasp around Buzbee's ankle was cold; his legs were getting stronger from pulling the chain around with him. He stood out on the porch, and the air, when he breathed deeply, went all the way down into his chest: he felt good. He felt like wrestling an alligator.

He had knocked Hollingsworth to the ground, tried to get him to tell him where the key was. But Hollingsworth, giggling, with his arm twisted behind his back—the older man riding him, breathing hard but steadily, pushing his son's face into the floor —had told Buzbee that he had thrown the key away. And Buzbee, knowing his son, his poisoned loneliness, knew that it was so.

The chain was too big to break or smash.

. . .

Sometimes Buzbee cried, looking at it. He felt as if he could not breathe; it was as if he were being smothered. It was like a thing was about to come to a stop.

He watched the field all the time. Jesse raced by, out on the road, checking his watch, looking at it, holding it in one hand, pedaling hard: flying, it seemed.

Buzbee heard Hollingsworth moving behind him; coming out to gab. It was like being in a cell.

Buzbee could see the trees, the watery blur of them, on the other side of the field.

"Pop," said Hollingsworth, ready with a story.

Pop, my ass, thought Buzbee bitterly. He wanted to strangle his own son.

He had so wanted to make a getaway—to have an escape, clean and free.

He looked out at the field, remembering what it had been like with the women, and the alligators, and he thought how he would be breaking free again, shortly, for good.

This time, he knew, he would get completely away.

The blue line of trees, where he had been with the women, wavered and flowed, in watercolor blotches, and there was a dizziness high in his forehead. He closed his eyes and listened to his mad son babble, and he prepared, and made his plans.

When he opened his eyes, the road was empty in front of him. Jesse was gone: a streak, a flash: already gone.

It was as if he had never even been there.

Buzbee narrowed his eyes and gripped the porch railing, squinted at the trees, scowled, and plotted, and tried to figure another way out.

Unstable Ground

•

ELLEN HERMAN

At the age of thirty-one, Teddy bought a house. The purchase made him nervous; signing the mortgage papers, his fingers trembled, leaving a crabbed, indecipherable name. The house was small, a wooden bungalow in the Hollywood Hills. Flagstone steps, settled with age into uneven lines, led to a porch that overlooked the city. The windows were so old that the glass rippled like water in the sun. Inside, the floors sagged slightly, the results of small shifts in the earth. The previous owners appeared to have left in haste. Their stray belongings lingered: a lone sock in the back of a closet, a crumpled wad of Kleenex in a kitchen drawer. People in Los Angeles seemed to change houses frequently, as if trading partners in an elaborate square dance.

Friends with stable incomes had assured him that real estate was the safest place for his new money: he'd sold his first movie screenplay, after years of ephemeral, sordid jobs, writing for TV shows aired in the middle of the night, or on obscure cable stations, or simply not aired at all. Now, for the first time, he was successful. But success made him worried. "What if I never sell a screenplay again?" he asked his girlfriend, Charlotte.

"Then the bank will have another house," she said. Charlotte had given up writing and was now a carpenter specializing in bookshelves, which she claimed would soon be obsolete. She was a strong woman with wiry hair and a perpetual sunburn that made her skin peel away in places, revealing tender, shiny pink patches. They hadn't officially moved in together, but somehow, she lived with him, her shirts tangling with his in the drawers, their hair mingling in the clogged drain of the shower. Most of the hair seemed to be Teddy's. He was convinced that he was going bald.

It was September, and hot. Heat blurred the air, dry heat that burned his lungs. The grass on his lawn, scorched and limp, sank into the dirt. A pall of smog dimmed the city. Teddy sat, damp with sweat, in his office; it seemed too hot to think. The screenplay he had sold was autobiographical: a bitter comedy about breaking up with his last girlfriend. Now, with an easy life, he groped for material. Each morning he sat at his word processor, trying to think of a second idea; words ventured forth, timid, on the black screen, and then with a stroke were obliterated.

"Don't sweat it," said Marc, his new agent. Marc was a heavyset man with flowing black hair; his clothes were voluminous, like those of a high-tech priest. In his office, indirect lighting fell in dim patches on the carpet. Cool air blew from invisible vents. The one decoration was a framed photograph of Marc's dog, Vinnie, an immense hairy creature who resembled a mastodon. Vinnie apparently bit anyone who intimidated him; he loved Marc with such ferocity that Marc had ceased to date women, of whom Vinnie was jealous and whom therefore he bit.

Teddy blinked in the murk and tried to adjust to the new indoor season. "I have this one idea," he said. He had thought of it on the way to the meeting, in desperation. "A woman wins the California Lottery and decides to give the money away."

Tilting back in his chair, Marc stretched his feet out on the desk. His ankles were hairless and tanned. "I love it," he said, without conviction.

Teddy's skin felt chilled and sticky. The idea, once spoken, sounded shopworn. "I'll think of something else."

"They're talking about using you to write that sequel to *Earthquake*."

"How can they do a sequel? Didn't everyone die in the end?"

"Not everyone," said Marc. "There were a couple of people left."

Earthquake II: The Aftermath, thought Teddy, driving home. Would he get the assignment? Would he want it? Why did Los Angeles feel compelled to tell itself the same story, time and again, like a victim of recurring nightmares? "95 degrees and counting!" said the deejay on the radio. In the background, a telephone rang, dimly. "Hello, hello?" shouted the deejay. Sun baked the top of Teddy's head, where the hair felt thin. Cars packed the street, sun rippling from their hoods. The sidewalks were deserted. "Kim, you have correctly named the past fifteen songs we've played!" the deejay shouted. "You have just won Five . . . Hundred . . . Dollars!" Screenplay, thought Teddy: Kim wins five hundred dollars. Kim is blonde, perky, the kind of girl who flips her hair back nervously. But it was hard for him to conjure interest in someone who had nothing better to do than listen to fifteen consecutive songs on the radio.

"Teddy," said Charlotte that night as they lay awake. "I have to tell you something." The lights of passing cars flashed across his walls. Cool, stale air drifted through the open window. Charlotte lay, one arm across his stomach, her breath warming his neck. All right, Teddy thought; she was leaving. He was prepared. All along he had known that love was risky; his last girlfriend, the one in the screenplay, had moved out after eight years. Better to make a clean break now, he was thinking, as Charlotte said: "I guess you've noticed how moody I've been."

"Charlotte," said Teddy, running his hand through her rough hair, which smelled of baby shampoo. "I know what you're going to say. It's all right."

"You mean it?" She propped herself up on her elbow and looked down at him; in the dark, her eyes glistened. "You know?"

"Yeah," he said. "I know."

"Then we'll have it? Together?"

"What?" The air seemed to thicken. His throat felt clogged. Charlotte's face bobbed above him, surreal. "Have what?"

"The baby," said Charlotte, and he inhaled slowly, as if preparing to dive deep into water.

There were hairs on his pillow in the morning, hairs on his towel. Even after a shower, he was still hot. In the paper, the weather report predicted monotony: yesterday, ninety, today, ninety, tomorrow, ninety, this weekend: continued hot. Pollution charts showed ominous hills of nitrous dioxide in quantities nearing what they called an "episode," as if the air quality were an ongoing TV series.

He paged through Charlotte's self-help book, *Women, Take Charge of Your Bodies*. Sun heated the kitchen. His fingers left damp indentations on the pages. In a drawing, a sharp instrument insinuated itself into a body part that resembled a doughnut. A blurred photograph in extreme closeup showed a fetus, curled and slick as a snail pulled out of its shell. "At twelve weeks," said the caption, "the baby already has fingernails and eyes." Charlotte was only eight weeks pregnant. Perhaps their baby was still eyeless. He thought of it, stirring in a deep, cool womb, waiting for him. Thinking. When did brain waves start? What inchoate dreams was this snail transmitting in the currents it sent out through the brownish air?

"Ted," said Marc on the phone. His voice was hollow and dim; he must be calling from his car phone. "Everyone's out at the studio. There's a new v.p., Mimi Stern. She's putting a lot of projects into turnaround." The euphemism "turnaround" meant rejection, as if his screenplay were the object of an expert judo flip.

"Are they still going to produce my script?"

"Sure," said Marc. Horns blared from his end of the phone. "Yeah, fuck you too, buddy!" he shouted, apparently at another car. "This asshole thinks he can make a left turn on red," he said to Teddy.

"What ever happened to that sequel idea? You know, *Earth-quake?*"

"Oh, forget that. They weren't serious."

"That's what I figured," said Teddy. And even though he hadn't really wanted the assignment, he hung up feeling queasy, as if he, not Charlotte, were the one with morning sickness.

The house smelled of Charlotte's cigarette smoke. Gray butts, stubbed out on plates, shimmered in clouds of ash. Through the windows, the city below was murky with the exhalations of cars. The house next door was for sale; strangers inside could be seen dimly through glass as they tapped on the walls, or bent to the floor as if searching for clues. No one seemed to want to buy it. He wondered why.

Teddy's brain felt desiccated. Unable to work, he got in his car and drove aimlessly, shooting down vacant side streets, slowing on boulevards thronged with traffic. On the radio, a woman wept quietly, having won a thousand dollars by guessing the deejay's middle name, Arthur. Sun, magnified by Teddy's glasses, burned his eyes. Where were all these people going in the middle of the day? Driving so slowly, no one seemed to have any destination. What a hot, restless city this was, the people always in transit, alone in their cars. "I can't believe I guessed right," sobbed the woman on the radio. "I must have ESP." Brain waves, thought Teddy, transmitted over radio waves. Could there be a screen-play—hopeless, hopeless. He gunned the engine and drove, for a moment, with his eyes shut.

"An abortion probably is the best thing," said Charlotte that night, pacing, her bare feet tapping the kitchen floor. Charlotte had dense, cracked calluses across the soles of her flat feet, and had once walked over red-hot coals just to prove she could do it.

"I think so," said Teddy, trying not to think of the tiny nude snail with fingernails and brain waves.

"I already have Lewis," said Charlotte. "Well, Don has custody, so I don't have him any more. But I did once." Don,
remarried, had been granted permanent custody, claiming in
court that Charlotte worked with dangerous tools.

"It just doesn't make sense for us right now," said Teddy.

"You're right," said Charlotte. "I'll make the appointment.
Soon."

In the morning, as Teddy brushed his teeth, blood turned the
foam pink. He examined his teeth in the mirror. Were his gums
receding? His teeth felt loose. Had they always been so crooked?
Perhaps they were migrating, like birds, to other parts of his
mouth. By the time he was thirty-two, he would be toothless and
bald—he would resemble his own baby. But of course, there
wasn't going to be any baby.

In the backyard, Charlotte hammered steadily at her latest
construction, a toy chest for Lewis. She had made the abortion
appointment for Friday. It was the sensible thing to do, thought
Teddy—what kind of life would a child have, with a father
whose brief months of success had already been forgotten by the
time he was born? Most likely, Teddy would spend the rest of his
life as a bartender. Lean, morose, in a dinner jacket and sagging
bow tie, Teddy would nod his balding head in feigned sympathy
as customers salted his counter with tears shed over their failed
romances.

The keys of his computer were sticky with dust. He stared at
the blank screen, which stared back at him in patient silence.
The thought that it might wait for his next screenplay, until at
last its electric circuits burned out, saddened and unnerved him.
So he flicked it off and drove instead. In the car, distracted, he
headed without thinking to his former apartment building. He
sat outside, the car engine humming beneath him. Who lived in
his old place? Looking at the flaking paint, the red tile coming
loose from the roof, the gutter choked with dead leaves, he en-

vied himself in his previous life. Then, unsuccessful, he'd at least had the comfort of knowing that things couldn't get any worse.

At home, the front door hung open. The TV flickered in the empty living room; a woman in lavish makeup was clutching at jail bars. Her hair billowed around her head, as if she were the target of a private gale. "We were so happy," she was saying tearfully to a jail guard. "Then Hugo kidnapped Fern, and left Otis in the cellar for dead."

"Whoopsie!" said a boy's voice from the kitchen. "That must not be the hard-boiled one."

Teddy rubbed his fists over his eyes until a dense plaid pattern throbbed before him.

"Is egg good for tables?" Lewis was asking, as Teddy walked into the kitchen. Slick yolk smeared the surface of the table and dropped to the floor in dollops. Eggshells crunched underfoot. Lewis, in a ragged Garfield T-shirt, had a magician's cape tied around his shoulders. "Uncle Ted!" he shouted. "Well, all right!"

"Pretty incredible, huh?" said Charlotte, who was standing over the sink, smoking. Her cigarette ashes fizzled as they hit the porcelain. "The bimbo Don married couldn't handle Lewis."

Lewis took a new egg from a carton and spun it. "She said she loved me, and wanted us to be best friends. But she said she needed R and R. Then she cried. I threw up." The egg spun a moment and wobbled, stopping short of the table's edge.

Charlotte mashed the butt of her cigarette into the counter. "So Don just gave him away. Now he's mine forever."

"Trishie and I were best friends," said Lewis. "But she's just too sensitive."

Music swelled in the other room, on TV. "Jasmine, that's impossible," said a woman's trembling voice. "Derek is impotent."

"Trishie and I used to watch this show together," said Lewis. "Before she got sensitive."

. . .

"I forget why the fuck I called," said Marc on the phone. His voice was hoarse, and trembled slightly. He cleared his throat twice, then said, softly: "Shit."

"Are you all right?"

"Sorry, man. It's my dog, Vinnie. I'm all rattled. I had to give him away. He bit me in the night. While I was sleeping."

"I'm so sorry," said Teddy. "Really."

"Wait a minute. Now I remember. Narla Green's assistant is going to call you. They want to hear your ideas for the American version of *Entre Nous*. They want it redone as a female buddy movie."

"I won't even ask why," said Teddy.

"Who knows why?" said Marc, and sighed, a low, rattling sigh so protracted that Teddy imagined him deflating, like an old balloon. "He wasn't even a nice dog," Marc said at last. "That's the crazy thing. But I miss him like hell. I really do."

Charlotte and Lewis made mud pies, filling the bathtub with dirt. Cakes of mud lay crumbling in the backyard like the droppings of an enormous beast. Now, mud clung to the hair in the bathtub drain. The sink backed up, belching out pools of stale gray water. In the backyard, a fine layer of silt seemed to be drifting down the hill, scattering twigs and pebbles across his lawn. Where the grass had been trampled down, he could see deep cracks in the ground. The house next door had been sold after all; a truck stood in the driveway, back lights flashing. On the lawn, a couch tilted, stacked with boxes; three lamps with bare sockets stood by the truck. Their lampshades, set on the grass, looked like the party hats of huge revellers who had evaporated in the night.

That night, Teddy slept badly, dreaming of vicious dogs. He awoke to find Charlotte gone. The pillow still held the hollow where her head had rested. The house felt ominously still. For the first time, it seemed too big for one person.

He padded down the hall. TV light filtered through Lewis's open door. Afraid of the dark, Lewis slept with the picture on and the sound off, in the company of silent chatter. Charlotte was hunched in the room, next to an open box. "Look at these sneakers," she whispered, handing him baby shoes. He held them in the palm of one hand. The laces were ragged and knotted. On TV, a haggard woman scavenged frantically in her medicine cabinet, mouthing words.

"Can you believe how small Lewis used to be?" said Charlotte.

The sneakers still smelled like cut grass. "It's hard to believe," Teddy said. Lewis, in bed, sighed and rolled over.

"I remember how I used to have to fight with him to put them on. It doesn't seem very long ago."

"Five years or so." The time stretched behind him. Five years ago, he had lived in his old apartment. Life had seemed long. On TV, the woman was now rummaging through a liquor cabinet, flinging out empty bottles, which smashed soundlessly against the wall.

"If I could do it over again, I'd be a better mother," said Charlotte, then sighed. "I guess everyone says that."

"You're a good mother, Char."

Charlotte wrapped tissue paper around the shoes, gently, as if tucking them into bed. "Being a mother is like one of those dreams where you're driving, but the sun is in your eyes and you can't see. The whole time, you're just praying you don't crash."

"So far, so good," said Teddy.

"It all goes so fast," said Charlotte.

"Mixing the perfect margarita," Teddy read in *Bartending for Professionals.* He and Charlotte were at the abortion clinic, waiting. The room smelled of Lavoris. Waxed floors gleamed ominously in all directions. Across from them, on an orange plastic couch, a teenage girl fanned herself with an information pamphlet. Teddy's gums felt swollen; he pressed his tongue against his teeth, trying to feel whether they were loose. Chilled air blasted from an air conditioner above his head. "The perfect margarita is one of bartending's greatest challenges," said the book.

"It's good that we're not going to have this baby," said Charlotte. She picked at a scrap of skin by her fingernail. A drop of blood appeared, then seeped into the tiny cracks of her skin.

"It wouldn't be practical," said Teddy.

"Neither of us has a steady income."

"We're not ready." Life was too uncertain. Something granted so easily might just as easily be taken away. Besides, how could he bring a child to life in a city whose air, hovering in a low cloud, was the color of weak tea? But anxiety burned in him. Their baby should be protected from the world—it should be shut off now, while it was still unformed, a minuscule heart in a bud of flesh. Like hope, the baby had sprung from nowhere, foolish, blind, fragile. Teddy's stomach ached. He flipped a page of his book. "The Tom Collins, if perfectly mixed, can be the crowning achievement of your career," he read. The text looked blurred before him, as if seen through thick heat.

"I keep thinking of names," whispered Charlotte. "Lucy. Rufus."

"You can't name our kid Rufus. He'll turn out weird."

"Teddy," said Charlotte. "With parents like us he's guaranteed to turn out weird. Might as well go with it."

"Charlotte Block?" said the receptionist, making a note in her book. "You can come on back."

Charlotte took a deep breath. "Say good-bye to Rufus," she said, but did not move.

He was certain he could hear a third heart thumping, feel eyes waiting to see. What kind of world might the baby live in, what kind of future hung in the distance, like a mirage? Time, all the rest of his unlived life, seemed to sweep before him like the world seen from above, glittering and shifting, filled with air and light, alive with uncertainty. The baby breathed through Char-

lotte's breath, suspended in her hope. The baby needed air.
"Let's get out of here," said Teddy, and they ran.

The floor pounded under their feet. "This is crazy!" shouted
Charlotte, gasping, as they emerged into the sunbaked air. Fist
over her mouth, she coughed, a deep, rumbling cough. The air
was golden with sun. Around him, the low roofs and palm leaves
gleamed, a dizzying sea of light. "I hope he gets your teeth and
your hair," said Teddy as they got into the car. "Since I'm not
going to have any."

"I hope he gets my tan," said Charlotte.

"Mimi got the axe already," said Marc. Splashing sounds came
over the phone, and the loud yips of a dog. "New management
at the studio kicks in tomorrow. You're up in the air again."

"I'm used to it," said Teddy.

"Okay, Vinnie. Stay still," said Marc. The dog let out one
affronted yelp.

"Vinnie's back?"

"Yeah. I missed him too much. You wouldn't believe how
filthy he got at the pound. I'm on the bathroom phone. Come
on, Vin. Get in the water." In the background, Vinnie growled.
"He hates water like poison," said Marc.

"Did that woman Narla Green ever—"

"Vinnie!" shouted Marc. "Vinnie, no! Christ!"

"Are you all right?"

He could hear Marc's gasping breath. "Fine," he said at last,
faintly. "A scratch. He's upset. He knows I tried to give him
away."

"You're sure you'll be okay?"

"Sure," said Marc. "He's bound to forget eventually. I'll just
hang in there."

"I think my movie career is already on the skids," said Teddy
over dinner. Lewis sat, one finger in his mouth, looking despon-
dently over his plate.

"Eat up," said Charlotte, ruffling Lewis's hair. "Don't you like steak?" Already, she had resolved to quit smoking for the baby; instead, she piled stick after stick of gum into her mouth. The gum, grown huge, made squelching sounds as she chewed. Teddy could not imagine how he would bear it for another seven months.

"I think I might become a lifeguard," said Teddy. He could sell the computer to pay for lifesaving lessons; it wouldn't be a bad life, flinging himself into the ice-cold waves to rescue people. He'd be the only toothless lifeguard in the world.

Charlotte blew a limp, gray bubble. "Great idea," she said.

Lewis turned red. He took a long breath. "I miss Trishie," he said, and cried into his peas. They sat for a long time, listening to his watery hiccups.

Charlotte removed her gum and stuck it under her plate. "Don't be sad, sweetie," she said finally.

Lewis looked up. A mashed pea adhered to his forehead. Tears slipped down his chin. "I will, too, be sad," he said. "You don't know." And he stalked out of the room.

Through the walls, Teddy could hear his muffled sobs, hear the click of the TV, the white-noise hiss of his mute company. "I can't believe he liked that bimbo," said Charlotte, scraping off plates. "Kids are too trusting."

Teddy stood by the kitchen window. Shadows flickered across the walls of the house next door, whose windows were dark, as if the house were in slumber. Through the leaves of palms, the city lights winked at him, a constellation of houses and cars under a murky sky. The lights of cars laced an intricate pattern, re-arranging themselves in tiny grids across the city. There were no stars to fix his eyes on here, only the faint light of real lives, fallible as his own. He stood, face to the glass, until his breath fogged the window and the city dissolved into mist.

Child in the Leaves

•

═══════ CHARLES DICKINSON ═══════

A mean little storm passed through Weatherwax on the first day of the leaf pickup, and a car went into a skid at lunchtime, striking a boy before coming to a stop in the leaves where the boy was hiding. The driver continued on, unaware of what had happened.

The boy's name was Randy Brennan. He was small for his age, which was eight and a half. His mother taught P.E. and coached the girls' volleyball team at the high school in Fillmore, six miles up the river. His father was a sculptor in unwieldy metals who supplemented his income by tending bar at the Sundial Lounge, a hundred feet from where Randy was lying.

The boy was supposed to be in school, but restlessness had been like a fever in him recently, and he kept going on little excursions of rebelliousness that only got him in trouble with his parents. At the time he was hit by the car, he was stretched out under the cold leaves confident he could not be seen; his coat was the wet-brown color of the raked leaves, and by keeping his head down he minimized the beacon signal of his red knit cap. He could lie there in the leaves on Weatherwax Avenue and keep watch over his father and never be seen.

. . .

Randy's father, Craig, was in the Sundial Lounge washing glasses one-handed. He had burned his left hand the night before with his acetylene torch. A glancing violet flame, barely a touch, had flashed across his skin while he was working in his studio. He had been having trouble lately knowing when a piece was finished. Each tended to grow cumbersome, to slip out of any sort of harmony, as he welded new elements to the work in a search for exactly what he was trying to accomplish. Tired and careless, working late without gauntlets, he was trying to salvage a piece that had consumed six months of his time. Frustrated that the teetering mess had resisted all his attempts at conjunction, he had glanced around him at the small, chilly converted garage imagining setting fire to the place. He had insurance; he could use the money to start fresh. But in the midst of this reverie he lost track of the position of the flame and touched it to the back of his hand. For a moment he looked at the burn with genuine curiosity. The skin was black and peeled back, as if the flame had run across his hand like a plow. The hairs on either side of this furrow had been turned to ash.

Now he wedged each wet glass between his hip and the rim of the sink counter, and then jabbed the soapy sponge-stick into the glass with his good hand. The pain that followed his brief, curious inspection of the burn had a life of its own. Francie had driven him to the emergency room, which was eleven miles down the river, in Lubbers. Randy and Glynnis rode in the back seat. Craig sat hunched forward, holding the burn in a coffee can filled with ice water, which had been Francie's idea.

Randy Brennan hurried down Weatherwax Avenue expecting a shout from his teacher, Mrs. Junkins, which would end his escape. But he was just one of thirty-four children in his classroom, and on the battlefield of recess, where two other classes of comparable size were also set loose, he and a dozen other children could walk away without any teacher noticing. The students had been turned out to beat the approaching storm, which was just a rumor on the radio, a nervous buzz in the air. The teachers wanted to get the children out in the cold wind to burn away some of the energy that would be merciless in the afternoon if not expended sooner.

Randy found himself behind the bus shelter across the street from the Sundial Lounge. The air was cold, silvery with the approaching sleet, and he thought about stepping into the tavern, surprising his father, having a sandwich and getting warm before being sent good-naturedly back to school. But his father would not understand. He would demand to know what Randy was doing away from school. He would greet him as a kid who had screwed up again.

Randy considered just sneaking up and looking in the Sundial's window. At lunchtime his father would be busy and not likely to notice him spying through the thin gap between the Weatherwax High basketball schedule and a community-blood-drive flyer. He wanted to see if his father's wounded hand was giving him as much pain as it had on the drive to Lubbers. He had never seen his father cry before.

If he waited long enough, school would be out, and he would see his father leave for home. He could nonchalantly come up behind him, and his presence would seem perfectly natural. His father might welcome the company, invite him into his studio. The chilly room, with its scorched-iron smell and jungle of metals and sculptures, was off limits to Randy unless he was in his father's company. Randy loved it in there. He had his own three-legged stool to sit on, out of the way. His father appeared to forget he was there, as if Randy were wearing a shirt the color of the garage wall and were hidden. Randy knew enough not to ask a lot of questions, lest he break his father's concentration and be told to leave. He liked the colors of the acetylene flames: violet, green, gaseous. He liked it when his father let him try on the cumbersome welder's helmet, its filmy window cutting the room down to strict dimensions, his breathing echoing in his ears; Randy thought this was what it must be like to drown. Now he had returned to the place where he had waited before. He could be out of sight and still keep watch over his father. He lay down in the leaves, on his back first. But his angle of vision was bad from that position, and little pins of sleet had begun to fall and sting his face. He rolled onto his stomach and pulled leaves out from under him and transferred them to the layer on top of him. He left a comparatively dry layer of leaves beneath him. He rested his head on his folded arms. In a minute he was out of sight.

The town of Weatherwax was built on a steep hillside. The leaf pickup began at the bottom of the hill, along Weatherwax Avenue, which hugged the river all the way through town. Each autumn day and into the early winter, the red municipal leaf trucks could be heard from three blocks away, their vacuums humming like bees, advancing back and forth up the hill, sucking up the leaves that the residents of Weatherwax had raked into piles at the curb.

Around noon on the first day of the pickup, a leaf truck pulled away from the Sundial Lounge, where the driver, Al Franks, had just eaten lunch. A thick hose extended from the storage bay out over the windshield of the truck. The hose was maneuvered with a joystick from the cab. Almost immediately, the hose mouth grabbed Randy Brennan between the shoulders and lifted him clear of the leaves, just far enough for Al Franks to realize what he had found.

A noise somewhere high in the house awakened Randy, and he lay without moving for several minutes, wondering if he had dreamed his father's burn. A little light had seeped into his room. Glynnis, who lately required nearly an hour to get ready for school each morning, would arise soon to dominate the downstairs bathroom and the hot water. Randy got out of bed and walked in his socks and pajamas down the hall to his parents' bedroom. The door was open an inch. He put his ear to this gap and listened. First he heard his mother's breathing, and this troubled him. Usually she could not be heard over his father's snores. But there she was, out of sight around the edge of the door, breathing in a deep, slow cadence.

Randy put a finger to the door and pushed. The foot of his parents' bed came into sight—the elongated plateaus and the rises of two pairs of feet under white covers. He pushed the door open farther. His mother was asleep on her back, her head nestled in a basket of her crumpled hair; his father was awake and looking over at him without evident interest, his bandaged hand held like a club over his head. After looking at Randy he returned his attention to his hand, turning it this way and that in the gray light, wiggling his fingertips a little, just staring at what he had done to himself. He glanced back at Randy and whispered with what the boy took to be impatience that he should go back to bed, it was too early to be up.

The night before, Randy was watching TV and his mother was going over Glynnis's homework when they heard Craig scream. Randy saw his father first. Looking through the living-room window, he saw him come crashing out the door of the studio, advancing on them through the fog-lamp light above the garage, his burned hand clutched desperately at the wrist with his other hand. The hand that he held looked strangely diminished, like the head of a doused match.

Randy's mother was the first to understand. She yanked a can of coffee from a cupboard and emptied it on the counter. She gave the can a quick rinse to let the water get colder, and had the can half full by the time her husband came bellowing into the room. She turned, almost as if greeting him with a gift, and he plunged the burned hand into the water, splashing them both, letting out another shriek. Randy's mother guided his father to the counter by pulling the can that way.

"Oh, God," she whispered. "You poor thing."

Expertly she cracked an ice tray against the counter opposite where her husband stood. She dumped the cubes and shards into the can. Randy thought he saw steam rising from the water, thought he heard it hiss.

"Let's get you to the emergency room," his mother said.

Firmly she ordered Randy and Glynnis into their coats. She shooed them from the kitchen to accomplish this chore, and to tear their eyes from the sight of their father hunched over the ice water. She took the car keys down off the hook that Randy had made in first grade and hustled her children out into the cold, clearing the way for her husband, who came last, slowly, carrying his cargo.

Before they left she asked, "Did you turn off the torch?"

Francie Brennan called her husband during her lunch break to gauge the pain in his hand. She would encourage him to leave the Sundial for the day; their family could survive without the forty dollars he might earn in the afternoon. But she knew he would refuse. Every dollar he made was important to him, because he saw it as one way to buy space in her life until he could pay his way as a sculptor.

She used the pay phone outside the gym, because there was more privacy there in the raucous halls than in the cramped P.E. office. Girls on her volleyball team crept past, winking, sticking out their tongues at her. They were tall, strong girls, agile leapers. She could not have chosen better players if she had recruited them, and as a result her team had not lost in almost two years, and her advice was sought by other coaches. She felt silly expounding on her philosophy of volleyball, when all the others needed was tall, leaping girls who had no other interests, really, except volleyball.

Someone, a strange voice, answered at the Sundial Lounge. The person said his name was Glen; he had reached over the bar and picked up the phone when nobody appeared willing to answer it. He did not know who Craig Brennan was; he knew only that he had the bar to himself and his beer glass was empty.

She called the house. They had a place a few blocks from the river, an architectural commonplace made remarkable by its positioning on the side of the hill. She would often look out the window while cracking an egg or pouring milk in the kitchen and imagine that she was living on a slant, that only an extended act of faith kept her from sliding to the downhill side of the house. Each morning she was surprised to see the car still in the street where she had parked it. She was convinced that one night all their preventive measures—the parking brake, the wheels turned in to the curb, and the stone chocks under the wheels— would be proved meaningless and the car would simply roll away down to the river.

No one answered her call at home. Her children were in school; she thought her husband was at work. Her inability to put her finger on his whereabouts, to exchange a few words with him before she had to go to class, set a small storm of nervous dread loose in her. Outside, in the courtyard, where the students went to smoke in better weather, she saw snow falling heavy and sharp as iron filings, and nearly of the same color. She phoned the Sundial one more time, and after many rings the same stranger picked up the phone and informed her that nothing had changed except that his glass was a little drier.

Still some miles from the hospital, Randy heard his father tell his mother, "I've melted the ice."

"We'll be there in a jiff, darling."

Randy looked over at Glynnis, who was watching the river. She had had the presence of mind to bring a book, and now had it open on her lap, though there was no light to read by. She ran her fingers lightly across it, back and forth, still looking at the river.

They spilled some water getting his father out of the car near the emergency room. His shirtsleeve had unrolled and fallen into the can, and the wetness had soaked up almost to his elbow. He stared down into the can of water as his wife guided him into the hospital. A nurse came forward, looked into the water, and removed Craig from his wife's care. She led him through double doors, leaving Randy and Glynnis and their mother behind.

Over the next three hours, Randy tried to behave. Glynnis, with her natural inclination toward the studious, hardly budged after she had taken a seat along the wall and found her place in her book. She understood that inevitably she would be informed, and in the meanwhile there was time to be put to good use.

Randy wanted to know what was happening every moment. He pestered his mother to question anyone who looked even remotely like a doctor. His mother finally was summoned inside the double doors, and he nearly exploded waiting for her to return. Glynnis barely raised her head (and kept a finger on her place) when their mother came back with news that their father had suffered a third-degree burn. He would be in a great deal of pain that night and for several days afterward. He was not to be bothered under any circumstances.

While they waited for him to be released, Randy moved around looking for a place where he would be most out of sight. He was wearing a blue sweater and green jeans with billowy military pockets on the legs. No colors in the waiting room matched his outfit, and he moved around feeling exposed, afraid his father would emerge and catch him in the open.

His mother was called back into the emergency room. She came out alone again, like someone sent ahead with a warning. "They gave him something for pain," she told her children. "I don't want you to make a sound. Got that?"

When Craig did finally come out, he did not seem to recognize anyone other than his wife. Something seemed to be missing, a piece of light from his eyes which Randy hadn't realized existed until it was removed. Randy's mother led Craig outside and helped him into the front seat. His injured hand had been swathed in bandages; it reminded Randy of the end of a bone.

As they pulled away from the hospital, his father leaned his head back against the seat. Within minutes he had begun to snore, and this sawing of the air, annoying under any other circumstances, comforted Randy, as if it were final proof that he had his father back.

Craig was turning his bad hand this way and that when he heard the siren. A police car. Close by. He was familiar with the town's cops. They came into the bar for free beer and roast-beef sandwiches at the end of their shifts, in exchange for quick responses to the occasional fights at the Sundial Lounge. A couple of guys drinking beer in a booth stood and pressed their faces to the front window to get a look at the cause of all the excitement. The glass fogged up in front of them before they could make a confident determination of events, but their curiosity was aroused sufficiently to draw them out into the cold without their coats on. Other drinkers straggled out. Something was going on down by the river. A leaf truck was parked there, as was a police car. Other people came running, slipping on the new snow and the wet leaves.

Jim Sarkisian, the owner of the Sundial Lounge, was the person who told Craig about Randy. He had left the bar in Craig's care, pulling on a sweater, eager to go and investigate. He was a man who never spent much time in his own business, and when he was on the premises he looked for any excuse to get out. He liked to go for walks with his patrons who had had too much to drink, throwing an arm over their shoulders and guiding them out to take the fresh air by the river, or, if they lived nearby, accompanying them right to their front door. He had survived two heart attacks, and his doctor had prescribed exercise, so he walked everywhere in town, even to his house up at the crest of the hill.

Jim knew Randy from those occasions when the boy came into the bar to visit his father. Craig didn't like his son to come there; the lights, the smoke, the music, the whole aura of the place were elements of his life that he did not want to advertise to Randy. But Randy came over to bring his father a forgotten lunch, or just to surprise him on a Saturday afternoon; he would come up behind him in the TV din of the football game, tap him on the hip and demand his attention for a few minutes.

A rumor had floated into the bar that someone had been hit by a car. A hit-and-run. The ambulance in Lubbers had been summoned. Craig drew a beer for the only customer left in the place. Craig's wife was at work; his children were safe in school. He wiped down the counter with a damp rag, then drifted to the window. Jim was coming back. He was running up a slight incline, into the wind, his head bowed and his hands in his pockets. He skidded a little reaching the door, then he was inside, looking wildly around for Craig.

"What?" Craig said, scared by the dread in Jim's eyes.

"Go down there," Jim said, gently drawing the towel from Craig's fingers. "I think it's Randy."

"He's in school."

"You're probably right. Go make sure, though."

Craig took a moment getting his coat out of the basement, and when he came back up Jim was gone, leaving the place empty except for the customer drinking the beer and reading the newspaper at the bar.

"You want a refill?" Craig asked conscientiously before heading for the door.

"No, thanks. I'll be fine."

Craig kept his injured hand in his coat pocket as he approached the scene. Randy's school was four blocks away—an easy distance for a kid to cover. And Randy had been restless of late, having trouble sleeping, picking fights with Glynnis. His whole attitude was one of wandering: his attention, his interest in school, his very participation in the family.

The figure on the ground was wearing a brown coat like Randy's, and a hat like his, too—a red knit stocking cap. Craig verified it was Randy from a distance of about a yard as he broke through the rings of the curious and saw his son's face pointed to the sky. He was frowning, his eyes squeezed shut, a bruise float-ing like a thundercloud beneath the skin at the corner of his forehead. Craig dropped to his knees and cupped the small head under one hand. He looked for blood in the ears. A policeman—his name would have come to Craig under other circumstances—told him to be careful. Craig had to put his ear to Randy's mouth to get the satisfaction of feeling a warm breath. He scraped a leaf chip from the corner of his son's mouth.

Randy had asked his father if he could come out to watch him work. Dinner was over, Glynnis was in her room doing her homework. Randy saw the brief hesitancy in his father's eyes before he agreed. His mother told him to put on his old coat—it was cold and dirty in the studio. While he was digging for the coat in the closet he heard the back door slam, and his father was gone.

"Go on," his mother said when she saw him looking at the old garage through the window. "He said you could go. He's never going to drag you with him by the hand."

So he pulled on the old coat and his red hat and went out. His father was already busy in the corner, his back to him. His sleeves were rolled up. It was cold—a deep, metal cold that did not seem to bother his father.

"Bring that book of matches over here," his father said with-out turning around.

He used one match to light some candles, saving the flame until Randy was certain he would burn his fingers, then kneeling and using the last spark to fire up the pilot light on the gas heater.

Randy pulled his stool over so he could sit near the warmth. He wondered if he should speak. His father had a vaguely trian-gular piece of metal about the size of an unfolded scarf clamped in a vise. He worked at this piece with a file, rasping the tool over the metal's razor edge, making a shriek that hurt Randy's ears. After a few minutes of this his father set the metal on his workbench and began to dimple it with the rounded end of a ball-peen hammer. Randy liked the look of his father at work— the muscles in his arm as he raised the hammer, the tension across his shoulders and down his back. When his father was concentrating on his work, he was less apt to be paying attention to Randy, and Randy felt then most comfortable watching his father closely.

After nearly a half hour of work, his father carried the piece of metal across the studio to the sculpture. He intended to add the triangular piece to the work. He put on the gauntlets and the welding helmet, the mask cocked up on his head, and scratched the igniter in front of the torch's nozzle. A bright white flame appeared with a *puck* and a hiss of gas, and his father focussed the flame down to a clean blue point. Craig nodded sharply, and the mask fell over his face.

Randy tried to guess where the piece would fit, but he could make no sense of the sculpture; it had no shape, no expression, no story. He dared not ask for a title or an explanation. His father would announce the piece's completion by ceasing to work on it. He would simply begin something new; or, rather, he would tear down something from the tangle at the back of the garage and use the components in some new form.

After ten minutes of work, his father stepped back, raising the mask. His face was smudged and wet. As he and Randy watched, the weld that held the triangular piece to the sculpture began to fail, and slowly the weight of the metal tore it loose until it fell with a clang on the studio floor.

"Shit," his father said. And soon after he asked his son to go back into the house.

"What happened to your hand?"

"I burned it."

"That's quite a bandage for a burn."

"I burned it with an acetylene torch."

The ambulance driver glanced over at Craig, wondering if he was being dramatic.

The paramedics had been in touch with the hospital about Randy's condition, but they kept their voices down. Out of deference to me, Craig thought—an assumption that terrified him. If the boy was going to survive, wouldn't they announce that fact proudly to the father? It made sense to Craig. But the paramedics communicated in murmurs and the ambulance travelled with no undue speed, as if the outcome had been decided.

The Lubbers Hospital was on a bluff above the river, with a circular drive in front of the emergency-room entrance. Two men and two women stood in the cold waiting for the ambulance. They watched its progress up the drive, and when the ambulance braked in the orange light they leaped to work, all eight hands grabbing for the doors; there was a chaotic bumping of his son's body as they extracted the gurney. All of them had disappeared by the time Craig got out. He went into the anteroom and they weren't there. Waiting people blinked in his direction.

He put his face to a narrow window in one E.R. door and saw them all, plus a few new people, bunched around Randy like a family at dinner. He wanted to get a look at his son's face, but that was the focus of attention in the room and most of the medical personnel were clustered there, blocking his view. He was amazed that he remembered almost nothing of the hospital, although he had been there the night before.

A man in a Red Sox cap was using the waiting room's only working pay phone. Craig thought the intensity of his longing to get in touch with Francie would be transmitted to the man, persuading him to hang up, but Craig stood within a yard of the man's broad back for nearly fifteen minutes thinking black and dangerous thoughts, and still the man gabbed on.

He went to a vending machine and bought a cup of coffee, black. The challenges of having one good hand had worn thin for him: he was in pain. He carried the coffee by his fingertips back to the E.R. window and peered inside. Everyone was gone: doctors, nurses, his son. He pushed the door far enough open to insert his head, and a nurse at a table hidden to him from outside asked him firmly to remain in the waiting room. He asked about Randy Brennan, and she promised to have the doctor speak to him when there was useful information to impart.

When the coffee had cooled enough to hold in his palm, he approached the man on the phone. "I'll give you this coffee if I can use the phone," he said.

The man looked with some impatience at Craig and covered the mouthpiece with his hand, as though the other party had sensibilities too fragile to overhear the exchange to come. "I'm on the phone," he said.

"I need to reach my wife. My son's been hurt."

The man tipped back his Red Sox cap and looked into the coffee cup. "You already drank some. I saw you."

"No, it was too hot. I haven't touched it."

"I take cream."

"Let me buy you a cup," Craig said. He put the coffee down on a bench and searched in his pocket for some change.

"This call is important," the man said. "My Pearl just had a baby."

"Congratulations. I'll buy you coffee with cream," Craig said, "and I'll pay for you to call back whoever you're talking to."

The man hung up without a word of explanation to the other party, and Craig stacked change in his hand.

Francie was not at home. Glynnis answered, sounding young, and nervous about being alone in a dark house always threatening to tip over. "Where *are* you?" she asked with a pout in her voice.

"I'm at work," he said. "Where's Mom?"

"Volleyball practice. Are you at the Sundial?"

"Yeah. Have you talked to Mom?"

"I looked in there for you and they told me you had left."

"I went out. But now I'm back."

"Can I come down and sit with you until Mom gets home?"

"I'm working, honey. It's not a place for you."

"I don't like being alone," Glynnis said. "It's dark in all the rooms."

"You know how to turn on the lights," he said. "Make yourself some cocoa and turn on the TV. Mom'll be home before you know it."

"Do you want her to call you?"

"Read me the gym-office number there," he asked.

His daughter was quiet as she searched the sheet of numbers taped to the wall beside the phone. He hated the idea of her in the bar. She was eleven years old, turning pretty to a degree that startled him when he came upon her unexpectedly. The idea of that innocent beauty looking for him in the clamor of the Sundial left him feeling helpless—the thought of her wandering there without his protection.

She read him the number; he held it in his memory, then hastened to end the conversation before he forgot it.

He put in his money and dialled the P.E. office number. A woman—a stranger—answered, and when he stressed that it was an emergency she agreed to interrupt Francie in gym class. He tried to imagine the office; he had never been there. More clearly, he saw his wife turning pale at the mention of an emergency, saw her running toward the phone. She was a quick, graceful runner, and it would not take her long to get there.

Francie had Glynnis with her when she arrived at the hospital, and Glynnis was carrying a book. First thing, she went to her father.

"You lied to me," she said coldly. With that she reassumed her pose, her very seat, from the night before, head bowed, the book open in her lap.

Francie had a great many questions, but Craig had few answers. His lack of knowledge about what had happened, what condition their son was in, finally wore her down and she just sat playing with her rings and watching the door to the emergency room.

Craig kept seeing vaguely familiar faces, men and women in pale-green clothes who had briefly come into the circle of his awareness in the past. Several smiled at him as if they had seen him somewhere but couldn't place him. None of them stopped to provide word about their son.

"Go look again," Francie said. The first two dozen times he had gone to look, Glynnis accompanied him, standing on tiptoe to see through the glass. But an hour ago she had fallen asleep and collapsed with her head in her mother's lap.

Craig went to the window in the E.R. door and looked through it. Francie seemed to have some hope that he would see Randy in there, sitting up in bed telling jokes to the nurses. This time, as before, he saw no one resembling his son.

In time, the waiting room emptied to the point where they felt comfortable arranging Glynnis in a limp, sleeping line along one couch. Francie stretched out on a couch perpendicular to Glynnis's and stroked her daughter's hair. Craig stayed in a chair with his coffee, and that was where the doctor found them. Oddly, he first asked about Craig's hand.

He then spoke in clipped phrases that Craig and Francie could not recall precisely afterward. But the information was conveyed that Randy had a crack in his skull and a concussion, that his eyes were reactive to light, that the impact of the car's tire against his head had been oblique and had been cushioned by leaves and an out-thrown hand.

Francie left with Glynnis in time for the girl to get home and ready for school, after which Francie would return to the hospital. But she had not yet returned when Craig was allowed in to see Randy. The boy's head was wrapped in white, and there was an abrasion like a skid mark running from the bottom of his cheek up under the edge of the dressing. He had an L-shaped cast on his arm. He opened his eyes once, but Craig was looking away at that moment and didn't see.

. . .

He stretched out in the leaves and kept watch over his father—
this on the day before the leaf pickup began. He was worried
where he would hide when the leaves were gone. The weather
that day had been overcast early, with an afternoon burst of
sunlight that threw shadows into the mix of colors where he hid.
People walked past, within a few feet of him, and didn't see him.
The road hummed when cars went past, and he was positive the
people in those cars didn't see him, either.

Biographies and Some Comments by the Authors

ALICE ADAMS grew up in Chapel Hill, North Carolina, and graduated from Radcliffe; since then she has lived mostly in San Francisco. Her latest novel, *Second Chances,* was published in 1988; her new collection of stories (of which "After You've Gone" is the title story) will be published in the fall of 1989.

RICK BASS has had stories and essays published in *The Paris Review, Esquire, Antaeus, The Quarterly, Harper's, Gentlemen's Quarterly,* and many other magazines. The winner of a General Electric Award for Younger Writers, he has also received creative writing grants from the state arts commissions of Mississippi and Montana. His first work of fiction, *The Watch,* was published in January 1989, and a collection of essays, *Oil Notes,* will also be published this year.

About "The Watch," Bass says, "As with all good and lucky stories a writer stumbles onto—really stumbles—I can remember nothing about the actual process of writing it—only that it went quickly, that it ran away from me, and I had no control. The characters took off. I think I remember laughing out loud when I realized that Jessie was going to get fat and ride a go-cart; other than that, I can't remember much. I do remember being spooked a few days after finishing the story. I was living in the Mississippi backwoods, country much similar to that in the story, and while out driving, I saw three white chickens pecking in the gravel by a garbage dumpster, looking exactly like the three white chickens in the story, sans rooster. I'd never seen chickens in the woods before and never saw them again. It made me nervous, even frightened, for a while. I had the feeling that maybe some of the other parts of the story were out there in the woods too after that."

Rick Bass was born in Fort Worth, Texas. He has worked as a biologist in Arkansas, as a geologist in Mississippi and Alabama, and has taught creative writing at the University of Texas. He currently lives in the Yaak Valley of extreme northwestern Montana.

T. CORAGHESSAN BOYLE claims to have the longest middle name of any contemporary American writer. He is a native of Peekskill, New York, a graduate of the Iowa Writers' Workshop, a bon vivant, and, as *The New York Times* has it, "a snappy dresser." In particularly snappy moments, he has produced three novels—*Water Music; Budding Prospects;* and *World's End,* winner of the 1988 PEN/Faulkner Award—and three books of short stories: *Descent of Man; Greasy Lake;* and the forthcoming *If the River Was Whiskey,* in which "Sinking House" appears. He writes, "Like my characters, I find life a baffling and usually unpleasant mystery."

JOHN CASEY: " 'Avid' is part of a cycle of nine stories which I wrote between 1979 and 1983. In 1979 I was thinking of fairy tales (as per an old suggestion of R. B. Cassill) and having wonderful conversations with my mother-in-law. I didn't take matter from her text but the method of her sympathy, which is the countercharm to the inexorability of fairy tales. The nine stories are part of a trilogy set in Rhode Island, written between 1979 and 1988.

"*Spartina,* a novel about fishing, smuggling, and class rage, will be published in May 1989."

John Casey is the author of the novel *An American Romance,* and *Testimony and Demeanor,* a collection of stories. His work has appeared in such publications as *The New Yorker, Sports Illustrated, Redbook, True, Harper's, Esquire, New Times,* and *Shenandoah.*

CHARLES DICKINSON is the author of two novels, *Waltz in Marathon* and *Crows,* and a collection of short stories, *With or Without.* His stories have appeared in *The New Yorker, The Atlantic*

Monthly, Grand Street, and *Esquire.* His story "Risk" was included in the 1984 O. Henry Awards collection. "Child in the Leaves" will be translated into Russian and published in the Soviet Union as part of the United States Information Agency's magazine, *America Illustrated.* Dickinson's third novel, *The Widows' Adventures,* will be published in 1989. He lives with his wife and children in Palatine, Illinois.

MILLICENT DILLON: "The telling of stories has always been mysterious to me. I did not begin to write until I was almost forty. I published a book of short stories, *Baby Perpetua and Other Stories,* and a novel, *The One in the Back Is Medea.* Then I published a biography of Jane Bowles, *A Little Original Sin.*

"I am now completing an antibiography of Isadora Duncan and Mary Cassatt, and a novel, *The Dance of the Mother.*

" 'Wrong Stories' is a story about the telling of stories. It is, in itself, what I know and don't know about 'story.' "

HARRIET DOERR: "Like an interrupted meal, my college education was split in two. I consumed the first course in the late 1920s and dessert in the late 1970s. Writing courses ventured upon in the second and final phase led me to attempt and eventually complete a novel, *Stones for Ibarra.* By that time I had lived, mesmerized and astonished, in Mexico for a number of years, and the book I'm working on now is set in Mexican dust on a Mexican hill.

" 'Edie,' however, takes place in California, where I was born in 1910 and have spent most of my life. But the landscape of this story is unfamiliar to me. I never knew these Ransoms, never entered their house, not even for tea. I never stood on their terrace to see the view. As far as I know, these particular children never existed.

"Once I had a nurse named Edie."

ERNEST J. FINNEY: "In the short story there is only time to thump the reader's heart once. But some characters insist on more than that: they develop claims on you, demand more space for their definition. My story 'Peacocks' became part of a novel, *Winterchill*, which made me realize another possibility for the short story form—chains of stories, where each sets up reverberations against the other, where what isn't said in the space between each story is almost as important as what *is* said within the stories' boundaries. I'm not the first to discover that, of course, but happening upon it, because of those demands my characters set upon me, turned out to be a great release.

"I am a native Californian, and I write stories and novels about this state. I live some of the time in the Sierras, tending a small apple orchard, mostly Grimes Goldens, and part of the time in the Central Valley."

STARKEY FLYTHE, JR., has published poetry and fiction and has been an NEA and S.C. literature fellow. He served with the U.S. Army in Ethiopia and was editor of *The Saturday Evening Post* for ten years. His stories have previously been included in *The Best American Short Stories* and in *Prize Stories: The O. Henry Awards.*

BARBARA GRIZZUTI HARRISON: "I am the author of *Unlearning the Lie: Sexism in School; Visions of Glory: A History and a Memory of Jehovah's Witnesses; Off-Center,* a collection of essays; *Foreign Bodies,* a novel; and a forthcoming nonfiction book entitled *Italian Days.*

" 'To Be' 'came' to me along with a cluster of short stories— short stories always come to me in clusters, never alone—in Rome; it formed itself around a sentence of Van Gogh: 'Happiness is round.' I had nothing but that sentence. (I was at the time writing a nonfiction book—with elements of fiction—about Italy and enjoying great happiness.) Although it lends itself to this reading, it is not autobiographical, though I drew from experience, real and imagined. Its subject, insofar as I understand what I've written, is happiness . . . it also serves to settle old scores."

ELLEN HERMAN: "I grew up in Winnetka, Illinois. After graduating from Bryn Mawr with a degree in English, I spent three years in New York as a writer, then a project director, of interactive videos. Since moving to Los Angeles four years ago, I've worked as a free-lance writer in many fields, including film and TV. My short stories have appeared or will appear soon in *The Massachusetts Review, The Missouri Review, The Greensboro Review, Seventeen,* and others. I live in Hollywood with my husband, who is a screenwriter. Currently, I'm finishing a novel, *The Cure for Regret.*"

BANNING K. LARY'S biographical information is furnished by *Witness* magazine: "Death of a Duke" won first place in fiction in a PEN prison-writing contest. Banning K. Lary cannot be located.

SUSAN MINOT was born in 1956 in Boston, Massachusetts. She received a B.A. in Creative Writing from Brown University, then an M.F.A. in Fiction at Columbia University. After selling her first story to *Grand Street,* she was hired there as an assistant editor. Before that, she worked as a house painter, environmental canvasser, and waitress. Her first stories appeared in *The New Yorker, The Paris Review,* and *Grand Street. Monkeys,* her first novel, was published in 1986, and eventually sold to twelve countries. She lives in New York City, where she sometimes teaches.

"Île Sèche" was written during a very cold January at the Hôtel Louisiane in Paris.

JOYCE CAROL OATES is the author of a number of works of fiction, nonfiction, and poetry, including most recently the novel *American Appetites* and *(Woman) Writer,* a collection of essays. *On Boxing.* She lives in Princeton, New Jersey, where she teaches at the university and helps edit *Ontario Review.* Previous stories of hers have frequently been included in the O. Henry Awards volumes, most recently in 1988. The idea for "House Hunting" grew out of an eerie personal experience while she and her husband were looking for a house.

Born in St. Louis, CATHERINE PETROSKI grew up in southern Illinois and lived in Austin and Chicago before moving to Durham, North Carolina, in 1980. She has twice been awarded fellowships by the NEA and by Yaddo, and her short fiction has been syndicated by the PEN Fiction Project and broadcast on NPR. The first of her three books was a collection, *Gravity and Other Stories* (1981), and she has a new book of stories and a novel in progress. Of "The Hit," she says, "For years I had mulled over the public personas of campus visitors—poets and scientists, senators and magnates—until after a reception one night I couldn't *not* write about them anymore. Yves Roland's story began almost to write itself, though I realize now I had been writing it internally for a long time."

JEAN ROSS: "I grew up in North Carolina and attended the University of North Carolina at Greensboro and at Chapel Hill. I have published fiction in *Shenandoah, The Missouri Review, The North American Review,* and *Esquire.* I live in Gainesville, Florida, with my husband, Donald Justice, and am the mother of one son. The idea for this story came as I read the biography of an American writer, but the people and events in it are entirely imaginary."

JAMES SALTER: "I had wanted to write 'American Express' for a long time. A fragment of it had been in my mind for years. Later I made some notes while traveling in Europe. Eventually there were fifteen or twenty pages of details, and finally I sat down and composed the story, following Charles Olson's four cardinal rules: be romantic, be passionate, be imaginative, never be rushed. To these I added one of Leautaud's: never stop simplifying.

"What I wrote turned out to be different from what I expected. Only a few of the original details survived. I rewrote endlessly, driven by an instinct that I would somehow be able to satisfy myself. The characters are real, although they did not exist precisely as shown. The moments are real, even those that did not happen. As someone once remarked, art is to reality as wine is to grapes. An astute observation.

"I cannot seem to write things quickly, stories especially. The question always arises: is this the absolute story or merely another version? I dislike versions, although I like the studies painters make before doing a large canvas.

"I was born in Passaic, New Jersey, between the two great wars of the century, the year after a very good vintage. There, I think, is the essence of it, coming after a great vintage, although we never drank wine at home—that all came later.

"The city of my youth was New York, much changed now. I lived there until I went into the army. Fifteen years in uniform passed. I was thirty-two when my first book was published and forty-two before my first story appeared, in *The Paris Review.* As a boy at school, I felt I would like to be a poet. The impulse deteriorated into prose. Julian Beck and John Simon were my classmates. Kerouac, dark and magnetic, just preceded us. The thing that has held true is that few pleasures do not seem evanescent compared to reading a great line."

FRANCES SHERWOOD'S short story collection, *Everything You've Heard Is True,* will be published this spring. She has had ten stories in literary magazines, has finished one novel, *Green,* and is working on a new one. An assistant professor of English at Indiana University, she graduated from Brooklyn College and was a teaching fellow in the Johns Hopkins Writing Seminars, where she received her M.A., a Stegner Fellow in Fiction at Stanford University, and a resident fellow at Yaddo. She grew up in Monterey, California, is divorced, and now lives in Indiana.

Sherwood did not begin writing until she was in her thirties. Until then she was raising children and working. "Money always seemed such a problem and writing such a luxury, I really didn't take myself that seriously. Then I started to read Grace Paley and encountered a wonderful story in *The New Yorker* by Linda Arking, called 'Certain Hard Places.' I knew then what I had to do. Now I'm mad it took so long. Several times I've just about given up—you know, stories coming back rejected—but getting into super writing programs has helped. Somehow I've managed to keep the faith.

"Bits and pieces of 'History' have been carried along for a long time. One paragraph was in something I wrote in college for a class; another part was in an early draft of my novel *Green.* Other ideas came along later. One day I sat down and wrestled with the whole thing, got it into one piece. It went through several drafts. I let it sit, sent it out. It came back from several places. One comment was very helpful, and I realized I hadn't ended the story soon enough. I cut about two pages off, reworked it, and that was it. To me it is a nostalgic story, then, for many reasons. It is a Washington, D.C., story and, in a way, a story I didn't want to have to write. I think it contains a kind of truth that we don't like to admit."

CHARLES SIMMONS was born in 1924 in New York City and raised there. He was graduated from Columbia College in 1948 after serving three years in the United States Army. He now lives in New York and Eastern Long Island. He was an editor of *The New York Times Book Review* for, as he puts it, "longer than I care to remember." During that time he wrote many reviews as well as magazine and newspaper articles. He also published about a dozen stories but stopped writing them when he began his first novel, *Powdered Eggs,* which won the William Faulkner Award in 1964. His subsequent novels are *An Old-fashioned Darling, Wrinkles* (part of which was published as a short story in a previous O. Henry Awards collection), and *The Belles Lettres Papers.* All four titles have just been reissued.

After finishing his most recent novel Simmons took up short stories again. Simmons says of "Clandestine Acts": "This story was there for me to write for a long time. I did it now, I think, because I discovered an ending. By that I mean I had achieved an acceptable attitude toward it. If I had tried earlier it might well have been soft. There is a right time in one's life to do a story, which is when one finally understands it. At that point the story suddenly hardens up and conveys to the reader a sense of the author's excitement and satisfaction."

DAVID FOSTER WALLACE was born in 1962, received his undergraduate degree from Amherst College and his M.F.A. from the University of Arizona. His first novel, *The Broom of the System,* was published in 1987. "Here and There" is part of a collection of stories and novellas, *Girl with Curious Hair,* to be published this year.

Magazines Consulted

A.I.D. Review, Box 103, Oklahoma City, Okla. 73101

The Agni Review, P.O. Box 229, Cambridge, Mass. 02238

Alaska Quarterly Review, Department of English, 3221 Providence Drive, Anchorage, Alaska 99508

Amelia, 329 "E" Street, Bakersfield, Calif. 93304

The American Voice, The Kentucky Foundation for Women, Inc., Heyburn Building, Suite 1215, Broadway at Fourth Avenue, Louisville, Ky. 40202

Antaeus, Ecco Press, 26 West 17th Street, New York, N.Y. 10011

The Antioch Review, P.O. Box 148, Yellow Springs, Ohio 45387

The Apalachee Quarterly, P.O. Box 20106, Tallahassee, Fla. 32304

Arizona Quarterly, University of Arizona, Tucson, Ariz. 85721

Arrival, 48 Shattuck Square, Suite 194, Berkeley, Calif. 94704

Ascent, Department of English, University of Illinois, Urbana, Ill. 61801

Asimov's Science Fiction Magazine, Davis Publications, 380 Lexington Avenue, New York, N.Y. 10017

The Atlantic Monthly, 8 Arlington Street, Boston, Mass. 02116

Avenue, 145 East 57th Street, New York, N.Y. 10022

Balcones, P.O. Box 50247, Austin, Tex. 78763

Black Ice, 571 Howell Avenue, Cincinnati, Ohio 45220

The Black Warrior Review, P.O. Box 2936, University, Ala. 34586

Boulevard, 4 Washington Square Village, 9R, New York, N.Y. 10012

California Quarterly, 100 Sproul Hall, University of California, Davis, Calif. 95616

Canadian Fiction Magazine, P.O. Box 46422, Station G, Vancouver, B.C., Canada V6R 4G7

Capital Region Magazine, 4 Central Avenue, Albany, N.Y. 12210

Carolina Quarterly, Greenlaw Hall 066-A, University of North Carolina, Chapel Hill, N.C. 27514

The Chariton Review, The Division of Language and Literature, Northeast Missouri State University, Kirksville, Mo. 63501

The Chattahoochee Review, DeKalb Community College, North Campus, 2101 Womack Road, Dunwoody, Ga. 30338-4497

Chelsea, P.O. Box 5880, Grand Central Station, New York, N.Y. 10163

Chicago, WFMT, Inc. 3 Illinois Center, 303 East Wacker Drive, Chicago, Ill. 60601

Chicago Review, 970 East 58th Street, Box C, University of Chicago, Chicago, Ill. 60637

City Lights Review, City Lights, 261 Columbus Avenue, San Francisco, Cal. 94133

Clockwatch Review, 737 Penbrook Way, Hartland, Wisc. 53021

Colorado Review, Department of English, Colorado State University, Fort Collins, Colo. 80523

Columbia, the Magazine of Columbia University, 3 Claremont Avenue, New York, N.Y. 10027

Columbia, the Magazine of Poetry and Prose, 404 Dodge Hall, Columbia University, New York, N.Y. 10027

Concho River Review, c/o English Department, Angelo State University, San Angelo, Tex. 76909

Confrontation, Department of English, C. W. Post of Long Island University, Greenvale, N.Y. 11548

Cosmopolitan, 224 West 57th Street, New York, N.Y. 10019

Crosscurrents, 2200 Glastonbury Rd., Westlake Village, Calif. 91361

Cutbank, c/o Department of English, University of Montana, Missoula, Mont. 59812

Delta Epsilon Sigma Journal, Belmont Abbey College, Belmont, North Carolina 28012

Denver Quarterly, Department of English, University of Denver, Denver, Colo. 80210

Descant, Department of English, Texas Christian University, Fort Worth, Tex. 76129

Epoch, 254 Goldwyn Smith Hall, Cornell University, Ithaca, N.Y. 14853

Esquire, 2 Park Avenue, New York, N.Y. 10016

Farmer's Market, P.O. Box 1272, Galesburg, Ill. 61402

Fiction, Department of English, The City College of New York, N.Y. 10031

Fiction International, Department of English, St. Lawrence University, Canton, N.Y. 13617

Fiction Network, P.O. Box 5651, San Francisco, Calif. 94101

The Fiction Review, P.O. Box 1508, Tempe, Ariz. 85281

The Fiddlehead, The Observatory, University of New Brunswick, P.O. Box 4400, Fredericton, New Brunswick, Canada E3B 5A3

The Florida Review, Department of English, University of Central Florida, Orlando, Fla. 32816

Formations, 832 Chilton Lane, Wilmette, Ill. 60091

Four Quarters, La Salle College, Philadelphia, Pa. 19141

Gallery, 401 Park Avenue South, New York, N.Y. 10016

Gargoyle, P.O. Box 30906, Bethesda, Md. 20814

The Georgia Review, University of Georgia, Athens, Ga. 30602

Grain, Box 1154, Regina, Saskatchewan, Canada S4P 3B4

Grand Street, 50 Riverside Drive, New York, N.Y. 10024

Granta, 13 White Street, New York, N.Y. 10013

The Greensboro Review, University of North Carolina, Greensboro, N.C. 27412

Hard Copies, Department of English and Foreign Languages, California State Polytechnic University, Pomona, Calif. 91768

Harper's Magazine, 2 Park Avenue, New York, N.Y. 10016

Hawaii Review, Hemenway Hall, University of Hawaii, Honolulu, Hawaii 96822

High Plains Literary Review, 180 Adams Street, Suite 250, Denver, Colorado 80206

The Hoboken Terminal, P.O. Box 841, Hoboken, N.J. 07030

The Hudson Review, 684 Park Avenue, New York, N.Y. 10021

Indiana Review, 316 North Jordan Avenue, Bloomington, Ind. 47405

Iowa Review, EPB 453, University of Iowa, Iowa City, Iowa 52240

Kairos, Hermes House Press, 900 West End Avenue, #10-D, New York, N.Y. 10025

Kalliope, a Journal of Women's Art, Kalliope Writer's Collective, Florida Community College at Jacksonville, 3939 Roosevelt Boulevard, Jacksonville, Fla. 32205

Kansas Quarterly, Department of English, Kansas State University, Manhattan, Kansas 66506

Karamu, English Department, Eastern Illinois University, Charleston, Ill. 61920

The Kenyon Review, Kenyon College, Gambier, Ohio 43022

Ladies' Home Journal, 641 Lexington Avenue, New York, N.Y. 10022

The Literary Review, Fairleigh Dickinson University, Teaneck, N.J. 07666

Mademoiselle, 350 Madison Avenue, New York, N.Y. 10017

The Magazine of Fantasy and Science Fiction, Box 56, Cornwall, Conn. 06753

Magical Blend, P.O. Box 11303, San Francisco, Calif. 94101

Malahat Review, University of Victoria, Victoria, British Columbia, Canada V8W 2Y2

The Massachusetts Review, Memorial Hall, University of Massachusetts, Amherst, Mass. 01002

McCall's, 230 Park Avenue, New York, N.Y. 10017

Memphis, 460 Tennessee Street, P.O. Box 256, Memphis, Tenn. 38101

Michigan Quarterly Review, 3032 Rackham Building, University of Michigan, Ann Arbor, Mich. 48109

Mid-American Review, 106 Hanna Hall, Bowling Green State University, Bowling Green, Ohio 43403

Midstream, 515 Park Avenue, New York, N.Y. 10022

The Missouri Review, Department of English, 231 Arts and Sciences, University of Missouri, Columbia, Mo. 65211

Mother Jones, 1663 Mission Street, San Francisco, Calif. 94103

MSS, Box 530, Department of English, SUNY-Binghamton, Binghamton, N.Y. 13901

The Nebraska Review, The Creative Writing Program, University of Nebraska-Omaha, Omaha, Neb. 68182-0324

New Directions, 80 Eighth Avenue, New York, N.Y. 10011

New England Review and Breadloaf Quarterly, Middlebury College, Middlebury, Vt. 05753

New Letters, University of Missouri-Kansas City, Kansas City, Mo. 64110

New Mexico Humanities Review, The Editors, Box A, New Mexico Tech., Socorro, N.M. 57801

The New Renaissance, 9 Heath Road, Arlington, Mass. 02174

New Virginia Review, 1306 East Cary Street, 2-A, Richmond, Va. 23219

The New Yorker, 25 West 43rd Street, New York, N.Y. 10036

Nimrod, Arts and Humanities Council of Tulsa, 2210 South Main, Tulsa, Okla. 74114-1190

The North American Review, University of Northern Iowa, 1222 West 27th Street, Cedar Falls, Iowa 50613

North Dakota Quarterly, University of North Dakota, Box 8237, Grand Forks, N.D. 58202

Northwest Review, 129 French Hall, University of Oregon, Eugene, Ore. 97403

Oak Square, P.O. Box 1238, Allston, Mass. 02134

The Ohio Review, Ellis Hall, Ohio University, Athens, Ohio 45701

Omni, 1965 Broadway, New York, N.Y. 10067

The Ontario Review, 9 Honey Brook Drive, Princeton, N.J. 08540

Orim, Box 1904A, Yale Station, New Haven, Conn. 06520

Other Voices, 820 Ridge Road, Highland Park, Ill. 60035

The Paris Review, 541 East 72nd Street, New York, N.Y. 10021

The Partisan Review, 128 Bay State Road, Boston, Mass. 02215/552 Fifth Avenue, New York, N.Y. 10036

The Pennsylvania Review, University of Pittsburgh, Department of English, 526 C.L., Pittsburgh, Penn. 15260

Phylon, 223 Chestnut Street, S.W., Atlanta, Ga. 30314

Playboy, 919 North Michigan Avenue, Chicago, Ill. 60611

Playgirl, 801 Second Avenue, New York, N.Y. 10017

Ploughshares, Box 529, Cambridge, Mass. 02139

Prairie Schooner, Andrews Hall, University of Nebraska, Lincoln, Neb. 68588

Provincetown Arts, P.O. Box 35, Provincetown, Mass. 02657

Puerto Del Sol, English Department, New Mexico State University, Box 3E, Las Cruces, N.M. 88003

The Quarterly, 201 East 50th Street, New York, N.Y. 10022

Raritan, 165 College Avenue, New Brunswick, N.J. 08903

Reconstructionist, Church Road and Greenwood Avenue, Wyncote, Pa. 19095

Redbook, 230 Park Avenue, New York, N.Y. 10017

Sailing, 125 E. Main Street, P.O. Box 248, Port Washington, Wisc. 53074

Salamagundi, Skidmore College, Saratoga Springs, N.Y. 12866

Sequoia, Storke Student Publications Building, Stanford, Calif. 94305

Seventeen, 850 Third Avenue, New York, N.Y. 10022

The Sewanee Review, University of the South, Sewanee, Tenn. 37375

Shenandoah: The Washington and Lee University Review, Box 722, Lexington, Va. 24450

The Short Story Review, P.O. Box 882108, San Francisco, Calif. 94188

Sidewinder, Division of Arts and Humanities, College of the Mainland, 8001 Palmer Highway, Texas City, Tex. 77591

Sinister Wisdom, P.O. Box 1023, Rockland, Maine 04841

Sonora Review, Department of English, University of Arizona, Tucson, Ariz. 85721

The South Carolina Review, Department of English, Clemson University, Clemson, S.C. 29631

South Dakota Review, Box 111, University Exchange, Vermillion, S.D. 57069

Southern Humanities Review, Auburn University, Auburn, Ala. 36830

The Southern Review, Drawer D, University Station, Baton Rouge, La. 70803

Southwest Review, Southern Methodist University Press, Dallas, Tex. 75275

Stone Drum, P.O. Box 233, Valley View, Tex. 76272-0233

Stories, 14 Beacon Street, Boston, Mass. 02108

StoryQuarterly, P.O. Box 1416, Northbrook, Ill. 60062

St. Andrews Review, St. Andrews Presbyterian College, Laurinburg, N.C. 28352

St. Anthony Messenger, 1615 Republic Street, Cincinnati, Ohio 45210-1298

The Sun, 412 West Rosemary Street, Chapel Hill, N.C. 27514

This World, San Francisco Chronicle, 901 Mission Street, San Francisco, Calif. 94103

The Threepenny Review, P.O. Box 9131, Berkeley, Calif. 94709

Tikkun, Institute of Labor and Mental Health, 5100 Leona Street, Oakland, Calif. 94619

TriQuarterly, 2020 Ridge Avenue, Evanston, Ill. 60208

Twilight Zone, 800 Second Avenue, New York, N.Y. 10017

Twin Cities, 7834 East Bush Lake Road, Minneapolis, Minn. 55435

University of Windsor Review, Department of English, University of Windsor, Windsor, Ontario, Canada N9B 3P4

U.S. Catholic, 221 West Madison Street, Chicago, Ill. 60606

Venus Rising, P.O. Box 21405, Santa Barbara, Calif. 93121

The Virginia Quarterly Review, University of Virginia, 1 West Range, Charlottesville, Va. 22903

Vogue, 350 Madison Avenue, New York, N.Y. 10017

Washington Review, Box 50132, Washington, D.C. 20004

Webster Review, Webster College, Webster Groves, Mo. 63119

Welter, English Department, University of Baltimore, 1420 North Charles Street, Baltimore, Md. 21201-5779

West Coast Review, Simon Fraser University, Burnaby, British Columbia, Canada V5A 1S6

Western Humanities Review, Building 41, University of Utah, Salt Lake City, Utah 84112

Wind, RFD Route 1, Box 809, Pikeville, Ky. 41501

Witness, 31000 Northwestern Highway, Suite 200, P.O. Box 9079, Farmington Hills, Mich. 48333-9079

Woman's Day, 1515 Broadway, New York, N.Y. 10036

Yale Review, 250 Church Street, 1902A Yale Station, New Haven, Conn. 06520

Yankee, Dublin, N.H. 03444

Yellow Silk, P.O. Box 6374, Albany, Calif. 94706

Zeta, 150 West Canton Street, Boston, Mass. 02118

Zyzzyva, 55 Sutter Street, Suite 400, San Francisco, Calif. 94104